"With her talent for perfectly blending wit, passion, excitement, and history, Chase hits the mark with a sprightly, highly engaging, action-packed love story that's filled with witty repartee and a bad-boy hero to die for. Put this at the top of your must-read list!"

—*Romantic Times* (4½ stars, Top Pick)

"Imbued with a wicked wit." —*Booklist*

"Humor, adventure, a unique setting, a toe-curling hero, a geeky heroine—this book has it all. An instant classic."

—*Rakehell*

"[With] wonderful storytelling, heady chemistry between the hero and heroine, and Ms. Chase's delicious wit, this is a spectacularly good book." —*The Romance Reader*

"A thoroughly enchanting read." —*Romance Reviews Today*

Simply wonderful reviews for
Miss Wonderful

"*Miss Wonderful* is Loretta Chase at her magical best as she spins a deliciously witty tale of an overworked woman, an under-challenged man, and a romance that shimmers with passion, humor, and tenderness." —Mary Jo Putney

"Chase takes a delightfully romantic story, filled with wit and unforgettable characters, and sets it against a rich historical backdrop with some marvelously heated love scenes for a joyous reading experience. *Miss Wonderful* is a delicious pleasure; we can welcome Chase back with a rousing cheer and heartfelt thanks for a superior read."

—*Romantic Times* (Top Pick)

LORD PERFECT

LORETTA CHASE

BERKLEY SENSATION, NEW YORK

THE BERKLEY PUBLISHING GROUP
Published by the Penguin Group
Penguin Group (USA) Inc.
375 Hudson Street, New York, New York 10014, USA
Penguin Group (Canada), 90 Eglinton Avenue East, Suite 700, Toronto, Ontario M4P 2Y3, Canada
(a division of Pearson Penguin Canada Inc.)
Penguin Books Ltd., 80 Strand, London WC2R 0RL, England
Penguin Group Ireland, 25 St. Stephen's Green, Dublin 2, Ireland (a division of Penguin Books Ltd.)
Penguin Group (Australia), 250 Camberwell Road, Camberwell, Victoria 3124, Australia (a division of
Pearson Australia Group Pty. Ltd.)
Penguin Books India Pvt. Ltd., 11 Community Centre, Panchsheel Park, New Delhi—110 017, India
Penguin Group (NZ), Cnr. Airborne and Rosedale Roads, Albany, Auckland 1310, New Zealand
(a division of Pearson New Zealand Ltd.)
Penguin Books (South Africa) (Pty.) Ltd., 24 Sturdee Avenue, Rosebank, Johannesburg 2196, South
Africa

Penguin Books Ltd., Registered Offices: 80 Strand, London WC2R 0RL, England

This is a work of fiction. Names, characters, places, and incidents either are the product of the author's
imagination or are used fictitiously, and any resemblance to actual persons, living or dead, business establishments, events, or locales is entirely coincidental. The publisher does not have any control over
and does not assume any responsibility for author or third-party websites or their content.

LORD PERFECT

A Berkley Sensation Book / published by arrangement with the author

PRINTING HISTORY
Berkley Sensation edition / March 2006

Copyright © 2006 by Loretta Chekani.
Excerpt from *Captives of the Night* copyright © 1994 by Loretta Chekani.
Excerpt from *The Lion's Daughter* copyright © 1992 by Loretta Chekani.
Cover art by Judy York.
Cover design by George Long.
Interior text design by Stacy Irwin.

ISBN: 0-425-20888-5

BERKLEY SENSATION®
Berkley Sensation Books are published by The Berkley Publishing Group,
a division of Penguin Group (USA) Inc.,
375 Hudson Street, New York, New York 10014.
BERKLEY SENSATION is a registered trademark of Penguin Group (USA) Inc.
The "B" design is a trademark belonging to Penguin Group (USA) Inc.

PRINTED IN THE UNITED STATES OF AMERICA

10 9 8 7 6 5 4 3 2 1

To Walter

Chapter 1

Egyptian Hall, Piccadilly, London, September 1821

HE LEANT AGAINST THE WINDOW FRAME, OF-fering those within the exhibition hall a fine rear view of a long, well-proportioned frame, expensively garbed. He seemed to have his arms folded and his attention upon the window, though the thick glass could show him no more than a blurred image of Piccadilly.

It was clear in any case that the exhibition within—of the marvels Giovanni Belzoni had discovered in Egypt—had failed to hold his interest.

The woman surreptitiously studying him decided he would make the perfect model of the bored aristocrat.

Supremely assured. Perfectly poised. Immaculately dressed. Tall. Dark.

He turned his head, presenting the expected patrician profile.

It wasn't what she expected.

She couldn't breathe.

BENEDICT CARSINGTON, VISCOUNT Rathbourne, turned away from the thick-paned window and the distorted view it offered of the lively scene outside—of horses, vehi-cles, and pedestrians in Piccadilly. With an inner sigh, he directed his dark gaze into the exhibition hall, where Death was on display.

"Belzoni's Tomb," exhibiting the explorer's discoveries in Egypt a few years ago, had proved a rousing success since its debut on the first of May. Against his better judg-ment, Benedict had formed one of the nineteen hundred at-tendees on opening day. This was his third visit, and once again, he had much rather be elsewhere.

Ancient Egypt did not exert over him the hold it did over so many of his relatives. Even his numskull brother Rupert had fallen under its spell, perhaps because the present-day place offered so many opportunities for head-breaking and hairsbreadth escapes from death. But Rupert was most certainly not the reason for Lord Rathbourne's spending another long afternoon in the Egyptian Hall.

The reason sat at the far end of the room: Benedict's thirteen-year-old nephew and godson Peregrine Dalmay, Earl of Lisle and sole issue of Benedict's brother-in-law, the Marquess of Atherton. The boy was diligently copying Belzoni's model of the interior of the famous Second Pyra-mid, whose entrance the explorer had discovered three years ago.

Diligence, Peregrine's schoolmasters would have told anyone—and had told his father, repeatedly—was not one of Lord Lisle's more noticeable character traits.

When it came to things Egyptian, however, Peregrine was persevering to a fault. They had arrived two hours ago, and his interest showed no signs of flagging. Any other boy would have been wild to be out and engaging in physical activity one and three-quarters of an hour ago.

But then, had this been any other boy, Benedict would not have had to come himself to the Egyptian Hall. He would have sent a servant to play nursemaid.

Peregrine wasn't any other boy.

He looked like an angel. A fair, open countenance. Flaxen hair. Clear, grey, utterly guileless eyes.

A group of boxers under "Gentleman" Jackson's super-vision had been employed to keep Queen Caroline and her sympathizers out of the king's coronation in July. These fellows, if they stuck together, might have contrived to keep the peace while Lord Atherton's heir was about.

Other than these—or a large military force—the only mortal with any real influence over the young Lord Lisle was Benedict—the only one, that is, apart from Benedict's father, the Earl of Hargate. But Lord Hargate could intimidate anybody—except for his wife—and he certainly would not stoop to looking after troublesome boys.

I should have brought a book, Benedict thought. Stifling a yawn, he directed his gaze to Belzoni's reproduction of a bas-relief from a pharaoh's tomb and tried to understand what Peregrine, along with so many other people, found so stimulating.

Benedict saw three rows of primitively drawn figures. A line of men whose beards curled up at the end, all leaning forward, arms pressed together. Lone hieroglyphic signs between the figures. Columns of hieroglyphs above their heads.

In the middle row, four figures towed a boat bearing three other figures. Some very long snakes played a part in the scene. More columns of hieroglyphs over the heads. Perhaps these figures were all talking? Were the signs the Egyptian version of the bubbles over caricatures' heads in today's satirical prints?

On the bottom, another line of figures marched under columns of hieroglyphs. These had different features and hairstyles. They must be foreigners. At the end of the line was a god Benedict recognized: Thoth, the ibis-headed one, the god of learning. Even Rupert, upon whom an expensive education had been utterly wasted—Lord Hargate might have fed the money to goats with the same result—could recognize Thoth.

What the rest of it meant was work for the imagination, and Benedict kept his imagination, along with a great deal else, under rigorous control.

He turned his attention to the opposite side of the room.

He had an unobstructed view. For most of the Beau Monde, the exhibition's novelty had worn off. Even their inferiors would rather spend this fine afternoon outdoors than among the contents of ancient tombs.

Benedict saw her clearly.

Too clearly.

For a moment he was blinded by the clarity, like one stepping out of a cave into a blazing noonday.

She stood in profile, like the figures on the wall behind her. She was studying a statue.

Benedict saw black curls under the rim of a pale blue bonnet. Long black lashes against pearly skin. A ripe plum of a mouth.

His gaze skimmed down.

A weight pressed on his chest.

He couldn't breathe.

Rule: The ill-bred, the vulgar, and the ignorant stare.

He made himself look away.

THE GIRL STOOD at Peregrine's shoulder. He tried to ignore her but she was standing in his light. He glanced up and quickly back at his sketchbook—enough to see that she had her arms folded and her lips pursed as she stared at his drawing. He knew that look. It was a schoolmaster look.

She must have taken the glance as an invitation because she started talking. "I wondered why you chose the model of the pyramid," she said. "It is all angles and lines. So uninteresting to draw. The mummy in the sarcophagus would be more fun. But now I understand the trouble. Your draughtsmanship is not very good."

Very slowly and deliberately Peregrine turned his head and looked up at her. He was startled at first, when he got a good look. She had eyes so blue, they looked like doll eyes, not real ones.

"I beg your pardon?" he said in the icily polite voice he'd learnt from his uncle. His father was a marquess, a peer of the realm, and his uncle had only the courtesy title of Viscount Rathbourne at present, but Uncle Benedict administered far more devastating set-downs. He was famous for it. At his most excessively polite, it was said, Lord Rathbourne could freeze boiling oil at fifty paces.

The icy politeness didn't work so well for Peregrine.

"There's a perfectly good cross section of the pyramid in Signor Belzoni's book," she said quite as though he'd begged her to rattle on. "Wouldn't you rather have a souvenir of one of the mummies? Or the goddess with the lion head? My mother could make you a superlative copy. She's a brilliant draughtsman."

"I don't want a *souvenir*," Peregrine said witheringly. "I'm going to be an explorer, and one day I shall bring home heaps of such things."

The girl stopped pursing her lips. The severe look went away. "An explorer like Signor Belzoni, do you mean?" she said. "Oh, that would be something grand to do."

Try as he might, Peregrine could not tamp down his enthusiasm in the proper Lord Rathbourne fashion. "Nothing could be grander," he said. "There are more than a thousand miles along the Nile to explore, and people who've been say that what you see is like the tip of an iceberg, because most of the wonderful things are buried under the sand. And once we learn to read the hieroglyphs, we'll know who built what and when they did it. At present, you see, ancient Egypt is like the Dark Ages: a great mystery. But I'm going to be one of the ones who finds out its secrets. It'll be like discovering a whole new world."

The girl's blue doll eyes opened wider. "Oh, then it's a *noble quest*. You're going to shed light on the Dark Ages of Egypt. I'm going on quests, too. When I grow up, I'm going to be a knight."

Peregrine almost stuck his finger in his ear to be sure it was in working order. He remembered his uncle was in the vicinity, though, and picturing the look Lord Rathbourne would give him, resisted the impulse. Instead he said, "Sorry. Say again? I thought you said you were going to be a knight—as in shining armor and such."

"That's what I said," she said. "Like the Knights of the Round Table. The gallant Sir Olivia, that's who I'll be, setting out on perilous quests, performing noble deeds, righting wrongs—"

"That's ridiculous," Peregrine said.

"No, it isn't," she said.

"Of course it is," Peregrine said—patiently, because she

was a girl and probably had no notion of logic. "In the first place, all that King Arthur and the Knights of the Round Table folderol is a myth. It has about as much basis in fact or history as the Egyptians had for their sphinxes and gods with ibis heads."

"A myth!" The great blue eyes opened wider still. "What about the Crusades?"

"I didn't say knights never existed," Peregrine said. "They did and do. But the magic, monsters, and miracles are nothing more than myths. The Venerable Bede doesn't even mention Arthur."

He went on, citing historical references to the simple warrior leader who might or might not have been the source of the legendary Arthur. Peregrine explained how, over the centuries, a romantic tale developed, and along the way, mythical creatures, miracles, and various other religious associations got stuck onto the story, because the Church was the great power and stuck religion onto everything.

He then offered his views on religion, the same views that had led to his being chucked out of one school after another. Out of consideration for her weaker and less amply educated feminine brain, though, he gave a simpler and shorter version.

When he paused for breath, she said scornfully, "That's only your opinion. You don't *know.* There *might* have been a Holy Grail. There *might* have been a Camelot."

"I know there weren't any dragons," he said. "So you can't slay any. Even if there were dragons, you couldn't."

"There were knights!" she cried. "I can still be a knight!"

"No, you can't," he said, more patient than ever, because she was so sadly confused. "You're a girl. Girls can't be knights."

She snatched the sketchbook from his hands and swung it at his head.

DISASTER WOULD NOT have occurred had Bathsheba Wingate been paying full attention to her daughter.

She was not paying attention.

She was trying desperately to keep her gaze from straying to the bored aristocrat . . . to the long legs whose muscles the costly wool trousers lovingly outlined . . . the boots whose dark gleam matched his eyes . . . the miles of shoulders bracing up the window frame . . . the haughty jaw and insolent nose . . . the dark, dangerously bored eyes.

Bathsheba might as well have been a giddy sixteen-year-old miss when in fact she was a sober matron twice that age, and she might as well have never seen a handsome aristocrat before in all her life when in fact she'd met any number and even married one. She was not herself and she didn't know or care who she was.

She only stood for a long time, trying to pay attention to the Egyptians instead of him, and oblivious of the minutes passing during which Olivia might easily re-create some of the more harrowing scenes from the Book of Revelation.

Bathsheba forgot she even had a daughter while she stood as though trapped, her heart beating so fast that it left no time or room to breathe.

This was why she failed to notice the signs of trouble before it was too late.

The crash, the outraged yelp, and the familiar voice crying, "You great blockhead!" told her it was too late at the same time they broke the spell. She hurried toward the noise and snatched the sketchbook from Olivia's hands before she could throw it across the room—and break a priceless object, beyond doubt.

"Olivia Wingate," Bathsheba said, careful to keep her voice low, in hopes of attracting as small an audience as possible. "I am shocked, deeply shocked." This was a hideous lie. Bathsheba would be shocked only if Olivia contrived to spend half an hour among civilized beings without making a spectacle of herself.

She turned toward the flaxen-haired boy, her daughter's latest victim. He shifted up into a sitting position on the floor near his overturned stool, but that was as far as he came. He watched them, grey eyes wary.

"I said I was going to be a knight when I grew up and *he* said girls couldn't be knights," Olivia said, her voice shaking with rage.

"Lisle, I am astonished at your flagrant disregard of a fundamental rule of human survival," came an impossibly deep voice from somewhere nearby and to Bathsheba's right. The sound shot down to the base of her spine then up again to vibrate against an acutely sensitive place in her neck. "I am sure I have told you more than once," the voice went on. "A gentleman *never* contradicts a lady."

Bathsheba turned her head toward the voice.

Ah, of course.

Of all the boys in all the world, Olivia had to assault the one belonging to *him*.

SHE WAS THE sort of woman who made accidents happen, simply by crossing a street.

She was the sort of woman who ought to be preceded by warning signs.

From a distance, she was breathtaking.

Now she stood within easy reach.

And now . . .

Once, in the course of a youthful prank, Benedict had fallen off a roof, and briefly lost consciousness.

Now, as he fell off something and into eyes like an indigo sea, he lost consciousness. The world went away, his brain went away, and only the vision remained, of pearly skin and ripe plum lips, of the fathomless sea in which he was drowning . . . and then a pink like a sunrise glowing upon finely sculpted cheekbones.

A blush. She was blushing.

His brain staggered back.

He bowed. "I do beg your pardon, madam," he said. "This young beast is far from fully civilized, I regret to say. Get up from the floor, sir, and apologize to the ladies for distressing them."

Peregrine scrambled to his feet, countenance indignant. "But—"

"He will do nothing of the kind," said the beauty. "I have explained to Olivia time and again that physical assault is not the proper response to disagreements unless one's life is in danger." She turned to the girl, a freckle-faced redhead who bore not the slightest resemblance to her mama—if mama she was—except in the eye department. "Was your life in danger, Olivia?"

"No, Mama," said the girl, blue eyes flashing, "but he said—"

"Did this young man threaten you in any way?" said her mother.

"No, Mama," the girl said, "but—"

"Was it merely a difference of opinion?" said her mother.

"Yes, Mama, but—"

"You lost your temper. What have I told you about losing your temper?"

"I am to count to twenty," the girl said. "And if I have not regained it by then, I must count to twenty again."

"Did you do so?"

A sigh. "No, Mama."

"Kindly apologize, Olivia."

The girl ground her teeth. Then she took a deep breath and let it out.

She turned to Peregrine. "Sir, I most humbly beg your pardon," she said. "It was a ghastly, unspeakable, heinous act I perpetrated. I hope the precipitous fall from the stool did you no permanent or disfiguring injury. I am so deeply ashamed. Not only have I attacked and possibly maimed an innocent person but I have disgraced my mother. It is my ungovernable temper, you see, an affliction I have suffered since birth." She fell to her knees and snatched his hand. "Can you be so good, so generous, kind sir, as to forgive me?"

Peregrine, who had listened to this speech with increasing bewilderment, was, for perhaps the first time in his life, struck dumb.

The mother rolled her outrageously blue eyes. "Get up, Olivia."

The girl clung to Peregrine's hand, her head bowed.

Peregrine threw a panicked look at Benedict.

"Perhaps now you comprehend the folly of contradicting ladies," said Benedict. "Do not look to me for rescue. I hope it will be a lesson to you."

Speechlessness being alien to Peregrine's character, he swiftly recovered. "Oh, do get up," he told the girl crossly. "It was only a sketchbook." The girl didn't move. Voice moderating, he added, "Uncle is right. I ought to apologize, too. I know I'm supposed to agree with whatever females as well as my elders say, for some reason or other. If there is a proper reason. No one has ever explained the rule's logic, certainly. At any rate, you barely hit me. I only fell because I lost my balance when I ducked. Not that it matters. It's not as though a girl could do much damage."

Olivia's head came up, and her eyes shot deadly sparks.

The boy went on, oblivious, as usual. "It wants practice, you know, and girls never get any. If you did practice, you'd strengthen your arm at least. That's why schoolmasters are so good at it."

The girl's expression softened. She rose, the subject having diverted her, apparently. "Papa told me about English schoolmasters," she said. "Do they beat you very often?"

"Oh, all the time," Peregrine said.

She sought details. He provided them.

By this time, Benedict had recovered his composure. So he believed, at any rate. While the children made peace, he allowed his attention to revert to the breathtaking mama.

"Her apology was not necessary," he said. "However, it was most—er—stirring."

"She is dreadful," the lady said. "I tried several times to sell her to gypsies, but they wouldn't take her."

The answer startled him. Beauty so rarely came coupled with wit. Another man would have rocked on his heels. Benedict only paused infinitesimally and said, "Then I daresay there's no chance they'd take him, either. Not that he's mine to dispose of. My nephew. Atherton's sole progeny. I am Rathbourne."

Something changed. A shadow appeared that had not been in her countenance before.

He had presumed, perhaps. She might be as beautiful as sin and she might have a sense of humor, but this did not mean she was not a stickler for certain proprieties.

"Perhaps a mutual acquaintance is idling about who

would introduce us properly," he said, glancing about the gallery. At present, the space held three other persons, none of whom he knew or could possibly wish to know. They looked away when his gaze fell upon them.

Then a shred of sense returned and he asked himself what difference a proper introduction would make. She was a married woman, and he had rules about married women. If he sought to further the acquaintance, it would only be to violate those rules.

"I greatly doubt we have a mutual acquaintance," she said. "You and I travel in different spheres, my lord."

"We're both *here*," he said, his tongue getting the better of Rules Regarding Married Women.

"As is Olivia," she said. "I can tell by her expression that she is nine and a half minutes away from getting one of her Ideas, which puts us eleven minutes away from mayhem. I am obliged to remove her."

She turned away.

The message was plain enough. As plain as a bucket of ice water thrown in his face. "I am dismissed, I see," he said. "A fitting return for my impertinence."

"This has nothing to do with impertinence," she said without turning back to him, "and everything to do with self-preservation."

She collected her daughter and left.

HE VERY NEARLY followed her from the room.

Unthinkable.

True, nonetheless.

Benedict had even started that way, heart pounding, when Lady Ordway burst from a doorway and surged toward him in a flutter of ribbons, ruffles, and feathers. These, given her advanced state of pregnancy, created the effect of an agitated brood hen.

"Tell me I am not seeing whatyoucallems," she said. "Those things they see in the desert—not oases, Rathbourne, but when one sees an oasis that isn't there."

He directed an expressionless gaze into her cheerfully stupid, pretty face. "I believe the word you seek is *mirage*."

She nodded, and the ruffles, ribbons, and feathers of her bonnet danced giddily about her head.

He had known her forever, it seemed. She was seven years his junior. Eight years ago, he had very nearly married her instead of Atherton's sister Ada. Benedict was not sure matters would have turned out more happily if he had. Both women were equally pretty, equally wellborn, equally well-dowered, and equally intelligent. Both were more handsomely endowed in all the other categories than in the last.

Still, precious few women had the wherewithal to offer true intellectual stimulation. In any case, it was Benedict who had failed his late wife, he was all too well aware.

"I thought it was a mirage," said Lady Ordway. "Or a dream. With all these strange creatures about, one might easily think oneself in a dream." She gestured at the objects about her. "But it was Bathsheba DeLucey truly. Well, Bathsheba DeLucey that was, for she was wed before I was. Not that the Wingates will ever acknowledge it. To them, she doesn't exist."

"How tiresome," he said while he stored away the not-unfamiliar names. "Families feuding over an ancient triviality, no doubt."

He was sure he'd gone to school with a Wingate. That was the Earl of Fosbury's family name, was it not? As to the DeLuceys, Benedict couldn't remember having met any. He knew his father was acquainted with the head of the family, the Earl of Mandeville, though. Lord Hargate knew everybody worth knowing, as well as everything worth knowing about them.

"It is far from *trivial*," Lady Ordway said. "And pray do not tell me it is un-Christian to visit the sins of the elders upon the children. In this case, if one accepts the children, the elders will come, too, and they are so very dreadful, as you know."

"I never met the lady before in all my life," Benedict said. "I know nothing about her. The children had a dispute, and we were obliged to intervene." He glanced at Peregrine, who'd returned to his drawing, altogether unaffected by recent events. Youth was so resilient.

Benedict, meanwhile, was still short of breath.

Bathsheba. Her name was Bathsheba.

Fitting.

Lady Ordway, too, looked at his nephew. Lowering her voice, she explained, "She comes of the ramshackle branch of the DeLuceys."

"We've all got one of those," Benedict said. "The Carsingtons have my brother Rupert, for instance."

"Oh, that scamp," said she, with the same smile and in the same indulgent tone most women adopted when speaking of Rupert. "The Dreadful DeLuceys are another story altogether. Thoroughly disreputable. Imagine Lord Fosbury's reaction when his second eldest, Jack, declared he was marrying one of them. It would be like your telling Lord Hargate that you intend to marry a gypsy girl. Which, really, is what she was, for all they tried to make a lady of her."

Whoever had tried to make a lady of Bathsheba Wingate had succeeded. Benedict had detected nothing common in her speech or manner, and he had a fine ear for the nuances that betrayed even the best-schooled imposters and posers.

He had assumed he was speaking to one of his own class. A lady.

"Beyond a doubt that was how they lured poor Jack into parson's mousetrap," Lady Ordway said. "But the marriage did not enrich her family as they had hoped. When Jack wed her, Lord Fosbury cut him off with a shilling. Jack and his bride ended up in Dublin. That was where I last saw them, not long before he died. The child looks like him."

At this point, the lady found it necessary to catch her breath and fan herself. These measures proving inadequate, she availed herself of the nearest bench. When she invited him to join her, Benedict complied without hesitation.

She was silly and wore too many frills, and rarely said anything worth listening to—and one must listen, for she was one of the multitude who believed "conversation" and "monologue" were synonyms. On the other hand, she was an old acquaintance, a member of his social circle, and married to one of his political allies.

More important, she had prevented his committing an appalling breach of both propriety and sense.

He had very nearly followed Bathsheba Wingate out of the Egyptian Hall.

And then . . .

And then, he was not sure what he would have done, so bedazzled had he been.

Would he have stooped to teasing her until she told him her name and direction?

Would he have sunk so low as to follow her secretly?

An hour earlier, he would have believed himself incapable of such gross behavior. That was the sort of thing infatuated schoolboys did. In his youth he had experienced the usual assortment of infatuations, naturally, and behaved in the usual absurd manner, but he'd long since outgrown such foolishness.

Or so he'd thought.

Now he wondered how many crucial rules he might have broken. Her being a widow rather than a married woman made no difference. For a short time he had not been himself but a sort of madman, bewitched.

Impetuous behavior is the province of poets, artists, and others who cannot regulate their passions.

And so he sat patiently with Lady Ordway and listened while she went on to the next topic, not at all interesting, and the next, which was less so, and told himself to be grateful, because she had broken the spell and rescued him from a shocking folly.

Chapter 2

BATHSHEBA WAITED ONLY UNTIL THEY'D EX-
ited the Egyptian Hall before she took her daughter to task.
Children, Bathsheba had found, were like dogs. If one did
not administer a punishment or lecture immediately after
the crime, one might as well forget the matter altogether,
for they certainly would.

"That was outrageous, even for you," she told Olivia as
they made their way across the busy street. "In the first
place, you accosted a stranger, which you have been told
countless times a lady never does, except when her life is
in danger and she requires help."

"Ladies never do anything interesting unless they're
about to be killed," Olivia said. "But we are allowed to aid
persons in need, you said. The boy was frowning as though
he was having a difficult time. I thought I could help him.
If he were unconscious, lying in a ditch, you wouldn't expect me to wait for an introduction, surely."

"He was not lying in a ditch," said Bathsheba. "Furthermore, striking him with his sketchbook meets no criterion
of charity I ever heard of."

"I thought he looked afflicted," Olivia said. "He was

scowling and biting his lip and shaking his head. Well, you saw why. He draws like an infant. Or someone very old and palsied. He's attended Eton and Harrow, can you credit it, Mama? That isn't all. Rugby, too. And Westminster. And Winchester. They cost heaps of money, as everybody knows, and one must be a nob to get in. Yet not one of those great schools could teach him to draw even adequately. Is it not shocking?"

"They are not like schools for girls," Bathsheba said. "They teach Greek and Latin and little else. In any event, the topic is not his education but your improper behavior. I have told you time and again—"

She broke off because a gleaming black phaeton had rounded the corner at a speed that threatened to overturn it, and was racing straight at them. Pedestrians and street vendors scrambled to get out of the way. Bathsheba hauled Olivia to the curb and watched it fly past, her hands clenched while she longed for something to throw at the driver, a drunken member of the upper orders with a trollop giggling beside him.

"What about that one, with his fancy piece?" Olivia said. "He's a nob, isn't he? It's so easy to tell. The way they dress. The way they walk. The way they drive. No one minds what they do."

"Ladies know nothing about fancy pieces and they never use the word *nob*," Bathsheba said between her teeth. She made herself count silently to twenty, because she still wanted to run after the phaeton, tear the driver from his perch, and knock his head against the carriage wheel.

"It only means he's got rank or money," Olivia said. "It isn't a bad word."

"It is slang," Bathsheba said. "A lady would refer to him as a *gentleman*. The term serves for men belonging to the gentry and the aristocracy as well as the peerage."

"I know," Olivia said. "Papa said a gentleman was a fellow who didn't work for his living."

Jack Wingate had never worked for a living and simply couldn't do it, even when it was a choice between working and starvation. For all of his life before he met Bathsheba, someone else had paid the bills, shouldered the responsibilities, and made a path through the difficulties. For the rest of his short life, she was the someone else.

Still, in every other way, he had been everything she could want in a husband, and he'd proved to be the best of fathers. Olivia had adored him and, more important, *listened* to him.

"Your father would make one of his wry faces and say, 'Really, now, Olivia,' if you spoke of *nobs* to him," Bathsheba said. "One does not use the word in polite conversation."

Wishing Jack had taught her the trick of getting through to their daughter, Bathsheba went on to explain how certain words were interpreted. This word would prejudice people against one, by indicating lower-class origins. She explained—for the thousandth time, it seemed—that such judgments were an unfortunate fact of life, with practical and often painful consequences.

She concluded with, "Kindly discard it from your vocabulary."

"But all those gentlemen can do as they please, and no one scolds *them*," Olivia said. "Even the women—the *ladies*. They drink to excess and gamble away their husbands' money and go to bed with men who aren't their husbands and—"

"Olivia, what have I told you about reading the scandal sheets?"

"I haven't read one in weeks, ever since you told me to stop," the girl said virtuously. "It was Riggles the pawnbroker who told me about Lady Dorving. She pawned her diamonds again to cover her gaming debts. And everyone knows that Lord John French is the father of Lady Craith's last two children."

Bathsheba hardly knew where to begin responding to this declaration. Riggles was an undesirable acquaintance, not to mention indiscreet. Regrettably, Olivia had been on easy terms with such persons practically since birth. Jack always dealt with them, because he'd had the most practice with pawnbrokers and moneylenders. And he always took

Olivia, because even the stoniest heart could not resist her enormous, innocent blue eyes.

When he fell ill, and Bathsheba had so many other cares, the then nine-year-old Olivia took over financial negotiations, carrying the remaining bits of jewelry and plate, household bric-a-brac, and clothing to and fro. She was even better at it than Jack had been. She had his charm and her mama's obstinacy combined, unfortunately, with the Dreadful DeLucey talent for bamboozlement.

Bathsheba and Jack had left the Continent and moved to Ireland to get Olivia away from the unwholesome influence of Bathsheba's family.

The trouble was, Olivia was drawn to shifty characters, rogues and vagabonds, spongers and swindlers—persons like her maternal relatives, in other words. Apart from her teacher and classmates, the pawnbrokers were the most respectable of her London acquaintances.

Undoing the education her daughter received on the streets was becoming a full-time occupation for Bathsheba. They *must* move to a better neighborhood very soon.

All they needed was a few shillings' increase in monthly income.

The question was where to find the money.

Bathsheba must either obtain more commissions or acquire more drawing students.

Neither students nor commissions were easy for a woman artist to come by. Needlework was, but it would earn a contemptibly small wage, and the working conditions would ruin her eyesight and health. She was ill-qualified for any other occupation—any other respectable occupation, that is.

If she was not respectable, her daughter could not be. If Olivia was not respectable, she could not marry well.

Later, Bathsheba counseled herself. She would fret about the future later, after her daughter was in bed. It would give her something productive to think about.

Instead of *him*.

The Earl of Hargate's heir, of all men.

Not merely a bored aristocrat, but a famous one.

Lord Perfect, people called him, because Rathbourne never put a foot wrong.

If he hadn't identified himself, Bathsheba might have lingered. It was hard to resist the dark eyes, especially, though she couldn't say why, exactly.

All she knew was that those eyes had very nearly made her lose her resolve and turn back.

But to what end?

Nothing good could come of knowing him.

He was not at all like her late husband. Jack Wingate was an earl's younger son with no sense of responsibility and as little affection for his family as she had for hers, though for different reasons.

Lord Rathbourne was another species. Though he, too, was a member of one of England's most prominent families, his was also one of the most tightly knit. Furthermore, all she'd ever heard and read about him led to one conclusion: He was the embodiment of the noble ideal, everything aristocrats ought to be but so seldom were. He had high standards, a powerful sense of duty—oh, what did the details matter? The scandal sheets never mentioned him. When his name appeared in print—as it did regularly—it was on account of some noble or clever or brave thing he'd done or said.

He was *perfect.*

And this paragon had turned out to be anything but the pompous bore she'd pictured.

To such a man—as was the case with nearly all responsible men of rank—her only possible role was mistress. In short, she must erase him completely from her mind.

They had reached the fringes of Holborn. They'd soon be home. Bathsheba must think about purchasing food. She'd barely enough money left for tea. She debated whether those supplies could be stretched to make supper, with something left over for tomorrow's breakfast. This awareness—along with the recollection of the dark eyes and the deep voice and long legs and broad shoulders, and the ache of regret the recollection caused—made her speak more sharply than usual.

"I wish you would remember that, unlike Lady This or Lord That, you are not in a position of privilege," she told her daughter. "If you wish to be accepted among respectable people, you must abide by their rules. You are growing too old to be a hoyden. In a few years, you will be ready to marry. All your future will depend upon your husband. What man of integrity, with a position to uphold, will wish to place his future happiness and his children's in the hands of an undisciplined, ignorant, and ill-mannered girl?"

Olivia's expression became subdued.

Instantly Bathsheba was sorry. Her daughter was bold and energetic, adventurous and imaginative. One hated to quell her strong spirit.

But one had no choice.

With a proper education, the right manners, and a little luck, Olivia would find a suitable husband. Not an aristocrat, no, certainly not. While Bathsheba did not regret marrying the man she loved, she'd rather Olivia did not experience the hardships that resulted from such a misalliance.

Bathsheba's hopes were modest enough. She wanted Olivia to be loved, well treated, and securely provided for. A barrister or a physician or other professional man would be perfect. But a respectable tradesman—a linen-draper or bookseller or stationer—would be acceptable, too.

As to wealth, it would be enough if the marriage spared her daughter her own worries and the dispiriting exercise of making a small, erratic income stretch beyond its limits.

If all went well, Olivia would never have to fret about such things.

All would not go well unless they moved to a better neighborhood very soon.

AS ONE MIGHT expect, Lady Ordway lost not a minute in spreading word of Bathsheba Wingate's appearance in Piccadilly.

The subject was on everyone's lips when Benedict went to his club later that afternoon.

All the same, he was not at all prepared when it came up at Hargate House that evening.

He and Peregrine had joined Benedict's parents, his brother Rupert, and Rupert's wife Daphne there for dinner.

When the family adjourned to the library afterward, Benedict was astonished to hear Peregrine ask Lord Hargate to look at his drawings from the Egyptian Hall and judge whether or not they were acceptable for one who intended to become an antiquarian.

Benedict casually crossed the room, picked up the latest *Quarterly Review*, and began leafing through its pages.

Lord Hargate rarely wasted tact upon family members. Since he, like the rest of the Carsingtons, regarded Peregrine as a member of the family, he wasted no tact on the boy, either.

"These are execrable," said his lordship. "Rupert can draw better, and Rupert is an idiot."

Rupert laughed.

"He only pretends to be an idiot," Daphne said. "It is a game with him. He deceives everyone else, but I can hardly believe he has deceived *you*, my lord."

"He does such a fine impression of an imbecile that he might as well be one," said Lord Hargate. "Still, he can draw as a gentleman ought. Even at Lisle's age, he could acquit himself creditably." He looked across the room at Benedict. "What have you been thinking of, Rathbourne, to let matters reach such a pass? The boy needs a proper drawing master."

"That's what *she* said," Peregrine said. "She said my drawings weren't any good. But she's a girl, and how could I be sure she knew anything about it?"

"She?" said Lady Hargate. Her eyebrows went up as she turned her dark gaze to Benedict.

Rupert looked at him with the same expression, except for the laughter in his eyes.

He and Benedict bore a strong physical resemblance to their mother and—from a distance—each other. The other three sons—Geoffrey, Alistair, and Darius—had inherited their father's golden brown hair and amber eyes.

"A girl," Benedict said dismissively while his heart

pounded. "At the Egyptian Hall. She and Peregrine had a difference of opinion." This ought to surprise no one. Peregrine had differences of opinion with everybody.

"She has the same color hair as Aunt Daphne and her name is Olivia and her mother is an artist," Peregrine volunteered. "She was silly, but her mother seemed a sensible sort."

"Ah, the mother was there," said Lady Hargate, her gaze still on Benedict.

"I don't suppose you happened to notice, Benedict, whether the mama was pretty?" Rupert said, so very innocently.

Benedict looked up from the *Quarterly Review*, his face carefully blank, as though his mind had been upon the contents of the journal. "Pretty?" he said. "Rather more than that. I should say she was beautiful." His gaze reverted to the periodical. "Lady Ordway recognized her. Said the name was Winshaw. Or was it Winston? Perhaps it was Willoughby."

"The girl said it was Wingate," Peregrine said.

The name fell into the room the way a meteor might fall through the roof.

After a short, reverberating silence, Lord Hargate said, "Wingate? A redheaded girl? But that must be Jack Wingate's daughter."

"She would be about eleven or twelve by now, I believe," said Lady Hargate.

"I am more interested in the mama," said Rupert.

"Why am I not surprised?" said Daphne.

Rupert looked at her innocently. "But Bathsheba Wingate is famous, love. She is like one of those irresistible females Homer talks about who lure sailors onto the rocks."

"Sirens," Peregrine said. "But they are mythological creatures, like mermaids. Supposedly they lure men to death through some sort of music, which is ridiculous. I do not understand how music can lure one to anything, except to sleep. Furthermore, if Mrs. Wingate is a murderess—"

"She is not," Lord Hargate said. "Inconceivable as it may seem, Rupert employed a metaphor. A surprisingly apt one."

"It is a tragic love story," Rupert said teasingly.

Peregrine made a face.

"You may go to the billiard room," Benedict said.

The boy was off like a shot. As Rupert knew, nothing, in Peregrine's view, could be more detestable and nauseating than a love story, especially a tragic one.

When the boy was out of earshot, Rupert told his wife how the beautiful Bathsheba DeLucey had bewitched the Earl of Fosbury's second and favorite son and destroyed his life. It was the same story Benedict had heard repeated at least a dozen times this day.

Jack Wingate had been "mad in love," everyone agreed. Bewitched. Completely in Bathsheba DeLucey's thrall. And the love had destroyed him. It had cost him his family, his position—everything.

"So you see, she was the siren who lured Wingate to his doom," Rupert concluded. "Exactly like one of the stories in the Greek myths."

"It sounds like a myth," Daphne said scornfully. "Society thinks women scholars are monstrosities, recollect. Society can be criminally narrow in its views."

Daphne would know. Even though she'd married into one of England's most influential families, the majority of male scholars dismissed her theories regarding the decipherment of Egyptian hieroglyphs.

"Not in this case," said Lord Hargate. "The trouble began in my grandfather's time, as I recall. It was early in the last century, at any rate. Every generation or so, the DeLuceys had produced a naval hero, and Edmund DeLucey, a second son and a highly competent naval officer, promised to be another. However, at some point, he contrived to get himself dismissed from the service. He abandoned the girl to whom he was betrothed and embarked on a career as a pirate."

"You're roasting us, Father," Benedict said. He had heard about Jack Wingate's tragic love ad nauseam. He had not until now heard the DeLuceys' history.

His father was not joking, however, and the details were appalling.

Unlike many pirates, according to Lord Hargate, Edmund

survived to a ripe old age, in the course of which he wed and sired a number of offspring. Every last one of them inherited his character. So did their descendants, who had a genius for attracting mates of good family and loose morals.

"That branch of the DeLuceys has produced nothing but frauds, gamesters, and swindlers," the earl said. "They are completely untrustworthy, and they have made themselves famous for their scandals. Generation after generation it continues. Bigamies and divorces are nothing out of the way for them. They live mainly abroad these days—to avoid their creditors and to sponge off anyone fool enough to take notice of them. An infamous family."

And Benedict had very nearly pursued one of them.

Even when he got away from her he couldn't escape her. People wouldn't stop talking about her.

She was a siren, a femme fatale.

But she had dismissed him.

Or had she?

It's nothing to do with impertinence and everything to do with self-preservation.

Was that a dismissal or a lure?

Not that it mattered. He would never know the answer because he would not try to find out.

Even before he was wed, he conducted his amours quietly. He had been scrupulously faithful while wed. He had waited a decent interval after Ada's death before acquiring a mistress, and the affair never became public knowledge.

Bathsheba Wingate was a walking legend.

His father's voice called him back to his surroundings.

"Well, Benedict, what do you mean to do about Lisle?"

Benedict wondered how much of the conversation he'd missed. He said smoothly, "The boy's future is not in my hands." He returned the *Quarterly Review* to its place.

"Don't be absurd," said Lord Hargate. "Someone must take charge."

And it must be me, as usual, Benedict thought.

"You know Atherton cannot manage matters," his mother said. "Peregrine not only respects you but he is attached to you. You have an obligation to him. If you do not intervene, that child will go straight to the devil."

My life is one endless chain of obligations, Benedict thought—and immediately reproached himself for thinking it. He was fond of Peregrine, and he knew, better than anybody, how much damage Atherton and his wife were doing.

Benedict knew what Peregrine needed, what he responded to. Logic. Calm. And simple rules.

Benedict believed in all these things, especially rules.

Without rules, life became incomprehensible. Without rules, one's passions and whims prevailed, and life flew out of control.

He promised to intervene to the extent of finding a drawing instructor and perhaps, in time, a tutor.

When that was settled, Peregrine was summoned to rejoin the family.

The rest of the evening proceeded peaceably, apart from Daphne's arguing with her father-in-law about the British Museum's scandalous treatment of Signor Belzoni. No one intervened, though the debate grew ferocious. Lady Hargate looked on amused, and Rupert proudly watched his wife. Even Peregrine sat silent and fiercely attentive, for Egypt was the one subject dear to his heart.

In the carriage, on the way home, Benedict asked why the boy hadn't sought his opinion of the scorned drawings.

"I was afraid you would be tactful," said Peregrine. "I knew Lord Hargate would tell me the plain truth. He said I needed a drawing master."

"I shall find one," Benedict said.

"The red-haired girl's mother is a drawing master," Peregrine said.

"Is she, indeed?"

Temptation rose before Benedict. She smiled her siren smile and crooked her finger.

He had turned his back on Temptation before, countless times. He could easily do it again, he told himself.

THE FOLLOWING AFTERNOON, Lord Rathbourne stood gazing at a card in the window of a print shop in Holborn, his countenance expressionless, his heart beating hard and fast.

Because of a piece of paper.

But that was ridiculous. He had no reason to be agitated.

The paper merely bore her name—her initial at least, and her late husband's surname. It was not even engraved but handwritten. Most beautifully handwritten.

> *Watercolor and drawing lessons by the hour.*
> *Experienced instructor, trained on the Continent.*
> *Sample work on display.*
> *For further particulars, enquire within.*
> *B. Wingate*

He looked down at Peregrine.

"It's where the freckle-faced girl said it would be," his nephew said. "One of her mother's works is supposed to be in the window as well. She said I might judge for myself whether her mother was skilled enough to teach me. Not that I can judge, when I know nothing at all about drawing, according to *her*." He frowned. "I did have a horrible suspicion even before she told me, and I wasn't surprised when Lord Hargate said my drawing was *execrable*."

While the boy searched eagerly for Mrs. Wingate's work among the assorted artistic atrocities in the print seller's window, Benedict wished his father would mince words once in a while.

Had he spoken a degree less damningly of Peregrine's efforts, the boy would not be so desperate at present for a drawing master. He was on fire to get started—there wasn't a moment to lose—his bad habits would only get harder and harder to break—and the lady took students—and she was sensible and agreeable, was she not?

Benedict should have simply said that Bathsheba Wingate was out of the question.

Instead, he'd given in. To curiosity.

A foolish indulgence.

True, Atherton did not involve himself overmuch in the details of his son's education . . . or his life. He only wanted the boy in a suitable school, and left effecting that miracle to his secretary.

At present, Atherton was with his wife at their place in Scotland. He did not propose to return to London until the new year.

He was not behaving very differently from the normal run of aristocratic parent.

The trouble was, Peregrine was not the normal run of aristocratic progeny. He fit no more easily into the world into which he was born than his namesake falcon might fit in a canary cage. His ambition in life wasn't simply to follow in the footsteps of his father and his father's father and a long line of Dalmay men before them.

While the possibility of being different had never occurred to Benedict, he could respect the ambition and admire the dedication to the one goal.

Still, this did not satisfactorily explain why he was here, in one of the drearier parts of Holborn, no less.

He did intend to find Peregrine a drawing master.

But it could not be Bathsheba Wingate. Atherton would draw the line at his son's taking lessons from one of the Dreadful DeLuceys—especially this one.

"There it is!" Peregrine pointed to a watercolor of Hampstead Heath.

As Benedict took it in, the pressure on his chest returned. It was as though a fist pressed against his heart.

This was everything a watercolor should be: true not only in line and form and tint, but in spirit. It was as though the artist had snatched a moment in time.

It was beautiful, hauntingly so, and he wanted it.

Far too much.

Not that his desire for it signified in the least. What signified was, the artist couldn't teach Peregrine. One didn't hire notorious women to educate impressionable children.

A drawing *master,* Lord Hargate had said, not a drawing *mistress.*

"Well, is it any good?" Peregrine said anxiously.

Say it's barely adequate. Pedestrian. Mediocre. Say anything but the truth and you can walk away and forget her.

"It's brilliant," Benedict said.

He paused to reestablish the connection between his brain and his tongue.

"Too good, in fact," he went on. "I cannot believe she will waste her time giving lessons to unruly children. Obviously she must be seeking more advanced students. I am sure the girl meant well. It was flattering of her, in fact, to offer her mother's services. However—"

The shop door opened, a woman hurried out and down the steps, glanced his way . . . and tripped.

Benedict moved instinctively to block her fall, and caught her before she could plunge to the pavement.

Caught her in his arms.

And looked down.

Her bonnet, dislodged, hung rakishly to one side.

He had an unobstructed view of the top of her head, of thick curls, blue-black in the afternoon light.

She tipped her head back, and he looked down into enormous blue eyes, fathoms deep.

His head bent. Her lips parted. His hold tightened. She made a sound, the smallest gasp.

He became aware of his hands, clamped upon her upper arms, and of the warmth under his gloves . . . and of her breath on his face—because his was inches away from hers.

He lifted his head. He made himself do it calmly while he fought to breathe normally, think normally.

He searched desperately for a rule, any rule, to make the world come out of chaos and back into order.

Humor will relieve an awkward moment.

"Mrs. Wingate," he said. "We were speaking of you. How good of you to drop by."

HE RELEASED HER, and Bathsheba backed away and straightened her bonnet, but the damage was done. She could still feel the pressure of his fingers through layers of muslin and wool. She still felt his breath on her lips, could almost taste him. She was too aware of the scent of him, of maleness and skin-scent teasing her nostrils. She tried to ignore it, tried to concentrate on the safer fragrances of starch and soap.

He smelled clean, scrupulously clean. It had been a very

long time since she'd been so close to a man who was scrupulously clean and starched and crisply pressed.

And now she knew he had a small scar under his chin, directly below the left corner of his mouth. It was thin, very slightly curved, and three-quarters of an inch long.

She didn't want to know he had a scar or what he smelled like. She didn't want to know any more about him. She had hardly noticed men in the three years since Jack's death, and before that, she'd never taken much notice of anyone but Jack. It was Fate's perversity that made her take such excruciatingly detailed notice of Lord Perfect.

"Lord Rathbourne," she said, still feeling short of breath, still burning with embarrassment. Of all the men's arms in all the world, she had to fall into *his*.

"You said we don't travel in the same spheres," he said. "But we must, for here we are."

"Yes, and I must be going," she said, turning away.

"We were seeking a drawing instructor," he said.

Arrrgh.

She turned back.

"For Lisle," he said. "My nephew. The one who—er—annoyed Miss Wingate yesterday. This one, in point of fact." He nodded at the boy.

"That girl only said my drawings weren't very good," said Lord Lisle. "She didn't tell me how bad they were—but Lord Hargate said my drawings are *execrable*."

Lord Rathbourne simply glanced down at him, and the boy hastily added, "Miss Wingate, I mean. She was so good as to offer her expert opinion. She was too kind, it turns out."

Bathsheba had been wrong yesterday about Olivia getting an Idea in nine and a half minutes. Clearly, she'd already had one and begun acting on it.

It was not hard to guess how Olivia's mind must have worked: *Here is a nob, who must have pots of money.* Naturally, like her DeLucey forebears, she had viewed the young Lord Lisle as a *mark*.

Not that Bathsheba was any more noble. At the mention of drawing lessons, she had paused, hadn't she, and commenced calculating how many drawing lessons at what rate would take her to a new neighborhood in a month or less.

"Olivia has altogether too many opinions," she said. "Worse, she rarely keeps them to herself."

"The fact remains," said Rathbourne. "My nephew cannot draw. If he cannot draw, he cannot realize his ambitions."

"Ambitions?" Bathsheba repeated, so astonished that she stopped calculating. "What need he do more than live, to realize his ambitions?"

She turned to the young Lord Lisle. "One day you will be the Marquess of Atherton," she said. "You may draw—and paint—and sculpt—as ill as you like and no one will dream of finding fault. Your acquaintances will say you are *sensitive* or you have an eye for beauty. They will beg for one of your works, which they will display in the stables or the guest bedchamber reserved for visitors they wish to be quickly rid of. Why on earth should you make yourself bored and cross with drawing lessons?"

"I know I'll be the Marquess of Atherton someday," the boy said. "But I'm going to be an explorer as well. In Egypt. An explorer must be able to draw."

"You can hire someone to do the drawing for you," she said.

"You had better take the hint, Lisle," said Rathbourne. "The lady is not eager to have you as a drawing student."

"You were not listening properly," she said. "That is not what I said."

"I know what you said," the boy said. "You think I will not take it seriously."

"You must make sure you are very serious," she said. She made herself look seriously at the matter, too, recalling certain harsh facts of life that erased the gleaming heaps of coins from the picture. "As your uncle is no doubt aware by now, I should have to make special arrangements for you. In any case, it is not at all wise to continue this discussion here."

She allowed herself to meet Lord Rathbourne's gaze. Did she see relief in those dark eyes?

It was only the briefest flicker, but it was emotion of some kind, and what else could it be?

She should have realized: If Rathbourne had learnt her name, then he must know everything else about her. She doubted there was a single member of the British aristocracy who did not know who Bathsheba Wingate was.

In that case, *he* was not serious about hiring her. He'd come only to indulge the boy . . . and perhaps himself.

Perhaps he had another sort of association in mind, and the boy offered a convenient excuse.

No one expected a man, even a perfect one, to live a celibate life. The world would still consider him the embodiment of the noble ideal if he kept a mistress, as long as he was discreet about it.

"What kind of special arrangements?" Lisle said.

"We are keeping the lady from her other students," Rathbourne said. "You and I shall discuss the subject further at another time, Lisle."

"Please do," she said, lifting her chin. "If you choose to pursue the matter, you may write to me in care of Mr. Popham the print seller. Good day." She hurried away, face hot and eyes itching with the angry tears she refused to shed.

Chapter 3

AS BATHSHEBA SUSPECTED, OLIVIA DID HAVE AN Idea and she did see Lord Lisle as a mark.

The Idea had been gradually taking shape in her mind since they'd come to London, nearly a year ago.

London wasn't as much fun as Dublin. Here, her mother made too many rules. Here, one must be bored witless every day in the classroom of a pinch-faced, droning schoolmistress.

In Dublin, when Papa was alive, life was jollier. Mama wasn't so strict. She laughed more. She invented interesting games and told wonderful stories.

All that changed when Papa died.

Though he'd told them not to grieve—he'd never had so much fun in all his life as he'd had with his wife and daughter, he said—it was impossible not to miss him. Olivia had cried more than he would have liked. Mama had, too.

But three years had gone by, and Mama still wasn't herself.

Olivia had no trouble understanding why: They were too poor, and poor people were usually unhappy. They were hungry or sick or living in the meanest lodgings or in workhouses or debtors' prisons. Other poor people cheated, robbed, and assaulted them. The bad ones got themselves imprisoned or transported or hanged, and the good ones suffered as much as if they'd been bad.

Not only was it disagreeable to be poor, it wasn't at all respectable.

For aristocrats, it was a completely different story. They had no worries. They did whatever they pleased, and no one arrested them or even objected when they behaved badly. They lived in enormous houses, with hundreds of servants looking after them. Aristocrats never worked. If one of them painted a picture, he didn't have to sell it to make money. He didn't have to give drawing lessons to shopkeepers' whining, spoiled brats, as Olivia's mother did.

Yet Mama was an aristocrat, too. Her great-great-grandfather was an earl, and *his* great-grandson lived near Bristol at a place called Throgmorton, an enormous house with hundreds of servants. Mama's mother was Sir Some-body's daughter. Her grandmother was Lord Somebody Else's second cousin. Practically all of Mama's relatives had blue blood in their veins.

The trouble was, there were two kinds of DeLuceys, the good ones and the bad ones, and Mama had had the tragic misfortune of being born into the bad side of the family.

Her side were the Dreadful DeLuceys ... shunned by the other lords and ladies and sirs because ... well, they were quite wicked, actually.

Mama wasn't at all wicked, and this was the great tragedy and cause of all her cruel sufferings and grievous poverty.

All of this made her a Damsel in Distress, exactly like the ones in the stories that Lord Lisle claimed were myths.

But he didn't understand anything.

They weren't myths, and if he'd known Mama's story, he would not have said such stupid, aggravating things, the great thickhead.

There were knights, too, and they didn't have to wear shining armor, at least not these days, and they didn't have to be men.

Olivia was the knight who would rescue her mother.

That was the Idea.

She was not yet certain exactly how to carry it out. She could see, though, that money was crucial.

This was why, at the Egyptian Hall, once her temper had cooled and she could think clearly, she decided to cultivate Lord Lisle.

He was the first aristocrat who'd come close enough to talk to since Papa died. Knowing it might be a very long time before she got that close to another one, Olivia had made the most of the opportunity.

As you'd expect, Mama didn't approve.

She came home very cross on Wednesday evening.

"I met up with Lord Rathbourne and Lord Lisle at Popham's today," she told Olivia as she took off her shabby cloak.

"Lord Rathbourne?" Olivia repeated. She pretended to be trying to remember who this was.

"You know perfectly well who he is," said her mother. "You assaulted his nephew. Then you tried to recruit the boy as a drawing student."

"Oh, *him*," said Olivia. "I told you I felt sorry for that boy. Obviously he was in desperate need of lessons."

"And we, obviously, are in desperate need of money," said her mother. "But you are barking up the wrong tree."

Olivia quickly began to lay out the tea things. Her mother watched, her face so stern. But she didn't look well. She had deep shadows under her eyes and her skin was too pale. Poor Mama!

"You are right, Mama," she said soothingly. "Everyone knows aristocrats never pay their tradesmen. I should have realized they'd treat teachers the same."

"That is not the point," her mother said. "You are grown up enough to understand our position. You know we are lepers and outcasts from the Great World."

"Lord Rathbourne didn't look disgusted when you spoke to him," Olivia said. He had looked at her as Papa used to do. And Mama had *blushed*.

"He was *acting*," her mother said. "He is a perfect gentleman, and a perfect gentleman is always polite. He would no more agree to my teaching his precious nephew how to draw than he would consent to your best friend the pawn-broker teaching him sums."

Well, this was disappointing.

But it would take more than one setback to daunt Olivia. Already she had an Idea.

THE LETTER ARRIVED on Thursday in a furtive manner calculated to awaken Peregrine's curiosity. The young under-footman slipped it to him, whispering that his lordship would have his head if he heard of it, but he didn't know how to say no to the young lady.

Possessing more than average intelligence, Peregrine had little trouble deducing the young lady's identity from the servant's description. The letter's clandestine arrival intrigued him to a painful degree. However, he knew better than to open it when anyone else was about. One of the other servants would see. The more who knew, the more likely the butler would find out. He would tell Lord Rathbourne.

Peregrine tucked the letter into an inner coat pocket and bore several hours of silent agonies before he was at last alone in his room, unwatched, and could open it.

Written in a large, elaborate, and untidy script, the thing took up a great deal of paper.

My Lord,

It is exceedingly wrong—and Fast, I believe—for a Young Lady to write privately to a Young Gentleman. Nonetheless, I must bow to a greater Necessity: <u>To Tell the Truth.</u> I know I risk lowering your Opinion of me. Not that I can imagine how you could think any Less than you do, for you must be aware by now that <u>Tragic Circumstances</u> have made me a <u>Leper and an Outcast</u> from the Great World to which you belong. ~~Until the Family Curse is lifted~~ My dear Mama has told me of meeting with you and His Lordship your Esteemed Uncle yesterday at Popham's Print Shop. She has chided me for my Audacity and explained why I should not have tried to enlist you as a *drawing student. Furthermore, she tells me I shall <u>Never See You Again.</u> I know this is of no consequence to you, for I am merely an Insignificant <u>Girl,</u> one you hardly know or would wish to know better. Yet our Meeting left a most <u>Forceful Impression</u> upon me. Since our Elders have decreed that we are <u>NEVER TO MEET AGAIN,</u> I must take the Liberty of telling you through these Secretive Means how greatly I <u>admire</u> your Honorable and Courageous Ambition to be a GREAT EXPLORER instead of another Idle Aristocrat. I most <u>earnestly</u> wish you well in your Endeavors to learn to Draw.*

> *Yours sincerely,*
> *Olivia Wingate*

P.S. Please do not attempt to communicate with me. ~~One day the Family Curse shall be lifted, and then~~ In India, there is a class of people known as Untouchables. ~~Until~~ Henceforth you must consider me one of Them.

The letter was ghastly, even for a girl. She'd overembellished the script with curls and corkscrews. The wretched excess of capital letters and thick underlines indicated sentimentality, an overly romantic turn of mind, and an emotional temperament.

Peregrine's parents were all these things; his paternal grandparents were more so. The Dalmays were always breaking out into dramatic scenes, and he was always being made to feel guilty without ever having the least idea what he was guilty of. But then, logic seemed to have no place in his relatives' thinking processes—if they had processes, which Peregrine sometimes doubted.

This was one of the many reasons he preferred his uncle's house and his uncle's company. Lord Rathbourne was calm. His household was calm. When he was vexed, he did not fly into a passion. He did not storm about and spout long, vehement speeches that made no sense. He never lost his temper, although once in a while he might become annoyed. Then his drawl might grow a trifle more pronounced and his countenance so calm that it might have been made of marble. But he never made a to-do. Ever. About anything.

With his uncle, Peregrine did not spend his time tensed, waiting for the next storm to break. With his uncle, Peregrine always knew exactly where he stood and precisely what was expected of him.

Until Wednesday evening, that is.

Before going to his room to dress to go out, Lord Rathbourne stopped by the study where Peregrine was writing out a Greek exercise. After making two corrections, his lordship told Peregrine that Mrs. Wingate "would not suit" as a drawing master.

Surprised and puzzled, Peregrine could not help trying to ascertain the logic of this decision.

"I do not understand, sir," he said. "What was unsuitable about her? Didn't you say that her watercolor was brilliant? You seemed to admire it very much. You seemed to find her agreeable. Of course, it is difficult to tell when you are polite because you want to be and polite because it is a gentleman's duty. When I do it, the difference is so obvious. But she was not boring or silly at all. Quite the opposite. Did she not strike you as unusually intelligent for a female?"

Lord Rathbourne did not answer any of these questions. Instead, his face acquired a marble calm. When he spoke, his drawl was quite pronounced. "I said she was not suitable, Lisle. That is the end of it."

"But, sir—"

"I can think of few exercises more tiresome than being catechized by a thirteen-year-old boy," Lord Rathbourne said.

Peregrine recognized the exceedingly bored tone. It meant the subject was closed.

This was a shock. Usually his lordship was the most logical and reasonable of adults.

If Peregrine had not been so completely flummoxed, he wouldn't have stared so hard. Then he would not have seen it. But he did stare and he did see it: a muscle twitch. Only the once, and very quick and slight, at the far corner of his uncle's right cheekbone.

Then Peregrine knew there was a Serious Problem (as Olivia would have written) regarding Mrs. Wingate.

If Lord Rathbourne would not tell him what it was, it must be very serious indeed.

If he would not speak of it to Peregrine, no other adult would. If Peregrine was so foolish as to ask someone else, he or she would say, "If it was proper for you to know, Lord Rathbourne would have told you."

Peregrine tried through all of Friday and Saturday to put the letter out of his head. The girl was silly—ye gods, she wanted to be a knight!—and since he'd never see her again, her family secrets didn't matter.

The trouble was, his chosen vocation was the finding out of secrets. He'd recently returned to his Greek and Latin studies with a zeal he'd previously been unable to muster. This was because he'd found out they were crucial to unlocking the secrets of the ancient Egyptians. Aunt Daphne—she wasn't really his aunt, but all of Lord Rathbourne's family had adopted him—had promised to teach Peregrine Coptic, one of the keys to deciphering hieroglyphs, if he could get through Homer creditably.

Thus, by Sunday, Peregrine knew that he would go mad if he didn't find out why Olivia Wingate was a <u>Leper and an Outcast,</u> and what the ~~Family Curse~~ was.

This is why, on Sunday night, long after his uncle had bade him good night and gone out, and most of the household had gone to bed, Peregrine began writing to Olivia Wingate.

THE LETTER FROM Lord Rathbourne arrived in care of Mr. Popham the print seller late on Friday. Bathsheba waited until she was at home to read it. With trembling fingers she opened it.

His lordship's secretary had written it. The message declining her services was short and scrupulously polite.

She stared blindly at it for a long time after she'd absorbed the meaning. A too-familiar icy feeling trickled through her veins. Then the heat came, setting her face aflame.

She told herself it wasn't the same, but the memory burned in her mind as though freshly branded there, though three years had passed.

It was a few months after she'd buried Jack. A note arrived from her father-in-law, written by his secretary. It accompanied the long letter he'd received, he believed, from her. This letter, which Bathsheba had never written, maundered on about Jack's death and his "beloved daughter Olivia." The writer sought forgiveness. And money, of course. It was horrible. "Let us be reconciled in Jack's memory and for his child's sake" . . . and more in that vein. For pages and pages the letter wheedled and begged, a shameless attempt to take advantage of Jack's death and his father's grief.

It was written in her mother's hand.

Mama hadn't even had the decency to exploit the situation in her own name. If she had, Bathsheba might never have known about it, never suffered a moment's distress on that account.

But no, Mama must pretend to be Bathsheba.

And so it was Bathsheba who received Lord Fosbury's curt reply. It was Bathsheba who was mortified.

And when she wrote to Mama, the answer was as she might have expected: "I did it for you, my love, because you are too proud and overscrupulous."

That was the last letter Bathsheba had from her mother. Her parents moved on to St. Petersburg, where Papa died of a liver ailment. Mama remarried soon after and went away without a word to anybody, including her daughter. Bathsheba wished she missed her family, but she didn't. Her childhood was filled with incidents like the letter to Lord Fosbury. Small wonder she'd been willing to endure anything, in order to have a life with Jack instead.

"What is it, Mama?" Olivia said.

Bathsheba looked up. She had not heard the girl come in. "Nothing," Bathsheba said. She tore Lord Rathbourne's secretary's note into very small pieces and threw it on the fire.

"You've been weeping," Olivia said.

Bathsheba hastily wiped her eyes. "I must have got a cinder in my eye," she said.

It *was* nothing, she told herself. She had known this would happen. She'd merely lost a potential pupil. She'd find others. This was nothing like the humiliation of Lord Fosbury's note. It was ridiculous to feel angry ... disappointed ... hurt.

The visit to the Egyptian Hall had been her first venture into a part of London that Society frequented. Her exchange with Lord Rathbourne had been her first conversation with a gentleman since Jack's funeral. The newness of the experience had unsettled her, that was all.

This explanation wasn't completely persuasive, but it got her through the rest of Friday, Saturday, and Sunday.

On Monday she conducted her drawing class as usual, in the room she rented two floors above the print shop. When the class was over, she went down to the shop as she usually did, to find out if anyone had enquired about drawing lessons.

A tall, familiar figure stood at the counter.

She stood and stared like a gawking girl who'd never learnt any manners at all, her gaze roaming over the broad shoulders and down the straight back and down and down along a mile-long stretch of muscled leg and up again, over the immaculate, elegantly garbed masculine figure. She gazed entranced at the strip of white neckcloth visible above the coat collar and the thick, dark hair curling against the neckcloth and the small, curving shadow the brim of his hat made at his ear.

"Ah, here she is," said Mr. Popham. She blinked as his head came into view. The tall, aristocratic figure had completely obscured the print seller's small person.

The gentleman turned. Rathbourne, yes, of course. Who else could be so ... perfect, even from the back? Who else would regard her so composedly, displaying not a flicker of surprise—no hint of unseemly interest?

He did not gawk like an imbecile.

"Mrs. Wingate," he said. "You have arrived in the very nick of time. Popham and I had almost come to blows."

"Oh, no, indeed, I am sure not, my lord," said Mr. Popham, much flustered. "Merely a hesitation on my part, as I was not at all certain ..." He trailed off, clearly at a loss.

"I expressed a desire to observe your drawing class," said his lordship. "Mr. Popham tells me it is conducted upstairs."

"The class is over," Bathsheba said. "I thought your interest was as well. I received a note to that effect. Or did I dream it?"

"You are displeased with me," he said. "You are thinking that when a man makes up his mind, he ought to make up his mind."

She was thinking she discerned an infuriatingly faint hint of a smile at the right corner of his mouth. "What is required to help you make up your mind once and for all?" she said. "The class is over. My next is on Wednesday. Do you wish to make another tedious journey to the other side of the moon to observe it?"

"Holborn is not the other side of the moon," he said.

"It is not a sphere in which you customarily travel," she said.

"Perhaps you would wish me to wrap the painting now, my lord, while you continue your conversation with Mrs. Wingate?" Mr. Popham said. "Then it will be ready for you when you leave. Or were you desiring to have it sent on?"

"No, I shall take it with me," Rathbourne said, his dark gaze never leaving Bathsheba.

Popham disappeared into the back room.

"Your watercolor of Hampstead Heath," Rathbourne said. "That is the problem, you see. That is what brings me to Holborn. That is what has made me so indecisive. It has haunted me since last Wednesday. I strongly doubt I should easily find another instructor as gifted. The true talents devote their time to creating and exhibiting their works. The more pedestrian make their living by teaching. I wondered whether I ought to take advantage before you come to your senses and leave off wasting your time and talent teaching brats like my nephew."

Had he complimented her beauty, Bathsheba could have listened unmoved. Though she knew she was well past her bloom, she was accustomed to that kind of flattery and thought little of it. Her looks were not her doing.

Her art was, and she had worked at it. She was particularly proud of the painting of Hampstead Heath. He could not have directed his praise more aptly.

She was hot everywhere, blushing like the veriest schoolgirl. "My usual pupils are nothing like your nephew," she said. "The classroom is nothing like what he is used to, either. And talented or not, we both know I am not suitable. You might be willing to overlook my background, but his family will go into fits."

"His family always goes into fits," Rathbourne said. "I try to ignore them as much as possible. Would you be so good as to show me the classroom, please, and allow me to try to imagine it populated with students? I am not an artist, and my imagination is limited. I hope it is a smallish class."

"Eight students on Mondays," she said. "This way, then." She led him out of the shop and up the narrow stairs.

"Imagining eight is within my capabilities," he said, and his deep voice seemed lower yet in the cramped, dim surroundings. "Girls? Boys? Both?"

"Girls." It was two flights up, but she was used to the climb and should not be breathing so hard. She was grateful he asked no more questions until she opened the classroom door.

The sparsely furnished room was large and amply supplied with windows. "The light is good, you see," she said, "especially in the early afternoon. It's always kept clean. Several of us—all women—share the rent and use the space alternately. We employ a diligent cleaning woman."

She showed him the easels, neatly stacked in a corner of the room. "My girls are the daughters of prosperous tradesmen. Some are a little spoiled, but I have managed to teach them the importance of maintaining order in the work space."

He walked to a window, clasped his hands behind his back, and looked out. She noticed his head was bare. She glanced about and saw his hat on a chair. He must have taken it off when he entered the room. She didn't know why she was surprised, or if surprise was what she felt. The afternoon light played over dark hair clean and free of

pomade. It had a hint of curl, which would be far more pronounced when it was wet.

Do not *picture him wet,* she commanded herself.

His deep voice dragged her back from the brink of danger. "What else do you teach them?" he asked. "What is
your method?"

She explained how she began with simple still life exercises, allowing her students to bring a few objects from
home and arrange them as they wished. "Perhaps some
fruit or a cup and saucer at first," she said. "Later, I might
arrange a bonnet, a pair of gloves, and a book. There are
outdoor exercises, too, when the weather permits. Trees,
doorways, a shop front."

"You do not take them to the Royal Academy to copy
other artists' works?" he said, still looking out of the
window.

"That is not the best method for my students," she said.
"They do not aim to become artists. Their main desire is
to acquire refinement and ladylike accomplishments. Their
parents want them to rise in the world. I teach my students
to see. I teach them mechanics and techniques. In learning
these, they acquire the capacity to discern quality. What they
learn from me they might apply to other subjects or hob-
bies." She tried to imagine what an adolescent lordling
would gain from such instruction.

"You teach fundamentals, in other words," said Rathbourne.

"Yes."

"That is what Peregrine lacks," he said, turning away
from the window finally. The sunlight outlined the almost-
curls and burnished his chiseled features. "He lacks the
foundation. He has had drawing masters. Apparently, their
methods did not suit him. Perhaps yours will."

"He would require private lessons," she said, ruthlessly
suppressing the seed of hope trying to sprout within her. He
had said only "perhaps." It was the diplomatic thing to say.
The room must seem shabby to him, her methods amateur-
ish, her students nobodies. "I cannot teach him in classes
with the girls. His presence would be disruptive. He will
make some girls shy and others bold and all of them silly."

"Peregrine *is* a disruptive presence," said Rathbourne. "It hardly matters who is about. Girls, boys, adults. Teachers, family, clergymen, sailors, soldiers, members of Parliament. My nephew is a doubting Thomas. He wants everything proved. He is inquisitive, argumentative, and obstinate. He will ask you *Why?* a hundred times in an hour. If you do not triple your usual fee at the very least, you will be a great fool."

He could not be serious. Thrice her fee for one boy? Lord Lisle couldn't be more difficult to manage than Olivia, however much he tried, however much his parents had spoiled him. Olivia had inherited altogether too much of the Dreadful DeLucey character.

"In that case, I shall quadruple it," Bathsheba said.

"He said you were sensible," said Rathbourne, coming away from the window. "Would you be willing to take him, then, in spite of my warning?"

She did not even blink. Her father had taught her how to play cards. "Have you made up your mind, then?" she said.

He looked about the room. "Society won't like it," he said. "Society's sympathies lie with your late husband's family."

"Oh," she said. She felt so weary, suddenly. She felt like Sisyphus, pushing the great stone up the hill, only to have it roll back down again. The stone was her past, and it rolled over the sprout of hope and crushed it. She'd felt the same way the other day in front of the print shop when she'd realized that her name was closing another door against her.

"These ancient grudges and prejudices are so tiresome," he said. "If Peregrine's parents find out you are teaching him, they will fly into fits. Emotional extravagance is their nature, you see. They cannot help it. Perhaps this is why they are at a complete loss what to do about him. Their solution is to leave him to me while they retire to their lair in Scotland. But if my in-laws leave him to me, they must live with my decisions." His gaze came to her then, and he smiled a very little. "All I need do is make up my mind. Do you know, you look at this moment as your daughter did when she became annoyed with Peregrine? Perhaps you wish to strike me with a sketchbook?"

"Would that help you make up your mind?" she said.

The smile became more pronounced, and she wished he had kept it hidden away, because the actual thing, rather than the hint of it, made her heart go much too fast and her brain much too slow.

"I have decided that the boy needs you," he said. "I have decided that he is more important than old grudges and scandals."

HE'D COME TO his senses, Benedict believed.

He'd been aware of her entering the print seller's before he acknowledged it. He'd heard the light step, sensed her presence. He'd taken his time turning to her, steeling himself first.

Then he'd looked, and the spell was broken, he thought.

She was not the most beautiful creature in all the world, as he'd believed. She did not appear too young to have a daughter near Peregrine's age. The face Benedict had found so unforgettable was careworn, the eyes not so brilliant as he remembered.

Consequently, he could be certain that he was choosing strictly as his conscience commanded, unaffected by the Great World's opinion or the scenes he'd endure should Atherton learn of it. One must choose what was best for Peregrine.

The instant Benedict said the words, he knew he'd made the right choice.

What he did not expect was to see the rightness reflected in her countenance. First her eyes lit, then her expression softened, then the taut line of her mouth dissolved into a luscious curve of a smile. The careworn expression fled, taking all signs of age with it. The blue of her eyes was brilliant, almost blinding, and she seemed all alight somehow.

If he'd been a fanciful man, he might have imagined he'd uttered a magical incantation to effect such a transformation.

But he never allowed himself to be fanciful.

"You truly are perfect," she said wonderingly.

Perfect. So everyone said of him. How low their standards of perfection were!

"Yes, it is a great bore," he said. "I ought to say, 'Nobody is perfect,' but that is even more boring. My comfort is, if word of this gets about, people will stop saying I am perfect. How exciting. At last I shall have a fault."

"I had no idea it was so difficult to acquire one," she said. "Luckily, you came to the right place. As you may have heard, my branch of the DeLucey family possesses them in abundance."

"If I need another one, I shall know where to come," he said.

"I recommend you grow accustomed to the one first," she said. "At present, it is a secret fault. Some people consider these the best kind."

"One fault, one secret," said Benedict. "I feel quite dissipated."

"I'm honored to help," she said. "But to return to business: Shall Lord Lisle come here for his lessons? I know it is out of the way, but that may be an advantage. He is less likely to cross paths with anyone who knows him."

"That advantage occurred to me," said Benedict. "It will be simple enough to send him with a servant." A discreet one. "On foot, I think."

"But it is nearly two miles from Cavendish Square," she said.

"You know where I live," he said.

"Who does not?" she said.

Who, indeed? Benedict wondered. Privacy was one luxury out of his reach.

"Two miles is nothing," he said. "Peregrine needs the exercise, especially now. He has recently realized that a high competence in Greek and Latin is essential to the antiquarian. As a result, he has become obsessed with the classical authors. If he truly means to go to Egypt, he will need to be fit physically as well as mentally. He will need to become accustomed as well to being among people who do not *travel in the same spheres* as he."

He allowed himself a smile over the phrase. She did not know *everything* about him—or very much about London—if she thought him a stranger to Holborn. Then he dragged his gaze from her remarkable face to the window, and the view beyond, of the buildings opposite. This was all for Peregrine. He must keep his mind on Peregrine.

She seemed to have no difficulty keeping her mind on business. She named the days and times the classroom was available for private instruction, wrote down the supplies needed, and obtained the name and direction of Benedict's man of business, to whom she'd send her bill.

After this, he had no excuse for lingering. In another ten minutes he'd collected the watercolor from Popham and set out for a more exclusive establishment well west of Holborn, to have the drawing mounted and framed.

It would hang in his bedroom, Benedict decided.

Chapter 4

TEN DAYS PASSED, AND FOUR LESSONS. NOT once in this time did Benedict darken Mr. Popham's door.

The obvious choice to accompany Peregrine to his drawing lessons was the footman Thomas, whom Benedict had brought down from Derbyshire. This was the only servant Benedict could trust to keep the matter to himself.

Discreetly dressed in everyday clothes rather than livery, Thomas would adjourn to a nearby coffeehouse while the lesson went on. At the end of the allotted time, he would collect his charge at the print shop door.

The task was well within Thomas's abilities because Benedict had given Peregrine one simple rule: "You will go quietly to and from your drawing lessons. If any Incidents occur—before, during, or after—the lessons will cease. No excuses will be accepted. Is that clear?"

"Yes, sir," said Peregrine.

Benedict let him go, certain the rule was sufficient. Anything deemed crucial to his vocation, like Latin and Greek, received Peregrine's full and fierce attention. Mrs. Wingate did not need Benedict at hand to subdue his nephew.

It was Benedict who needed subduing.

Day Eleven, a Friday, found him dangerously bored and restless.

It was not as though he had nothing to do. He was following a troubling criminal case at the Old Bailey. He had a speech to prepare in support of a proposal for a metropolitan police force. Though most of Fashionable Society had left London, they had not left a desert behind. He suffered no shortage of invitations to dine and dance, attend lectures, concerts, plays, operas, ballets, and exhibitions.

He was desperately bored, all the same.

So bored that he had twice this afternoon caught himself starting to pace, a practice he considered suitable only for hysterical women and other high-strung persons.

Caged animals pace. Children fidget. A gentleman stands or sits quietly.

Benedict sat quietly in his study, in the chair behind his desk. His secretary, Gregson, sat opposite. They were reviewing the last ten days' correspondence.

His lordship had been too bored to attend to it until now. He didn't want to do it now, either. If he continued to ignore it, however, the small piles of letters and cards would grow into great untidy heaps. That was the sort of thing irresponsible persons like his brothers Rupert and Darius allowed to happen.

The responsible gentleman keeps his affairs in order.

"This one is from Lord Atherton, sir," said Gregson, taking up a thick one. "Perhaps you prefer to open it."

"Certainly not," said Benedict. "Then I should see what is inside, and you know he always puts in thrice as many words as any subject needs, along with a surfeit of dashes and exclamation points. Please be so good as to pare it down to the essentials."

"Certainly, sir." Gregson perused the thick epistle. " 'I had a most distressing encounter,' " he read.

"No distressing encounters," Benedict said.

Gregson returned to the letter. " 'I was outraged to learn—' "

"No outrages," said his lordship.

" 'Priscilla's mother—' "

"Nothing to do with Lady Atherton's mama, I beg you, Gregson. Perhaps you had better summarize."

Gregson rapidly scanned the next few pages. "He has found a place for Lord Lisle."

Benedict stiffened. "What place?"

Gregson read: " 'You will be as relieved as we were, I am sure, to learn that arrangements have at last been made for my errant son. Heriot's School in Edinburgh has agreed to take him.' "

"Heriot's School," Benedict said. "In Edinburgh."

"In a fortnight's time, his lordship will send servants to collect Lord Lisle and take him to his new school," said Gregson.

Benedict got up from the desk and walked to the window. He stood quietly. By gazing steadily into the garden below and watching the chrysanthemums bob in the September breeze, he was able to maintain his composure. Nothing of the inner storm could be seen on the outer man.

Certainly he did not say what he was thinking. He rarely did. Despite years of discipline, his thoughts regarding his fellow creatures and their doings sometimes had a rampaging quality. In his mind, in fact, he sometimes sounded like Atherton on one of his rants.

Unlike Atherton, however, Benedict had taught himself to keep the rampage inside. What little he expressed he restricted to dry observations, sarcasm, and a raised eyebrow.

Life is not an opera. Scenes belong on the stage.

Benedict did not storm about the study, berating his muddleheaded brother-in-law. He merely said, "Send Lord Atherton a note, Gregson. Tell him that he may spare his servants a journey. I shall take the boy to Scotland in a fortnight."

Half an hour later, Lord Rathbourne was on his way to Holborn.

THANKS TO THE crush of traffic, Benedict did not reach the print shop until well after Peregrine's lesson was over and the boy was on his way home. Mrs. Wingate had departed as well, Mr. Popham told Benedict.

Benedict tried to tell himself to communicate with her

by letter. He rejected the idea—as he'd done a dozen or more times on the way here.

A letter simply wouldn't do. She had taken offense at the last one, declining her services.

Benedict remembered the scornful way she'd referred to it, the haughty lift of her chin, the disdain in her blue eyes. He had wanted to laugh. He had wanted to bring his face close to that beautiful, angry one and . . .

And do something he shouldn't.

To Popham he said, "I must speak to her. It is urgent. Regarding one of her pupils. Perhaps you would be so good as to give me her direction."

Mr. Popham turned red. "I pray your lordship will n-not take offense, b-but I am not at liberty to give the lady's direction."

"Not at liberty," Benedict repeated evenly.

"N-no, y-your lordship. I beg pardon, your l-lordship. I trust your lordship will understand. The—er—difficulties. For a widow, that is, especially a young one, living on her own. Men can make such n-nuisances of themselves. Not your lordship, certainly—that is to say, but . . . er. The difficulty is, I did faithfully promise the lady to make no exceptions. Sir."

What Benedict wanted to do was reach across the counter, grab the little man by the neck, and strike his head against the counter until he became more cooperative.

What Benedict said was, "Your scruples do you credit, sir. I quite understand. Kindly send a note to Mrs. Wingate, seeking her permission for me to call. I shall wait."

Then he disposed himself upon a chair at a table and began perusing a portfolio of lithographs.

"I sh-should be h-happy to, your lordship," Popham stammered. "But there is a d-difficulty. My assistant is making a delivery, and I cannot leave the shop unattended."

"Then send a ticket porter," said Benedict without looking up from the prints.

"Yes, your lordship." Popham stepped out of the shop. He looked up the street. He looked down the street. No ticket porter appeared. He returned to the shop. At intervals, he went out again, and looked up and down the street.

It was a small shop. Though Benedict was not a small man, he did not take up a great deal of space physically. However, being an aristocrat—a species virtually unknown in this part of Holborn—he seemed to take up a good deal more space than ordinary people did.

Not only did he seem to occupy every square inch of the shop, but he made customers stare and forget what they'd come in for. Several walked out, too awed and intimidated to buy anything. That wasn't the worst of it.

He had taken a hackney in lieu of one of his own carriages, in order to travel without calling attention to himself. But he'd paid the driver to wait, and the vehicle dawdling in front of the shop was slowing traffic. Idlers gathered about to gossip with the driver and among themselves. Passing drivers expressed their ire loudly enough to be heard inside the shop. Popham grew redder and more agitated.

Finally, when half an hour had passed and the assistant had not yet returned, he gave Lord Rathbourne the address.

FROM HOLBORN THE hackney driver turned left into Hatton Garden then right into Charles Street. Here, at a public house named the Bleeding Heart, Benedict disembarked. He asked the driver to wait farther down the street, where the vehicle would not impede traffic so much.

He crossed the street, then paused at the narrow way leading down into the yard.

The neighborhood was an exceedingly poor one. Contrary to Mrs. Wingate's beliefs, however, Lord Rathbourne was no stranger to London's more downtrodden areas. He had been involved in several parliamentary inquiries into the condition of the lower classes. He had not obtained his information solely by reading.

He did not hesitate, either, because he feared contagion, though his wife had died of a fever caught during one of her evangelical missions into a neighborhood like this.

He paused because reason returned.

What on earth could he say in person that he could not say in a letter? What did it matter to him whether

Mrs. Wingate took it ill or not? Had he simply leapt at the excuse to see her? Had he let the rampage in his mind rule his actions?

This last question made him reverse direction.

He made his way back down Charles Street. He walked briskly, keeping his eyes on the way ahead and his mind firmly where it ought to be. This was business. He would write Mrs. Wingate a note informing her that Peregrine was returning to school and could not continue his lessons with her. She would be paid for the full schedule of lessons they'd agreed upon, naturally. Benedict would thank her for all she'd accomplished with the boy so far. He would allow himself a word of regret, perhaps, about the abruptness—

Curse Atherton! Why could he not go on in an orderly fashion, instead of one minute throwing up his hands and proclaiming the cause hopeless and the next—

A jarring sensation, then a jumble of sensations: Benedict heard the short shriek, saw the parcels tumbling about him, felt a bonnet strike his chin and a hand grab his coat sleeve, all at the same time.

He caught her—it was definitely a she, and he knew which she it was in the next instant, even before he saw her face.

IF SHE'D BEEN paying attention to where she was putting her feet instead of gawking at him, Bathsheba would not have missed the step. He was not looking her way, but straight ahead, his mind clearly elsewhere. If only she'd kept her wits about her, he would have passed, and she would not have made a spectacle of herself.

Again.

She saw his eyes widen when he recognized her, and the unguarded expression she saw in those dark depths sent a jolt of heat through her.

The look vanished in an instant, but the heat remained, tingling in her veins and softening her muscles.

He swiftly set her on her feet. He was a good deal slower to let go. She was aware of bands of heat where the long,

gloved hands clasped her upper arms. She was aware of
warmth radiating from the large, hard body inches from
hers. She saw the textures of wool and linen and took in
the strong contrast of color: brilliant white against deep
green. She inhaled the clean scents of soap and starch, the
more exotic fragrance mingling with them, of a discreet
and costly masculine cologne . . . and far more insidious,
the scent of *him.*

"Mrs. Wingate," he said. "I was hoping our paths would
cross."

"You would have done better to look rather than simply
hope," she said. "Had I not had the presence of mind to
throw myself in your way, you might have missed me
altogether."

His grip tightened. She realized then that she was still
holding on, her hand still clutching his forearm. It was like
grasping warm marble.

She let go, dragged her gaze from his, and focused on
her parcels, strewn about the pavement. A passing vehicle
had crushed her basket under its wheels.

"You may release me," she said. "I should like to collect
my purchases before an enterprising street urchin makes
off with them."

He released her and gathered her parcels.

She watched him perform the lowly task with his usual
perfect grace. Even his coat did not appear to stretch at the
seams when he bent, though it fit him like skin. Weston's
work, very likely. And what his lordship had paid for it
would probably keep her and Olivia comfortably for a
year, perhaps two or three.

The crowd forming about them watched him, too, with
undisguised curiosity. Bathsheba belatedly collected her
wits.

"A footman, out of work," she explained. "One of my
late husband's relatives turned him off, poor fellow."

"He's come to the wrong neighborhood, Mrs. W," said
an onlooker. "There ain't hardly work enough for ordinary
folk hereabouts."

"Pity, ain't it?" said another. "Big, strong fellow like

that. The Quality likes them tall, strapping fellows, I heard. Is it true, ma'am?"

"Yes," she said. "Tall footmen are *de rigeur.*"

When he'd retrieved all her parcels, she started away at a brisk pace, leaving the audience to argue about what *de rigeur* meant.

When they'd turned a corner and the crowd was out of earshot, he said, "I'm a footman?"

"You should not have come to this neighborhood dressed so fine," she said. "Clearly you have no idea how to travel incognito."

"I had not thought about it."

"Obviously not," she said. "Luckily, one of us comes of a long line of accomplished liars. Your being a footman accounts for both your elegant dress and your air of superiority."

"My air of—" He broke off. "You are walking in the wrong direction. Is not Bleeding Heart Yard the other way?"

She stopped. "You found out where I live."

He nodded over the bundles stacked under his jaw. "It is not Popham's fault. I bullied him. I wish I had not. I despise bullying. But I was . . . exceedingly annoyed."

"With Popham?"

"With my brother-in-law. Atherton."

"Then why did you not bully your brother-in-law?"

"He is in Scotland. Did I not tell you that?"

"My lord," she said.

"Ah, here is a quiet churchyard," he said, indicating the place with his chin. "Why do we not go in? We shall be private without giving an appearance of impropriety."

She was not so sanguine about what appeared improper and what didn't. Still, if he had his hands full of bundles . . .

She went in, and paused at a spot close by the gateway.

He set her purchases down on a gravestone. "I am obliged to take Peregrine to Scotland in a fortnight," he said. "His father makes anarchy of our neat arrangements. He has had a fit of responsibility and decided to foist his offspring upon Heriot's School in Edinburgh."

She suppressed a sigh. *Good-bye, shiny coins,* she thought. "Is that not a good school?" she said.

"Peregrine will never fit in any of our great British schools," he said, his voice clipped. "But one cannot explain this to Atherton by letter. One can scarcely explain anything to him at all. He is too impatient, impulsive, and dramatic to reason matters out."

To Bathsheba's surprise, Lord Rathbourne began to pace the pathway. He did it gracefully, of course, being perfect, but with a contained energy that seemed to make the air churn about him.

"If he would only view the matter in a rational way," he went on, "he would see that the methods of the British public school are antithetical to Peregrine's character. One learns everything by rote. One is expected to do as one is told without question, to memorize without making sense of what one memorizes. When Peregrine insists upon knowing why and wherefore, he is deemed disrespectful at best, blasphemous at worst. Then he is punished. Most boys require only a few beatings to learn to hold their tongues. Peregrine is not most boys. Beatings mean nothing to him. Why can his father not see this, when it is obvious to a mere uncle?" the uncle concluded, shaking his fist.

"Perhaps the father lacks the uncle's ability to imagine himself in the boy's place," she said.

Rathbourne halted abruptly. He looked down at his clenched hand and blinked once. He unclenched it. "Really. Well. I should have thought Atherton had imagination enough for half a dozen men. More than I, certainly."

"Parents have a peculiar sort of vision," she said. "They can be blind in some ways. Does your father understand *you*?"

For a moment he looked shocked, and she was as well, to discern so strong a sign of emotion. She'd seen at the start that his was a tell-nothing countenance.

"I sincerely hope not," he said.

She laughed. She couldn't help it. It had lasted but a moment—he was back to looking inscrutable—but for that brief time he had seemed a chagrined schoolboy, and she thought she would have liked to know that boy.

Dangerous thought.

He stood for a time, looking at her and smiling the almost-smile. Then he approached. "Did you really fall in my way on purpose?" he said.

"That was a joke," she said. "The truth is, I was shocked witless to see you in Charles Street. I wish you would give warning the next time you decide to come looking for me. I had rather not walk into a shop front and black my eye or fall over a curb and break my ankle."

He had come too near, and his gaze was a magnet, drawing hers. She was caught for but a moment—time enough only for her to breathe in and out—yet it was time enough to lure her in deeper. Looking into those eyes, so dark, was like looking down a long, shadowy corridor. Too intriguing. She wanted to find out what was at the end of it, *who* was at the end of it, and how great a distance it was from the man on the outside to the man on the inside.

She looked away. "I did not mean you ought to come looking for me," she added. "I was not issuing an invitation."

"I know I ought not to have come," he said. "I could have written to you. Yet here I am."

She could not let herself be drawn in again. She focused on the gravestone behind him, where her parcels lay.

"Yes, well, I must be going," she said. "Olivia returns home from school soon, and if I am not there, she finds things to do. Usually it is something one had rather she didn't."

"Ah, yes, how remiss of me." He moved away, to the gravestone, and started collecting her belongings. "I should not have troubled you in the first place, and I have compounded the offense by trespassing too long upon your time."

He hadn't trespassed for long enough. She hadn't found out a fraction of what she wanted to know.

Think of your daughter, she told herself. *Curiosity about this man is a luxury you cannot afford.*

"I prefer to carry them now, my lord," she said. "A foot-man will be out of place in Bleeding Heart Yard. It would be best if we went our separate ways."

* * *

BENEDICT DID NOT want to go his separate way.

He wanted to stay where he was, talking to her, looking at her, listening to her. She had laughed—at what must have been a comical look of horror on his face when she asked whether his father understood him.

The sound of it wasn't what he'd expected. It was low, deep in her throat.

Wicked laughter. Bedroom laughter.

The laughter seemed to hang in the air about him as he returned to the hackney. It hung there during the short journey home. It followed him into the house and up to Peregrine's room.

He found the boy kneeling in the window seat, bent over a colored plate from Belzoni's book. It illustrated the ceiling of the pharaoh's tomb, with an assortment of strange figures and symbols in gold on a black background, possibly a representation of the nighttime sky and constellations as the ancient Egyptians saw them.

Benedict refused to puzzle over it. The ancient Egyptians were too aggravating for words.

He told the boy what Atherton had decided.

Peregrine frowned. "I do not understand," he said. "Father said he was done with sending me away to school. He said I was welcome to grow up illiterate and ignorant. He said I did not deserve a gentlemanly education when I could not behave as a gentleman ought. He said—"

"Obviously, he has changed his mind," Benedict said.

"It is exceedingly inconvenient," Peregrine said. "I am not done studying Belzoni's collection. In any case, it makes no sense to leave so soon. The term will have already started by the time I get to Edinburgh. If one must be a new boy, it is better to start at least with the other new boys. Now I shall be the newest new boy, and I shall waste a lot of valuable time fighting when I might be here, improving my Greek and Latin and organizing my tables of hieroglyphs."

Peregrine would not be bullied. He would not be any boy's lackey. As a consequence of this, and of eternally being the new boy, he spent a good deal of time making his position clear by means of his fists.

"I am aware of this," Benedict said. "The fact remains, your father commands, and you must obey." He did not mention the word or two he intended to have with Lord Atherton. Benedict did not hint at his intention to bring Peregrine straight back, if it was humanly possible, and hire a proper tutor for him, as should have been done ages ago.

He did not want to get his nephew's hopes up. In any case, a son must obey his father.

Parents must be treated with respect, whether one wants to strangle them or not.

Whatever else Benedict was prepared to do on Peregrine's behalf, he would not encourage disobedience.

"I thought he had washed his hands of me and put you in charge," Peregrine said. "Lord Hargate must think so, because it was you, not Papa, he told to find me a drawing master. And what is to become of my drawing, I cannot think. I shall never get on at this rate. I have only now begun to make progress. No, it is true," he said when Benedict's eyebrows went up. "Mrs. Wingate says so, and she does not flatter me, you know. 'Lord Lisle, you have been drawing with your feet again,' she will say when I have made a muck of things." He smiled. "She makes me laugh."

"I understand," Benedict said. She made him *want* to laugh. She'd done it at the Egyptian Hall, when she'd quizzed her daughter about attacking Peregrine. He'd wanted to laugh in front of Popham's shop—at her blank astonishment when informed that Peregrine had an ambition—and at her response to this. He'd wanted to laugh today, when she'd joked about throwing herself at Benedict.

She was droll. She said and did things he didn't expect.

He could still hear her laughter.

"Well, I suppose there is no help for it," Peregrine said. He closed the book. "Still, I have a fortnight. I shall have to make the most of the time."

Benedict had prepared himself for a good deal more trouble. Peregrine had not sought a fraction as many whys and wherefores as expected. Perhaps he'd at last realized that his father's behavior seldom had any rational basis, and had given up looking for one.

Perhaps the boy was maturing, learning, finally.

"If you please, sir, may I go to the British Museum tomorrow?" Peregrine said. "I should like to have another go at the head of Young Memnon. I had asked Mrs. Wingate if we might have an extra lesson on a Saturday, there or at the Egyptian Hall, but she hasn't time. She will be in Soho Square for most of tomorrow morning and early afternoon, she said."

"A portrait commission, probably," Benedict said. One of the tradesmen whose daughters she taught must have recognized her talent.

"I believe she's looking for lodgings there," said Peregrine.

Benedict supposed that Soho Square might seem to some an improvement over Bleeding Heart Yard. Yet both addresses teetered on the edge of unsavory neighborhoods. "I should advise her against it," he said. "She is unwise to move so close to Seven Dials. It is as bad as if not worse than Saffron Hill."

Peregrine frowned.

"Not that it is any of our concern where she chooses to live," Benedict went on. "You want to visit the British Museum. You had better go with Thomas. There is no reason for me to hang about while you practice drawing."

"Indeed not," said Peregrine. "You would be dreadfully bored. Naturally I assumed I must behave as though it were a lesson day. Even if one of the museum directors happens by, I shall say nothing to him about the red granite sarcophagus in the courtyard—the one Aunt Daphne is so troubled about—though it truly is shameful, sir, the way they have treated Signor Belzoni—"

"So it is, and sooner or later, Rupert will start throwing the directors out of windows," Benedict said. "You, however, will hold your tongue."

The last thing in the world he needed now was to become involved in the wrangling about Belzoni's acquisitions: what belonged to whom and who ought to pay for it. He had carefully deflected all Daphne's attempts to lure him into fighting that exasperating battle. He had enough battles to fight as it was. The primary one at present involved Peregrine's future.

"I shan't breathe a word about it, sir, upon my honor," said Peregrine.

"Very well, then, you may go with Thomas."

Then, relieved to have one troublesome matter settled so easily, Lord Rathbourne left.

He did not see the guilty look his nephew cast after him.

Chapter 5

PEREGRINE'S GUILT WAS ON ACCOUNT OF THE
Wingate lady he'd failed to mention, the one sitting on a
portable stool next to his. They were sketching an enormous red granite pharaoh's head with a partially broken
crown: the head of Young Memnon that Belzoni had sent
back from Egypt.

Unlike the Egyptian Hall, the museum was rarely
crowded, because it was so difficult to get tickets. It was
easier, some said, to obtain vouchers to Almack's Assembly Rooms, Society's most exclusive gathering place.

How Olivia Wingate had obtained a ticket Peregrine did
not and had rather not know.

Though the place was deserted today, the two spoke in
whispers, and made sure to keep their pencils moving
busily.

"It will be easy enough for me to write to you in Edinburgh," Olivia was assuring him.

It was better she didn't write to him, Peregrine told himself. Her letters were dangerous.

He shouldn't be here with her. Not one of the adults
in his life would approve of her. For one thing, she was

deceitful. Today, for instance, her mother believed Olivia was here with a school friend and the friend's mother.

While Peregrine hadn't told his uncle about her, he hadn't told any outright lies. His conscience nagged and pinched all the same. She, on the other hand, didn't seem to own a conscience.

He knew this, knew she was trouble. But he couldn't seem to help himself. She was as horribly irresistible as a ghost story. One couldn't stop until the end.

"Do the grown-ups read all your letters?" she said.

He shook his head. "Not the ones from family and schoolmates."

"That makes it simple," she said. "They'll probably know a relative's hand, so I'll pretend to be a former school-mate. I'll use his name and direction and make my writing look like a boy's."

Oh, it was tempting. Olivia's outrageous letters would certainly offer an escape from dreary school days. But wasn't what she suggested a *crime*? If Uncle found out . . .

"You are very pale," she said. "I am not sure you get enough exercise. Or perhaps you are not eating well. I should not let going away to Edinburgh spoil my appetite, if I were you. It's a lovely place, and not all of the Scots are as dour as people believe."

"You're proposing to do *forgery*," Peregrine whispered. "It's a capital offense. You could be hanged."

"Shall I stop writing to you, then?" she said, unconcerned.

"Perhaps it would be best."

"Perhaps you are right. I shall have to sort out the details on my own."

Peregrine knew he shouldn't ask, but it was impossible not to. He lasted barely a minute before the question burst from him. "What details?" he said. "Regarding what?"

"My quest," she said.

"What quest?" he said. "You are not going to be a knight until you grow up."

He was more teachable than his uncle thought. Peregrine knew better than to repeat his error of telling her she would never be a knight. That would only make her lose her temper. He was not afraid she'd injure him. He was afraid the row would attract attention. That would make an Incident, and the few drawing lessons he had left would turn into no drawing lessons at all.

"I can't wait until I grow up," she said. "Now that you are leaving, Mama and I are back where we started. We shall never get anywhere, relying on drawing lessons. I shall have to take matters into my own hands and find the treasure."

Over the course of several clandestine letters, Peregrine had learned, in appalling detail, precisely why Olivia and her mother were <u>Outcasts and Lepers</u>. He was aware that the ~~Family Curse~~ was ill fame. The Dreadful DeLuceys deserved their bad reputation, Olivia had cheerfully admitted—all except her mother, who was nothing like the others. If anything, Olivia considered her mama far too proper.

If Olivia was one of the milder examples, Peregrine thought, "Dreadful" was a gross understatement.

She had filled her letters with references to this wicked relative or that. She had never before mentioned treasure, however.

"What treasure?" he said, unable to help himself.

"Edmund DeLucey's treasure," she said. "My great-great-grandfather. The pirate. I know where he hid it."

BATHSHEBA SET OUT on Saturday morning with a list of possible lodgings and an optimistic spirit.

She worked her way in an orderly fashion up and down the streets projecting from Soho Square and round the square itself.

Meanwhile, the day, which started out mild and clear, grew steadily less so. By early afternoon a sharp breeze had driven down the temperature, and dreary grey clouds obscured the sun. By midafternoon, the breeze was stiffening into a wintry wind and the clouds were darkening, along with her mood.

The rooms she could afford in Soho, she found, were shabbier and more cramped than those she had now. At least in Bleeding Heart Yard, some of the ancient buildings retained vestiges of their bygone grandeur. Not all of their large rooms had been divided and divided again into narrow little ones.

Moreover, the neighborhood, acceptable at the heart, quickly deteriorated, much as her present one did. A few minutes' walking southeastward from Soho Square brought one into St. Giles's, a notorious back-slum.

In short, Bathsheba had wasted a Saturday. Instead of looking forward to a new home, she could only look forward to spending more precious hours on a task she was beginning to believe futile.

Thanks to Lord Lisle's ridiculously expensive lessons, her finances had improved markedly, but she feared they had not improved enough to make any significant difference in her circumstances.

London had turned out to be a great deal more costly than she'd expected. Not for the first time she wondered whether she'd done the right thing in coming here. Dublin was cheaper and friendlier.

Yet Ireland was poorer, and obtaining artistic work had been even more difficult there. Good, affordable schooling for Olivia certainly was easier to find in London.

In less than a year, Miss Smithson of New Ormond Street had eradicated all traces of Olivia's brogue. She spoke as a lady ought to speak. If only one could teach her to behave as a lady ought to behave. In school, among her classmates and under Miss Smithson's basilisk gaze, Olivia was a model of ladylike deportment. Unfortunately, like so many of her maternal relatives, she was a chameleon, adapting easily to her surroundings. Out of school, among a different class of persons, she was another girl altogether.

Matters would not improve if they returned to Ireland.

London was the place of opportunity. But it did not offer opportunity cheap or make the way easy.

It was not going to make way for Bathsheba Wingate today, obviously.

Time to give up and go home.

She started down Meard's Court as the first cold drops of rain began to fall. She was used to rain and cold, but today, weary in both body and spirit, she minded it very much.

The rain pattered on her bonnet and the shoulders of her cloak. Soon it would beat harder, she thought, glancing up at the blackening sky. She would be wet through by the time she had walked home.

When she reached the corner of Dean Street, she found herself gazing southward toward St. Anne's Church. There was a hackney stand at the church.

But if she splurged on a hired vehicle she must scrimp for dinner.

She put the hackney out of her mind and hurried across Dean Street, her gaze darting north and south. If she had been looking straight ahead she might have been run over, for the grey veil of rain turned her into a dark blur. But she didn't look straight ahead. She very sensibly watched the street for oncoming carts and carriages.

And so she ran straight into the man on the walkway.

She heard a grunt, and felt him stagger a little. She grabbed two fistfuls of coat to keep him from toppling over. This was not the most intelligent move, but she acted instinctively. It took her brain another moment to point out that he was taller and heavier than she was and would only take her down with him.

By this time, he'd regained his balance.

"Oh, I do beg your pardon," she said, releasing the coat. Out of maternal habit, she smoothed it down where she'd wrinkled it. "I was not looking—"

That was when she lifted her head and did look, finally. Rain drizzled into her face and the daylight was all but gone, yet she had no trouble recognizing the coal-black eyes gazing down at her over the patrician nose or the firm mouth with its provoking promise of a smile.

She simply stared, one hand falling away, the other still resting on his coat.

"It is I who ought to beg your pardon," Lord Rathbourne said. "I seem to have acquired a troublesome habit of standing in your way."

"I did not see you," she said. She snatched her hand away from his coat. Once, only once, could she not meet up with him in a civilized and graceful way? Embarrassment swept over her in a hot rush, sharpening her tone.

"I shouldn't see you here. What could possibly bring you to Soho?"

"You," he said. "I have been looking for you for hours. But I shall not keep you standing in the rain while I explain myself. Let us make a dash to St. Anne's Church for a hackney. We can speak more comfortably then."

Involuntarily, her gaze shot southward again, to the church.

Oh, it was tempting.

But riding in a closed carriage with a man who turned her into a witless sixteen-year-old was asking for trouble.

"No, thank you," she said. "I think it best if we travel in different directions." Once more she set herself walking eastward.

She was distantly aware of a rumble. In the next instant, her feet left the ground, and before she could make her brain believe it was happening, he had scooped her up and was carrying her down Dean Street.

They'd reached Compton Street before she recovered her wits and untangled her tongue. "Put me down," she said.

He kept on walking.

He was not even breathing hard.

She was. The arms bracing her were like iron bands. His broad chest and shoulders blocked out the wind and much of the rain. His coat was damp, but warmed by the body under it.

While she had realized he was fit—the cut of his clothes had told her so—she'd greatly underestimated his strength. She knew he was tall and well proportioned. She hadn't realized, though, how very much of him there was.

Too much.

Overpowering.

An image came into her head of warriors in armor storming castles, slaughtering the men, and carrying off the women.

His ancestors were such men.

"Put me down," she said. She squirmed.

He only tightened his grasp, crushing her more closely against him.

She grew hot and addled. She knew she ought to fight, but her will was ebbing away. Or maybe what she felt was her morals disintegrating.

Belatedly she recollected their surroundings: a public byway. If she renewed her struggles, all she'd do was attract attention.

People had clustered in doorways for shelter. They had nothing to do but stare at passersby.

Someone might recognize him. Or her. If word of this got out . . .

It did not bear thinking of.

She kept her head down and tried to occupy her brain with composing devastating set-downs and plotting retribution. She found that her mind had gone on holiday and left her body in charge.

Her body was warm and sheltered. It wanted to get closer to the stronger one, the source of heat. It wanted to crawl inside his coat.

Luckily, they had only a short distance to cover, and he walked briskly. In a few minutes, they reached the hackney stand.

"The lady's slipped and hurt her foot," he told the driver at the head of the queue. "I should prefer to travel with a minimum of sudden starts, stops, and bumps, if you please." He tossed her into the vehicle, growled something else at the driver, and climbed in beside her.

"I'm sorry about that," he said, when the vehicle was in motion. "Well, not completely sorry." His mouth curved a very little.

She tried to think of a cutting answer. Her mind was sluggish. Her heart, meanwhile, was beating dementedly.

"I was too impatient, perhaps," he said. "Yet it seemed absurd to stand in the rain, arguing with you. I only wanted to make an offer."

She stiffened. This she could understand, all too well. This was not confusing. The heat drained away, leaving her chilled, and she said, with all the icy dignity she could muster, "A *what*?"

He made a dismissive gesture. "Not *that* kind of offer," he said.

"It would seem that you've mistaken me for someone who was born yesterday, my lord," she said.

"It would seem you are completely blind to the obvious, to suppose I should deceive you about such a thing," he said.

"I am not blind," she said.

"You are not using your head," he said. "Try a little common sense. I am not a younger son. I haven't the luxury of being the family scapegrace. That is Rupert's job. My world is a small one, where liaisons are nearly impossible to keep secret. They might, however, be kept quiet, if they are too boring to interest the gossips and the scandal sheets. You are much too exciting. If I became intimately involved with you, I should be made a public spectacle—as Byron was, but worse. The caricaturists would be thrilled. I should not be able to stir a step without seeing my exaggerated image, captioned with what passes for witticism these days. The prospect does not enchant me."

Bathsheba was aware that Lord Byron had been ridiculed mercilessly. She had seen some of the cruel caricatures.

With Rathbourne, it would be worse. The higher a man stood in the public eye, the keener the world's delight in his fall.

"Oh," she said, deflated. Disappointed, too. For a moment she had almost believed that she made Lord Perfect as witless and immature as he made her.

"My offer is a respectable one," he said. "I know of a set of rooms in Bloomsbury that might suit you. The landlady is a war widow. The rent should be within your means, if I have calculated correctly. If one multiplies one-fourth the rate you charge for Peregrine by your eight students on Mondays and—"

"You *calculated* my income?" she said.

He explained that much of his parliamentary work involved computation. Consequently he understood what a budget was and how to balance it. He was aware, furthermore, that some people had to live on very little money. He and a few colleagues had founded enterprises aimed at bettering the condition of war widows, veterans, and others for whom neither the government nor the parish provided adequately or at all.

"Oh, yes, your famous philanthropy," she said, her face burning. She did not want to be one of his charity cases.

"This is not philanthropy, madam," he said coldly. "I am merely saving you the trouble of finding Mrs. Briggs on your own and wasting time roaming unsatisfactory neighborhoods like Soho. The rest will be up to you. Would you like to see the place?"

The chill tone was calculated to subdue the listener. It made Bathsheba want to shake him. She had her pride, after all, which rebelled at being treated like an unintelligent, lesser being. Still, Olivia's future was more important than her mama's pride.

Bathsheba swallowed it in a gulp. "Indeed, I would," she said.

She had not understood the directions he'd given the hackney driver, and the rain was so heavy now that the world outside was a blur. When the hackney stopped, and Rathbourne alit to help her out, she must simply trust that he was taking her to Mrs. Briggs of Bloomsbury Square, and not his private love nest.

She could see that the blood of his savage ancestors still ran in his veins. She could see that he was a good deal too accustomed to telling others what to do and too little used to their contradicting him.

She had trouble, however, seeing him as one who lured women to their undoing through deceit and trickery.

To lure a woman, all he had to do was stand there, looking bored with being perfect.

Her instincts proved correct. Mrs. Briggs turned out to be a respectable lady of middle years. The rooms she offered, while far from luxurious, were neatly kept and furnished. The price was a bit higher than Bathsheba liked, yet lower than what she'd assumed she must pay in this part of London. Within an hour, all was settled, and she was in another hackney with Rathbourne, on her way home.

En route, he gave her financial advice. His assuming that she was financially incompetent was annoying, but she supposed he couldn't help it. He was in the habit of arranging the lives of the less fortunate. In any case, he had experience with this sort of thing, and only a fool would refuse to listen.

She was surprised, though, when he took out one of his calling cards and on the back wrote the names and addresses of shops to whom she ought to bring her watercolors and drawings. Were her art hanging in Fleet Street or the Strand, it was more likely to attract those with the means to purchase it, he told her. Moreover, she must raise her prices. "You do not value your work sufficiently," he said.

"I am a complete unknown," she said. "I do not belong to any prestigious art society. One must value the work accordingly."

"Your name, as I pointed out earlier, is far from unknown," he said. "What you are is naïve."

She almost laughed. She had lost the last of her naïveté by the time she was ten years old, thanks to her parents. "I am two and thirty, and I have lived everywhere," she said. "While I may not have seen *everything*, there is not a great deal I haven't."

"You don't seem to understand your potential customers," he said. "This makes me wonder if you are truly one of the Dreadful DeLuceys. You have failed to take advantage of common human weaknesses. It has not occurred to you to exploit your notoriety. You seem unaware that the more expensive an item is, the more people value it. Such is the case, in any event, with Fashionable Society. When you set a rate of quadruple the usual to teach Peregrine, my respect for you increased proportionally."

It was no use trying to read his face. Even if his were not a tell-nothing countenance, the light was too dim. She could not decide whether or not he was being sarcastic. He sounded bored.

"I advise you to make them pay," he said. "You cannot change Society. Despite my privileged position, I cannot, either. Even I must live according to the rules, as I said before. It is tiresome, but the price of breaking the rules is excessive. In addition to causing my family distress, I should lose the respect of people necessary to passing bills, instituting reforms, and supporting various other efforts that give my life purpose. You have already paid a high price because your late husband broke Society's rules. What do you owe the Beau Monde, then? Does it not owe you? Why should you not require ample payment for the work that supports you and your daughter?"

The bored drawl could easily make one believe the subject was merely tedious to him. He sounded the way he'd looked in the Egyptian Hall, at the moment she'd first seen him: the very model of aristocratic ennui.

The carriage interior was small, though, and she sat too near him not to sense something amiss: a tension in the air, perhaps. Or maybe it was the way he held his head and shoulders. Whatever it was, she doubted that the man on the inside was fully in harmony with the one on the outside.

"Perhaps I have fallen into a bad habit of being humble," she said. "How shocked Papa and Mama would be!"

Neither of her parents would have hesitated to exploit others' weaknesses. Neither of them knew what a scruple was.

"There is that," he said. "Another trouble is, you are not a Londoner. You do not know how to take proper advantage of the place. Like most of my acquaintance, you know your bits of London, but you do not know her in all her infinite variety."

"London is like Cleopatra to you?" she said, smiling at the image of the bored aristocrat fascinated with this vast, smoky metropolis. " 'Age cannot wither her, nor custom stale her infinite variety.' Is that your view?"

He nodded. "You know your Shakespeare," he said.

"But not my London, it would seem."

"That would be impossible," he said. "You have lived here for how long? A year?"

"Not quite."

"I have spent the greater part of my life here," he said. "I am obnoxiously knowledgeable."

He proceeded to demonstrate, with a detailed description of the environs of Bloomsbury, including the shops and vendors worth patronizing and those best avoided.

They reached the Bleeding Heart Tavern all too soon for Bathsheba. She could have listened to him for a good deal longer. He loved London, clearly, and the picture he painted

transformed it for her. This afternoon it had seemed a cold
fortress, shutting its gates to her. He opened it up, and turned
it into a haven.

That was not all he'd done for her this day, she realized.
A short while earlier, she'd felt bowed down by the weight
of her cares. Rathbourne had lightened them.

This had never happened to her before.

Her parents spent their money as fast as they got it, and
went on spending when there wasn't any. When creditors
and landlords became difficult, Mama and Papa packed up
and moved, usually in the dead of night.

Though Jack was far more honorable, he was no more
helpful. He had loved her passionately, but he was hope-
lessly irresponsible. The practical problems of everyday
life were completely outside his experience. He couldn't
see them, let alone analyze and solve them. He had no notion of the value of money. The concept of living within
one's means was beyond his comprehension.

This man, who did not love her, had sorted out her
finances, guided her to precisely the sort of home she'd
hoped for, and advised her how to make and save money.
He'd even taken London apart for her, as though it were a
mechanical toy, and shown her how it worked.

The carriage stopped. She was not ready to part from
him but she had no excuse to stay.

"Thank you," she said, and laughed a little. "Two paltry
words, not a fraction of what I feel. If only I were Shakespeare. But I am not. *Thank you* must do all the work of
reams of clever verse."

She meant the words to do all the work.

But her spirits had lifted, and for a moment anything
was possible, and so she dared to lean toward him and
lightly kiss him on the cheek.

He turned his head at that moment, and then his mouth
was moving over hers and his hand was curling round the
back of her neck, and she was on her way to perdition.

BENEDICT SHOULD NOT have turned his head.

He should not have sought those plum-ripe lips.

But he had, and the instant his mouth touched hers, his famous self-control unraveled.

He grasped the back of her neck and drew her closer and kissed her as he'd wanted to do from the first moment he saw her.

He felt her stiffen, and *No danger,* some distant part of his brain assured him. She would thrust him away, and probably slap him for good measure.

She did not thrust him away.

Her body abruptly went all soft and pliant, and her mouth moved under his, answering. Her silken hair tickled the back of his hand, begging to twine about his fingers. The scent of her skin stole inside him like a dangerous vapor, and the longing to which he'd refused to yield came to wild life inside him.

His body remembered the feel of hers when he carried her, the easy way she fit in his arms, the soft curves tucked against his hard frame. His body had craved more, and it had cost him an effort, later, to speak without revealing the depths of his frustration.

But that was before. This was now, and all he cared about was now. He cupped her face and drank deeply. He tasted dreams and youth and longing—a taste like a night of too much wine, a taste like too many lonely nights.

Of course he wasn't drunk or lonely and he knew better than to yearn for his youth and its dreams, its passions. All that was behind him. Years behind. Lost.

He should have recognized the danger then, understood what was stirring to life within him, and stopped.

But he was past the moment of logical thinking. He was unable to recognize that what he tasted was danger, and so he failed to understand why it called more insistently than common sense. He understood only that this tasted like a woman and smelled like a woman and felt like a woman—and she was a forbidden woman, all the more irresistible.

Her hands stole up his coat and caught hold of the fabric. He felt her fists on his chest, and his heart thundered with excitement, like a boy's when a girl first says yes. He brought his hands to her jaw, to untie the bonnet. He pushed it from her head. He dragged his hands through her hair, and the glossy curls coiled about his fingers as he'd wanted, and they were softer and silkier than he'd imagined. Everything about her was more than a man could imagine, and he wanted more.

He crushed her against him and deepened the kiss, to find the secret taste of her. He let his hands rove over her back and down to her waist, but as he slid them over her breasts, she broke away.

She pushed him from her with surprising strength. "No! Enough!" She turned away and picked up her bonnet from the carriage floor. "Oh, this is very bad."

She shoved it on her head and hastily tied the ribbons. "This was *unforgivably* stupid. What is wrong with me? I cannot believe— What an *idiot*. I was supposed to kick you or tread on your foot. I vow, one would think I had never learnt a thing about men. This was a terrible *mistake*!"

He found his voice and some vestige of his mind. "Yes, it was," he said.

He collected his famous composure and helped her out of the carriage.

The perfect gentleman, as always.

"Good-bye," he said.

She hurried away without answering. In the next instant, she'd vanished into the night.

He swore once, under his breath, then set himself to gathering the shattered pieces of what used to be his perfectly regulated world.

Chapter 6

Friday 5 October

TO AVOID FURTHER INVOLVING THE UNDER-
footman in the secret, Peregrine had made a post office of
sorts by prying loose some bricks near the back garden
gate. There either Olivia or an accomplice deposited her
letters and collected Peregrine's. Though she was a girl,
she moved about London far more freely than Peregrine
did.

Unlike him, she did not have servants watching her constantly. She made any number of detours to and from
school, none of which she remembered to mention to her
mother, and all of which horrified and fascinated him.

He squeezed into the shrubbery, where he would not be
seen, and opened the letter.

Queen Square
Thursday 4 October
My Lord,
Farewell!
The Time has come for me to Depart upon my Quest.

"No," Peregrine said. *"No."*

He had written two long letters to her, explaining what was wrong with her Idea about finding Edmund DeLucey's treasure. First and foremost, young ladies—and she *was* a lady by birth, and must never forget this—did not set off on jaunts unaccompanied. Second, she must consider the grief she would cause her mother, who was an agreeable, sensible, and intelligent parent, unlike some. He had written third, fourth, fifth, and sixth points, too—a complete waste of ink.

"I might as well have written to the head of Young Memnon," Peregrine muttered.

> *Be assured, sir, that I have read and thought about* Every Word *you have written to me. However,* Matters Have Reached a *Crisis. We moved to Queen Square on Monday. Our new Lodgings are more than comfortable, and I for one am glad to put a distance between my home and St. Sepulchre's Workhouse. Yet Mama grows more Un-*happy *every day. I fear she is Sickening, the Victim of a* Wasting Disease. *She pretends to eat and sleep, but it is all a Sham, for she grows pale and thin. I am glad Papa is not alive to see it, because he would be Heartsick.*
>
> *Even you must agree that I have* Not a Moment To Lose *but must set out AT ONCE. Rest assured that I have taken your words To Heart and shall not make this Journey* Alone. *Sir Olivia travels with her Trusty Squire, Nat Diggerby. His uncle drives a cart to market on Mondays and Fridays. We have arranged to meet him tomorrow at the Hyde Park Corner Tollgate. He will take us as far as Hounslow. A Wise Plan, you must agree.*

"No, I don't, you idiot girl," Peregrine said. "What becomes of you after Hounslow—if you get that far? Do you never stop to think that your *Squire* Diggerby might be taking you to his 'uncle' the pimp or his 'aunt' the brothel keeper?"

Peregrine could hardly believe she was so naïve, given how much else she knew. He supposed the deficiency was on account of never having attended public school, where boys learned, along with Greek and Latin, all they needed to know about pimps, bawds, and prostitutes.

He hadn't time to fill in the gap in her education.

The impulsive creature was leaving *today*.

He had to stop her.

BATHSHEBA GAVE UP waiting for Lord Lisle after half
an hour. Evidently she'd misunderstood his schedule.
She'd thought he'd said he was leaving on Saturday for
Scotland. He must have said Friday, and she had only half-
listened, her mind elsewhere.

She could not recall whether he'd said good-bye. But
why should a boy of thirteen think it necessary to take any
special leave of his drawing teacher? His uncle had taken
polite leave already, a few days after their last encounter.
His secretary had written a courteous thank-you letter, en-
closing payment for the remaining lessons.

She gathered her belongings, closed up the classroom,
and set out for home: a new home, thanks to Lord Rathbourne . . . whom she'd never see again.

He would keep away, and she was safe now, quite safe.

Also bored and out of sorts . . .

. . . until some hours later, when she was taking the
table linens out of the cupboard and found the letter Olivia
had left for her.

PEREGRINE ARRIVED AT Hyde Park Corner tired, hot,
and cross. He'd lost his way several times, and twice he'd
had to run away from louts who took exception to his
costly attire. In normal circumstances, Peregrine would have
run straight at them, in order to beat them bloody. He
couldn't take the time, and having to run away like a coward did not improve his temper.

He was angry with himself, too, for not having the good
sense to hire a hackney and spare himself a great deal of
aggravation.

This was not the best frame of mind in which to approach
Olivia, who stood talking to some women selling pies. Beside her stood the boy version of a bull: Nat Diggerby, no
doubt. His head went straight down to his shoulders, with

no discernible neck between, and his shoulders were so wide he must have to go through doors sideways. He stood like a bull, too, head tilted downward, while only his eyes moved, watching the scene about him.

Peregrine straightened his own shoulders, puffed out his chest, and marched up to them. Instead of the persuasive and tactful speech he'd rehearsed, he said, "Miss Wingate, I've come to take you home."

Her big, blue doll eyes widened. "Why? Has something happened to Mama?"

"No, something has happened to you," Peregrine said. "A head injury is my guess. It's the only way to explain this cork-brained scheme of yours."

Scowling, the bull-boy moved in front of Olivia. "Here, bugger off, you," he said.

"Bugger off yourself," Peregrine said. "I wasn't talking to you."

The boy grasped the front of Peregrine's coat.

"Take your hand away," Peregrine said.

"Oooh, will you listen to him?" said the boy. "Ain't he the fine lady, though?"

"No, I ain't," Peregrine said, and slammed his fist into Bull-Boy's jaw.

BENEDICT WAS AT his club when he was informed that one of his servants wished to speak to him.

This was not a good sign.

The last time a servant had come to the club for him was when Ada had collapsed upon her return home after a prayer meeting.

Still, Benedict appeared calm and composed when he entered the antechamber where Thomas waited.

At his entrance, Thomas's face worked.

A very bad sign.

Ignoring the cold spreading in his gut, Benedict told him to say what the matter was in as few words as possible.

"It's Lord Lisle, my lord," Thomas said, blinking hard. "I don't know where he is. He went in the print shop door like he always does. I went into Porter's Coffee House to wait, like I always do. I come out like I always do, a few minutes early. He never come out, sir. I waited a quarter hour past the time, then I went up. The classroom was locked up tight, and no one answered when I knocked and called. I went down to the shop and asked Mr. Popham if the drawing lessons was over for today. He said there wasn't any. Mrs. Wingate went home early, he said, on account her pupil never came."

The cold spread further, numbing feeling. Time itself seemed to slow, as though frozen, too. "I see," said Benedict. Then he ordered his hat and coat and left with his footman.

During the short walk home, his feelings safely closed down, Benedict disciplined his mind to analyze the problem as though it were like any of the other problems he was called upon every day to sort out and solve.

By the time he entered his house, the thousands of wild possibilities he might have entertained had narrowed to the two likeliest, in the circumstances:

1. Peregrine had run away.
2. Despite all their precautions, someone had found out who Peregrine was and had kidnapped him.

Benedict went up to the boy's room with Thomas. A search revealed no signs of a planned departure. No clothes were missing, Thomas said, except for those Lord Lisle had worn today. Questioned more closely, however, the footman did produce two relevant pieces of information. First, the boy had struck up an acquaintance with a red-haired girl at the British Museum two weeks ago. Second, Peregrine was in the habit of visiting the garden several times a day.

Benedict destroyed several shrubs and a flower bed before he discovered the loose bricks near the back garden gate. Stuck to one was a broken piece of sealing wax and a fragment of paper.

Benedict returned to the bedroom. His gaze went to the window seat, which looked out into the garden. He often found his nephew there, bent over a book. A few minutes later, Benedict found the cache of letters, folded between the pages of Belzoni's *Narrative*.

* * *

IT DID NOT take Lord Lisle long to leave Nat Diggerby in a stunned heap by the side of the road. It was time enough for a crowd to gather, though, which gave Olivia a chance to slip away unnoticed.

The crowd aroused the curiosity of passersby, and traffic slowed in consequence. The road on both sides of the tollgate became jammed with vehicles, horses, and pedestrians. Among those forced to wait was a young farmer driving a small wagon. Olivia approached him. Tears filled her great blue eyes. From her trembling lips fell a poignant tale about an ailing mother in Slough.

Moved, the farmer offered her a ride in his cart as far as Brentford.

She climbed in.

Before the cart was through the tollgate, Lord Lisle came running alongside. "You beastly girl!" he said. "I won't let you do this."

"Oh, look, it is my poor brother," she told the farmer. "He is mad with grief. I told him to stay in London. He is sure to find work eventually. But he . . ."

She went on to tell a tragic tale of family woes. The farmer swallowed it whole. He told Lord Lisle he was welcome to join his sister if he chose.

Lord Lisle looked wildly about him. A couple of soldiers had got hold of Nat Diggerby and were dragging him to the watch house.

Lord Lisle climbed into the cart.

BATHSHEBA LIT ANOTHER candle and read the letter again, because the first time, she thought her eyes were playing tricks on her.

After the second perusal, she was furious.

Olivia's scheme was all too familiar. It was the same method her parents used to deal with their difficulties. They'd count on a crackbrained scheme to solve all their problems at once, rather than tackle them directly, one at a time. They'd chance their money on a throw of the dice, rather than pay the rent with it.

She flung the letter down. "Only wait until I get my hands on you, my girl."

But Bathsheba must find her first.

The letter did not reveal her destination. Olivia said she was going to find Edmund DeLucey's legendary treasure, however, and that was clue enough.

She would head for Throgmorton, the Earl of Mandeville's country house, because that was where Jack had said the treasure was, and why listen to boring Mama when Papa's stories were so much more exciting and romantic?

The only question was how great a head start she had. Not more than a few hours, Bathsheba guessed. Had Olivia missed school, Bathsheba would have heard from Miss Smithson by now. With any luck, one might catch up with the girl in a matter of hours rather than days.

Still, to pursue her, Bathsheba needed money, which meant she needed a pawnbroker. She was not sure where the nearest one was. But Mrs. Briggs would know. Meanwhile, Bathsheba must find something to pawn.

She began to tear the rooms apart. She emptied cupboards and drawers, pulled bed linens from the mattresses. She flung everything into a heap in the center of the room. She was wrapping up her few pieces of cutlery when someone knocked on the door.

She rose, pushed her hair out of her face, and walked to the door, praying the visitor was the watchman, the beadle, or a constable, with Olivia in tow. She opened the door.

The man standing in the dimly lit hall was not the watchman, the beadle, or a constable.

"Mrs. Wingate," said Lord Rathbourne, looking excessively bored. "I believe your daughter has made off with my nephew."

THE PLACE WAS a shambles, and so was Mrs. Wingate.

Her coiffure was tumbling to pieces, the raven-black curls falling over her forehead and bouncing against her neck. Her face was flushed. She had a smudge on her nose and another on her cheek.

She glared at him.

Benedict wanted to snatch her up and kiss the scowl away.

He had to drag his mind back to reality, and remember why he'd come: *Peregrine.*

. . . who wasn't here, as Benedict saw in the instant it took him to survey the room. His spirits sank. All the evidence had indicated his nephew would try to stop Miss Wingate, rather than go along with her.

Still, Benedict had endured nearly two weeks of stultifying boredom, and it was impossible to gaze at Bathsheba Wingate, tousled and cross, and feel completely cast down.

"I beg your pardon for giving no warning," he said. "I should have asked Mrs. Briggs to announce me, but she had company. I was disinclined to wait in her parlor, making her guests uncomfortable, while she came up to ask whether you were receiving visitors. I have let her believe I have come to inspect the place. May I enter?"

"Yes, why not?" With a dismissive wave, Mrs. Wingate moved away from the door. "I was about to go to the pawnbroker, but this . . ." She dragged her hand through the glossy black curls. "Lord Lisle is gone, too? With Olivia? But they scarcely know each other."

"It seems they have become well acquainted," he said. "They have been corresponding secretly for weeks."

After briefly explaining this day's discoveries, he took out from his inside breast pocket the most recent of the letters he'd found and gave it to her.

She scanned it quickly, then paused, her color mounting. " 'Pale and thin,' indeed," she said. "That is her overactive imagination at work."

Benedict did not think so. Though Mrs. Wingate wasn't pale at the moment, her face seemed thinner, more drawn. While she read on, his gaze slid lower. She had seemed more rounded the last time he saw her. . . .

Kissed her.

Touched her.

Think about the weather, he told himself.

She briskly folded up the letter and gave it back. "She will have hidden his somewhere about," she said. "I see no reason to waste time looking for them. Time will be better spent finding her—and Lord Lisle, if he is with her, which I can scarcely believe. He is such a logical boy. He does question everything, as you said. I cannot believe he did not question Olivia. I should have thought he had better sense than to be drawn into one of her madcap schemes."

Benedict returned the letter to his coat pocket. "I had the same thought," he said. "I could not believe Peregrine had fallen in with her plan. Her latest letter, you must have noticed, names one Nat Diggerby her chosen escort and refers to Peregrine's misgivings about her quest. He must have tried to dissuade her. In which case, one might reasonably suppose he went to stop her. I came here, hoping he'd retrieved her and brought her home."

"Not on his own, he couldn't," she said. "If he'd asked my advice, I should have recommended he take a law officer with him. Or a large body of soldiers."

Any other mother would be in fainting fits or hysterics, Benedict thought. She did not even appear anxious. She was definitely out of temper, though.

"Not being a thirteen-year-old boy, I shall not require a regiment," Benedict said. "Not that I should dream of alerting the authorities. The last thing I need is for anyone to hear of this." If any member of his set found out, the story would be all over London within hours. It would reach Atherton in Scotland within days. That was not a pretty prospect.

"The footman Thomas should be sufficient for my purposes," he went on. "Between us, I reckon we can recover a pair of children." He started for the door.

She moved quickly to block his way. Her blue eyes flashed, and he almost took a step back—in surprise, that was all.

"You are distressed," she said. "I excuse your obliviousness on those grounds."

"You excuse my *what*?"

"This is Olivia's doing," she said, "and Olivia is *my* problem. I understand how her mind works. I know where

she is going. I am the one who will search for her." The
color came and went in her cheeks. "However, you can save
me time if you would lend me the money to hire a vehicle."

His jaw almost dropped. He caught himself in time.

"You have taken leave of your senses if you believe I
should sit at home twiddling my thumbs while you hunt for
my nephew," he said. "He is not your responsibility but
mine."

"Your wits are wandering if you expect *me* to sit at
home," she said.

"One of us must go," he said. "One of us must remain.
We cannot travel together."

"Obviously," she said. "But you are too overset to think
clearly."

"Overset?" he echoed incredulously. "I am never overset."

"You are not using logic," she said. "You want to keep
this quiet, do you not?"

"Of course I—"

"I should attract far less attention than you," she cut in
impatiently. "You cannot make enquiries about a pair of
children without causing talk. Everything about you screams
who and what you are. You will act bored and sound sarcastic, and behave in that superior way, and simply *assume*
you are in command. It will be as plain to everyone who
you are as if you had a sign hanging from your neck, proclaiming your title and antecedents."

"I know how to be discreet," he said.

"You do not know how to be ordinary," she said.

As though *she* could be ordinary, Benedict thought, with
that face and body. She would turn heads wherever she
went. She would have men trailing after her, their tongues
hanging out.

He clenched his hands. She, setting out after dark, traveling alone, in a hired vehicle, without an escort, without
so much as a maid . . .

Unthinkable.

"You cannot travel alone," he said in the frigid accents
anyone else would have recognized as ending the discussion.

"I have traveled alone for the last three years," she said.

He wanted to shake her. He made himself unclench his hands. He summoned his patience. "You had your daughter with you," he said. "People behave differently toward solitary women than they do toward mothers traveling with their children."

"This is absurd," she said, turning away abruptly. "It is a waste of time, arguing with you. I shall do as I planned." She marched to the heap of belongings on the floor and started to make a bundle.

She had said she was on her way to the pawnbroker.

Benedict wondered how he could stop her, short of knocking her unconscious or wrestling her into a straitwaistcoat or tying her to a heavy piece of furniture.

"Stop that," he said, in a tone he usually reserved for rambunctious MPs. "Never mind the pawnbroker. We shall combine forces."

"We cannot—"

"You leave us no choice, you obstinate woman," he said. "I shall be hanged before I let you set out alone."

WHILE HE WAITED for her to collect her bonnet and spencer and whatever other items she deemed necessary, Benedict tried to reconnect his tongue to his brain.

He *never* spoke to women in that way.

He was always patient with them.

But she . . .

She was a problem.

Matters did not improve once she'd emerged from the house, after having stopped briefly to speak to Mrs. Briggs.

"A curricle?" she said, pausing on the steps to take stock of the vehicle standing at the curb. "An open vehicle?"

"Did you suppose I should take a coach and four?" he said. "Do you imagine I should wish to bring a coachman along on such a journey?"

"But this will never do," she said. "It is far too smart."

"It is hired, it needs a coat of paint, and it is at least ten years old," he said. "You haven't the least idea what smart is. Get in."

She clutched his arm, her gaze riveted upon Thomas,

who held the horses. "We cannot travel with a servant," she said.

Patience, Benedict counseled himself. "Someone must look after the horses," he said patiently. "You will not know he is there. He will sit in the seat at the back, gazing at the passing scene and thinking his own thoughts."

She tugged on his arm, to pull him toward her, and stood on her toes to whisper in his ear, "You must have been completely distracted to bring him here. Servants are dreadful gossips, worse than old ladies. By this time tomorrow, everyone in London will know what you have been doing and with whom."

Her breath tickled Benedict's ear. He was acutely aware of the slim hand clutching his arm.

He picked her up and tossed her onto the carriage seat.

When he climbed in beside her, she said, "May I remind you that this is the nineteenth century, not the ninth? That sort of behavior went out of fashion with chain mail and wimples."

Thomas hastily took his place in the servant's seat.

Benedict gave the horses leave to start before he answered her.

"I am not accustomed to explaining myself, Mrs. Wingate," he began.

"Obviously," she said.

He started to grind his teeth. He made himself stop, and reminded himself of the rule: *Women and children, possessing smaller brains and thus a smaller capacity for reason, require a correspondingly greater degree of patience.*

Now he said, patiently, "Thomas is not a London-bred servant. He is a countryman, who grew up on the family property in Derbyshire. Though he is now my footman, he is as competent with horses as any of my grooms. I took him into my confidence weeks ago, when Peregrine began his drawing lessons. I would not have entrusted so delicate a business to him had I not complete confidence in his discretion."

Mrs. Wingate let out a huff, sat straighter, and folded her hands in her lap. "I beg your pardon for questioning your judgment," she said. "It is nothing to me, after all, if it proves faulty. I am not the one responsible for the Marquess of Atherton's heir and sole offspring. I am not the one who will be toppled from my pedestal if the world learns I have not only permitted but encouraged my nephew to associate with the most shocking persons. I am not the one who—"

"I wish you were the one who had heard of the rule *Silence is golden,*" he said.

"I am not a politician," she said. "I am accustomed to saying what I think."

"I should have thought that anxieties about your daughter would fully occupy your mind."

"I greatly doubt Olivia will come to any harm," said her mama. "I only wish I could say the same for those who cross her path."

Chapter 7

THOUGH THE CURRICLE WAS MUCH TOO DASH-
ing a vehicle for people who wished to remain anonymous,
Bathsheba had to admit it had certain advantages, like
speed and maneuverability.

They halted near Hyde Park Corner shortly before the
church bells chimed six o'clock.

While not as busy as it would be during the daylight
hours, the area was by no means deserted. The waterman
still carried buckets to the hackneys lined up at the coach
stand. Some soldiers gossiped under a street lamp. A milk-
woman carried her empty pails back toward Knightsbridge.
The tollgate keeper would continue to work through the
night.

At least some of these people had been about during the
afternoon. If Olivia had been here, some one of them
would have noticed.

Here, therefore, Bathsheba alit, while Rathbourne drove
on, as he'd finally and not very graciously agreed after a
short, fierce argument. She would meet him a short distance down the road, opposite the Horse Barracks.

The first person she spoke to was the waterman. He had

no trouble recollecting Olivia. He wasn't the only one. As one might expect, she'd caused a scene.

Not long afterward, Bathsheba was climbing back into the carriage. "Well?" Rathbourne said.

"My daughter's so-called squire, Nat Diggerby, has been brought before the magistrate for causing a disturbance," she said. "Olivia, in true DeLucey style, abandoned him and found another pigeon. A pie seller heard my daughter tell a young farmer a heartbreaking tale of a sick mother."

She described the ensuing scene, adding, "Lord Lisle must have a chivalrous streak. Olivia would have left him without a second thought. But it appears that someone has inculcated in him a sense of responsibility."

She strongly suspected the someone was Rathbourne. Despite the light way he spoke of the boy, she'd sensed a strong bond between them from the first. His rage with Lord Atherton's method of dealing with Lisle had made clear how important his nephew was to Rathbourne. Olivia's mad act might jeopardize that relationship.

Typical, Bathsheba thought gloomily. Whenever a Dreadful DeLucey appeared on the scene, someone's life was sure to change, and seldom for the better.

"Though his parents have failed to recognize it, Peregrine is mature for his age," Rathbourne said as he set the horses in motion. "He would consider it unthinkable to allow a twelve-year-old girl to travel completely unprotected."

"Among the lower orders, a twelve-year-old is, to all intents and purposes, an adult," Bathsheba said. "Olivia has not lived a sheltered life. Furthermore, she has inherited my family's talent for talking or cheating her way out of any difficulty. The tale of the sick mother is a perfect example. I wonder why I waste money sending her to school, when she might be making us a fortune by writing melodramas for the stage and the more sensational periodicals."

He glanced at her. "You cannot be as cold and cynical as that," he said. "I will not believe it."

"One cannot be softhearted about Olivia," she said. "She will only exploit it. She is a dreadful child. One can either face the fact or one can live in a delusion and watch her go straight to the devil. I refuse to let her go to the devil. Therefore I cannot be sentimental about her, or pretend she is a normal girl."

There was a silence. Bathsheba let it stretch. Her hard-heartedness had shocked him, naturally. Being an aristocratic male, he had no inkling what it was like to raise a difficult child. Few of the women of his class had any idea. Someone else looked after their children.

She did not point this out. She did not want him to feel sorry for her. She did not even want him to like her—the sensible part of her didn't, at any rate. The sensible Bathsheba was glad this crisis had started them quarreling. Hostility would keep them at a safe distance from each other.

After a time, he spoke. Growled, rather. "They left in a farmer's cart, you said. Did you happen to find out their direction?"

"The farmer offered to take them to Brentford," she said. "She must be headed to Bristol."

"Bristol is an odd place for a pirate to bury treasure," he said.

"There is no treasure," Bathsheba said. "It's legend, nothing more. Edmund DeLucey wasn't really a pirate, either. I have explained it all to Olivia time and again. A precious waste of breath."

"And the truth is?"

"My great-grandfather had the Idea of becoming a pirate, yes," she said. "But it quickly palled. Edmund was a dandy or a macaroni—or whatever they called them in those days. Pirates, he soon discovered, were crude, ill-dressed, and dirty brutes. Not at all in Edmund's style. Furthermore, because they were far from intelligent, they were constantly getting themselves maimed, hacked to pieces, drowned, and hanged. Smuggling suited Edmund far better. Playing cat and mouse with the English authorities was vastly entertaining. He especially delighted in daring forays into the mouth of the Severn, not many miles from his family's ancestral home."

"Ah, indeed," Rathbourne said. "I'd forgotten. The—er—other DeLuceys—"

"The good ones," she supplied.

"The less exciting ones," he said. "The ancestral pile is near Bristol, if I recall aright."

"Every member of my family knows where Throgmorton is and all about it, though they know better than to come within fifty miles of it," she said. "Meanwhile, they never tire of boasting about Edmund DeLucey. Perhaps because Jack, too, had a rebellious streak, he never tired of hearing about him. He started repeating the tales to Olivia when she was a baby. Those were among the bedtime stories he told her. I had assumed that as she grew up, she must realize the buried treasure was make-believe, like the tales from *The Thousand and One Nights*."

"A treasure is not completely unreasonable, in the circumstances," Rathbourne said. "A smuggler might easily amass a fortune."

"He might," she said. "But would he bury it?"

"That seems doubtful," he said.

"It makes no sense," she said. "Edmund was a wastrel. Why bury it instead of spend it? I have made this point repeatedly. I cannot tell you how many times the three of us had the same exchange. It became a game at bedtime. 'Where do you think Edmund DeLucey buried the treasure, Mama?' Olivia would say as we tucked her in. 'Men like that don't bury treasure,' I would say. 'They spend it as fast as they get it, on drink, gaming, and women.' Then she would ask Jack: 'Where do you think he buried the treasure, Papa?' And Jack would say, 'Right under his family's noses. That's where I'd hide it, if I were him. I'd go in the dead of night and bury it at the base of the mausoleum where all the revered ancestors lie a-moldering: all my ill-got gains, on hallowed ground. And I'd laugh and laugh every time I thought about it.'"

She heard Rathbourne suck in his breath.

"Do I shock you, my lord?" she said.

They'd reached the Hogmire Lane tollgate. He halted the vehicle.

"Well, yes, I am shocked, actually," he said slowly. "Your husband put his child to bed. He told her bedtime stories. Astonishing."

* * *

THE TOLLGATE KEEPER had seen too many farm carts to recall one in particular, with or without young passengers.

Still, this was the usual route to Brentford, so Benedict drove on. To his vexation, he had to do so far more slowly. This stretch of road, while set with paving stones and therefore less dusty than the section they'd just traversed, was also a good deal narrower and more congested.

Benedict tried, as he'd tried before, to concentrate on driving, always a chancy thing after dark. The carriage lanterns illuminated the vehicle somewhat but not the way ahead. The street lamps made a halfhearted twilight. He tried to keep his eyes and mind on the road while Bathsheba Wingate's voice rippled and flowed about him.

He was used to letting women's voices go on and on about him while his mind wrestled with important matters: the war widows and veterans, the inadequacies of present policing methods, and the vagaries of English law.

He could not get his mind to turn away from Bathsheba Wingate. He listened to her, to every word. He couldn't ignore her. He was too intensely aware of her next to him on the seat: the not-nearly-wide-enough seat. While the carriage was in motion, the only way to keep from touching was to hug the side of the vehicle, which he could hardly do while driving, even if it wasn't ridiculous, which it was.

And so they touched, frequently, hip briefly pressing against hip, thigh brushing against thigh.

And every touch reminded him of the last time they'd touched: the kiss, weeks ago . . . the taste of her mouth and the scent of her skin and the mad hunger she awoke in him.

To distract himself from physical awareness, he focused on what she said. The result was, he now wanted to know more about Jack Wingate.

The image Benedict received from her did not match the one Society had painted: the victim of a heartless siren, a man destroyed by a fatal passion. Benedict had pictured a broken man living in lonely exile from the world to which he properly belonged.

The Jack Wingate she spoke of sounded like a man who'd ended up where he truly belonged. His remarks about burying the treasure made him sound more like a Dreadful DeLucey than his widow did, in fact. Intrigued, Benedict wanted to probe.

He was very good at probing subtly and manipulating others into imprudent speech. But that was strictly for political purposes. It was justified if used to promote worthy causes or to crush opponents. Employing such methods in a personal conversation was disgraceful.

Prying into others' private affairs is the preferred occupation of small minds.

He certainly never meant to offer glimpses of his own private life. The trouble was, her nearness was a constant distraction and irritation, and the words spilled out before his irritated and distracted brain had properly examined them.

This must be why, shortly after they'd passed Kensington House and a press of vehicles brought them to a standstill, he said, "I am deeply shocked. I had always believed that nursemaids put one to bed and told one bedtime stories. Fathers, on the other hand, want to know why you tied your little brother to a bedpost and cut off most of his hair with a penknife."

He'd hardly said the words before he wished he hadn't. But he hadn't time to fret. A space appeared in the solid mass of vehicles, and he quickly guided the curricle into and through it.

Though focused on the maneuver, he felt her shift in the seat, turning toward him. He was as aware of her gaze on his face as if it had been her hand there . . . and he knew she hadn't missed a word.

"Why did you?" she said.

"We were pretending we were in the American Colonies," he said, striving for a tone of cool amusement. "I was a Red Indian chief." He was *always* the Red Indian because he was the dark one. "Geoffrey was my English captive, and I scalped him."

She laughed, and the wicked, haunting sound almost made him smile.

"You were not a perfect child," she said.

"By no means," he said. He'd *hated* Geoffrey's golden curls and golden eyes and angelically sweet countenance. "I should have scalped Alistair, too, if I could have got my hands on him. But he was safe with a nursemaid elsewhere."

She said nothing. He need say nothing, either, but, "The nurses called my brothers 'little golden angels,'" he went on. "They were not angels by any stretch of the imagination, but they looked the part."

"You should have scalped the nurses, too," she said. "For stupidity."

"I was a child, no more than eight or nine years old," he said. "Geoffrey and Alistair were fair and I was dark. If they were golden angels, what was I?"

"What else could you think?" she said feelingly. "In your place, I should have done exactly the same."

He glanced at her. "No, you would not."

"Because I am a female?" she said, eyebrows aloft.

"Girls do not behave that way."

"How little you know my sex," she said. "All children are little savages, even—or perhaps especially—girls."

"Not *all* children," he said. "Not for long, at any rate. Certainly not when one is the eldest. As soon as the next child arrives, we have responsibilities. We are not quite children anymore. 'You must take care of your brother, Benedict,' they say. 'He is smaller than you.' Or, 'You ought to know better, Benedict,' they say. 'You are the eldest.'"

"Is that what your father said?"

"More or less. I remember little of the lecture, except the end. He sighed and said he wished he had daughters."

"That was nothing more than parental exasperation," she said. "Few men—and no noblemen—would wish to have daughters instead of sons."

"He meant it," Benedict said. "He's said it countless times since then."

"Still?"

"Yes."

"Why? You have all got past the trying stage. You are all grown up."

"Not to his satisfaction," Benedict said.

She turned fully in the seat to stare at him. "Even you? Lord Perfect?"

"I am perfect by average standards," Benedict said. "My father's standards are not average. Nothing about my father is average. I am not sure anything about him is even human." He added quickly, "At any rate, he did not tell bedtime stories. I was unaware parents did such a thing."

"Then it's unlikely Jack's parents did," she said. "The Dreadful DeLuceys must have corrupted him."

"Not necessarily," Benedict said. "You said he was rebellious. Maybe, like Peregrine, your husband wanted a different sort of life. Maybe it was in his nature to be unconventional."

And among the DeLuceys, Jack Wingate must have experienced the kind of freedom he could never have in respectable Society. He'd found a world without rules.

"He had no trouble adapting, admittedly," she said. "Still, Jack could distinguish between truth and fiction. I am not sure my relatives can. They spin brilliant tales, and perhaps their lies are so convincing because they believe them. I think it is the same for Olivia. That is the only way I can explain this mad quest of hers."

"She needs a governess," he said—and cursed himself immediately the words were out. It was an idiotish thing to say. Why not suggest a pack of servants, while he was at it—and a house in the country, away from London and its pernicious influences?

Face hot, he waited for a sarcastic comment from her regarding the obliviousness of the upper orders.

"I could not agree more," she said, startling him again as she too easily did. "That is next on the list. Miss Smithson runs a fine school but it is not the same. I had a governess. A dragon. Even Papa was afraid of her. But that was the idea. If she could not intimidate my father, she hadn't a prayer of making an impression on me."

"Are you saying that you were not a properly behaved child, either?" he said.

"From whom would I have learnt to behave properly?" she said.

"You must have learnt from somebody," he said. "You are a lady."

She turned away, facing forward once more, and folded her hands in her lap.

"You are," he said. "There is no question—and I am an expert on the subject."

"I had to be a lady," she said tightly. "My mother had ambitions for me."

"Thus the dragon governess," he said.

"I admit I have ambitions for Olivia," she said.

"You aim to keep her from going to the devil," he said, dodging a clumsily driven gig. "A noble ambition."

"You needn't be tactful," she said. "I can guess what you're thinking."

"I doubt it," he said. Even he wasn't sure what he was thinking. He was aware of the busy road and of his impatience at the delay. He was aware of anxiety about Peregrine and Olivia, of time passing and night settling in. He was aware of the woman beside him, of warmth and physical nearness . . . and, perhaps more dangerous yet, of his fascination with her, with what she said and how her mind worked.

Her mind! A woman's mind!

But there was no getting round it. He was too aware of the growing mental intimacy and too uneasy with it to pretend it wasn't there. He was too aware of something in the air—or about the darkness—or about her—that lowered his guard and made him say things he would never dream of saying aloud to anybody, especially a woman.

He was aware at the same time of a distance as vast as if an ocean rolled between them and of a rage almost like despair because he must not bridge the distance. Perhaps the rage worried him most.

In any case, it was all too much. He couldn't think because he needed order to think, and what he had at present was disorder, chaos.

"My mother was determined to see me married into a noble family," she said, voice still taut, body still rigid on the seat beside him. "I was to be the key that opened the doors of Society to the Dreadful DeLuceys."

Her tone and posture told him far more than her words what her mother's ambition had cost her. She had been hurt—or shamed perhaps—and deeply so, else Bathsheba Wingate would have spoken with her usual droll wit. He wanted to know more . . . but Reason told him it was better not to know. He felt too much for her as it was.

"All mothers want their daughters to marry up," he said, making his voice light in hopes he could make the conversation become so, too. "They plot and scheme, and they are thoroughly unscrupulous." He paused. "My father is, too, in that regard."

She started. "Your *father*?"

"I know," Benedict said. "It is shocking. But he does not confine his manipulations to politics. He has determined that all my brothers must marry wealthy wives—and so far, he's had his way. Even with Rupert, whom he declared a hopeless case."

"And what about you?" she said.

"Oh, I have always been excused from vulgar financial considerations," he said. "I shall inherit everything."

The topic appeared to have diverted her from whatever deep unhappiness it was, for her posture eased a bit.

"All the mothers must have pushed their daughters at you," she said. "They must still do."

He shrugged. "I am not sure I was aware then of the mamas and chaperons scheming and plotting. It's more obvious now, looking on from the outside. I had not thought about it, but it must be hard on the girls—at least those with a modicum of sensitivity or intelligence. Not that I was one to notice such subtleties at the time. I noticed their faces and figures first, then whether their voices were agreeable or not, then their deportment."

He felt her relax, her gaze coming back to his face. "You are roasting me," she said. "You make it sound as though finding a bride was the same as choosing a horse at— What is the name of the auction house? Taver—"

"Tattersall's," he said.

"Tattersall's, then. Is that how men view the famous Almack's assemblies? Do you take no account of the girls' characters or their personalities?"

"If they were not girls of good character, they would not be on the Marriage Mart," he said. "And they most certainly would not be admitted to Almack's."

He would not have dreamt of seeking a girl who was not admitted. Not being obliged to marry for money hadn't meant Lord Hargate's heir could marry where he pleased. Or when he pleased. Benedict knew the rules, knew what was expected of him.

And Ada? Had she followed rules or her heart? He had no idea—and that said everything, didn't it?

"In other words, they were virgins of good family, and that was all you needed to know about their character," Mrs. Wingate said. "Good bloodstock—"

"I'm the Earl of Hargate's heir," he cut in tightly. "I hadn't the luxury of being swept off my feet, if that is what you are getting at."

"That is not what I meant," she said. "You speak of marriage, a lifelong commitment, yet love does not come into the picture."

"How absurd," he said. "I could not wander the world like one of Byron's heroes, looking for the love of my life, if there is such a thing."

"What about the *like* of your life?" she said. "What about a friend and companion? Good grief, Rathbourne, how did you choose?"

"I fail to see how the matter can be of any import to you," he said in the glacial tone he had learnt from his father. It was famous for leaving its victims bereft not only of speech but, in some cases, of the will to live.

She waved it away with one slim, gloved hand. "Don't be silly," she said. "It is vastly interesting. I feel like a visitor to an exotic land, trying to understand the ways of the natives. I didn't choose. I was only sixteen, and I simply fell over head and ears in love. But it is wrong of me to quiz you. Clearly, the subject is too painful for you to talk about." Her tone softened. "I forgot that you have not been widowed for very long."

Benedict's heart was pounding, and it wanted all his self-control not to relay his agitation to the horses via the ribbons. Luckily, they'd finally reached the Kensington tollgate. Fuming, he waited for the gatekeeper to collect the money and open the gate.

At last it opened. As he drove through it, Benedict belatedly recalled Thomas. He'd completely forgotten about the footman, riding in the back. Benedict's ears burned as he recalled his revelations about his younger brothers.

It didn't matter that the footman could not possibly hear their conversation over the constant rumble of wheels and clatter of hooves on the cobblestones, the horses' snorts and whinnies, and the drivers' complaints and curses. Benedict was too upset to be reasonable.

"I ought not be required to remind you," he growled, "that we are not alone."

"I told you not to bring the servant," she said coolly.

"I wish I had not brought you," he said. "You—Devil take it! You made me forget to ask the tollgate keeper about the children." He brought the carriage to a halt. Before he could summon Thomas to take charge of it, she jumped down.

"I shall ask," she said. "You are too agitated."

Without being told, Thomas leapt down to tend the horses.

Meanwhile, without a backward glance, Mrs. Wingate walked on toward the tollgate, hips swaying in the most blatantly provocative manner—much to the delight of the mob of men, who performed torturous maneuvers with their vehicles to make way for her.

Benedict did not wait to see how many collisions she caused—nor did he drag down any of the men from their vehicles and throw them into any walls, because this would be undignified and precisely the sort of thing Rupert would do—but caught up with her in a few swift strides.

"I am not agitated," he said. "I am perfectly capable of—"

"I should not have mentioned Lady Rathbourne in that thoughtless, light way," she said. "I beg your pardon."

"There is no need to become maudlin," he said. "Ada died two years ago and she—and she . . ." He let out an angry sigh. "Oh, very well. She was a stranger to me. There, is your tender heart comforted?"

BATHSHEBA WISHED SHE had not answered her door this evening. Rathbourne was proving even more trouble-some than she had feared. She might have borne the phys-ical proximity with some degree of composure. The mental proximity was making dangerous cracks in her defenses.

"No, I am not at all comforted, because you are talking nonsense," she said. "For how long were you wed?"

"Six years," he said.

"Then your wife could not be a stranger." She stopped walking. "I must insist you return to the carriage. You are attracting too much attention."

He glanced about them at the vehicles emerging from the tollgate. "So far as I can ascertain, the onlookers are all men," he said, "and they are all looking at you."

"I am merely a handsome piece of goods to them," she said. "While they stare at me, their brains are not engaged. Do you want them to start thinking—and wonder which aristocrat that is, dogging my footsteps and glowering at me?"

He glowered at her some more, bowed curtly, turned away, and strode back to the carriage.

He was waiting by the carriage, pocket watch in hand, when she returned not many minutes later.

"Well?" he said.

"We're still headed in the right direction," she said. She hurriedly climbed into the carriage before he could throw her in. It was not that she minded being flung about in that imperious way. It was rather that she liked it too much: the ease with which he lifted her, the power and heat she felt radiating from him, and above all, the feel of his hands upon her.

Much too dangerous. As it was, she'd been unable to banish the memory of that kiss weeks ago. She remem-bered too well the feel of his hand at the back of her neck and what that simple touch did to her, melting will and morals and muscles simultaneously.

A moment later, she had positioned herself as close to her side of the vehicle as she could without being obvious about it, and they were once more on their way. This time they traveled at a speedier pace, the road having grown less congested. While he focused on driving, she told what she'd learnt from the tollgate keeper.

It turned out that he knew the farmer she'd described. His name was Jarvis, and he traveled from Brentford to London and back regularly. Though the tollgate keeper could not say precisely when he'd arrived, he reckoned it was between one and two hours earlier. He vaguely remembered children in the cart, but had not paid close attention. Jarvis often had his own or neighbors' children with him.

"If that is the case, it makes no sense to continue stopping to inquire about them until we reach Brentford," Rathbourne said. "If the road remains reasonably clear of drovers, carts, and wagons, we might easily get there by eight o'clock. They might be as little as an hour ahead of us at this point. We have an excellent chance of finding them before they can negotiate another ride—a task they'll find a good deal more difficult in a hamlet like Brentford than at busy Hyde Park Corner. If my nephew has failed to persuade your daughter to turn back, he'll be aware that I must soon be after him, in which case he will exercise his ingenuity to slow their progress."

"That sounds reasonable enough," she said. "The trouble is, Olivia is not reasonable."

"She is twelve years old," Rathbourne said. "She has no money, and her companion objects to the journey. Even if she were in more promising circumstances than these, she can only go so far in a few hours."

PEREGRINE SOON DISCOVERED he'd have better success in slowing Olivia Wingate down if the rest of the world were not so gullible.

The farmer had suggested they stop at the Pigeons Inn

in Brentford and mention his name to the landlord, who would look after them and help them find a ride west.

Peregrine decided he would insist they pause there to eat. This would give him time to find a way to leave a message for Uncle Benedict.

Surely Lord Rathbourne had realized hours ago that Peregrine was gone. He would not have many clues, unfortunately. Had it occurred to Peregrine that he'd fail to retrieve Miss Wingate, he'd have left clues. It had not occurred to him.

Still, Uncle being so clever, he would quickly deduce what had happened. No doubt he was already on their trail.

After all, crime was one of his lordship's pet interests. He knew all the Bow Street Runners and their thief-catching methods. He had studied countless disreputable persons and criminals in the course of his parliamentary inquiries. Finding Miss Wingate and Peregrine would be child's play.

If Peregrine dawdled long enough, his uncle would catch up with them.

The trouble was, Olivia didn't go straight to the inn. First, she stood by the side of the road, waiting for it to empty. Then, to Peregrine's horror, she pulled off her frock. Under it she was wearing boy's clothes. She took from the shawl containing her traveling things a cap, stuck it on her head, and tucked her hair up inside it. She rolled the frock up and stuffed it into the shawl and tied up the parcel again.

Next, when they reached the inn, she didn't go inside, but into the inn yard. She wandered about the place, walking and talking like a boy. Knowing that it was most unwise to unmask her in such a place, Peregrine could only hang about in a state of painful suspense until he realized what she was about, at which point he dared do nothing.

She became friendly with a pair of young grooms who were playing a complicated dice game.

She asked them to teach her the game.

Peregrine didn't dare warn them. Either they would laugh themselves sick or there would be a fight—which might bring a constable. If Peregrine's parents found out he'd been taken up by a constable, he'd never be entrusted to his uncle's care again.

Consequently, in what must have been a fairly short time though it seemed like years to Peregrine, the dreadful girl obtained not only all the unsuspecting grooms' money, but a ride to Hounslow in their master's recently repaired carriage.

Chapter 8

THE LANDLORD AT THE PIGEONS INN IN BRENT-ford had seen nothing of a girl and boy. Though he knew Farmer Jarvis, he had not seen him this day, he said. Jarvis must have gone straight home instead of traveling the short distance out of his way, as he often did, to stop at the Pigeons for gossip and a tankard of ale.

Benedict and Mrs. Wingate learnt no more from the others they questioned. Thomas the footman had better luck during his conversation with some servants in the inn yard. When he rejoined his master, the footman described the encounter between two "lads" and a pair of servants belonging to one of the local gentry families.

"One of the lads sounded like Lord Lisle," he reported. "Same height, same color hair. The other had red hair and freckles."

Benedict looked at Mrs. Wingate.

"Dressing as a boy would be simple enough for Olivia," she said. "She might have obtained clothes cheaply and easily at a pawnshop or secondhand clothes dealer. She wouldn't have too much difficulty raising small amounts of money. She has the DeLucey affinity for games of chance, and my lectures fall on deaf ears."

However she'd done it, Olivia had obtained a ride as far as Hounslow.

On to Hounslow Benedict drove, more swiftly than caution decreed. They had lost valuable time searching Brentford. Now at least Benedict needn't fall farther behind, slowing to study the market carts he passed.

It was past nine o'clock. By the time they reached Hounslow, most of the populace would be asleep. Still, he knew he'd find abundant signs of life at the inns. Mr. Chaplin kept extensive stables in Hounslow, and everyone stopped there to change horses. With so many travelers coming and going, one was more likely to obtain word of the children.

So at least Benedict assured himself, trying to ignore his growing uneasiness. Despite what Mrs. Wingate said about her daughter, he'd left London certain he'd find his nephew in a few hours. He'd believed his search would end in Brentford. He'd refused to consider the alternative: a search continuing for days—during which Peregrine and Olivia might meet with an accident or evildoers.

And all the while Benedict would be berating and hating himself for not taking better care of his nephew. All the while Mrs. Wingate would be sitting next to him, hour after hour, her hip bumping his, her thigh brushing his, her voice stealing under his skin.

Meanwhile, the longer they traveled together, the greater the chance of their encountering someone who'd recognize them . . . and setting off the scandal of the decade.

When he first caught sight of the buildings thickly clustered along the roadside, Benedict nearly shouted with relief. Hounslow. At last.

The numerous inns proved sufficiently awake. At the George, by the time the ostler had put fresh horses in the traces, Mrs. Wingate had news. The two "lads" were now traveling with a cottager from Cranford Park, the Earl of Berkeley's estate. One of the inn servants, a nephew of the cottager, gave them directions to his relative's home, where he was sure the "boys" would spend the night.

This seemed the likeliest possibility to Benedict. At this hour, the stream of market carts was dwindling. Soon the stagecoaches and the Royal Mail would have the road mainly to themselves. The latter had passed Benedict long since—not that he believed even Olivia's cunning could obtain a seat on a mail coach. Passengers were strictly limited and tickets expensive. So near to London, it was unlikely that even the stagecoaches would have room for additional passengers. So, at least, Benedict hoped.

He drove on, at a gallop as often as it was feasible, through a lonely length of road. Hounslow Heath stretched alongside them on the left, but no highwaymen burst out of the darkness, luckily for the highwaymen. Benedict had a pair of pistols under the seat, and he was in no mood for interruptions.

Near Cranford Bridge, he turned into the road through Berkeley's property. The directions were accurate, and they easily found the cottage.

They also found the two boys who'd come to spend the night. They were boys in truth, and neither of them was Peregrine.

"COUNT TO TWENTY," Bathsheba advised when they finally returned to the king's highway. It was nearly midnight, they'd wasted an hour and a half, and Rathbourne, as one would expect, was seething.

She knew he was anxious, too, about his nephew, but for most men, fear was too disturbing an emotion to entertain. Like others, he swept it under the heavy rug of anger.

"I am not a child," he said.

"Good," she said. "Then you will not throw a tantrum when I tell you we must stop at the inn."

"We've stopped at every accursed inn in every be-damned clump of hovels that calls itself a village," he said. "And where has it got us? One village idiot after another who can scarcely attach a predicate to a subject, who can't tell the difference between a girl and a boy or distinguish between a lad of twelve and one of ten. They called that boy—and he not eight years old, I'll wager—a redhead. His hair was *brown*, the precise color of Derbyshire cow sh—"

"That one," she said as he drove straight past the White Hart Inn.

He swore, but, unlike many men, he did not let his emotions affect his driving. With his usual smooth economy of motion, he brought the carriage back to the inn's entrance.

She could not get him to wait in the carriage, though. Leaving Thomas in charge of the vehicle, they entered together. They found the landlord fully awake. A stagecoach, the Courser, had left not half an hour earlier, after disgorging a family of five. This had been their first ride on a stagecoach, and they hadn't liked it.

"I told them it wouldn't be no different on any other stage they took," the landlord said. "If they didn't like traveling with every Tom, Dick, Harry, and his brother who hasn't washed since the bath he took to celebrate Waterloo, they should've gone by mail coach or hired a post chaise. Was it a room you wanted? If it was, you're out of luck. They've taken my last bed, all five of 'em."

"My brother and I are trying to find our two young cousins," Bathsheba said. "They were visiting us in London. After seeing a traveling theater troupe, they took it into their heads to join the actors. We believe they are headed toward Bristol." She described Olivia and Lord Lisle and pointed out that one or both of the children might be in "costume" or disguise.

"Oh, them," the landlord said. "They said they was going home to their sick mother. Least, that was what the younger one told the coachman. The taller one didn't say much. Looked like he'd et something that didn't agree."

Rathbourne, who'd stood by, silently vibrating with impatience, came to attention, his dark eyes alight. "They spoke to the coachman?" he said. "They boarded the stage?"

"Well, the driver had room, didn't he?" said the landlord. "And they had the fare—enough, at any rate, to get them to the next stage, Salt Hill."

* * *

SALT HILL WAS less than nine miles away, and the horses were fresh, Rathbourne having decided to make the change at the White Hart. A mail coach might cover the distance in less than an hour. Rathbourne seemed determined to drive at mail coach speed, which Bathsheba minded not at all. The longer it took to find the children, the more time her conscience had to torment her. Had she used her limited funds more wisely, Olivia might have had a governess by now, and none of this would have happened.

"You are very quiet," he said after they'd traveled a while in silence. "The speed doesn't frighten you, I hope."

The recent news seemed to have lightened his mood. Bathsheba no longer felt as though she was sitting next to an about-to-erupt volcano. "I was thinking about the children," she said. "I've done a poor job with Olivia. I've allowed her too much freedom."

"Most of the girls in my world have too little freedom," he said. "Small wonder so many grow into women of narrow understanding. You asked before whether I gave any thought to finding a friend and companion as a wife. How could I expect to find among those child-women a true companion?"

"It was unfair of me to criticize your choice," she said. "I did not choose my spouse on any rational basis, and he certainly didn't use his head in choosing me."

"No girl of the upper classes would dare to set out on a 'Noble Quest,' though one or two might dream of it," he said. "None would have the least idea how to get from one place to another on her own. We ought to admire Olivia's pluck at least. And she has got Peregrine onto a stagecoach. Without her, he was unlikely to have the experience in his lifetime."

"Indeed, only think of what he might have missed," she said. "Now he will have the thrill of traveling on a vehicle dangerously overcrowded, filthy, and prone to overturning. He will be crammed in with persons in dire need of a bath or sobriety or both. It is no better outside than in. Inside, you cannot sleep because you are jolted and jostled constantly. Outside, you dare not sleep, because you will fall off. No matter who your fellow passengers are, at least one of them is sure to be sick on the way. Even outside, the smell is appalling—and let us not forget the fleas and lice one's fellow passengers share so generously."

"Peregrine is a boy," Rathbourne said. "They don't fret about dirt or vermin, and their sense of smell is far from delicate. Recall that he's shared a dormitory with other boys. Boys are disgusting creatures. Your daughter is far more likely than my nephew to be uncomfortable."

Olivia was by no means the most fastidious girl in the world, Bathsheba reflected. And the children would certainly be safer on the stage than walking along a dark road. Still, time was passing, and she and Rathbourne were drawing farther and farther from London.

"I was so sure we would find them by now," she said.

"As was I," he said.

"What shall we do if they are not in Salt Hill?" she said.

"They cannot go far in the small hours of the morning with no money," Rathbourne said. "Your daughter will have told one of the innkeepers a poignant story and obtained a space by the hearthside, if not a bed with one of the servants. Should the innkeepers prove hard-hearted, she will practice her wiles on one of the stable men, and we'll find our runaways sleeping in the straw."

After a pause, he added, "When we learnt they were on the stage, and therefore relatively safe, it dawned on me that I was fretting over Peregrine as though he were a small, helpless child. This is far from the case. He is a precocious boy, and boys are wonderfully resilient. I reminded myself that he is all of thirteen years old, intelligent and curious, and has never had a proper adventure."

"Did you?" she said. "When you were a boy?"

The instant the words were out, Bathsheba wished them back. She *wished* she would stop prying and probing.

It took him a while to answer, and she hoped he was devising a polite way to turn the subject to something less personal.

"I had a great many adventures," he said. "I ran away at every opportunity."

That brought her head around, and she stared at his perfect profile. "You're joking," she said. "How does an earl's son contrive to run away? And why would he?"

"If it were easy to do, it wouldn't be worth doing," he said. "But outwitting the adults was a game to me. I ran away when I felt bored or annoyed or . . . well, when I was sick to death of being *good*. Once I went missing for three days."

Bathsheba could picture his youthful self all too easily. She had no trouble imagining the glint in boyish eyes of the devil in him.

Was that what called to her, in those dark eyes?

Her heart began to race.

"Olivia and Lisle will *not* go missing for three days," she said.

"That would certainly complicate matters," he said.

"Complicate?" she said. "It would be *disastrous*." Three days, traveling with him . . . talking, discovering more about him . . . sitting so close, feeling the warmth and strength of him . . . listening to his deep voice in the dark . . . looking at his long, gloved hands.

"I cannot be gone overnight in your company," she went on, her voice sharp. "I told Mrs. Briggs I was called away to a sick relative, and you had kindly offered to drive me. I said I might be back rather late."

"At this rate, I doubt we'll be back before dawn at the earliest," he said. "We shall require an alibi. You told me weeks ago that you came of a long line of accomplished liars. I must agree that you are highly accomplished. I noticed how beautifully you lied to the innkeeper at the White Hart. You even had me almost believing you were my sister." He turned and met her gaze. "Almost."

He was smiling that provoking not-quite-a-smile, the one that could be anything: amusement, mockery, cynicism, condescension. Yet she heard a smile, or laughter, in his voice. The sound was like a whisper in the dark, and she felt the whisper glide down her neck and on down her spine.

"I said the first thing that came to mind," she said.

"I have no doubt you can think of something equally simple and convincing to account for an extended disappearance," he said. "Ah, that will be the bridge over the Coln River ahead."

She turned her gaze forward. His eyes were sharper than hers. To her, the road ahead was unfathomable gloom.

"There's a lurid tale about the Ostrich Inn of Colnbrook," he said. "Do you know it?"

"This is the first I've ever heard of the place," she said.

"Oh, it is quite famous," he said. "Some centuries ago, the inn was called the Hospice. The wealthy merchants who went back and forth between Bath, Reading, and London often stayed there. The strange thing was, sixty of these fellows went in and never came out. They simply vanished, along with all of their goods. You would have thought the authorities would have become suspicious, but no. Then, one night, a rich merchant named Thomas Cole, who'd often stayed there without mishap, disappeared. Unlike the others, however, he reappeared. His body, well boiled, was found floating in the river a few days later."

"Well *boiled*?" Bathsheba said. "Are you serious?"

"You are aware that the heads of evildoers were often stuck on pikes as a lesson and warning to others?" he said. "You may be unaware that the heads were often boiled first, so they would keep longer."

"That is revolting," she said.

"They still do it in Egypt," he said. "My father received a skull in a basket from Muhammad Ali, Pasha of Egypt, during the summer. It belonged to the fellow who'd allegedly murdered my brother Rupert. As it turned out—and much as one might have expected—Rupert defied the laws of probability. He turned up, very much alive, not long after the head was delivered."

"Such strange things happen in your family," she said. "You did not mention trying to scalp Rupert. Was he another golden angel?"

"Gad, no," he said. "From a distance, some people cannot tell us apart."

Before she could ask further impertinent questions, he said, "To return to Thomas Cole. The authorities finally investigated the Ostrich. It turned out that in one of the rooms, the bed was attached to a trapdoor directly above a boiling vat. When one released the bolt under the trapdoor, the bed tilted, and its occupant slid into the vat."

"They boiled him?" she said. *"Alive?"*

"Yes," Rathbourne said. "I reckon the innkeeper and his wife must have made sure the guest went to bed very drunk. Then he wouldn't be able to try to save himself or even cry out."

"That is unspeakable," she said.

"People can do unspeakable things," he said. "They do them for absurd reasons or no reason at all. In this instance, however, justice triumphed. Innkeeper Jarman and his wife were arrested and tried, found guilty, and hanged, drawn, and quartered. Afterward, the place was known as Thomas Cole-in-the-Brook."

By this time they had crossed the bridge and entered Colnbrook's narrow street. They passed hostelries bearing the usual, familiar names: the White Hart and the George, both quiet at present. A little way farther on stood the infamous Ostrich, windows still alight. The sounds of drunken laughter wafted out into the night air.

The curricle was mere yards from the entrance when the door opened, and a trio of men stumbled out into the street. One staggered directly into the horses' path and fell on his face. Rathbourne smoothly drew the carriage to a halt, a few feet short of the inert man.

"Whyn't you watch where you're going?" one of the men shouted as he lurched toward his friend. "Bleedin' menace. You might've killed him, y' bloody great cod's head."

The third man stumbled in front of the horses and caught hold of the bridle of the offside horse. "S'all right," he said. "They won't be goin' nowhere."

"I am perfectly capable of holding a pair of horses," Rathbourne said composedly. "You would do better to get your friend out of the road."

The third man cordially invited Rathbourne to do something anatomically impossible.

The second man made himself more useful. He hoisted up his semiconscious friend, helped him out of the road, and shifted him onto the bench in front of the inn.

Meanwhile, oblivious to the animal's uneasiness, the third man continued hanging on to the bridle while he speculated about Rathbourne's sexual inadequacies, his affinity for young boys and mature sheep, and the number of ugly and deformed men his mother had reason to believe had fathered him.

Despite the provocation, Rathbourne remained the unflappable aristocrat. "I wonder, could there exist any more repellent sight than a drunk at one o'clock in the morning?" he said to Bathsheba in a bored undertone. "Or a being on earth less capable of reason?"

More audibly, he said, "I do apologize for the inconvenience, sir. Your friend is safe now, however. I am sure you and your other friend will be more comfortable resting on the bench with him. While you three enjoy a refreshing nap, we shall take our disagreeable selves out of your way."

The third man offered to stuff a part of Rathbourne's anatomy down his throat.

"I daresay I should waste my breath reminding you that a lady is present," Rathbourne said.

"Oh, a fine lady she is, too," said Drunk Number Two, abandoning his friend on the bench. "I know what kind of ladies come out at this time of night, don't I?"

He walked unsteadily to the curricle, contorting his face into what Bathsheba supposed was meant to be a wink. "Why don't you leave old carbuncle face there and his catch-fart to amuse each other like they like best? Why don't you come down to me instead, my pretty blackbird." He grasped her seat handle with one hand and grabbed his crotch with the other. "I've got something bigger and stronger for you to perch on."

"Not tonight," said Bathsheba. "I have a headache."

"Take your hand away from the carriage," Rathbourne said in a low, hard voice.

"Yes, sir, your majesty," said Drunk Number Two. He let go of the seat handle and grabbed her ankle. "I like this part better anyway."

Before Bathsheba could react, Rathbourne was up. He stepped over her, dropping the reins and whip into her lap, and dropped onto Drunk Number Two, who crashed to the ground under him. Rathbourne rose, picked him up, and threw him into the bench, knocking to the ground the first drunk, who'd been struggling to sit up.

Drunk Number Three let go of the horse and started toward him. Rathbourne spun on his heel and came around the front of the carriage. He grasped the man by the lapels and threw him against the inn door.

It all happened so quickly that Bathsheba had barely taken up the reins to hold the horses before it was over. Two men lay on the ground near the bench. The third was sinking into a heap against the doorpost.

She stared at Rathbourne.

He met her gaze and shrugged.

He started toward the carriage.

The inn door opened then, and a mob irrupted into the street.

THOUGH HE HAD been outnumbered before, his assailants were barely able to walk, let alone fight. Bathsheba had remained where she was, surprised but not worried.

But when half a dozen others set upon Rathbourne at once and knocked him down, she grabbed the whip and jumped down. She threw herself into the fray, lashing about her as best she could. When that proved impractical in the crowd, she began striking any head within reach with the whip handle.

"Get away from him, you scurvy coward!" she shouted at one, kicking him for good measure. Someone tried to wrench the whip from her, but she thrust her elbow into his soft parts, and he shrieked.

Perhaps it was the surprise, or perhaps her frenzy frightened them, but the men backed away long enough for Rathbourne to get up. He was no sooner on his feet, though, than one of the bigger ones lunged at him. An instant later, one of the others joined the fun. But she reckoned Rathbourne could handle two clodpoles, and turned her attention to keeping off the others.

At this point she became aware that Thomas was in it, too. As she watched him knock two men's heads together, she did wonder about the carriage and the horses. It was only a passing thought, though. Still more men were coming toward them, evidently from the inns they'd passed earlier.

She didn't have time to decide whether they were coming to join in and whose side they'd be on. Someone was trying to drag her out of the melee. She twisted free and balled up her hand into a fist, and landed it hard on his nose. He staggered backward, clutching his bleeding nose. Then another fellow claimed her attention, and she returned to fighting.

She was aware of Rathbourne, striking this one then another, a blur of movement at times. She saw two or three men fly into walls and windows, and heard the crash of breaking glass. She was aware of men on the ground, and others stumbling into lampposts. She glimpsed Thomas, pulling a man away from the carriage.

She noticed, too, the horses rearing, and people getting out of the way. She saw the curricle moving—and no one driving it—but the men from the inns were rapidly nearing, and she couldn't let Rathbourne be overwhelmed.

She didn't know how long it lasted—only a few minutes, probably, though it seemed she'd been at war for days.

Then a voice made itself heard above the others, and words rang out: "I command you in His Majesty's name to disperse, and to keep silence while I make proclamation to that effect."

The voice repeated the command two more times, and silence fell.

The voice went on: "Our Sovereign Lord the King charges and commands that all persons being assembled immediately do disperse themselves, and peaceably do depart to their habitations or to their lawful business, upon the pains contained in the Act made in the first year of King George I for preventing tumultuous and riotous assemblies. God save the King."

Men started backing away, muttering among themselves. The latecomers left first. Then those of the earlier group who were still on their feet began to retreat, some limping.

She looked toward Rathbourne, who stood alone. His coat was torn, his neckcloth and hat were gone. His hair stood up on end in one place, and damp ringlets had formed near his forehead. His face was so dirty, she could not tell how badly it was bruised. He met her gaze then, and gave a short, low laugh, and shook his head.

She went to him. It was instinctive. It was instinctive, too, reaching up to gently touch his face. "Are you hurt?" she said.

He gave the short laugh again, and took her hand, and lightly touched it to his cheek. "Am I hurt, she asks," he said. "You mad creature. What did you think you were doing?"

"I wasn't thinking," she said. "They knocked you down. . . . It wasn't fair. I was angry."

He let go of her hand in order to smooth back her hair.

She hadn't thought before and didn't stop to think now. She bowed her head and rested it on his chest. That was instinctive, too.

"I was afraid they'd hurt you," she said softly.

"And what of you, madam ninnyhammer?" he said. "Did you not think you might be hurt?"

"I didn't think," she said. "I didn't care."

She felt his hand slide down to rest at the back of her neck. She felt his chest rise and fall under her cheek. She was aware of her heart still pumping madly, and her lungs working hard, too, her breathing fast and uneven.

Then she heard his voice, very low, in her hair. "I believe the local constable draws nigh, the one who read the Riot Act so movingly. Get ready to lie through your teeth."

Chapter 9

MOST OF THE CROWD MELTED AWAY INTO THE night—those who were capable of moving, at any rate. The three original inebriates still lay more or less where they'd fallen.

Thomas, too, was nowhere in sight, Benedict noticed. He hoped the footman had gone after the runaway carriage.

The vehicle being out of reach at the moment, Benedict and Mrs. Wingate could not melt away. They had no speedy way out of Colnbrook and, unlike the locals, no nearby haven.

The man who'd read the Riot Act introduced himself as Henry Humber, landlord of the Bull Inn and local constable. He was a barrel-chested man of about forty who, it seemed, did not get to exercise his authority enough. The way he studied the fallen men and the broken windows, and peered here and there and made notes in a little book, boded very ill. Humber meant to raise difficulties, Benedict was sure. The two men he had with him—both large, muscled fellows—were obviously there to discourage opposition.

Nonetheless, it would have been simple enough to deal with the matter, if Benedict could have told the truth.

All he had to do was adopt the drawling voice and icy manner he used to crush upstarts and fools, and say he was on urgent business. All he had to do was write the name and direction of his solicitor on the back of one of his cards and give it to the constable. Benedict was not so far from civilization that his name would not be known. Those who recognized his name would know who his father was.

Then he would be allowed to continue on his way. If necessary, someone would make sure he had a vehicle and fresh horses. He would be offered refreshment and, very likely, an apology for the "misunderstanding."

Benedict could not tell the truth. He could not be who he was or behave as he normally would. Alone, he might easily survive the social consequences of a fracas with a lot of yokels some eighteen miles from London. People would assume he had been attacked or grossly provoked. Everyone knew that Lord Rathbourne—unlike his black sheep brother Rupert—was not in the habit of fighting and making a spectacle of himself.

Benedict was not alone, however. He had a woman with him, a beautiful and notorious and far too exciting woman.

Also a brave or possibly mad woman.

He still could scarcely believe she'd leapt out of the carriage and straight into the fight. She'd laid the horsewhip about her with remarkable energy and effectiveness. She had certainly amazed the men. Benedict had heard a couple of them scream like girls, and he'd seen more than one scurry to safety at the fringes of the crowd. If he hadn't been so busy himself, he would have laughed.

Equally unbelievable and less laughable was his own behavior.

He had got into a fight—a public brawl—with a lot of drunken peasants.

Because of a woman.

He had been perfectly rational, he'd thought. He'd seen that the men were deeply intoxicated. He knew one could not reason with drunkards or expect them to behave rationally. He knew his wisest course of action was to get away from them.

Benedict had ignored the insults and obscenities they hurled at him. He'd found it harder to ignore their coarse remarks to Mrs. Wingate, but he'd gritted his teeth and endured them.

Then the fellow had touched Mrs. Wingate.

And Benedict had to kill him.

Now she stood close, clutching his arm. The light from the inn windows and the men's lanterns was enough to reveal her increasing indignation as Humber muttered about outsiders coming into peaceable villages and making disturbances and disruptions.

Her great, blue eyes widened and flashed, her fine bosom rose and fell, and her soft mouth was parted in outraged astonishment.

Aroused, as any man would be, by this stirring picture of barely contained passion, Benedict was a moment too slow to warn her to keep her temper.

As he opened his mouth to do so, she burst out, "I cannot believe my ears. Three drunken men accosted us in the dead of night as we were innocently passing through the town. One of them put his hands on me. My husband defended my honor. A mob spilled into the streets and tried to kill him. And *we* are at fault?"

Humber said the men had obviously been too far gone in drink to stay on their feet, let alone hurt anybody, and people came out into the street simply to protect their friends. He indicated the casualties about him and the windows of nearby buildings. A few men had fallen or been flung against the windows, breaking the glass.

Before Mrs. Wingate could muster further arguments, Thomas emerged from the gloom, leading the horses. They were still attached, Benedict was relieved to see, to the curricle, which did not appear badly damaged.

"That's yours, is it?" said Humber. "And that's your servant? Well, he must come along with you, and your rig must go to the Bull." He turned back to Benedict. "You'll have it back once you've sorted matters out with magistrate on Monday."

"Monday?" Benedict and Mrs. Wingate said at the same time.

"Squire Pardew won't hold sessions until then," said Humber. "The missus putting her foot down as to miscreants in the parlor on Saturdays and the Sabbath."

Like many local magistrates, the squire held petty sessions in his parlor. Like his fellows, he'd have only a passing acquaintance with the law, and his judgments would be based on what he deemed common sense, colored by his personal biases and, very probably, those of his wife.

This did not necessarily make for poor justice, and it did not trouble Benedict. What troubled him was the name, with which he was all too familiar, and the possibility that someone had already woken the magistrate and told him of the brawl. Pardew might be on his way even now. He was a prodigious busybody and gossip.

Benedict bent his head and murmured to Mrs. Wingate. "We cannot linger here. I cannot risk an encounter with Pardew. He knows me."

More audibly Benedict said, "To my great regret, Monday will not—"

"Ooooh," said Mrs. Wingate. She let go of him, took a few staggering steps toward Humber, and fainted.

BENEDICT DID NOT suspect anything at first. When she put her hand to her head and began to sway, he stopped breathing as well as thinking. Still, he moved to catch her. But she fell against Humber, who caught her instead.

Benedict's heart recommenced beating while with narrowed eyes he watched her shift and squirm until she ended up facing the innkeeper, her bosom pressed to his chest.

Humber showed no eagerness to return her, and Benedict promptly considered killing *him*.

At that moment, however, a large woman carrying a lantern came into view. She wore a man's cloak over what had to be her nightdress. She still wore her sleeping bonnet, apparently deeming it sufficient protection against the night air. She strode toward them purposefully, her countenance hard.

"Humber," she said. "What keeps you so long?"

Mrs. Wingate let out a little moan.

Humber hastily transferred the limp, curvaceous armful to Benedict. "Bertha," said the innkeeper. "What do you want to be out looking for me for at this hour? You'll catch your death, you will."

"How was I to sleep with all the uproar?" Bertha demanded.

Mrs. Wingate moaned again.

Benedict gazed down at the woman languishing in his arms. She'd lost her bonnet, and her hair had come undone. Her head was flung back, exposing her white throat, and thrusting her firm, round bosom upward. Her soft lips were parted, her eyes closed. . . .

He knew the pose was a sham, but that was about all he knew. His brain wasn't working half so well as other, lower parts of him.

She was dirty and disheveled from the recent scuffle, and that only made it worse.

He wanted to tear off every last soiled, worn garment, strip her to the skin, and . . .

. . . *wash* her.

. . . Slowly . . .

. . . from the top of her head to the tips of her toes.

With an effort—and it was no light one—he reclaimed his mind.

"My dear," he said thickly. "Speak to me."

She fluttered her eyelids and, by degrees, began to recover. *Pretended* to begin to recover.

Since Benedict desperately needed to collect his wits, he looked about for a place to set her down.

Drunkards One and Two lay peacefully near the bench where they'd fallen, both snoring loudly. Benedict nudged Number One out of the way with his foot, and sat Mrs. Wingate on the bench. Before he could draw away, she tugged his hand.

Though he needed to put some distance between them, Benedict sat down gingerly beside her. Remembering he was supposed to be her spouse, he put his arm about her shoulders and tried not to think about baths.

"My dear, I fear my trouble grows worse," she said. "It is not a good sign: another spell, so soon after the last one." She gave a little sob.

Ah, she was dying, that was it.

"No, no, you are better," Benedict said, patting her hand. "It was the shock—all those men—the shouting and violence. You were alarmed."

Not half as alarmed as the men at the receiving end of the whip handle, he'd wager. It was made of good, solid blackthorn.

She shook her head. "No, I grow weaker," she said, with a wonderful, sad bravery. "I had so hoped to see dear Sarah before . . . before . . . well, you know."

Benedict didn't know, but he had the general idea, and played along. "You shall see her soon, my dear, I promise."

"Oh, I wish it could be so," she said. "It was the one last thing I wished for. But by Monday . . . it may be too late. I am not sure I shall be strong enough."

The tender scene had diverted the other couple's attention, as Mrs. Wingate no doubt intended.

"The lady's ailing?" said Mrs. Humber. She glared at her spouse.

"Well, who could've guessed it?" said he. "She felt— Mean to say, she *looked* plenty robust to me. And I heard she was lively enough with the horsewhip only a little while ago."

Benedict gently leaned Mrs. Wingate against the wall of the inn, then rose and joined the pair. "If you could see her in the harsh light of day, you would recognize the signs," he told them in a low voice. "I cannot say where she found the strength to come to my aid. It was reckless of her, not wise at all, in her condition . . . but she has great c-courage." He let his voice break.

"She's amazing spirited for a invalid," said Humber.

"She is determined to see her sister, though she knows the journey might be fatal," Benedict went on. "I dare to hope that some better instinct guides her. Perhaps the doctors are wrong, and the reunion and change of air will strengthen her. It is desperation, you see, that leads us to travel so late. She fears she will not see her sister in time."

Mrs. Humber's scowl deepened.

"She weren't a bit sick before," Humber said. "You didn't see her then, Bertha."

"I seen plenty," said Mrs. Humber.

"And only look at what *he* done," said Mr. Humber, nodding at his fallen neighbors. "Then there's all the broken windows. Squire will want to—"

"Squire, indeed," said Mrs. Humber. "Much he cares about a lot of your sotted friends knocking heads. Let *them* pay for the broken winders. Don't you be telling me about Squire. I wasn't born yesterday, was I?"

"Now, Bertha," Humber said.

"Don't you 'now Bertha' me," she said.

She turned to Benedict. "I'm sorry for your trouble, sir," she said. "But if I was you, I wouldn't be traveling so late with the lady. The night air won't do her no good, for one thing. And for another, at this hour it's mostly drunken fools and lechers up and about. Pretty creeturs like her is bound to bring out the worst in 'em. You be on your way, now—and I'd keep her better covered up if I was you."

Moments later, Benedict, Mrs. Wingate, and Thomas were safely in the curricle and on their way out of Colnbrook.

None of them noticed Squire Pardew riding up to the highway. He halted at the edge of the road to let the curricle pass. He remained there, in the shadows, frowning as he watched it drive away.

"THAT WAS A near thing," Rathbourne told Bathsheba as they crossed the next bridge. "I had it in mind to signal to Thomas, then scoop you up and make a mad dash for the carriage. I reckoned that if we took them by surprise, Humber's ruffians would be too slow to stop us, and we might gallop to freedom."

"That was a better idea than mine," she said. "But I saw a woman coming, and falling into his arms was what came into my head."

"Your idea was brilliant," he said. "By gad, that was a delicious scene. Better than any stage farce." He transferred the reins to his whip hand, then threw the other round her shoulders and hugged her. She felt his chin on her head. "You were wonderful," he said, his deep voice dropping to a rumble. "Mad, to leap to my rescue—but wonderful then, too."

She wanted to tuck herself in closer. Now that it was over, she found she was trembling. "I was afraid you would be hurt," she said.

His hold tightened. "Were you, indeed?" He cleared his throat. "Not half as afraid as those men when you leapt down amongst them, I daresay," he went on in lighter tones. "What a picture you made!"

"I have had practice," she said. She remembered who and what she was, then, and made herself draw away.

Rathbourne seemed to recollect himself, too. He did not try to draw her back but gathered the reins into his left hand again, straightened his posture, and returned his attention to driving.

"My family traveled the Continent during wartime," she said. "My father taught me how to use a pistol and a whip—in case we met with any roaming bands of soldiers, he said. As it turned out, we had more trouble with his numerous victims than from marauding soldiers."

"If your daughter is half as resourceful as you, I cannot be in the least anxious about Peregrine," he said. "I know he can defend himself, if it comes to that. He is more than handy with his fists, as Nat Diggerby discovered. In any case, they will be safe enough on the stage."

"Safe enough, yes," she said. "But we are running out of time. How far is it to Salt Hill?"

"About three miles," he said.

"Drive faster," she said.

RATHBOURNE DROVE FASTER, to no avail.

At the Windmill in Salt Hill, Mrs. Edkins, the landlady, told them that only one passenger had disembarked from the Courser. This was an elderly lady, who was at present asleep in one of the rooms. It proved unnecessary to wake and question her, since Mrs. Edkins had spoken to her at length.

The innkeeper told Bathsheba and Rathbourne what her elderly guest had told her. In Cranford Bridge, the Courser had taken up two boys making their way home from London to see their dying mama. The old lady had taken pity on them and given them a few coins. It was not very much—she did not travel with a great deal of money—but it would cover the fare to Twyford.

Bathsheba looked at Rathbourne. "How far is Twyford?" she asked.

"About twelve miles," he said. "How annoying. I had hoped to have a bath before too long. It seems I must make do with the inn yard's pump."

"Testing the horses' mettle and had an accident, did you?" said Mrs. Edkins, eyeing him up and down. Notwithstanding his dirty face, missing buttons, draggled neckcloth, scarred trousers, and scuffed boots, her gaze was warm with admiration.

"We had a run-in with a lot of drunken oafs in Colnbrook," Bathsheba said.

"You should have seen our opponents," Rathbourne said, black eyes gleaming, "after my wife was done with them."

He turned away and started down the narrow passage leading to the back of the inn. Bathsheba watched him go, marveling at his ability to appear merely attractively rumpled, while she . . .

The thought trailed into nothing as her gaze slid down from his broad shoulders to his narrow hips. He was walking oddly.

She hurried after him. "Are you hurt?" she said.

"Certainly not," he said. He kept walking. "I only want a dash of cold water to revive me."

He seemed to be favoring his right side. "You are hurt," she said. "You must let me look at you. You might have cracked a rib."

"I have cracked nothing," he said. "It is no more than a protesting muscle. My throwing-fellows-into-doors muscle has grown stiff and weak from lack of use."

"Mrs. Edkins!" she called.

The landlady hastened into the passageway.

"My husband is hurt," Bathsheba told her. "I shall want some hot water."

"No, you most certainly shall not," he said. "Mrs. Edkins, you are on no account to trouble about hot water or anything else." He threw Bathsheba a quelling look. "It is past two o'clock in the morning. You will not keep everybody awake and turn this hostelry inside out because I have a muscle spasm." He turned away, wincing as he did so.

"Pay no attention to him, Mrs. Edkins," said Bathsheba. "He is a man, and you know how men are."

"Indeed, I do," said the landlady. "And it's no trouble at all. We are up at all hours here, with all the coaches and carriages coming and going. I'll have that hot water for you in a trice. And a bite to eat, maybe, and something to drink, to fortify the gentleman?"

"No," said Rathbourne in his most lordly tones. "Absolutely n-n—" His mouth twitched. He made a choked sound.

Bathsheba stared at him, alarmed.

And then it exploded from him, a great roar of laughter that shook the walls of the passageway.

ONCE HE'D STARTED, it was as though a dam had burst.

Benedict couldn't stop laughing. Again and again he saw the recent episode in his mind's eye, and again and again he returned to the moment when Drunk Number Two had made his spectacularly crude suggestions to Mrs. Wingate, and she had said in that marvelously matter-of-fact voice, "Not tonight. I have a headache."

Thence Benedict's mind strayed to her falling into Humber's arms—and the expression on Mrs. Humber's face—and her succinct remark, "I seen plenty."

Then he would go on laughing, helplessly, doubled over at times.

Benedict leant an arm against the wall and tried to catch his breath—but he saw Mrs. Wingate beating a fellow on the head and shoulders with the whip handle, saw the fellow raising his arms to shield himself—and that set him off again, into whoops.

He had no idea how long it went on. He only knew that it did eventually abate, leaving him short of breath and lightheaded. It wanted effort to stand erect and wipe his eyes, and stagger down the passageway to the back of the inn and outside to the pump.

He could feel the women's eyes upon him as he went.

Still, they only watched. They didn't follow to try to nurse him, so that was all right. Thomas did follow a short time afterward, but that was Thomas's job.

Outside, when Benedict had rinsed off the worst of the filth and cooled down several degrees, Thomas proffered a towel and said he was glad to see that the master had not taken any serious hurt.

"Certainly not," Benedict said. "I had no trouble with those louts—except the once when they knocked me off my feet. I might have suffered some damage then, if Mrs.—er—my dear wife—had not intervened." He squelched a chuckle.

"Mrs. Woodhouse, sir," said Thomas. He drew closer and lowered his voice, for as Mrs. Edkins had noted, the place was not entirely asleep. The inn yard in particular tended to be more awake than other parts, with vehicles arriving at intervals throughout the night to change horses. Salt Hill was another popular stop.

"Madam told the landlady that you are Mr. and Mrs. Woodhouse," Thomas explained. "But I couldn't make out whether she gave you a Christian name of John or George."

"It hardly matters what she christened me," Benedict said. "We shall be gone in a trice."

Thomas cleared his throat.

Benedict looked at him. The inn yard was adequately lit. Still, it was difficult to read the footman's expression.

"What is it?" Benedict said.

"Mrs. Woodhouse has obtained a private parlor," said Thomas. "I would have come sooner, but she wanted the fire built up."

"And you obeyed her," Benedict said. "Though you knew it was my wish to be gone as soon as possible."

"Yes, sir."

"Are you afraid of her, Thomas?"

"I seen her jump right out of the carriage when the men knocked you down," said Thomas. "She was quicker than I was, or it would've been me, like it should've been. I couldn't help thinking she had your best interests at heart. And if it comes to being afraid or not, my lord, I'd just as soon not be in her black books. So I built up the fire, like she wanted."

"I see," said Benedict.

"She ordered hot water and bandages and food," the footman went on doggedly. "She says you must eat something—as soon as she tends to your injuries."

"I have no injuries," Benedict said. "Did I not say so?"

"My lord, meaning no disrespect, but the ladies are always wanting to pill, plaster, or poultice us," said Thomas. "It don't matter whether a man needs it or not. He might as well go along, as it makes the lady happy and saves the time of arguing."

Though he saw the simple wisdom of Thomas's viewpoint, Benedict also saw the suicidal stupidity of letting Bathsheba Wingate put her hands on him, even to apply a medical remedy. His self-control was showing alarming cracks as it was: the brawl, the hug in the carriage, the laughing fit. At present he was far from calm and he was growing fatigued, which would not help his self-control a whit.

If she touched him, if she stood too close for too long while he had no other important task, like driving, to occupy him and take his mind off her, he was all too likely to make a fatal error.

Benedict could not follow Thomas's advice.

He could not indulge Mrs. Wingate's fears about injuries or her feminine need to nurse.

His mind made up, Benedict returned the towel to his servant. In lieu of a comb, Benedict dragged his hand through his hair, which he had no doubt was standing up in curly clumps. He was tempted to ask Thomas how bad it was, but resisted the urge.

It was not fair. He and Rupert had inherited their mother's

coloring, but Rupert's hair never fell into ridiculous ringlets or sprang up on end in this absurd manner.

Not that he was in the least envious of Rupert, who was always in one ridiculous scrape or another and whose life was chaos. How the logical, brainy Daphne tolerated the unpredictability, disorganization, and disorder, Benedict would never understand.

In any event, the state of Benedict's hair didn't signify. He was not attending an assembly at Almack's. He was not on display as a matrimonial prize. He was not trying to find and win the Perfect Wife.

Furthermore, Duty and Reason both forbade his trying to make himself attractive to Bathsheba Wingate.

And so, hoping he did not too closely resemble Grimaldi the clown, Benedict made his way back into the inn and to the private parlor, determined to put everything, including Bathsheba Wingate, in its proper place.

Chapter 10

BATHSHEBA HAD CLEANED OFF THE WORST OF the dirt, too, but in a more ladylike way, using the washbowl and pitcher Mrs. Edkins supplied.

The landlady had not provided a looking glass or hairpins, however, and Bathsheba was trying to arrange her hair without benefit of either when the door to the private parlor was flung open.

"You have corrupted my footman," Rathbourne said.

His damp neckcloth had been hastily tied. The collar of his shirt hung limp. His coat and waistcoat were unbuttoned.

Gleaming black curls dangled over his brow. Here and there others stood up like corkscrews.

He had not simply washed his face but stuck his head under the pump, she saw with despair. He was *wet*.

She longed to drag her fingers through that unruly mass of curls. She longed to peel off his damp clothes and let her hands roam in places where they ought not to be.

It was the dratted fight in Colnbrook that was to blame. His reaction when the drunkard touched her . . . the way the men had come after him and he'd knocked them about and tossed them here and there and made it all seem effortless . . . the danger . . .

She'd loved it.

She'd found it arousing.

Typical DeLucey reaction.

She shoved a hairpin into the rat's nest on her head. "I am a DeLucey," she said grimly. "We corrupt everyone."

"You will not corrupt me," he said. "You must make do with enslaving Thomas and making him cater to your mad whims. I am not Thomas, however, and I am not accustomed to being dictated to. Come, we must be off."

She stiffened. "I am not accustomed to being dictated to, either," she said. "I refuse to stir from here until I have made sure you haven't fractured a rib."

"I have not fractured any ribs," he said.

"You cannot be sure," she said. "Before, in the passageway, you favored your right side."

"I was trying not to laugh," he said.

"You walked oddly afterward," she said.

"I was dizzy from laughing so hard," he said.

She had felt dizzy watching and listening. When he'd laughed, he'd made her heart ache because he looked so much like a boy and so much like a rogue, and so utterly imperfect and *human.*

He *was* human, breakable like anyone else. Those paroxysms might have worsened his injuries.

"It will only take a moment," she said. "Can you not indulge—"

"I am not an idiot, Mrs. Win—Mrs. *Woodhouse*," he said. "If I had broken a rib, I should know it. On account of the pain, you see. My being so manly and stoical does not mean I never feel pain. I have wit enough as well to recognize when I am not in pain. I am not."

"There is often a delayed reaction," she said. "Sometimes hours pass before the shock or excitement fully wears off and the pain—"

"I am not shocked or excited and we are not hanging about here for hours," he said. "I am going, madam. You may come along or remain, as you choose." He turned away and went out of the door.

He expected her to follow, like a sheep.

Bathsheba folded her arms and glared at the doorway.

A moment later, he stomped back into the room. "You are being obstinate for the sake of being obstinate," he said. "You are determined to challenge me at every turn. This is the same as you did in London. Well, you cannot have your way every time."

"But you can?" she said.

"I refuse to remain here arguing with you," he said. "It is completely absurd."

"I will not be treated like a child," she said. "You may not take that tone with me. You may not ridicule my reasonable concern. Fractured ribs can prove fatal."

His expression abruptly softened. "Yes, of course it is a reasonable concern. I should not make light of it."

She relaxed, unfolding her arms.

He moved toward her, face penitent. "You may tell me all about it," he said, reaching for her hand. "In the carriage."

She backed away, but he moved quickly, too, and scooped her up.

"Oh, no," she said. "You will not use these primitive tactics with me. I will not be flung about like a sack of corn. Put me down." She punched his chest.

"Look out for my fractured ribs, my love," he said with a laugh.

"I am not your love, you overbearing, sarcastic bully," she said, trying to wriggle free. "You are not my lord and master. You will not—"

"You are making a scene," he said.

"I have not even begun to make a scene," she said as they came to the door. "Take one more step and I—"

His mouth came down on hers.

THE WORLD TIPPED out of balance, went dark.

He slammed the door shut, fell back against it, his mouth clamped on hers.

No! No! a voice inside Benedict's head roared.

Too late.

Her mouth instantly yielded and her hands came up and curled tightly on his shoulders.

She took his kiss and gave him back more, laced with defiance. The same defiance that had flashed in her blue eyes became molten liquid in his mouth.

She squirmed in his arms until he eased his grasp and let her down, but her mouth never left his. He drank liquid fire while she slid down slowly, the friction of those soft curves against his hard frame setting every fiber and cell of his body vibrating.

He had to let her go. *Now.*

All he had to do was unhook his arm from her waist. But he didn't. He held her against him while the kiss became a wicked game between them, taunting, daring, demanding.

Passion.

Passion was not allowed. Ever. Passion was madness, chaos. He had scores of rules against it.

NO. Kick me. Step on my foot. You know how to fight.

She held on to him, one slim hand that might as well have been a vise curled over his upper arm.

He heard the voices of Reason and Duty shrieking out rules, but she drowned them out with the whisper touch of her fingers gliding over the back of his hand, the hand he'd laid flat against the door, to keep it still until he found the strength to draw the other away from her, too.

Her fingers curled round his wrist and he couldn't help but turn his hand to twine his fingers with hers. The intimacy of the touch made him ache and the ache made him angry. She was made for him. Why could he not have her?

He broke the kiss, burying his face in her neck. He tasted her skin and drank in her scent, and it was all as he'd remembered and remembered despite trying so determinedly to forget.

Then he could not keep his hands still. He dragged them over her back and traced the curve of her waist and the sweep of her hips. And it was as though he dared her, or perhaps she felt it, too, the same mad need he felt, because her hands moved, too, and made turmoil wherever they went. They slid under his coat and inside his waistcoat and teased over the thin shirt when she *knew*, she had to know, he needed her hands on his skin.

He felt over the back of her dress, but the fastenings weren't there. He found them in front instead, and it was a moment's work to undo the tapes, to push away the thin fabric of her shift and thrust his hand inside the top of her stays and clasp her breast, skin to skin.

She sucked in her breath.

Tell me to stop don't tell me to stop.

She pulled away and tugged at the corset, loosening it, and looked up at him, eyes dark and challenging. She brought her hands up to his head and drew him down, and he heard her soft gasp of pleasure when he trailed his lips over the smooth swell of her breasts.

That was the end of thought.

After that was only mindless *I want* and *must have, must have* and *mine, mine, mine.*

The beast in charge.

He dragged up her skirts, up and up, petticoats bunching and whispering against his sleeve until at last his hand slid over the top of her stocking, and then up, where there was soft, soft skin, and up farther still, until he found the core of her, warm, silky, slick.

He reached for his trouser buttons, but she was there first, and when her palm brushed over his throbbing groin, he had to sink his mouth onto her shoulder to keep from crying out, like the merest boy learning pleasure for the first time.

He was impatient, mindless, but her hand was there and that was too tormentingly pleasurable to push away, for all his impatience. He felt one button come loose, then the next. His cock thrust against the cloth toward her hand and he was reaching to help her—to help himself—he couldn't wait—when she cried out, and pulled away, then swore, low and fierce, in French.

ONE FEROCIOUS JAB of pain: That's what it took to bring Bathsheba to her senses.

She pulled away from him, her hand throbbing. She turned away, too, her face aflame.

"What?" he said, his deep voice thick. "What?"

She could have wept. She could have laughed. "My hand," she said. "My hand, thank heaven. Damn you to hell, Rathbourne. You know we cannot do this."

"Damn me to hell?" he said. "Damn *me* to hell?" Then, more gently he said, "What is wrong with your hand?"

"I think it broke somebody's nose," she said. "And now it throbs like the very devil."

"Let me see."

She wanted to put distance between them while she put her clothes back in order and gave him time to do the same. Her bosom was falling out of her stays, part of her petticoat had bunched up under her waistband, and her skirts were all twisted about.

But she had never learnt to be ashamed or shy about her body, and at the moment she didn't care what he could see. She would have let him see all he wanted and have all he wanted, and she'd have done it happily, nay, eagerly.

Because she was besotted and it was completely hopeless. *She* was completely hopeless, a DeLucey through and through, no matter what she did.

She let him take her hand and look at it.

"Your fingers are swollen," he said. "Did you say you punched somebody on the nose?"

"Yes," she said.

"Because of me," he said.

"Yes, certainly, because of you," she said. "I was not going to let you fight them alone, Rathbourne. Not that you should have fought them in the first place. It was ridiculous to make such a fuss over that drunkard groping at my leg. I was perfectly capable of kicking him if he became too annoying. Still, it was lovely of you. Chivalrous."

"It was not lovely of me," he said. "It was ridiculous. If I had not behaved in that imbecile, Rupert-like way, we should be well on our way by now, with none of us sporting any injuries and none of us imagining the other had any injuries, and most important, neither of us coming within a hairsbreadth of doing what we both know perfectly well we must not do."

"Well, we didn't do it," she said. She didn't try to sound cheerful about it. She hadn't even enough self-command to not sound regretful.

"No, we did not." He stared at her hand. Then he bent his head and brought it to his lips and gently touched them to each knuckle. He released her hand and looked her up and down. He let out a long sigh. "I was the one who took your clothes apart. It seems I had better put them together again."

"I can do it," she said.

"The pain made you cry out when you were simply trying to unfasten a trouser button," he said. "How do you imagine you will be able to manage your tapes and corset strings?"

Good question.

As she'd predicted, there was a delayed reaction to the fight. But she was the one in pain, not he. Too bad the pain had not started some minutes sooner. Then she would not have had to face the fact that she was another DeLucey harlot.

"I imagine it would take me several hours and a good deal of cursing and screaming," she said. "Perhaps you had better do it."

She stared at the notch of his collarbone while he briskly pulled the corset back into place, arranged and smoothed her shift, stuffed her breasts back where they belonged, and laced up the stays.

While he tied her petticoat, she swallowed and said, "I daresay proper ladies do not unbutton gentlemen's trousers."

"They do not do that," he said as he tugged her frock straight, "nearly so often as one could wish."

THOUGH THEY HAD the fare to take them to Twyford, Peregrine and Olivia did not get that far.

In Maidenhead, when the coach stopped to change horses, Peregrine squeezed himself out from where he was wedged between two fat and not overclean male passengers. They had been sleeping soundly, mostly on him. He'd inhaled their stinking breath and been deafened by their explosive snoring for the last five miles. He would not have minded so much if he'd had something interesting to do or to look at but he hadn't, and so he was bored and cross as well as tired and hungry.

"I'm stopping here," he told Olivia. "You can stay or you can go on. I really don't care."

He climbed out and walked out of the inn yard and into the street and gulped in cool night air.

Then he looked about him. He had never before been out so late at night, alone, in a strange town. Except for the bustle in the inn yard, the place was quiet. It was very late, and everyone was asleep.

He wanted to be quiet, too, so he could think. In fact, he wanted to be asleep, like everyone else.

He'd spent the afternoon and night in a state of tension, unsure what Olivia would do next, wondering when calamity would strike.

Now he realized it had already struck. Running away with Olivia Wingate, no matter how worthy his reasons, was going to bring unpleasant consequences.

Had Lord Rathbourne caught up with them early on, as Peregrine had hoped, matters might have been settled without a great fuss. He had only to explain, and Uncle would understand why he'd done what he'd done. Uncle Benedict was a reasonable and rational man.

But it was tomorrow already. It was Saturday, the day Peregrine was supposed to set out with his lordship for Scotland. Even if Peregrine could afford to hire a post chaise—which he couldn't—he doubted he could get back to London fast enough to avert disaster. By now all of Uncle Benedict's servants would know something was wrong. Once the servants knew, all the world would find out.

Peregrine should have realized that anything to do with Olivia Wingate spelled disaster. He should have let her go with Nat Diggerby.

But then Peregrine would have missed the adventure.

And the truth was, he was not in any hurry to go to Edinburgh and be bored and aggravated at yet another school, out of which he would soon be chucked.

What troubled him was annoying Lord Rathbourne, who might decide Peregrine was more trouble than he was worth, and upsetting Mama and Papa because they might become hysterical enough to forbid any more visits with his lordship. Otherwise Peregrine wouldn't have minded continuing with Olivia on her mad Quest. For a young man who planned to travel the Nile, traveling the road to Bristol would be a useful experience.

But there was Lord Rathbourne to consider, and since he hadn't caught them yet, Peregrine decided he must stop and wait to be caught.

Meanwhile he wanted food. And a bed.

Maidenhead, a good-sized market town, boasted a number of inns. He returned to the Bear, the largest and busiest. As he neared the entrance, he saw Olivia there, waiting, her arms folded. "You are supposed to be my squire," she said. "Squires are steadfast and true. They don't abandon their knights."

"I'm hungry," he said. "I want to sleep."

"You can't do it *here*," she said. "This is the biggest inn in Maidenhead. It will cost the earth, and I know they'll never let us have one of their grand rooms out of charity." She glanced appraisingly about her at her surroundings. "You can't expect me to earn any money at this time of night."

"Earn?" he said. "You mean *bamboozle*."

She shrugged. "Your father gives you money. I have to work for mine."

Peregrine was not sure that sharp practices and outright deceit ought to be called *work*, but he was too tired to debate semantics. "As a matter of fact, my father does give me money," he said. "And I do have a bit with me."

Her eyes narrowed.

"In the first place, it isn't very much," he said. "In the second, it's no use looking at me that way because I never lied to you about it."

"You never said you had money," she said.

"You never asked," he said. "Have you asked once for my advice or help or opinion?" Without waiting for an answer he went on, "I'll buy you supper and maybe a bed if we're lucky, if you promise not to tell anybody else about our dying mother—or any other people who don't exist."

"Why?" she said.

"It isn't sporting."

"It isn't *what*?"

"Sporting," he said.

"You mean it isn't *proper*," she said mockingly.

Peregrine wrenched the door open. "I mean," he said, "it's like a great, big fellow picking on a little fellow. That's what I mean." He waved her inside.

"Oh," she said, and went.

She became quiet after that, which suited Peregrine. He wanted to eat and he wanted to sleep. After he'd had some rest he'd be ready to talk, perhaps.

He did rest, very comfortably, though the inn was indeed expensive and they ended up in a cupboard-sized room on hard cots meant for servants.

Though it was more Spartan than anything he'd ever experienced before, even at school, Lord Lisle was sound asleep when Lord Rathbourne drove through Maidenhead at half past three o'clock in the morning.

BENEDICT HARDLY NOTICED Maidenhead.

He devoted the first tautly silent moments of travel to trying to revive his famous self-control, gather the remaining shreds of his moral fiber, and evict the alien spirit that had taken possession of him.

Then Mrs. Wingate spoke, and everything went to pieces.

"I think it would be best if we separated in Twyford," she said. "I shall take Olivia to Bristol and attempt to settle the treasure nonsense once and for all."

"To Bristol?" he echoed incredulously. "Did you hit your head in Colnbrook as well as your hand?"

"You and I cannot return to London together," she said, "and you know you must hurry back if you wish to avoid causing a stir. You were to set out for Scotland today, were you not?"

"That is not the point," he said. "The point is, you cannot travel to Bristol alone."

"I shall have Olivia with me," she said.

"You haven't any money," he said.

"I have a little," she said.

"It must be a very little," he said. "When I came to your lodgings, you were preparing to visit the pawnbroker with a sack of your belongings."

"Olivia and I have always traveled with very little money," she said. "It is not as though I plan to hire a post chaise. We can walk."

"To *Bristol*? Are you mad? That is nearly a hundred miles." He recalled the men's reaction to her provocatively swaying hips at the Kensington tollgate.

She was proposing to swing those hips over a hundred miles of road along which mainly men would be traveling.

"It is out of the question," he said. "I will not permit it."

She turned in the seat to look at him. Her knee bumped his thigh. He set his jaw.

"Where on earth did you obtain the mad idea that you had any say over my doings?" she said. "Oh, never mind. I had forgotten. With you, it is force of habit, ordering everyone about. Very well, my lord. Go ahead and tell me everything I may and may not do. I had rather spend the next few miles laughing than fretting about my exasperating daughter."

"You say she is exasperating, yet you mean to indulge her," Benedict said. "What have you in mind, exactly? A visit to your relatives' mausoleum in the dead of night? I have an interesting picture in my mind of the pair of you in hooded cloaks, Olivia carrying a dark lantern and you with a spade on your shoulder."

"Like many great estates, Throgmorton is open to visitors on certain days," she said. "I shall take her to the mausoleum and let her see how scrupulously the grounds are tended. She will see for herself that, had any treasure been buried there, the gardeners or men making repairs would have found it ages ago. After that, perhaps we shall amuse ourselves looking for smugglers' caves."

"In other words, you do not mean to return to London for some time." He ought to be glad. He would not be tempted to hunt for her when he returned from Scotland. In time, this damnable infatuation would pass.

"Certainly not," she said. "You will be in Edinburgh with your nephew. What is there for me—for anyone—in London when Lord Rathbourne is not there?"

He glanced at her. She turned away again, her countenance sober, but not before he saw the glint of mirth in her eyes.

"You are laughing at me," he said.

"On the contrary, my lord," she said, "I am trying desperately to contain my grief at your impending departure. I am smiling bravely, not laughing. Well, I am not laughing very much."

Troubled as he was, he couldn't help smiling, too. But then, he was bewitched.

She looked away, to the road ahead, and her expression sobered. "It will not be a laughing matter if we do not take care," she said. "You know we must separate as soon as we recover the children, and you must take Peregrine to Scotland without delay. If you are only a day or two late, his parents will not make a fuss."

"They always make a fuss," he said. "His parents are the least of the difficulty. By now my household will be aware that something is amiss. Someone will talk and some sort of rumor will begin making the rounds. I shall need a good lie."

"I shall need one as well, for Mrs. Briggs," she said, "to explain my extended absence."

"Write her a note when we get to Twyford," Benedict said. "You are needed to nurse your sick relative. I shall see that the note arrives quickly. As to my story: Perhaps I shall say that Peregrine took it into his head to join a traveling acting troupe or a band of gypsies. Or perhaps he became enslaved by the charms of a peddler's daughter and followed her. That is the sort of romantic idiocy his parents would accept implicitly."

"They do not know Lord Lisle very well, do they?" she said. "Even I, knowing him for only a few weeks, would never believe it for a moment."

"What I cannot believe is that his parents had anything to do with producing him," Benedict said. "All the Dalmays are emotionally extravagant, and they tend to choose spouses of the same temperament."

"He is an aberration," she said. "It happens all the time. I only wish it had happened in Olivia's case."

"Then Peregrine would have missed an adventure," Benedict said. *And so would I,* he thought.

The end of it was approaching all too quickly.

"If only it were no more than that," she said. "But it is not, and I don't mean to let her off easily." After a pause, she added, "Rathbourne, what shall we do if it is found out that we traveled together?"

He had no trouble imagining that possibility. He knew that the darkness was not a completely reliable shield. He realized that someone might have recognized him at some point along the last twenty-odd miles.

He was well aware of how swiftly gossip could travel.

He remembered the men talking about Jack Wingate at the club. He could still hear the mingled contempt and pity in their voices. He could hear the disgust in his father's voice, when he spoke of the Dreadful DeLuceys.

Benedict had seen countless times what happened when some unhappy soul became the subject of scandal: the titters and whispers behind fans, the smirks, the not-so-subtle innuendoes, the not-at-all subtle caricatures hanging in shop windows or pinned inside umbrellas for all the world to see.

The prospect of becoming such an object was not pleasant to contemplate. The prospect of *her* being tittered and whispered about and caricatured was intolerable.

"Denial is the only sensible response," he said.

"Do you truly believe it could be so simple?" she said. "All we need do is say, 'It isn't true'?"

"No," he said. "We pretend a faux pas has been committed. We elevate an eyebrow. We allow ourselves a faint, pitying smile. If people persist in being tiresome, we adopt the expression and tones of one who is bored witless and endeavoring to be polite, and say, 'Indeed' or 'How very interesting.'" He demonstrated as he spoke.

"That is very good," she said. "But are you sure it will be sufficient?"

"It had better be," he said.

In the distance he made out a faint twinkle near the side of the road. "That looks to be Twyford," he said. "We had better decide how to proceed once we locate the children."

They devoted those last minutes to working out the logistics of going their separate ways.

It was a more melancholy experience than he was prepared for.

He had not long to be melancholy, however, because at Twyford, they learned that no one—man, woman, or child—had disembarked there from the Courser.

They drove on, to Reading.

*and restitched . . . the ones I've mended and mended and
mended until little remains of the original cloth . . . the
ones I've washed and washed until nothing remains of the
original color.*

Who was she trying to fool?

She'd gone to bed with a man to whom she was not
wed. She *was* a whore.

She might as well be a happy one.

She said, "I'll *make* it fit."

She took the clothes from him and sorted out the underthings. She would have declined his assistance but Thomas
had bought the type of garments women of the middle and
upper classes wore, the kind one couldn't manage single-
handed. Her usual dresses and corsets fastened in the front.
The new corset and frock fastened in the back.

"I shall need your help with the stays," she said after
she'd donned drawers and chemise.

"Then I had better fix my mind on sobering thoughts,"
Rathbourne said. He flung aside the waistcoat he'd been
about to put on, and came to her.

"Will scandal do?" she said. "Or a pair of missing children? Or both?"

He moved behind her and set to work. "Those will do
admirably. Let us review in an orderly fashion our possible
courses of action regarding the brats."

Orderly thinking was beyond her at present. She was
too aware of his hands at her back, of the intimacy of this
moment, the curious *domesticity* of it.

Fortunately, Rathbourne did not need any more help
with orderly thinking than he did with managing the intri-
cacies of women's attire.

"Here is what comes to mind," he said. "One, we continue
to do what we've done thus far. Two, we turn back to the last
place we had word of them. Three, we alert the authorities
and assemble a formal search party."

"Good grief."

"Have I pulled the stays too tight?"

"No, it was only . . ." She sighed. "Never mind. It is
foolish to worry about how much scandal we make."

"It is not at all foolish," he said. "There are degrees of

Chapter 11

THE SKY WAS LIGHTENING BY THE TIME BENE-
dict and Mrs. Wingate had made the rounds of the likeliest
inns in Reading. By this point, she was on the point of col-
lapse, though she refused to admit it.

They stood near the ticket office of the Crown Inn, she
watching every vehicle that came and went while quarreling with him about their next step.

"This grows ridiculous," he told her. "We have wasted
valuable time taking the word of innkeepers and servants
who are half asleep. It makes as much sense to wait in
Reading for the Courser to make its return trip, and speak
directly to the coachman."

"That will be hours," she said. "The children might be
halfway to Bristol by then."

"If you would only apply a little logic, you would see
how very unlikely that is," Benedict said as patiently as he
could. "They are two children with next to no money. They
must rely on their wits and the kindness or gullibility of
strangers. Even your daughter, spawn of Satan that you believe her to be, cannot travel at any great rate unless she
hires a post chaise. To afford it, she must take to highway

robbery. She would then need to find, in a short space of time on a small piece of road, a victim willing to hand over an unusually heavy purse."

Mrs. Wingate regarded him through slitted blue eyes. "Have you any idea, Rathbourne, how utterly detestable you become when you adopt that tone of patient superiority?"

"The trouble is, you are tired, hungry, anxious, and afflicted with an aching hand," he said. "The trouble is, you had confidently expected a happy outcome only to have your hopes dashed. Consequently, you are too low-spirited at present to appreciate that I am perfect and therefore cannot be detestable."

She gazed at him for a moment, up and down, then up again. Then, "Did your wife ever throw things at you?" she said.

"No," he said, blinking, not merely because the question surprised him but because he was trying to picture Ada doing it and couldn't.

"Was she an aberration then, like Lord Lisle?" she said. "You did say all the Dalmays were emotionally extravagant. Yet she never threw anything at you."

"She never did," Benedict said. "We never quarreled. We were strangers, as I told you before."

"She could not have been as emotional as you claim," she said. "Perhaps she merely seemed so, compared to you. A mild show of feeling or a lack of perfect logic must seem extreme to a man who is so determinedly in control of everything."

"Once upon a time, I imagined I was in reasonable control of my life," he said. "Now I have a missing nephew, a stupendous scandal looming like a great storm cloud on the horizon, and *you*."

And the dreadful truth was, he was enjoying himself.

The dreadful truth was, he was relieved they hadn't found the children yet.

It was madness to feel this way. Everything Benedict cared most about was at risk. He knew this; he never forgot that storm cloud on the horizon.

But it had been a very long time since he'd courted trouble. He'd forgotten how stimulating it could be.

"Lady Rathbourne must have been a stoic," Mrs. Wingate said. "That is the only way she could have borne six years of marriage to you without throwing something at you."

"A Dalmay is as likely to be stoical as I am to sprout fins," he said. "But if you wish to quarrel with me about my late wife or my in-laws or anything else, may we not do it over breakfast?"

"I am not hungry," she said. She dragged her hand through her tangled hair. "I am too frustrated to be hungry."

"If we do not stop to eat and rest, Thomas cannot stop to eat and rest," Benedict said.

Her gaze went to the footman, who was talking to one of the grooms. Her brow knit.

"He has been awake for more than four and twenty hours," Benedict said, ruthlessly flaying her conscience. "He has had little to eat since we left London, some twelve hours ago. He has ridden in the least comfortable part of the vehicle. He has fought off drunken ruffians. He—"

"Yes, yes, you have made your point," she said. "One hour, then."

"Two," he said.

She closed her eyes.

"Perhaps three hours would be better," he said. "Do you feel faint?"

"I do not feel faint," she said. She opened her eyes. "I was counting to twenty."

BATHSHEBA DID NOT quarrel with him about his late wife or anything else at breakfast. She had all she could do not to fall asleep on top of the eggs, bacon, potatoes, bread, and butter he'd ordered heaped upon her plate.

He had an even taller heap, which he swiftly demolished.

After breakfast, she staggered up to the room he'd hired for her and went straight for the bed, the upper mattress of which was level with her shoulders. She somehow clambered up the set of steps. She sank onto a mattress of cloudlike softness.

The next she knew, a chambermaid was talking to her and the sun was streaming in the window. The angle of light told her it was midmorning.

"You ordered a bath, ma'am," the chambermaid said. "Shall we bring it up now?"

Bathsheba sat up and looked about her. She'd stayed at countless inns, but never in a room as luxurious as this. A washstand, a dresser, and a set of shelves lined the walls. A mirror stood on the deep windowsill, and a tall horse dressing glass nearby. At the opposite end from the bed, more chairs surrounded a small table. Pristine white curtains draped the window and the bed. The bed linens were clean and dry. A fire burned in the grate, eradicating all traces of the previous night's and early morning's chill and dampness.

Now she was to have a bath. With hot water and good soap. In a tub in a great, sunny, warm room. Unheard-of luxury.

But not for Rathbourne.

"How I long for a bath," she had said—or mumbled, rather—at some point during breakfast.

And he had told Thomas and Thomas had told somebody and no one had seemed the least put out.

Now she watched a pair of servants carry in a tub. Behind them came a short parade of more servants carrying pitchers and buckets.

As soon as they had all gone out again, she latched the door and tore off her clothes.

AFTER BREAKFAST, BENEDICT and Thomas retired to the narrow servant's room adjoining the guest chamber Benedict had hired for "Mr. and Mrs. Bennett." Leaving Mrs. Wingate to sleep in solitary splendor atop three mattresses, Benedict took a nap on the narrow cot, Thomas on the floor beside him.

Sometime later, feeling sufficiently refreshed, Benedict rose and bathed, using the large basin Thomas had borrowed from next door.

At present, having done his best with his master's clothes, the footman was seeing about the carriage. Since that would take time, and the bill must be settled and the servants given their gratuities, Benedict decided Mrs. Wingate need not be wakened for another quarter hour or so.

He was about to sit down to pull on his boots when he heard loud whispering in the corridor outside.

"It can't be Lord Rathbourne," said one voice.

"Mistress says it were," said the other. "She seen him at the ticket office."

"She must've been dreaming."

"How could she when she don't never sleep? She said it were him, big as life, along with a servant."

"Mebbe he rode on."

"She says he never did. She says he come here. And now I'm the one as has to find out why he didn't stay at the Bear like usual nor even stop in for his breakfast. And what was wrong, she wanted to know, that he gives his custom to the Crown, when all these years him and his lordship his father and all the rest on 'em, whenever they comes to Reading, they always stops at the Bear?"

Benedict swore under his breath.

The landlady of Reading's Bear Inn should have been called Argus, for she definitely possessed more than the usual allotment of eyes.

He should not have come within a mile of Reading. He was too well known, and not only at the Bear.

"She can't expect you to ask *him*," the first voice said.

"Well, I wouldn't, would I, even if she told me to. Do I look daft to you? I'll ask his manservant what the matter is."

"If it *is* his manservant," said the first voice. "If she wasn't seeing things that wasn't there."

Not waiting for the man to knock or listen for signs of life within, Benedict noiselessly latched the door to the hallway, crossed the tiny room, silently opened the door to the guest bedchamber, and slipped inside.

Very quietly he closed the door behind him.

He heard a sharply indrawn breath.

He turned . . . and froze where he was.

Mrs. Wingate froze, too, in the act of rising from the bathtub to reach for the towel draped upon the chair.

He found his tongue. "I beg your—"

"Ohhh—" She slipped and started to topple.

He shot across the room, scooping her out of the tub and up into his arms while the bathtub rocked, sloshing water.

She was wet, and slippery as an eel, and she was struggling—to hold on or get away, he couldn't be sure. Trying not to drop her, Benedict bumped into the chair. He lost his footing on the wet floor and went down, landing on his back with her on top. The chair skidded across the floor.

He tried reaching for the towel, but the chair was more than an arm's length away. Meanwhile, she was straddling him, and her breasts, her naked breasts, dripped onto his face as she tried to hoist herself up. His hands slid down to cup her wet bottom. Her wet, utterly naked bottom.

She was wet and naked everywhere, every glorious curve glistening in the morning sunlight.

She went very still, her blue gaze locking with his, her hands splayed on the floor next to his arms, boxing him in.

Water dripped from her chin to his.

She bent her head.

She licked the water droplet from his chin.

He remained very still. *This is a test of character,* he told himself. *I can and will—I must—resist.*

She lifted her head again and gazed at him, blue eyes wide and dark.

His gaze slid lower. To where the skin was soft and white and . . . pink.

Pink, the color one found on a woman in all the wickedest places.

One tiny water droplet gleamed tantalizingly on a taut, rosy nipple.

He couldn't remember why he ought to resist.

He lifted his head and flicked his tongue over the droplet.

She shivered, and another droplet slid down the side of his neck. She bent and pressed her lips to the place. The water drop was cool, and he felt the coolness of her damp skin. But her mouth was warm, and the warmth spread outward from the place where she touched him. It shot down to the pit of his belly to make it ache, and the ache vibrated in his groin. He was hard and swollen even before their lips met, trembling with need. Theirs was a tremulous kiss, too, like the hesitant first step into a forbidden place.

Forbidden, yes, absolutely.

Also inevitable.

The taste and feel of her mouth—remembered, endlessly remembered, impossible to forget—swept away hesitation. He rushed in, like any fool.

He cupped her head to hold her in place so he could drink deep and long. She sank down onto him, and her body made a damp imprint on his clothes that did nothing to cool him and everything to inflame him.

He let go of her to tear off his clothes, heedless of buttons flying and fabric ripping. In one impatient instant he was as naked as she. Then he crushed her body against his, warming hers with his heat while he savored the lushness of her and the softness and silkiness of her and while his hands hungrily roamed the length and breadth of her: the graceful slope of her shoulders and the perfect swell of her breasts and the dusky rose nipples, taut buds against the palms of his hands.

She roamed him, too, in the same hungry way, and he kept himself in check, though the touch of those slim hands tore at the last particles of his self-restraint, and he had little other thought—if you could call the wild need thought—than to be inside her.

Still, in the back of his mind he knew this was once in a lifetime, and he must make it last as long as he possibly could. He would never have her again, and so he must have all he possibly could, and give all he had to give. And so he took possession with hands and mouth upon the soft upswell of her belly and over the span of her hips and down along the contours of her thighs. That was too near where he wanted to be, but he hadn't the will to retreat.

He slid his hand between her legs and held her there, possessively, held her where it was warm and damp and completely feminine and pink, where a delicious pink bud hid amid the moist curls. He stroked there, and she caught her breath and let it out on the softest moan, and moved against his hand.

He had to have her then, but he had to have her completely and absolutely. Surrender, unconditional.

He stroked along the soft folds and inside, where he felt the hot pressure of flesh against his fingers. He held himself in check, and pleasured her until her entire body vibrated, and he heard her surrender in one soft cry.

Then at last he drew up her legs and thrust into her. She wrapped her legs tightly about his hips and thrust back. When he answered in kind, she threw her head back and arched her body. She was fearless and uninhibited, taking pure animal joy in him, and he could not get enough of her. He could only give himself up to her.

He was lost and didn't want to be found. The world was bedlam and he didn't want sanity.

He wanted only her. He let passion take them where it would, rushing recklessly to the last jolting ecstasy. He clasped her tight in his arms and held on, through a short, sweet nothingness, and he was holding her still while the world slowly rocked back into place.

BATHSHEBA LAY SNUGLY in his arms for far longer than she should have done. She need only breathe to inhale the scent of his skin, and it made her feel as though she'd drunk one glass too many of champagne.

She lay securely wrapped in his arms, her head resting on his chest, one hand clinging to his shoulder, one leg tucked between his. She wanted to stay where she was, where she had wanted to be, it seemed, since the first moment she saw him. She wanted to make believe this was where she properly belonged.

But she was too aware of the midmorning sun, and the sounds outside of a town fully awake and busy.

She made herself draw away. Or try to. His arms tightened about her. She pushed at him. The muscular arms were immovable.

"You must let me go," she said.

"You are becoming emotional," he said. "I knew this would happen."

"I am not emotional," she lied. As the languor of love-making wore off, she was rapidly approaching a state of panic. She was ruined, utterly. She'd ruined everything. Olivia's future was—

"You are not thinking rationally," he said. "I can feel it. You are agitated, when you ought to be calm and content. After all, we have done what we both have been longing to do—"

"Speak for yourself," she said.

"If my touch disgusts you, you have a curious way of showing it," he said.

"I did not want to hurt your feelings," she said.

He laughed softly, his big chest rising and falling.

"Yes, of course, you are happy," she said tartly. "You got what you wanted."

"Did you not get what you wanted?" he said. He drew his head back to regard her. "If that is the case, I should be happy to correct any oversights."

"That is not what I meant," she said. "I meant that you are a man, and lovemaking means nothing to you. It is not the same for me. I cannot simply roll over and fall asleep, especially when all my carefully arranged world is falling to pieces—and I know I have no one to blame but myself."

There was a short silence, then, "I should not have to re-mind you that it takes two," he said. "I made no effort to free myself from your wicked toils."

She recalled what she'd done: the irresistible urge to lick the water droplet from his chin . . . the urge she'd given in to. What more brazen invitation could she have issued?

She ought to hide her head in shame, but shame was not in her character.

"No, you did not," she said. "You put up no struggle at all."

"I appear to be sadly lacking in moral fiber," he said.

"That is true," she said. She let her hand stray over his chest. "Naturally, I prefer that. The Great World will be vastly disappointed in you, however. You know what they will say, do you not?" she went on ruthlessly. If she did not face the facts, aloud, she'd let herself hope. For more. For everything to come right . . . when she knew it could only go wrong. "They will say a man of your strong character ought to have been able to resist the likes of a common harlot like me."

"You are not a common harlot," he said tightly.

"Very well. An uncommon harlot."

"Bathsheba," he said.

The sound of her Christian name in that deep baritone surprised and moved her, but not as much as the anger that flared in his dark eyes.

"I should never allow anyone to say such a thing of you," he said. "That includes you."

He took her hand and lifted it to his lips and kissed each knuckle. "Stop talking nonsense," he said. He returned her hand to his chest and lay his atop it.

His hand was warm and big, and the simple gesture calmed her. It was only then she realized that her hand no longer throbbed with pain.

"My hand is better," she said.

"That is because your humors are in better balance now," he said. He looked away, turning his head toward the bed. "How comfortable it looks." He frowned. "How hard the floor is."

"Was your bed not comfortable?" she said. "Where did you sleep?"

He loosened his hold, and she sat up. He sat up, too, and she let her gaze roam over him: miles and miles of naked, muscled male. For a time, he had been all hers. She ought to be content, but she was awash again in longing, exactly like a girl experiencing her first infatuation.

Oh, she would pay dearly for this.

"I slept," he said. "I bathed." He grimaced. "At least I did not come to you in all my dirt—not that I came here intending to ravish you—er, I mean, to be ravished." His dark gaze slid over her, lingering upon her breasts, and a fire trail burned its way from there to the pit of her belly.

She rose hastily.

He turned away and reached for his shirt. "I thought you

were still asleep," he said. "I was planning to hide under the bed. But there you were, rising like Venus from the waves—and may I say that Botticelli's Venus hasn't a patch on you?" He pulled the shirt over his head and stood up.

You'd think she'd never heard a compliment before. It was no use reminding herself she was two and thirty years old and she'd borne a child, for she blushed, exactly like the innocent maiden she wasn't, and something like pleasure danced in her heart.

The dancing stopped abruptly when he told her about the servants' whispering in the corridor.

"Pray do not make yourself anxious," he said. "The innkeeper did not see you."

His countenance seldom told her anything. Hers, she realized, was an open book to him.

Her uneasiness grew. "She saw *you*," she said. "We must not leave this place together." She moved to the chair that held her clothes. She took her chemise and drawers from the top of the heap and eyed them unhappily. "I wish I had brought fresh undergarments at least," she said.

He walked to the window and looked out. The shirt covered him too well, allowing a view only of the lower part of his long, muscled legs. Still, in the sunlight, the fine material was semitransparent. She could make herself miserable studying the planes and contours of his long, lean body . . . the narrow hip and taut bottom . . .

She swallowed a groan.

"The inn yard is busy," he said. "Saturday is market day in Reading. I am sure your wish can be accommodated."

"Are you mad?" she said. "You cannot go out in public to buy me underwear."

"I can think of very few labors I should more enjoy," he said, turning back to her, face sober, dark eyes glinting. "In the circumstances, however, I must assign the task to others. I shall let Thomas—"

"Not your *footman*!"

"I shall let Thomas choose a maidservant to attend to the matter."

"If it comes to that, I can purchase my own underthings,"

she said. "At least I am not known in Reading. But it is not necessary."

She might as well have talked to the chair. He'd already found the bell. He rang it.

"You cannot go out like that," he said. "And you do not wish to don the garments you were wearing."

"It does not matter what I wish," she said. "I am perfectly capable of making do."

"Why on earth would you want to?"

She grew exasperated. "That is exactly what Jack used to—"

A rap at the door made her break off and dart behind the bed curtains.

"Ah, Thomas," Rathbourne said, opening the door but a crack. The rest was conducted in whispers—a deep rumble on Rathbourne's part—then he closed the door.

Bathsheba emerged from behind the bed curtains.

"It will take a while," he said.

"You have taken leave of your senses!" she cried. "We have been too careless already. We have lost valuable time."

"I think it is time we admit we have lost the children," he said. "They might be behind us, ahead of us, beside us, or right under our noses, but we have not found them and are unlikely to do so in the immediate future. The more time passes, the more ways we might go astray. Our present course, for instance, will not serve us beyond Chippenham. We might continue making inquiries along the road to Bath—but from Chippenham there is a slightly shorter and more direct route to Bristol. We cannot investigate two routes simultaneously."

Her heart beat, too hard. Even without being aware of the alternate route from Chippenham, she'd come to the same conclusion. She'd held the thought—and the accompanying despair—at bay.

No wonder she'd yielded so easily to desire. Deep in her heart she'd known the cause was lost. Scandal was inevitable.

"There is no need to look so stricken," he said. "All is not lost. We simply need to look at the problem afresh."

Bathsheba did not want to look at the problem. She wanted to sink to her knees and bawl like a child. She didn't want to be a grown-up anymore. She didn't want to be a mama anymore. She didn't want to have to mend matters and clean up after others and make the best of things.

"Stop that," he said, reading everything in her countenance. Yet he said it gently, and came to her, and wrapped his arms about her. She broke then, and wept.

Only a little storm, and it soon passed, but he held her. When she'd quieted, he said, "You are fatigued."

"I am not fatigued," she said. "I slept for hours."

He let out a sigh. "You are behaving like a child who needs her nap."

"What do you know of children who need naps?" she said.

He muttered something, then picked her up and tossed her onto the bed.

She bounced up from the pillows. "I am not a child and I do not need a *nap*!"

"Well, I do," he said, and swung up and onto the mattress beside her.

"Then sleep," she said. She tried to scramble away, but one long arm hooked about her waist and drew her back.

"We cannot sleep together in the same bed," she said. "That is asking for trouble."

"I know," he said.

He pulled her on top of him.

SHE HAD TRIED so hard to think, to be responsible.

But he had only to claim her, in that imperious, possessive way of his, and her defenses—what was left of them—shattered.

"It is not fair," she said, lowering her head to within an inch of his mouth.

"No, it is not." Their lips met and clung and she was young again, blood running hot. They kissed, deeply and wickedly, and she flung herself headlong into the pure wild pleasure of it: the taste of him, the feel of him, the scent of him, this big, beautiful male animal.

His long, warm hands moved over her, and she moved helplessly under them. His hands . . . his touch . . . she thought she would die when he touched her and then she wanted only to die of that touch and of the gladness that coursed through her, the tingling current that raced over her skin.

Besotted. Enslaved.

She didn't care.

For this moment, he was hers. She broke the kiss and sat up and dragged his hands up over her belly to her breasts. She held them there and arched back, in pure animal pleasure.

"My God," he growled. "My God. You will kill me, Bathsheba." He pulled her down to him and kissed her. He ravished her mouth, then broke away to ravish her throat. She was impatient already to have him inside her, but before she could reach for him, he rolled her over and straddled her. He grasped her hands and held them flat on the bed on either side of her head. He gazed at her, dark eyes fathoms deep, his mouth hinting at a smile.

"You must let me kill you a little," he said.

He bent then, and made a trail of kisses along her shoulder and along her arm to the hand he held. He licked her wrist, and sensation shot through her and swirled to the pit of her stomach to make her ache with need. She writhed helplessly, lust-crazed.

It was torture, delicious torture.

He tortured the other side, then slowly worked his way down, and she had no words for what he did with his lips and tongue. All she knew was sensation, thrill after thrill of it, strange and wonderful. Every caress of his mouth, his hands, sent lascivious messages straight to her groin, and she was shaking by the time he brought his mouth there.

He had let go of her hands, and so she clung to the pillow, and tried to bury her cries there.

Then, finally, when she had reached the very last thread of sanity, when she thought she must scream, or fly to pieces, he rose up again. He drew one of her hands away from the pillow and down to his rod. It was velvety smooth and hot and immense and shuddering at her touch. She grasped it, and smiling up at him, she pulled him into her, and nearly screamed with the relief of it.

At last at last at last.

"Yes," she said as he drove into her, and *yes* and *yes* again because this was what she had been made for, born for: to possess him, to be possessed by him. No oughts and mustn'ts. No self-restraint and common sense. Only this: to be joined, to be one, to yield completely to passion.

Yes, yes, yes, want you want you want you . . .

And at last it came, the last, wild paroxysm, sparkling ecstasy, and *yes, yes, yes . . . I love you.*

Chapter 12

WHEN BENEDICT AWOKE, HE WAS AWASH IN HER scent. She lay tucked up against him, spoon style, her derrière pressed against his groin. His rod had taken notice even before he woke, for it was swelling in anticipation. His hand cupped one perfectly rounded breast. He buried his face in her neck.

He was bad and selfish.

The storm cloud hung over their heads.

He was about to be engulfed in the scandal of the decade.

He didn't care.

It was inevitable. They would both pay severely for the sin.

They might as well sin thoroughly.

She stirred, then, coming awake, too. "Rathbourne?" she said in a sleep-clogged voice.

"Yes, that is me, holding your breast. Pray do not wriggle about. I am very comfortable."

"It must be noon at least," she said.

"Must it be?"

"How long do you mean to pretend that nothing is wrong and we are not facing disaster?" she said.

"Everything is wrong," he said. "Disaster is nigh. All the more reason to enjoy these final moments. 'Always at my back I hear / Time's wingèd chariot drawing near.' Let us heed the poet Marvell, and make the most of this time."

"I think we did, Rathbourne," she said. "I am not sure there is any more 'most' to be made of it."

"For an artist, you have a shockingly limited imagination," he said.

"I am a mother as well," she said. "I was hardly awake before I was fretting about Olivia and Lord Lisle."

Ah, well, time to come back to earth.

He made no protest when she slipped out of his arms and sat up. It was more sensible to feast his eyes upon her naked body for as long as he could. She was certainly accommodating in that way. After they had made love the first time, she'd not tried to cover herself but moved about the bedchamber with no self-consciousness whatsoever—until Thomas came to the door. Benedict smiled.

"You think I am being a silly female," she said.

"I was thinking of you darting behind the bed curtains when Thomas came," he said.

She let out a sigh. "Sometimes I wish I were an aristocratic male," she said. "I wish I could leave it to someone else to do the worrying."

He sat up, too. He plumped up the pillows and reclined upon them, his arms folded under his head. "You were not so anxious before," he said. "I was impressed by your philosophical detachment regarding your daughter's disappearance."

"That was before," she said. "That was when I believed we'd find them within a few miles of London. I was confident we'd catch up with them before they met with an accident or fell into the clutches of an unscrupulous person. At that point, I supposed the most unscrupulous person in the picture was Olivia."

"Is she really as bad as all that?" he said.

"She has spent far too much time with people who don't know what a moral principle is," she said. "Such people are more agreeable company than a mama who is always lecturing and scolding. Jack at least had some influence with her." She laughed a little. "I know it is hard to imagine feckless Jack Wingate teaching a child manners and moral principles. But he was a *gentleman*, and he lived by a gentleman's code, and he knew how to scold in a way that—that . . ." She pressed her fist against her breast. "Olivia took it to heart. But it's been three years and more, and she remembers only the exciting things her papa told her, like the story of the treasure. And I don't know how to speak to her in the way he did."

I do, Benedict thought, and his heart squeezed, as though she held it in her fist.

"Then you've one less reason to fret," he said. "Whatever else she might be, Olivia does not seem to be a gullible child. Unscrupulous persons will not find it easy to deceive her. As to Peregrine, we both know he takes nothing and nobody on faith. This does not mean they face no risks. But it does put the odds in their favor."

There was a short silence. Then she gave an impatient huff and said, "Rathbourne, it is abominable of you to say something wise and reassuring when I had prepared myself to call you obtuse and start a quarrel."

"This is what I *do*," he said. "I have been doing it for as long as I can remember. I spend half my days sorting out muddles and calming people and making them see reason. That is the way I have been trained. That is the way my father gets things done. That is the way *I* get things done." He paused. "Not that I should object to quarreling with you. I find that most invigorating. I am almost sorry I did not prove sufficiently obtuse. But you must expect such disappointments when you deal with a man who is perfect."

"Perhaps I shall throw things at you from time to time, simply on general principle," she said. "Not because of anything in particular you've done or said, but because you *need* it."

He laughed then, and pulled her into his arms, and she kissed him, wickedly, but she soon wriggled free, and slipped out of the bed.

Benedict swallowed his frustration, as his life had taught him to do, and turned his mind to the problem he couldn't be wise or reassuring about.

LUCKILY FOR HER, Rathbourne left the bed, too. To Bathsheba he looked far too inviting, lying there with his arms folded behind his head, the pale light from the window gilding the muscled planes of his upper body and glinting in his tousled hair. It did not matter that he was decently covered from the waist down. The tangled bedclothes made him look indecent . . . and too deliciously rumpled by half.

If he had not left the bed, Bathsheba would have been in dire straits, for she doubted she possessed the moral character or willpower to resist the temptation to climb back in beside him . . . on top of him . . .

She made herself look away while she washed . . . again.

Then she faced her soiled clothes . . . again.

"No, no," he said, as she took up the dingy shift.

She looked at him.

He'd donned his shirt and trousers. For an aristocrat, he was remarkably efficient at looking after himself.

He crossed to the bell and rang. "The servants will have found something for you to wear by now. Thomas is most conscientious. Yesterday, as I prepared to set out, I blithely assumed I would not need a change of clothes. He merely gave me an indulgent look—as one would a child, for to good servants we are all children, you know. Then he packed fresh linen and I don't know what else."

"I wish he had packed for me," she said.

"He will see that you have what you need," he said.

She discovered a few minutes later that Thomas had more than seen to it.

He passed a large heap of clothing through the partly open door. He would have sent a chambermaid through the narrow opening as well, but Rathbourne told him he was perfectly capable of dressing "Mrs. Bennett."

The footman and whomever he'd recruited had bought

Bathsheba an entire change of clothes, including a frock. And a bonnet.

"He could not have found these at the market," Bathsheba said as Rathbourne held up two outer garments for her approval. "You sent him to a dressmaker—and I am afraid to think what it must have cost, because she would have had to sell something promised to another customer as well as make alterations in a hurry."

"Dressmakers always have orphan garments in their shops," he said. "Their customers are women, and women are famous for changing their minds. She would be glad to do hurried alterations and at last be paid. But never mind that. Do you like it?"

It was a simple white muslin round dress, but the bottom was prettily trimmed with flounces and puffings of fabric. Furthermore, Thomas or whatever maid he'd sent had bought a spencer as well, and this was a vivid blue and made of silk and satin. The bonnet matched.

Bathsheba had not worn anything so pretty since the last time her father had been in funds, which had not lasted long.

But she could not accept such a gift. To do so was to announce she was Rathbourne's whore.

"It's lovely," she said.

He smiled, and his was so boyishly pleased a smile that it snatched away a piece of her heart and left an ache behind, fierce enough to steal her breath away.

But that was a momentary feeling.

She was not in love, not at all.

She'd had one mad fancy at the height of passion but it was only that: a fancy, a wild thought.

She was besotted, yes, infatuated, yes, and probably had been since the first moment she saw him in the Egyptian Hall.

That was not love.

"The only remaining question is whether it will fit," he said. His dark gaze slid over her, as warm and wicked as his hands.

Now was the time to say *Thank you but no, I cannot accept this. Thank you, but I must make do with my own clothes . . . the ones I've taken apart and turned inside out*

scandal. A formal search will assure us of the highest possible degree. It will be fact—published fact, no less—not mere gossip. Denial would be out of the question." While he spoke, he wrestled her into her petticoat.

"There is one more possibility," he said. He tossed the frock over her head. "We might proceed to Bristol—to the end of the trail, in other words—and await them at the gates of Throgmorton Park."

It was like trying to choose the least of four evils.

Stalling, she twitched the frock into place. "It fits remarkably well, considering I was not present to be fitted," she said.

"I advised Thomas to find a maidservant of a similar size," Rathbourne said.

"I am not sure I am altogether comfortable with the idea of Thomas's taking such careful notice of my figure," she said.

"Don't be absurd," he said. "Thomas is a servant, true. He is also a man. The only men who do not take careful notice of your figure are dead or blind. So long as they keep their hands off, no one will have to kill them, and you need not be uneasy."

Startled, she started to turn to read his expression.

He gave the frock a tug. "Keep still," he said. "I'm not done."

Ah, well, she had as good a chance of reading Sanskrit as she had of reading his thoughts from his face.

She stood obediently still.

He tied the last of the tapes and stepped away. He eyed her up and down and frowned.

Uneasy, she moved to the dressing glass and studied her reflection. "It does not fit perfectly," she said, smoothing the skirt. "Still, it fits well, indeed, considering the circumstances."

"Ah, yes, the circumstances," he said. "The damned circumstances. We have neglected those long enough." He pulled on his waistcoat and buttoned it. "What is your preference, madam, regarding our course of action?"

* * *

LORD RATHBOURNE WAS not the only one who'd faced facts and decided to make the most of the remaining time.

By ten o'clock that morning, Peregrine knew he'd never reach Edinburgh in time to avert catastrophe. He could only assume his uncle had somehow gone astray.

Though the idea of Lord Rathbourne making an error was nearly unthinkable, Peregrine was obliged to think it. Had his lordship stopped in Maidenhead and made inquiries at the inns—the logical thing to do—he would have found them by now.

Since, therefore, catastrophe was inevitable, Peregrine reviewed his situation while awaiting breakfast in the inn's public dining room.

He did not want to go to Edinburgh.

He hated school and schoolteachers.

Since his parents would bar further visits with Uncle Benedict, Peregrine's life for the next several years would be disagreeable in the extreme.

Therefore, he had better make the most of the present.

Breakfast arrived as he reached this conclusion.

His mind at ease, he attacked his food with gusto. The room and the meals had made enormous inroads into his limited funds, but he would not worry about that. An explorer must be resourceful.

It might have taken him longer to achieve this state of mental equilibrium had Olivia not continued quiet.

Peregrine was too busy thinking, then eating, to notice this. It was only after he'd cleaned his plate that it dawned on him. "You've hardly said a word since last night," he said. "Are you unwell?"

"I've been thinking," she said.

He had much rather Olivia didn't think, but he had no idea how to stop her.

He nodded and tried not to hold his breath.

"How are we to get rides to Bristol if people don't feel sorry for us?" she said, lowering her voice. "If it's unsporting to have a dying mother, what are we to say? You can't expect us to tell the truth. You know we'll be taken straight back to London."

Peregrine considered. Last night his goal had been London, not Bristol. This morning his goal had changed. But she didn't know that.

"It wouldn't be unsporting to tell something *like* the truth," he said. "We could say we're going to Bristol to seek our fortune."

"That's not unsporting?" She raised one pale eyebrow.

"Well, it's true of you, certainly," he said. "And it won't make people cry—the way that old lady did who gave us the money for Twyford. That was shameful. For all we knew, she needed the money worse than we did. How do we know she wasn't poor, living on her widow's mite? Maybe she'll have to go without her bit of chop this week, because of us."

Olivia stared at him for a while. Then she looked at the table. Then she looked about the crowded dining room.

"Oh, very well," she said with a shrug. "We'll seek our fortune. But you'd better leave the talking to me, your nibs. Your accent gives you away."

He couldn't help his upper-class accent. Unlike her, he couldn't change his speech at will, mimicking the style of whomever he spoke to. "You'd better come with me to settle up with the innkeeper, then," he said.

The innkeeper, who studied them more carefully than made Peregrine comfortable, asked whether they wanted a horse.

Olivia looked at Peregrine. He shook his head.

When they left the inn he said, "I've only three shillings left. I'd like to save it in case of an emergency."

She stood on the pavement, looking down the High Street. "It's market day in Reading, I heard people say," she said. "We might have some luck there. But it's twelve miles. Have you ever walked twelve miles, m'lord?"

"Don't call me that," he said, looking about him. But no one stood in hearing range. "I can walk twelve miles. Easily." He'd never done so in his life, but he'd die before he admitted that to her.

In any case, he didn't have to prove his hardihood that day. Four miles down the road, a young couple in a dogcart offered them a ride.

Like the innkeeper, the lady seemed mightily curious about them. She kept turning to look at Peregrine. Though he had his back to her as they rode and he said as little as possible, he grew increasingly uneasy. As soon as they reached Reading, he was wild to get away from them.

Luckily, Olivia had noticed or sensed trouble of some kind, and when the couple offered to treat them to tea and biscuits, she suddenly remembered errands that couldn't be postponed.

It was midafternoon, and Reading was bustling. It was easy enough to lose their brand-new friends in the crowd.

Olivia led Peregrine to a large group gathered in front of a bench from which a grizzled peddler sold trimmings, laces, buttons, and other such articles indispensable to the feminine sex.

"We must do something about you," Olivia told Peregrine in a low voice. "You look too aristocratic." She squinted at him critically. "It's the profile. We shall have to find you a large cap—or perhaps a scarf would be better. We could wrap up your face and pretend you have the toothache."

Without appearing to push, she somehow made her way to the front of the crowd, towing Peregrine along.

A large woman was haggling with the peddler over a length of lace.

"Oh, my," said Olivia, "I can hardly believe my eyes. Is that the *Santiamondo* lace—made only in the one small village in Spain—and the pattern passed down through one family? But where did you get it?" she asked the peddler. "You can't find that lace in London for love or money, you know, because it's all the rage with the ladies. The Duchess of Trenton wore it to a ball at Carlton House. I read about it in the newspaper. She wore Santiamondo lace, and her famous diamonds."

The woman snatched up the lace, thrust the coins into the peddler's hands, and hurried away.

The peddler looked at Olivia. She looked back at him.

Another customer asked about a ribbon. Olivia spouted off some piece of nonsense about the ribbon. Every button and bauble had a story. By late afternoon, little stock remained.

When the peddler took down his bench and packed up everything in his cart, Peregrine and Olivia helped him. He invited them to dine with him.

They ate at an inn frequented by other peddlers and itinerants. The place was dark and smoky, the food plain and overcooked, but Peregrine was too fascinated by the company to notice.

He had never been in the midst of such people before.

He could barely understand some of them. It was like visiting a foreign country.

The peddler's name was Gaffy Tipton. "Now, I know you're no boy," he said, pointing his pipe at Olivia. "What I don't know is why you was so helpful."

She crossed her arms on the table and leaned forward and said in a low voice, "My brother and me, we're going to Bristol to seek our fortune. It's a good ways from here, though, and all we got is three shillings. We don't know any trades, except that I used to help a pawnbroker sometimes, and I know about dress trimmings and such. I know the names of all the great nobs, and I read about the parties and operas and plays they go to. I come and helped you today to show what I can do. I heard someone say you always come on Saturdays from Bristol. If you'd let us go back with you, we'd make ourselves useful."

Gaffy looked at Peregrine.

"He's very shy," she said.

"Is he now?" said Gaffy skeptically.

"I'm a good liar but we don't neither of us steal," she said. "If you let us go with you, I can be a girl again. If we go with you, people won't trouble us."

Peregrine blinked. It had never occurred to him that she might be worried about their safety. It had not occurred to him, either, that she could be as effective even when she told almost the whole truth.

After staring at Peregrine for an aggravatingly long time, the peddler said, "All right, then. I'll take you."

* * *

BENEDICT CLIMBED INTO the carriage beside
Bathsheba. "Bristol, then?" he said.

"As you said before, we cannot know whether they are
ahead of us, behind us, beside us, or right under our noses,"
she said. "We cannot even be certain we're traveling the
same road. The one thing we do know is that they're
headed for Throgmorton."

"It is a gamble," he said.

"I know," she said. "But whatever we do is a gamble,
and they will be at risk whatever we do."

"Bristol, then," he said, and gave the horses office to
start.

AT THIS SAME moment, Rupert Carsington stood in the
vestibule of his brother Benedict's town house.

"Not at home?" he said to the butler, Marrows. "Has he
left for Edinburgh already?"

"No, sir," said Marrows in the completely noncommittal
manner butlers had to master before they learnt anything
else.

"Urgent government business got in the way, most
likely," Rupert said. "Well, no matter. I can see him any-
time. I wanted to take my leave of the boy."

"Lord Lisle is not at home, either, sir," said Marrows.

"Really," said Rupert.

"Yes, sir."

"Where are they?"

"I cannot say, sir."

"Yes, you can, Marrows. I don't doubt you could say a
great deal. But it seems you'd rather I blunder about the
house looking for clues."

"Sir, I cannot say where they are," Marrows said.

Rupert walked past him into the hall.

"Sir, I do not *know* where they are," Marrows said. His
voice held a faint note of panic.

"Do you not?" said Rupert. "That's interesting." He
continued on to Benedict's study. "Maybe Gregson can
clear up the mystery."

Men who became secretaries to titled persons were

usually gentlemen of good family and limited means. Unlike the butler, Gregson could regard himself as one of his lordship's confidants. Unlike the butler, too, Gregson would not consider his position to require an impassive countenance and a stubborn determination to give no visitor, even a family member, any information of any kind whatsoever about anything.

Gregson sat at his lordship's desk, which was not its usual well-ordered self. At the moment it more closely resembled Rupert's desk. Letters, cards, and invitations lay carelessly strewn about. A stack of apparently untouched correspondence stood at the secretary's elbow.

"What's got into His Perfectionship, I wonder?" Rupert said as he entered.

"Sir." Gregson stood.

"Sit." Rupert waved at the chair.

The man remained standing.

Rupert shrugged and walked across the room to look out of the window. "What the devil is that back there?" he said. "Is my brother going to tear up the garden at last and put in a bowling green as I recommended?"

"There was some damage in the area near the back gate," said Gregson.

"Intruders?"

"Lord Rathbourne."

"My *brother* did that?"

"This is what the servants say. I did not witness the—er—"

"Demolition?"

"Thank you, sir. I did not witness the demolition."

"My brother wrecked the garden," Rupert said thoughtfully. "This grows more interesting by the minute. Any idea what's become of him?"

"I am not at all sure," Gregson said. "His lordship has been behaving rather oddly of late. As you know, he is scrupulous about keeping me apprised of his appointments. But late yesterday afternoon he departed without a word to anybody. It seems he took the footman Thomas with him. It is vastly puzzling. I was sure Thomas had gone out some hours earlier with Lord Lisle—to a drawing lesson, I believe. But no one has seen Lord Lisle since then."

"So Rathbourne found Lisle a drawing instructor, after all," Rupert said.

"Oh, yes, indeed, sir. Lord Lisle has been taking instruction from . . ." Gregson drew toward him a ledger and flipped the page. "Here it is. The instructor is a B. Wingate, care of Popham Print Sellers." He gave an address in one of Holborn's more dismal neighborhoods.

"B. Wingate," Rupert said, careful to keep his countenance blank. He had no trouble recalling the evening Peregrine had uttered the famous name at Hargate House.

Benedict thought himself the coolest of customers, but both Rupert and their mother had sensed something in the air.

Gregson, the innocent, had no idea who B. Wingate was, or he would have loyally protected his employer.

Not wishing to distress the man, Rupert returned his gaze to the scene outside and choked back a whoop of laughter.

Lord Perfect had answered the siren's call.

Wait until I tell Alistair, Rupert thought. *Wait until . . .*

It was then he realized he'd better not tell anybody.

Lord Hargate had ears everywhere, and he would not find the matter amusing.

His countenance sober, Rupert turned away from the window. "Gregson, I thank you for being so helpful," he said. "I must ask you, however, on my brother's behalf, to be as unhelpful as possible to everyone else."

The secretary looked alarmed. "Sir, I am sure I did not intend—"

"Rathbourne has been under a strain recently," Rupert said. "That would explain why he forgot to inform you. This Wingate is connected to a government matter. Highly secret. That's all I know. But if anyone else asks, I must beg you to know nothing at all about B. Wingate or my brother behaving strangely. A great deal may be at stake. Governments might topple. No telling. Best to play it safe and know nothing."

"But sir, if Lord Hargate inquires about Lord Rathbourne—"

"In that case, Gregson," said Rupert, "I should develop an incapacitating and highly contagious disease, if I were you."

Chapter 13

"I HAD NOT REALIZED IT WAS SO FAR," BATH-sheba said as they passed through the Walcot tollgate.

Though she knew Rathbourne had driven as fast as the horses were capable of traveling, night had long since fallen. Ahead sprawled the town of Bath, famed for its healing waters. Bristol lay another half dozen miles or more to the northwest, and Throgmorton "some ways from there," according to the tollgate keeper. When pressed, he could not say whether it was five or ten miles.

"Whatever it is, it might add another two hours to our journey, depending on the state of the country roads," Rathbourne said. "We had better stop in Bath. We might enjoy a proper night's rest and set out fresh in the morning."

"And when we reach Throgmorton, then what?"

"Ask me tomorrow," he said.

"I cannot wait until tomorrow," she said. "We need a plan of action. We cannot simply set up camp at the gates and wait for Olivia and Lord Lisle to turn up. What are the chances of their entering in the normal way?"

"We have plenty of time to discuss what can and can't be done," he said.

"I've been discussing it with myself," she said. "For most of the last several hours I've counted milestones and tried to sort out courses of action in an orderly manner, the way you do."

"Is that how you occupied yourself?" he said. "What a boring way to spend the journey. And what an appalling waste of time. Why did you not ask me to sort it out?"

Because she could not get into the habit of letting him solve her problems for her, she thought.

"You seemed preoccupied," she said. "I did not wish to disturb your meditations."

He shot her a surprised glance.

"I did not think you needed to be entertained," she said. "I do not need to talk constantly. I am happy to have a quiet time for thinking. Such times do not come often. And I wanted to work it out for myself."

"You are too accommodating," he said. "I am in the habit of traveling alone. I was not ignoring you. You are impossible to ignore. But I let myself become lost in thought. I wish you had reminded me to say something now and again to pass the time."

"I was not bored," she said. "I had a good deal to think about."

There was a short silence, then, "I am not the most attentive of men," he said.

"You have a great deal on your mind," she said. "Especially at present."

"I am not attentive," he repeated impatiently. "I finally recognized that . . . though it took me long enough. A valuable insight—and what use do I make of it? I have spent all this time with you—more time, I think, than I have spent in constant company with any woman since I was an infant. Yet now, when the last thing I want is to waste our remaining time together, I fall into old habits."

"It is not your duty to entertain me," she said. "You must watch the road and—"

"You wondered how my wife could be a stranger," he cut in, his voice taut. "This is how. Lack of conversation. Lack of—gad, I hardly know. I treated her like a handsome piece of furniture—she, a *Dalmay*. She needed to swim in an ocean of feeling. She needed attention. Small wonder she turned elsewhere."

Bathsheba was too surprised at the outburst to speak. She could only stare at him. His handsome profile was set in hard lines.

"It was not a man," he said. "Not in the way you think, at any rate. She fell under the spell of an evangelical preacher. He persuaded her—and a great many other misguided creatures—to bring salvation to the poor. They did this by handing out Bibles and preaching at people who regarded them as a joke or an insult. I have dealt with the poor, Bathsheba. They need a great deal, but I do not believe they feel any great want for aristocratic females dressed in the latest stare of fashion telling them they are proud, vain, and licentious."

She longed to touch him, to lay her hand on his arm. She could not. It was nighttime, but this was not a lonely stretch of road. This was a main thoroughfare through England's most famous watering place.

"I was mistaken," she said. "Perhaps she was emotional, after all."

"I *wish* she had thrown something at me," he said. "But I had no idea of the extent and depth of her—her *passion* for the cause. I hardly knew what she was up to. I didn't ask. I dismissed it as a typically muddled feminine whim. I should have put a stop to it. Instead, I now and again stirred myself to make sardonic observations that went over her head. Then I went on about my so much more important business and forgot about it."

"You didn't love her," she said.

"That is no excuse," he said angrily. "I married her. I was responsible for her. She was my oldest friend's *sister*, plague take me—and I *ignored* her. Thanks to my neglect, she went into the back-slums prophesying hellfire and damnation, and came out with a fever that killed her in three days."

"Jack rode a horse he was warned against," she said. "The beast threw him. It took him three months to die."

"It is not the same," he said.

"Because he was a man and she was a woman?" she said.

"Your marriage was a success, though all the world condemned it," he said. "Mine was a failure, though everyone applauded it."

"It takes two," she said, reminding him of what he'd said after the first time they made love. "Some unwise marriages do turn out well, for the participants, at any rate. Any number of arranged marriages turn out well, too. Why should not a marriage based on duty? A marriage of convenience? A political marriage? You are not unreachable, Rathbourne."

"Not for you," he growled. "But you are different."

"The difference is, I grew up learning to make do," she said. "You and Lady Rathbourne did not. I do not say you bear no responsibility. You should have made more of an effort. But so should she have done. Men are difficult creatures, yet a great many women—even the silliest, weakest-willed women—do manage to train them eventually."

A short, shocked silence.

Then he laughed, and she felt the bottled-up rage and grief dissipate.

"You wicked woman," he said. "I open up my heart to you. I reveal my secret shame—and you make a joke of it."

"You need a joke," she said. "You paint too black a picture of your marriage. A great many women would be thrilled to have husbands who ignore them. It is preferable to being humiliated or abandoned or beaten. You were not the perfect husband, yet I should calculate that you were far from the worst."

"Merely mediocre," he said. "That is a great comfort."

"That is the trouble with believing you are the center of the universe," she said.

"I do not—"

"You are like the king of your own small country," she said. "Because you use your power for good, you are weighted down with cares. It is hard work to be a paragon. And because you are perfect, your mistakes cause you far more anguish than they would do ordinary, fallible persons. You need a joke. You need a Touchstone."

"A touchstone?"

"From *As You Like It*," she said. "The jester."

He threw her a glance. "I see. And you have appointed yourself to the position."

That and others, she thought. Companion, lover, and fool. Oh, above all, fool.

"Yes, my lord," she said. "And you must allow me to speak freely. That is the special privilege of the court jester, your majesty."

"As though I could stop your saying what you liked, or doing what you liked," he said. "Yet I will *request* that you not address me as 'your majesty' nor yet 'my lord.' For this once in my life I need not be 'my lord.' For once I needn't be anybody in particular. I must have a new name for this stage of the journey. I shall be . . ." He considered. "Mr. Dashwood."

"I shall be Miss Dashwood," she said. "Your sister."

"No, you will not," he said. "You do not want a separate room at the inn."

"You do not know what I want," she said.

"Yes, I do. And so will everyone else. No one will believe we are sister and brother."

"They believed it before," she said.

He turned into the courtyard of an unprepossessing inn.

"That was *before*," he said. "Now it is impossible for you to conceal your lustful feelings for me."

He had no idea how much she was concealing. Lust was but a fraction of it.

She lifted her chin. "That was *before*," she said. "I experienced a momentary, aberrant emotion—"

"We shall see about that," he said.

No, we shall not, she answered silently. In only two days she had let herself become too attached. He could easily become a habit. If she was to have a prayer of extricating herself, she must start now. She would be unhappy, yes, but she'd been a fool to imagine she and Olivia could ever be happy in England.

Where could she go that wasn't haunted by the ghosts of her history?

He halted the carriage, and a pair of stable men stepped out into the well-lit yard.

"The Swan is far from fashionable," Rathbourne said in a low voice as he helped her alight. "We shall be the only patrons here who are not commercial travelers. An ideal situation for us. A number of my elderly relatives reside in Bath, and a great many others visit from time to time. Regrettably, none are decrepit enough not to recognize me."

Relatives, everywhere, she thought. Political allies and foes, everywhere. Every moment he spent with her put him at risk.

He ushered her inside.

While not as elegant as the inn in Reading, the Swan was by no means shabby or cramped. A neatly attired maid bobbed a quick curtsey before promising to summon the innkeeper.

"It may well be cleaner, drier, and better run than the fashionable establishments," Rathbourne said. "Yet no one with any pretensions to fashion would dream of coming here. They would not wish to risk rubbing shoulders with tradesmen—if, that is, they know of its existence. But we are well out on the Bristol Road at the edge of town. I learnt my lesson, you see, in Reading."

Bathsheba had learnt a great deal since then.

She had been unsure what to do until he confided in her about his wife.

Lord Perfect was not infallible. When he'd wed, he'd made an error of judgment that could have ruined forever his chances of finding true happiness.

She would not be another, worse error of judgment.

He would not see it that way, of course. Rathbourne was used to deciding and commanding and taking responsibility. He was chivalrous as well as imperious.

He would never let her act as she knew she must do.

The innkeeper approached and, as Rathbourne had predicted, proved a gracious host.

Yes, he had a suitable room for Mr. and Mrs. Dashwood. He would have the fire built up, to take off the damp. Perhaps the lady and gentleman would like to adjourn to a private dining parlor for refreshment meanwhile?

At that instant she saw the solution to her difficulty.

"I should like that very much," she said. She looked up at Rathbourne. "I am famished—and perishing of thirst."

BENEDICT HAD NOT meant the meal to go on for so long. He had meant to get her naked as soon as possible.

She distracted him, though, with stories about her life with her vagabond parents. At first he was vastly entertained, for she made their numerous misadventures into farces.

But as the anecdotes flowed, so did the wine. By degrees, as the wine loosened her tongue, the picture she painted of her girlhood grew darker, and he was no longer amused. Again and again he caught himself clenching his fists. Again and again he had to make himself unclench them.

"It is amazing you had any education at all," he said at one point. "You seem never to have remained in one place long enough or had peace and quiet enough for books and lessons."

It took all his self-control to keep his voice cool and steady. Her parents were despicable. Her childhood was a *scandal.* She might as well have lived in an orphanage for all the tender care she received.

"I realized at an early age that I couldn't count on my parents for my education, academic or moral," she said with a laugh. "I could always find a quiet corner, and there I would stay with a book. I learnt to make myself invisible. They would forget about me, and I'd be left in peace . . . unless they needed to soften somebody's head or heart. Then they'd bring me out, all blue-eyed innocence, and enact a touching scene. They found me particularly useful with irate landlords. I hated it, but I learnt not to spoil the scene. Otherwise I'd have to endure copious weeping from my mother and the entire speech from King Lear about ungrateful children from my father."

She pressed a fist to her forehead and declaimed, " 'Ingratitude, thou marble-hearted fiend, / More hideous, when thou show'st thee in a child, / Than the sea monster.' " She lifted her glass and drank.

The method was not dissimilar to that employed by Peregrine's parents. Still, however misguided, they at least had their son's best interests at heart. Benedict very much doubted her parents considered anybody's interests but their own.

He refilled the glass. "So that's where you learnt your Shakespeare," he said.

"I studied the bard in self-defense," she said. "They chose only the bits that suited them. I chose the ones that suited me. They were always acting. Nothing was ever genuine. When they played the loving parents, it was a play." She smiled at the glass in her hand. "My governess was real, though. My one and only model for proper behavior. Oh, and Jack was real. The genuine article."

Benedict hoped Jack Wingate had appreciated her as she deserved. If he could not bring her riches, the man should at least have brought her love, devotion, kindness, gratitude. It would be so easy to give her these things.

Easy, that is, for everyone except the Earl of Hargate's eldest son, who was allowed to do no more than bed her—and then only if he walked away soon after and forgot her.

She tipped her head to one side as though considering. "Perhaps I should not have appreciated my governess and Jack half so much had my previous life been . . . less imperfect." She shrugged, then lifted the glass and drank.

Benedict drank, too, and ordered more.

Had he been less imperfect, he would not have ordered so much wine. While he was not an abstemious man, he rarely drank to excess.

She, however, was made for excess.

And he was not as free of flaw as he ought to be.

The more she told him, the more he wanted to know about her. This might be his last chance.

Not that intellectual enlightenment was his sole aim.

He was a man, after all, his motives as sordid as any other's.

If getting her tipsy would quiet whatever qualms she felt about their recent lovemaking and would get her naked more quickly and easily, then he was not quite perfect enough not to order another bottle. And another.

And the stories continued. But as she was mimicking her parents' rage and horror when they found out that Jack had been disinherited, Benedict became aware of wanting desperately to throw something against the wall. Somebody, actually. Her father as well as Wingate's.

He told himself they'd had enough to drink, and the night was getting no younger. He wanted her relaxed, he reminded himself. He did not want her unconscious.

"That's enough, *Mrs. Dashwood*," he said, snatching the wineglass from her. He drained the contents and stood. The room tilted slightly. "Time for bed. Important day tomorrow. Decisions." He set the empty glass down with a *thunk*.

She smiled the same smile Calypso must have used on Odysseus, to keep the hero ensnared for so many years.

"That is what I like about you, Mr. Dashwood," she said. "You are so decisive. It saves me all the bother of thinking for myself."

"That is what I like about you, Mrs. Dashwood," he said. "You are so sarcastic. It saves me the bother of trying to be tactful and charming."

She stood. And swayed.

"You're drunk," he said. "I knew I should have stopped at the last bottle."

"I am a DeLucey," she said. "I can hold my liquor."

"That's debatable," he said. "But I can hold you, at any rate." He rounded the table and gathered her up in his arms. She wrapped her arms about his neck and rested her head on his shoulder.

As though she belonged there.

"Very well, but only for a moment, while I collect myself," she said. "Our rooms are on the first floor, remember. If you carry me up the stairs, you could do yourself an injury."

"I can carry you up a flight of stairs," he said, "and have plenty of strength remaining for any other little tasks you need performed."

"Hmmm," she said. "Let me think of some tasks."

He carried her out of the room—and nearly trod on Thomas, hovering in the corridor.

"Oh, there you are," said Benedict. "Mrs. Dashwood is a

trifle foxed, and I was worried she might fall into or onto somebody." Recalling the way she'd so gracefully propelled herself into Constable Humber's surprised but not unwilling arms, Benedict chuckled.

She nuzzled his neck. "The room," she said in an undertone. "You promised to put me to bed."

Ah, yes. To bed. Naked.

"The room," Benedict said. "Where's the blasted room?"

IT WAS NOT as large as the inn at Reading, and the bed held only two mattresses rather than three, but it was warm and dry and *private.* That was all Benedict cared about.

He set Bathsheba down, glanced about, and, seeing nothing out of order—except for the floor's tendency to roll under his feet—told Thomas to go to bed. She closed the door after the footman, and locked it.

She advanced on Benedict.

"I want you," she said.

"I told you so," he said. "But you must natter on about temporary insanity and—"

"Stop talking," she said. She grasped the lapels of his coat. "I have tasks for you to perform."

She slid her hand down to the front of his trousers. His rod, already in readiness, sprang to rigid attention.

She smiled the siren's smile up at him.

He grasped her waist and lifted her up and brought her wicked mouth level with his own. He kissed her, not delicately or seductively, but hotly. She grasped his shoulders and thrust her tongue against his, and the taste of her raced through him, more potent than any intoxicant.

She wriggled upward, her breasts rubbing his chest, and wrapped her legs about his waist. He staggered backward until he came against something solid. He braced himself there while his hands worked through layers of dress and petticoats and clasped her bottom, clad in the thin knitted silk of her drawers.

Still they kissed, deep, demanding kisses that turned him hot then cold then hot again. No enchantress's brew could be so potent as her passion. She made him mad and reckless and glad to be so.

She worked his neckcloth loose, and undid the shirt buttons and slid her hand inside over his skin, and laid it over his heart, his desperately pumping heart.

She slid her hand lower, over his belly, to the waistband of his trousers, and he was helpless, holding her up, while she pulled the trouser buttons from their buttonholes and brought her hand down over his drawers to his swollen, throbbing cock.

He groaned against her mouth and she broke the kiss.

"Now," she said. "I can't wait. Now. Let me down."

He wanted *now,* too, and he let her down, let her torture him with a slow easing down over his length.

She pushed him back, toward the bed, and he went, laughing and hot and addled, and fell onto it. She yanked up her skirts, untied her drawers, and let them fall to the floor. She stepped out of them and over them and climbed up onto him.

She tugged his trousers and drawers down to his knees.

He lifted his head and gazed down at himself. It was most undignified. His *membrum virile* stood up proudly, unconcerned with dignity. "My boots," he said, laughing. "May I not at least—"

"Keep still," she said, and straddled him. "Leave this to me."

He never left anything to women—even this—but she was different and he couldn't think and didn't want to think.

Then her soft hand was curling round his rod, sliding up and down, and he thought he would die and knew he'd never last. "You will kill me, Bathsheba," he said.

"You are killing me," she said. She pushed herself onto his aching cock, surrounding him with hot, moist flesh . . . and muscles, wicked muscles, pressing against him.

He cried out something, not words but some mad, animal sound. She lifted herself, then pushed down again. She moved slowly at first, sending waves of voluptuous pleasure coursing through him. By degrees the rhythm built, faster, more ferocious.

He watched her beautiful face while she made his body hers. He saw her hunger, the mirror of his own, and her joy, unlike anything he'd ever known before. Harder and faster she rode him, and the joy was in his veins and pumping through his heart. She rode him, wild now, and he was a runaway, racing with her he knew not where and cared not where. They raced to the edge of the world and beyond, and soared for a while, free and joy-filled, then floated down and into sleep.

When he woke in the morning, she was gone.

So, he soon discovered, were his purse and his clothes.

Chapter 14

BATHSHEBA COULD GUESS WHAT THE BUTLER was thinking.

The name Wingate would not be unfamiliar to him.

The elderly Earl of Mandeville, lord of these domains and head of the DeLucey family, was on speaking terms—although just barely—with the Earl of Fosbury, Jack's father.

A reasonable person could hardly hold the good DeLuceys responsible for what the dreadful ones did. However, Lord Fosbury had never been reasonable where his favorite son—whom he'd indulged to a shocking degree, and who in repayment had broken his heart—was concerned. In his opinion, Lord Mandeville should have prevented the marriage and arranged for Bathsheba to be taken somewhere far beyond Jack's reach.

In Lord Mandeville's opinion, Lord Fosbury was incapable of controlling his son.

Relations between the two families, therefore, were frosty.

Nonetheless, they were on speaking terms, which meant the butler dare not turn away any lady named *Wingate* . . .

even though she had arrived on horseback, with neither maid nor groom in attendance.

Bathsheba might have made up a lie about an accident or some such, but she was aware that members of the upper orders did not **explain** themselves to anybody, especially servants.

She merely **regarded** the butler with the same bored-to-death expression she'd seen on Rathbourne's face at times. She had learnt from her governess how to make that face. Rathbourne, however, had raised it to a form of high art.

Thinking of him caused her a twinge, which she ruthlessly crushed.

"Lord Mandeville is not at home," the butler said.

"Lord Northwick, then," she said. Northwick was the earl's eldest son.

"Lord Northwick is not at home," the butler said.

"I see," she said. "Must I name each of the family members by turn, and do you mean to keep me standing upon the step throughout the exercise?"

That made him blink. He begged her pardon. He ushered her inside.

"My business is urgent," she said crisply. "Are the family all at church, or is there a responsible adult at home to whom I might speak?"

"I shall ascertain whether anyone is at home, madam," he said.

He led her into a large antechamber and left.

She had paced it for a few minutes when she heard footsteps. She halted and donned Rathbourne's expression once again.

A young man hurried into the room. He was but a few inches taller than she and much younger—in his early twenties, she guessed. He was good-looking and well dressed, although it was clear he'd put on those fine clothes in great haste. He must have risen very recently. He—or his servant—had neglected to brush his thick brown hair. His eyes were the same intense blue as Olivia's.

"Mrs. Wingate?" he said. "I am Peter DeLucey. I saw you ride up the drive. I do apologize for keeping you. Urgent business, Keble said. I hope . . ." He trailed off, his gaze going from her to something behind her right shoulder.

She glanced that way. Then she turned more fully and studied it: a full-length portrait of a naval officer in the style of wig popular early in the previous century. He could have been her father. In a black wig, he might have been *her.*

"That can't be Great-Grandpapa Edmund," she said. "They burnt all his portraits, I was told."

When she looked back, the young man was dragging his hand through his hair. "I say," he said.

"I am Bathsheba Wingate," she said.

None of the ancestors about her fell out of their frames, and the ceiling did not crash to the floor, which did not open up to admit Beelzebub, who did not try to drag Mr. DeLucey back down into the inferno with him.

But Peter DeLucey *looked* as though all these things had happened.

Then, "I say," he managed to get out.

She silenced him with a wave of her hand. "Alas, we have no time for family reminiscences," she said. "My wicked daughter has run away with Lord Atherton's heir and sole offspring. She has entangled him in a hare-brained scheme to unearth Edmund DeLucey's treasure, which she believes is buried at the base of Throgmorton's mausoleum."

"T-treasure," he said. "Mauso—"

"I have been chasing them since Friday afternoon," she cut in impatiently, "but the brats have eluded me. Throgmorton is a large property. There is no predicting how or where they will get in. Once they get in, they will have numerous places to hide."

"I say," he said. "I can hardly take it in. Your daughter has eloped with Atherton's son?"

"He is thirteen," she said impatiently. "Olivia is twelve. It is not an elopement. They are *children.* Do attend. I have a plan for catching them, but I must have your help."

At that moment, she heard from without the clatter of hooves and carriage wheels.

Bathsheba caught her breath. It could not be Rathbourne. He would not find her for hours, if ever. She had made sure of that—and that he'd hate her if and when he did find her.

Peter DeLucey hurried to the door and listened. "Oh, now we're for it," he said. "The family's back from church."

One hour later

When he got his hands on her, he would strangle her, Benedict told himself.

The aftereffects of the previous night's debauch didn't improve his temper. His head was an anvil, and Hephaestus, forger of Zeus's thunderbolts, was beating on it with his giant hammer.

Seething, he made his way to the servants' entrance.

He could have gone to the front door and announced who he was . . . if he wanted to be bodily ejected from Throgmorton, and hear a lot of country louts laughing when he landed on his arse outside the entrance gate.

He had had to borrow both money and clothes from Thomas. The clothes didn't fit. Thomas was shorter than he and wider. Furthermore, thanks to the limited funds, Benedict had endured a long, hard ride on a bad horse, which did nothing to soothe his aching head.

To finish matters off nicely, he'd had to leave Thomas behind at the inn as surety for the bill that wicked girl might at least have paid.

Pure good fortune had got Benedict through the entrance gate in the first place. Not knowing what tale she'd told or who she'd claimed to be, he'd acted like a dolt of a country bumpkin and asked whether his mistress had come this way. Luckily for him, no other female callers must have arrived this day, for no one had asked who his mistress was.

Benedict was going to kill her.

But first he had to get at her.

He played the same thickheaded country lout at the servants' entrance and had no trouble getting in there, either. He found the place abuzz.

"You've come for Mrs. Wingate, I see," said the house-keeper. "They said she was in a state when she come. I reckon she wouldn't wait for you. She wouldn't wait for Mr. Keble, that's certain. He backed right down, I was told. Joseph said he never seen anything like it. He said she would've walked straight through Mr. Keble if he tried to stop her. And Mr. Peter won't take notice of anything but her face and figure, will he?"

"Both which is uncommon fine," said a footman coming in with a tray of untouched sandwiches. "That being why he can't take his eyes off her and sits there like a fish with his mouth opening and closing, like he never seen one of her kind before. Which I expect he never did, what with being wrapped in cotton wool all his life and gone away to school with a lot of spotty boys as horny as him."

Rathbourne regarded him stonily. Such talk would not have been tolerated in any servants' hall belonging to any member of the Carsington family.

"Did you hear anything more, Joseph?" everyone asked at once.

"Oh, she was telling 'em some Banbury tale like the fe-males dote on, all about stolen children and pirate treasure and everyone in dire peril," said Joseph. "As to the rest of 'em, who could tell what they was saying, when the fe-males start clucking and squawking like a lot of tetchy hens the instant *she* stops?" he said. "But Lord Mandeville just come, and he's looking like murder," he added with malicious glee. "I bet James sixpence the old fire-breather throws the strumpet out on that pretty rump of hers."

Benedict stood up from his chair and launched himself at Joseph.

"OUT!" LORD MANDEVILLE shouted. "Not another word. How dare you pollute this house—"

"Mandeville, were you not attending to the sermon this day?" said his wife. "We were counseled patience and for-giveness, as I recollect—"

"Forgive any of her lot, and they will cozen us out of our last farthing. When we are dead, they will steal the winding cloths," the old man said. "It is a trick, and you are a lot of confiding morons to believe it. Atherton's son, my foot."

"I agree the tale seems dubious, Father," Lord Northwick said in a bored voice. He was an elegant man in his forties whose keenly assessing blue eyes belied his jaded pose. "Nonetheless, one is obliged to give the lady a hearing."

"Lady?" His father sneered. "She plays a part, the way they all of them do. You're credulous fools, the lot of you." He swept a glare over his wife, daughter-in-law, and grandson. "Everyone knows the Athertons are in Scotland."

Bathsheba held on to her temper. "Lord and Lady Atherton are in Scotland," she said. "Their son stayed in London with his uncle, Lord Rathbourne. As I have explained—"

"Oh, I don't doubt you've *explained* to a nicety," Mandeville said. "And a precious tangle of black falsehoods it is. Not that any of this lot has wit enough to see it. The women of my household let their soft hearts get the better of their brains—such as they are—and my fool son and grandson notice nothing but your allurements."

"Really, Father—"

"But you won't cozen me, Jezebel," Mandeville went on, ignoring the sophisticated Northwick as one might a prattling child. "I've had doings with your kind before and learnt my lesson. I know your tricks and arts. It'll be a bitter cold day in hell before I—"

A loud crash in the hall made everyone jump.

"What the devil is that noise?" said Mandeville. "Keble!"

Keble hurried in, face flushed. "I beg your pardon, my lord, for the disturbance. We have the matter in hand."

Another crash, this time the sound of shattering crockery.

Mandeville started toward the door at the same moment a liveried footman sailed over the threshold. He landed at the earl's feet.

Bathsheba shut her eyes. No, it was not possible.

She opened them.

A tall, dark figure appeared in the doorway.

He wore clothing obviously belonging to someone else. The coat was too short, the trousers too wide.

"Who the devil is that?" Mandeville shouted.

Rathbourne drew himself up. "I am—"

"My brother," Bathsheba said. "My mad brother Derek."

He scowled at her. "I am not—"

"You naughty boy," she said. "Why did you not wait for me at the inn as I told you to do? Did I not promise to return as soon as I could?"

"No, you did not," said Rathbourne. His dark eyes glittered. "You took my clothes. You took my money. You went away without a word."

"You are confused," she said. She looked at the ladies and twirled her index finger near her temple. Returning to Rathbourne she went on, patiently, "I explained several times why you must not come with me."

The footman lying on the floor let out a weak moan.

Bathsheba threw Rathbourne a reproachful look. "That is one reason," she said.

"He called you a strumpet," Rathbourne said, sulky as a child.

"You lost your temper," she said. "What have I told you about losing your temper?"

A throbbing pause. The glitter in his eyes was diabolical.

"I must count to twenty," he said.

"You see," she said softly to the others. "He is like a child."

"He's a deuced big child," said Lord Northwick.

"He belongs in an asylum!" Lord Mandeville shouted, purple with rage. "Out! Out of my house, the pair of you, or I'll have you taken up and locked up. Set foot on my property again and I'll set the dogs on you."

Rathbourne looked at him.

Mandeville took a step back, his color draining away.

"Derek," Bathsheba said.

Rathbourne looked at her. She marched toward him, chin up, spine straight. "Lord Mandeville is overset," she said. "We had better leave before he does himself an injury."

She brushed past him through the doorway and continued on down the long hallway. After a moment, she heard angry footsteps behind her.

* * *

BATHSHEBA AND BENEDICT rode in furious silence until they passed the entrance gates.

Then, "You ruined everything!" she burst out.

"Everything was ruined long before I arrived," Benedict said, gritting his teeth against the headache, which recent events had not ameliorated. "I cannot believe you went to Throgmorton—as yourself—and expected anything from your relatives but insults and eviction."

"I was doing well enough until the irascible earl came home," she said. "The ladies were too curious about me to be rude, and the gentlemen—"

"Could not stare at your breasts and think at the same time," he said.

"I could have coaxed them all round—including the wretched old man—if you had not brawled with the footman," she said. "If you had to fight, could you not at least keep it belowstairs?"

"He ran away from me, the coward," Benedict said. "I was not in a forgiving state of mind. I woke up with Satan's own headache to find that someone had stolen my money and clothes, you see."

He took a long, steadying breath. "It is clear what happened. Getting me drunk and ravishing me was part of your cunning plan. You thought I would be too sick and debilitated after the excesses of last night to pursue you. You thought I'd never guess where you'd gone. You think I'm an idiot, obviously."

"I did only the getting-you-drunk part on purpose," she said. "The trouble is, I drank a good deal more than I intended, because you have a curst strong head. I ravished you because I was as drunk as a sailor. But yes, I do believe you are acting like an idiot. You have let lust cloud your thinking. You very nearly told the DeLuceys who you were, did you not? If I had not interrupted, you would have given them one of your Who-are-*you*-you-insignificant-insect looks and said, 'I am Rathbourne.' "

She mimicked him so well that he had the devil's own time keeping the scowl on his face.

"You told them who *you* were," he said. "You have put yourself at risk. If it is found out that I am not your mad brother Derek, you will be ruined."

He had nearly choked, struggling not to go off into whoops, when he found himself turned into her lunatic sibling.

"I am already ruined," she said. "I was ruined from the day I was born."

"Then what of Olivia?" he said. "What of her future?"

"I cannot make a future for her here," she said. "I was deluded to think so. If I wish her to have a fair chance at a proper life, I must take her abroad, where the name Bathsheba Wingate means nothing to anybody."

"I cannot believe you are seriously considering returning her to the same ramshackle existence you have deplored, time and again!" he shouted. And winced, because the shouting reverberated painfully in his skull.

"That is because I am facing facts and you are not," she said. "You are pretending that this is your life. But it is only a few days out of your life. Perhaps it does make an amusing change. Yet all you have done is run away, for a time, as you used to do long ago. The trouble is, you are no longer a little boy, and unlike in the past, you face grave consequences when you return. And you must return, Rathbourne. I can shake the dust of England from my feet. You cannot."

"You will not," he said. "I will not permit it."

"I wish you would try to remember that this is not the Middle Ages and I am not your vassal," she said.

"I won't let you be my martyr, either," he said.

"I was not—"

"If I had been born a younger son, I should have become a barrister," he said. "As it is, I have participated in any number of criminal inquiries. I have learnt how to put two and two together. Your motive is obvious, my girl. I am not sure whether it arises from a misguided maternal instinct or the DeLucey flare for drama. Whatever the source, I do not need your protection or self-sacrifice. The very idea is absurd. I am a man, and not a young one, wet behind the ears. I am thirty-seven years old. I should be hanged before I hid behind your skirts." He shot her a look. "What I should do *under* your skirts is another subject altogether, which I should be happy to discuss at another time."

"What is wrong with you?" she cried. "What will you do if you are found out?"

"What my ancestors did at Hastings and Agincourt," he said. "What my brother Alistair did at Waterloo. If other members of my family could face Death unflinchingly, I can certainly face ridicule and disapproval."

"I don't want you to, you obstinate man!"

"I know that, my dear," he said. "I realized it when I discovered you'd made off with my clothes and money. I was deeply touched by that display of affection. But now you must give them back."

THE LADIES STALKED out of the drawing room of Throgmorton House, followed immediately by Lord Mandeville's son and grandson. This left the earl no one to rage at but the servants, who quickly made themselves scarce, too. Then he was at leisure to seethe in solitude.

While the ladies sought haven in the conservatory, Lord Northwick and Peter DeLucey viewed the wreckage in the hall.

Two chairs had been overturned. An enormous Chinese porcelain dragon Lord Northwick had always hated lay on the floor in fragments, which a pair of frightened housemaids were in the process of sweeping up.

Joseph, braced up by James and Keble, limped toward the baize door leading to the servants' realm.

Lord Northwick led his son out of hearing range. "You must go after them," he said. "The lady and her . . . brother."

Peter stared at him.

"Now," said his father. "We have not a moment to lose."

"But Grandfather said . . . But you—you didn't believe her. I could tell. You wore that look—"

"I have changed my mind," said Lord Northwick. "Stop dithering and listen to me."

* * *

"MRS. WINGATE! I say, Mrs. Wingate!"

Benedict and Bathsheba looked behind them.

A lone rider galloped toward them.

As he drew nearer, Bathsheba said, "That is Lord Northwick's boy, Peter DeLucey. What now?"

They halted and waited for him.

"A message," he said breathlessly. "From my father. Apologies. Couldn't come himself. Press of duty. But he asks that you meet him tomorrow morning at the King's Arms Inn. I am to show you where it is and see that you are made comfortable. Father says . . ." The young man glanced uncertainly from Bathsheba to Benedict. "Father says he believes you, and we are to offer you every assistance."

"EVERY ASSISTANCE" INCLUDED arranging for rooms at the inn as well as a midday meal, which not only went a good way to helping Benedict recover from the previous night's debauch, but raised his opinion of the DeLuceys.

Still, he thought at first that this DeLucey's helpfulness was an excuse to loiter about ogling Bathsheba, for the young man could not take his eyes off her. He did not need to be asked twice to join them for the meal.

DeLucey was in no hurry to leave after the meal, either.

Benedict decided to drop a hint.

"I regret I must be on my way," he said. "Our manservant and carriage remain at an inn near Bath, and I am obliged to collect them. The innkeeper must be paid as well. My sister left in great haste, you see, and in her anxiety and agitation, she mistook my purse for hers."

"Oh, I can ride to the inn and do all that for you," DeLucey said.

"Certainly not," said Bathsheba. "We should never ask such a thing."

"You would be doing me a favor," the young man said. "Otherwise, I'll have nothing to do all day but be bored witless. Sundays at Throgmorton can be deadly. Grandfather loathes going to church, but he believes it is his duty to set an example. I wish he would stay home and let the ladies set an example instead. Being preached at always puts him in the foulest mood. Then someone is sure to stop him after the service with complaints or demands or some such, and make him late coming home. Meanwhile, he will fast before services, though his physician has told him time and again that it isn't good for him at his age. So naturally, by the time he does come home he is as hungry as a bear, which does not improve anybody's temper."

He colored. "I daresay he would not have welcomed you in any case, but this being Sunday, perhaps it was worse than it might have been."

It was well said, Benedict thought. The young man effected an apology of sorts for his grandfather without disparaging him, and with a degree of compassion.

Benedict's paternal grandmother had a deadly sharp tongue and no patience whatsoever. In Lord Mandeville's place, she might have displayed more self-control, but she would not have been any gentler.

The elderly must be allowed their crotchets.

Benedict had reminded himself of this rule a short time ago. This was why he had not heaved Lord Mandeville through the nearest window.

"It is the DeLucey temper," said Bathsheba. "Apparently, that family characteristic is found in all the branches. I am quite used to it."

"You have it," Benedict said.

"Yet it was not I who threw the footman through the drawing room door," she said.

"He was a vile person," Benedict said. "I shall not apologize for that."

"That might have been what turned Father in your favor," DeLucey said. "He has wanted Joseph dismissed this age, but Grandfather . . ." He trailed off, his blue eyes widening. "I say, sir, you are not really queer in the attic, after all." He turned his puzzled stare upon Bathsheba.

"I thought your family might excuse lunacy more readily than they would temper," she said.

"Sometimes my sister drives me mad," Benedict said. "Otherwise I am perfectly rational. Being rational, I see no reason for you to travel all the way to Bath to pacify an irate innkeeper while allaying my loyal servant's anxieties. After that, you would make the same tiresome journey back, during which you would feel as though you were alone, because Thomas would not dream of conversing with you. However, if you are in no hurry to return to Throgmorton, you are welcome to accompany me."

"It seems I am not needed, then," said Bathsheba.

Benedict blinked. He'd expected her to insist on going with them. He'd braced himself for the inevitable battle.

But she showed none of the usual signs of determination to do exactly what he didn't want her to do. Her face was white and drawn. The day must have caught up with her, he thought. She'd not only had insufficient rest, but she'd had to bear the brunt of Mandeville's fury, along with her other relatives' coldness and distrust.

She'd borne it well, Benedict thought. She'd held her head high. She had not let anybody ruffle her composure. She had behaved with dignity, every inch the lady.

"Mr. DeLucey and I shall manage without you," Benedict said. "While we're gone, dear sister, I hope you'll get as much rest as you can. The next few days promise to be challenging."

SINCE PETER DELUCEY had obtained separate rooms for the supposed siblings, that was the last Bathsheba saw of Rathbourne until the following morning, when she met him for breakfast in a private dining parlor on the inn's ground floor.

He rose when she entered the room, and his expression softened. "You look a good deal better than you did yesterday," he said. "I was afraid you'd made yourself ill, what with the debauchery and the noble self-sacrifice and bearding lions in their den and such."

"You are the most ungrateful man," she said. "I was trying to save you from yourself."

He laughed and came to her.

"It was sweet of you," he said. He brought his arms

round her but he did not draw her close. He only looked down at her, smiling a little.

"I am not sweet," she said.

He kissed her forehead. "Indeed you are. You are wicked, too. A dizzying combination."

A footstep outside made him draw away.

Someone tapped on the door.

"Yes, yes, come in," Rathbourne said.

Thomas entered. "Lord Northwick is here, sir."

"Yes, of course. We were expecting him. Don't make his lordship wait, Thomas. You know better than that."

"Which I was not wishing to interrupt anything," Thomas muttered as he went out again.

"Thomas thinks me an ingrate, too," Rathbourne said.

"I take back everything I said about him on Friday evening," Bathsheba said. "Thomas is a paragon. And a saint."

"Indeed, he is, poor fellow. He waited all the day yesterday for me in his underwear. That was your fault, by the way, but I—Ah, Lord Northwick. Good morning, sir."

His lordship stood in the doorway for a moment. Then he swept off his hat, revealing hair nearly as dark as hers, but threaded with silver at the temples. He was immaculately groomed, and dressed to the highest pitch of the tailor's art.

He entered and closed the door behind him.

"Good morning, Lord Rathbourne," he said. "Perhaps you would be so good, sir, as to tell me what, exactly, all this charade is about?"

Chapter 15

TEMPER, BATHSHEBA HAD DISCOVERED, WAS not the exclusive domain of her branch of the family. Now she was aware that the Dreadful DeLuceys weren't the only ones who knew how to make dramatic entrances.

She had been too agitated yesterday, too conscious of being unwelcome and too much occupied in steeling herself against the hurt and frustration, to study her audience very carefully. In any case, Mandeville, who'd come storming in like a Visigoth invasion, took center stage.

Still, she'd been aware of Northwick. Though he'd said very little and looked very bored, she had felt herself under an unusually keen scrutiny. Without question, he had made her far more uneasy than his openly hostile father had done.

Clearly, Northwick was nobody's fool.

She sank into the nearest chair, her heart pounding. She'd known Rathbourne must be found out sooner or later. But knowing it was not the same as seeing and hearing it happen.

He did not appear in the least discomposed. "Ah, then you were not taken in by the 'mad brother Derek' business," he said.

"I know Bathsheba Wingate has no siblings," Lord Northwick said. "I know Lord Rathbourne has several. One is named Rupert. I became acquainted with Rupert Carsington a few years ago when he and one of my cousins had a dispute with some fellows at a wrestling match. Mr. Carsington threw one of his assailants into a trough. I recognized the style of combat—and a strong physical resemblance. Now, perhaps you would be so good as to explain matters, sir."

"Apart from my not being Derek the deranged imbecile, it is all as Mrs. Wingate explained yesterday," Rathbourne said. "We have come in search of my nephew and her daughter. But pray be seated. You have no objections to breakfasting with your cousin, I trust?"

There followed a short, thunderous silence.

A test of some kind, or a challenge.

It was something men did, and the silent language was one Bathsheba did not fully understand.

Then Lord Northwick said, "No objections, sir, so long as everybody understands that I would trust my *cousin* only as far as I could throw one of those rocks at Stonehenge."

Rathbourne's face turned to marble.

Man language or not, it was time to intervene.

"That is fair enough," Bathsheba said. "Lord Northwick is not obliged to like or trust me. The main concern is finding the children."

"That is why I am here," Lord Northwick said. "I came because Mrs. Wingate said Atherton's boy was missing. I knew Lord Hargate's eldest son had wed one of Atherton's sisters. When you appeared, sir, I surmised that you were this eldest son. Such being the case, it seemed the story of the missing nephew must be true. Still, a number of questions remained. I wondered why you failed to identify yourself. I wondered why you were dressed in that bizarre manner. I wondered at your behavior. None of this accorded with anything I had ever heard or read previously about Lord Rathbourne."

Rathbourne said nothing, merely regarded him stonily.

He was not going to explain himself, even to a man of the same rank.

Lord Northwick shrugged. "In any event, my primary concern was and is Atherton's boy. I am not in the least surprised at his being led astray by the young person in question. My dear cousins have at one time or another led any number of people astray."

Including you, Lord Northwick might as well have added, for he looked it, plainly enough, at Rathbourne.

Rathbourne's expression became bored. "I believe the important question is where my nephew is being led to, and how we might most quickly intercept him. Mr. DeLucey gave me to understand that you were willing to assist us in this regard. Or did I misunderstand?"

Lord Northwick's gaze went from Bathsheba to Rathbourne. His jaw set and he said, "I believe I know my duty, sir. Naturally I shall render you every assistance."

London

The Dowager Countess of Hargate went to bed very late and woke very early. This, her grandchildren said, was how she contrived to know everything about everybody before anyone else did. The volume of her correspondence far exceeded that of King George IV, his Prime Minister, and the Cabinet combined. She spent a good part of her day in bed, reading and answering letters. This still left plenty of time for gossiping with her friends (known to her grandchildren as the Harpies), playing whist, and terrorizing her family.

By early afternoon on Monday, she had reached the terrorizing portion of her program, and sent for her eldest son.

Lord Hargate found her in her boudoir enthroned among vast heaps of pillows and dressed as always in the grand style popular in her youth, which involved enough silk, satin, and lace to drape St. Paul's, inside and out, twice over.

He had greeted and kissed her and was enquiring about her health when she waved a letter in his face and said, "Never mind that nonsense! What the devil are you about, Hargate? My grandson has run off with a black-haired hussy, I am told. He has been brawling and making a spectacle of himself on the Bath Road."

"Your informant is mistaken," Lord Hargate said. "Rupert is safe in London with his wife. They are making arrangements to return to Egypt, my dear. You know as well as I that Rupert will not run off with anybody but Daphne. He is completely—"

"Not *him*," said his mama. "How can you be so thick, Ned? Why should I trouble to send for you, was it only to announce that Rupert had done something ridiculous? I should be more likely to send for you if by some bizarre accident he did something sensible. To my knowledge he has done so only once in his life, when he married that clever red-haired girl with the fine fortune. Since this miracle occurred but a few months ago, I should not expect another in my lifetime."

"No doubt, then, your informant has confused one of my offspring with one of our cousins," said Lord Hargate. "Geoffrey has taken his family to Sussex to visit his in-laws. Alistair is in Derbyshire, awaiting the birth of my grandchild. Darius has gone to support him in his hour of trial. None of them could possibly have been anywhere upon the Bath Road in recent days."

"You leave one son unaccounted for," she said.

"You cannot mean Benedict," Lord Hargate said.

She gave him the letter.

BATHSHEBA REGARDED HER surroundings with a sinking heart.

Throgmorton was immense. Extensive gardens, formal and informal, surrounded the main house. These gave way to a vast park, then acres of plantations and farmland. Once the children got in—and that would be child's play for Olivia—they might stay for days, perhaps weeks, unnoticed.

The park was amply wooded. Temples, follies, ruins, grottoes, and other hideaways dotted the landscape. A rustic cottage, used in summer for picnics, hid within a pine bower. A fishing house stood at the edge of the lake. The extensive grounds had been designed for entertaining not only the family but large parties of guests. While Lord Mandeville and his family spent little time in London, they were by no means unsociable. Moreover, the house was open to touring visitors on Tuesdays and Thursdays. It was all too easy to enter and all to easy to wander.

The mausoleum was not part of the regular tour, and visible only from certain areas of the grounds. Though it stood on a rise in the southwestern part of the park, the surrounding trees sheltered it from view of the vulgar masses touring the house and gardens that sprawled over the eastern side of the property.

At present Bathsheba stood a short distance away on another, slightly higher rise, with Rathbourne and Lord Northwick. They were gathered in front of the New Lodge, a structure dating back, Northwick said, to Elizabethan times.

Thomas was at the mausoleum, studying the terrain. He was easy to see at present. As Northwick had promised, this was the best vantage point for observing his ancestors' resting place. From here she had a fine view of the place, a Roman temple adorned with finials and elaborate carving. A short, wide flight of steps led to a portico supported by Corinthian columns. A wide lane led down to the bottom of the rise, then branched into narrower pathways. One of these led up to the New Lodge, circled it, and went down the rise another way. Another followed the contours of the lower part of the hill. From this, others led into the wooded slopes and down to the pathway that circled the lake.

"The mausoleum is relatively new," Lord Northwick was saying. "Building began a few years after Edmund DeLucey changed professions. My grandfather—his brother William—often stayed here, to keep an eye on the builders, he said."

"It would make a fine spot for a secret rendezvous, I notice," said Rathbourne. "Did your grandfather meet a lover here or was it his black sheep brother?"

Northwick lifted his eyebrows.

"Rathbourne is a sort of detective," Bathsheba said. "He is an expert on the criminal mind."

"Do not tease Lord Northwick," Rathbourne said. "You know perfectly well I did not refer to criminal behavior."

"You seem to read my mind well enough," she said.

"That is because you are transparent," he said.

She turned away, her face too warm.

"I merely observed the location," Rathbourne's deep voice continued behind her. "It is well out of view of the main house and outbuildings. I considered that William was the eldest son. I, too, am the eldest, and have been trained since childhood to protect my younger siblings. Perhaps it is like Mrs. Wingate's maternal instinct, which is not always connected to logic. I merely supposed that William acted under a similar sense of fraternal affection or obligation."

"I had heard you were prodigious clever," said Northwick. "You suppose right. My grandmother always believed that William did meet with Edmund here. She said it was to lend Edmund large sums of money, which he never repaid."

"That seems far more likely than Edmund's making deposits at Throgmorton, as my family likes to imagine," Bathsheba said.

"It almost seems a pity to stop the brats," Rathbourne said thoughtfully. "I should dearly love to see how they would go about excavating the place. It would certainly be good practice for Peregrine." He'd already told Northwick of Peregrine's Egyptian ambitions.

"I must confess that I grow curious, too," said Northwick. "If it would not send my father into an apoplexy, I should indulge them. I should dearly love to know what they propose to dig with. But one must then have people on watch to make sure they did not bring any finials down on their heads or tumble down the steps. Yesterday I noticed some crumbling stone that needs to be attended to. That is not the only problem at Throgmorton."

"There are always problems," Rathbourne said. "No matter how diligent the estate manager, he is obliged to postpone work here in order to do it there. The supply of workers is not unlimited. One must accommodate the weather. Only so much can be done."

"You have some experience of managing an estate, I see," said Lord Northwick.

Rathbourne smiled faintly. "I was not allowed to be idle. My father taught me farming at an early age."

"Then you understand my concerns," said Lord Northwick. "Accidents will happen, no matter what precautions one takes. The trouble is, young people are not notably cautious. When they keep to the paths, in daytime, they ought to be quite safe. But I have visions of these two skulking about at night, a prospect that makes my blood run cold."

"Did you never skulk about at night, in your youth, Lord Northwick?" said Rathbourne.

Bathsheba glanced back at him. He was not smiling, but she heard the smile in his voice.

"Yes, and that is why I am so uneasy," said Northwick. "I have told the groundskeepers to keep the dogs leashed. I have warned everyone to exercise caution. Yet if one is suddenly awakened at night, it is all too easy to act first and think later."

The warnings were part of the "press of duty" that had kept him from meeting with Bathsheba and Rathbourne until today. Lord Northwick had immediately begun alerting his staff, the local constables, and just about everyone else in the vicinity. He'd even sent messages to the tollgate keepers around Bristol.

"You have taken every possible precaution," Rathbourne said. "Already I breathe easier."

"Though I hope Lord Lisle has better sense than to attempt to enter a property at night, I shall put someone to watch the mausoleum after dark," said Northwick. "That way you might get some rest. You should find everything in readiness within." He nodded toward the lodge. "A servant will bring your dinner while the rest of us are occupied at table. Is your footman sufficient for your needs, or shall I send one of my staff to assist him?"

"Certainly you need not send dinner," Rathbourne said. "We can dine at the King's Arms when we return."

"But you are not returning to the inn," said Northwick. "I have made the New Lodge ready for you. It is absurd to

waste time traveling to and fro. You will be far more comfortable here, I promise you. My lady and I have stayed
here more times than I can count, when we find the house
too confining."

Throgmorton House contained one hundred fifty
rooms.

What Lord Northwick sought, no doubt, was a refuge.

This was understandable. Even the members of the most
close-knit families could wear on one another's nerves.

What was surprising was his choosing to have his lady
with him.

Lord Northwick had a romantic streak, Bathsheba realized. And his wife was part of the romance.

He loved his wife, and this was their lovers' hideaway.

Yet he was allowing his despised cousin to contaminate
it with her presence.

She hadn't time to wonder at it.

Peter DeLucey burst into view, galloping toward them.
"They're on the way!" he called. "Seen this morning. At
the Walcot tollgate."

THE FIRST RAINDROPS began to fall as Peter DeLucey
was assuring them that both Peregrine and Olivia were reported to be in good health and spirits. They were traveling
with a peddler, one familiar to the tollgate keeper. The peddler's name was Gaffy Tipton.

"The word has gone out," Peter said. "With any luck,
one of our men will find Tipton and your young wanderers
before nightfall."

Soon after this promising news, Lord Northwick and
his son took their leave.

The sky grew steadily darker, and the rain's patter increased. Ignoring her protests, Benedict threw his coat over
Bathsheba's shoulders.

Soon the rain was pouring down in sheets, driving them
indoors. Inside or out, they couldn't see anything anyway.
The mausoleum vanished behind a grey curtain of rain.

"So much for keeping watch," Benedict said, coming
away from a window. "I wonder where Thomas has got to."

"Out of the wet, I hope," said Bathsheba.

"No doubt he felt the change coming in the weather and took sensible action," Benedict said. "He's a countryman, recollect."

She took off his damp coat and shivered.

"I'll build a fire," he said. "Let us pray the chimney doesn't smoke."

The chimney, like the rest of the old building, appeared to be well maintained, to Benedict's relief. He could not remember when last he'd built a wood fire. He needed as many circumstances as possible in his favor.

She stayed at the window.

A tinderbox sat on the stone mantel. He opened the box and eyed it warily. The tinder had better not be damp.

"I'll have you warm in no time," he said.

"I'm not cold," she said.

"You're shivering," he said. He set to work arranging wood and kindling.

"I think it's the shock wearing off," she said.

"What shock?"

"Lord Northwick," she said. "I never would have guessed he'd defy his father."

"Northwick is not a child," Benedict said. "A man in possession of sound moral principles will do what must be done. Ultimately he is responsible to his own conscience. As you have reminded me repeatedly, this is not the Middle Ages. Mandeville may want blind obedience, but Northwick is not obliged to give it."

He focused on striking a spark.

"He did not need to let his wicked relative pollute his love nest with her presence," she said. "And you know as well as I that it is a love nest. You heard the note in his voice when he spoke of his lady."

Benedict blew gently on the tinder. A bit of flame rewarded him. Carefully he transferred the little fire to the kindling.

"I heard," he said, his gaze on the sickly bit of flame. He'd heard the softened tone when Northwick said "my lady," and he'd envied the man. "Perhaps my infinite perfections cancel out your infinite imperfections. Or perhaps

Northwick noticed the languishing way you look at me, and took pity on you."

"I do not languish," she said.

Benedict glanced back at her, one eyebrow raised.

She came away from the window. "You have an overactive imagination," she said, chin aloft. "I find you no more than tolerable."

The kindling crackled. Flames leapt up to the wood and swiftly took hold. The fire began to dance, reaching up the chimney, snapping and popping. Meanwhile rain hammered on the roof and drummed against the windows.

"What a delicious liar you are," he said. "It is like living with Scheherazade. I can never guess what amazing fabrication you will utter next."

"It is not—"

"Behold, fair princess," he said. He rose and gestured sweepingly at his handiwork. "I have made fire for you."

She stared at the fire. After a moment, her beautiful mouth curved a little. "And what an elegant fire it is, Rathbourne. Wood, too. How extravagant."

"This is a love nest," he said. "Wood is more romantic. It smells better than coal. Nor is it as extravagant here as elsewhere. You noticed the plantations, I daresay."

"I noticed everything," she said. "I knew Throgmorton was a large property. I had not expected it to be quite so immense. It is like a small kingdom."

"Most great properties are," he said.

"I never rode over one in the company of an owner who told me its history and his plans for its future," she said. "That changes one's perspective."

"Northwick has a feeling for the place," Benedict said.

"Have you?" she said. "For your family's property?"

"The pile in Derbyshire, you mean?" he said. "Yes, I cannot help it, though my life seems to belong to London. But in London, one simply has a house. In the country, the house is part of a greater world, one that stretches back for generations. Everywhere I look, I find my ancestors' handiwork."

"That is what struck me today," she said. "Great estates always seemed like grand monuments before. I didn't truly see them as living entities."

"That is because you never had a chance to be part of one," he said.

"But Edmund DeLucey was. Jack was." She shook her head. "I had imagined I understood Edmund, because I thought I understood Jack. Each was a younger son, living in his brother's shadow. Each knew he'd never rule the family's kingdom. They were restless men, I thought, but too undisciplined for military life, where they might have done great things and become heroes. Instead they did something spectacularly shocking."

"Now, however, you cannot comprehend why they would sacrifice all this." Benedict nodded toward the window where, behind the rain-curtain, thousands of acres of property stretched.

"I don't know what to think." She moved to a chair near the fire and sat down, her countenance troubled. "If I had grown up in such a place, should I ever be truly happy in a poky pair of rooms in the shabby part of town? Or hurrying from one foreign place to the next, trying to outrun my creditors?"

"I should think it would depend," he said, "on who shared the rooms with you or with whom you ran."

She looked up and met his gaze. "You must not look at me like that," she said.

He went to her and crouched before her. "Like what?" he said. He took her hand and cradled it in his.

"As though you would live that way . . . with me," she said.

"Oh, I wouldn't," he said. "I couldn't. It isn't in me. I've always been the heir. I've been trained for a great deal, but not for privation. I've not been trained to run but to stand my ground. I've been trained for stability, you see, because so much depends on me." He glanced toward the window again. "The place in Derbyshire. Our little kingdom. Hundreds of lives—and that's not counting the livestock."

She studied his face for the longest time. He hid nothing. He was not sure he could any longer hide anything from her, even if he wished to. Still, he knew she wouldn't believe what she saw in his eyes.

Why should she, when he could scarcely believe it?

She gave up and, with a rueful smile, drew her hand away to lightly stroke his cheek. "No, you are too intelligent and responsible to make a shambles of your life and make your family wretched on account of a woman. That is one of the things I like about you, Rathbourne. Nonetheless, you have been rather more careless than makes me comfortable."

He turned his head and kissed the palm of her hand. "Learn to count," he said. " 'Intelligent' and 'responsible' make two things. Tell me what else you like about me."

She let her hand fall to her lap. "Certainly not. The list of your perfections is much too long . . . and I am too weary."

Uneasy now, he searched her countenance. Had she been this pale all day? Before, she'd been shivering. Was she unwell?

"I thought you would have slept soundly last night," he said. "I was not there to keep you awake."

"You were there, nonetheless," she said.

"You were fretting about me," he said. "How many times must I tell you—"

"Do not tell me again." She rose abruptly and moved away. "You are perfect, but you have an aristocratic blind spot," she said. "I am not sure where it comes from. Perhaps it comes of others always smoothing the way for you. Perhaps it has to do with the wall between you and ordinary people. Wealth and privilege insulate even a philanthropist like you, Rathbourne."

"I know that," he said. "Did I not say so a moment ago? I am not equipped to live an ordinary life, let alone an impoverished or vagabond life."

"You will be hurt!" she cried. "That is what you do not understand, and I do not know how to make you understand what it is like: the kind of desolation you will feel and the humiliation you will bear. I don't want you to know what it is like. I don't want you to be hurt because of m-me."

"My dear girl." He went to her and wrapped his arms about her.

"There, you see?" she said, her voice shaky. "You stupid man. You have let yourself care for me."

"Perhaps a little," he said.

"We are too compatible," she said. "That is the trouble, improbable as it is."

"That is true," he said. "I like your company almost as much as I like your face and figure. That is a shocking development, certainly."

She laid her head upon his chest. "I am not noble enough to resist you when you are near," she said. "I should have resisted you weeks ago. I knew it. I knew you would be trouble. But I shall not cry over spilt milk." She lifted her head and looked at him, blue eyes glittering with unshed tears. "That is what I told myself last night. What truly matters now is that we have both been discovered, and nothing on earth will make us undiscovered. A scandal is inevitable. Yet I have thought of a way to reduce the damage."

"I know what you are going to say," he said. "Save your breath. It is out of the question."

She pulled away from him. "The instant we find the children, I shall take Olivia and go away."

"No, you will not," he said.

"Be logical, Rathbourne," she said. "The quicker I am out of sight, the quicker out of mind."

"Not out of *my* mind," he said.

"You are not thinking clearly," she said. "Listen to me."

He set his jaw. "Very well. I am listening."

"Once our names are paired, most people will assume that you and I had an affair," she said. "However, if I go away, it will be only a brief affair: in your case, a mere peccadillo; in mine, merely the typical DeLucey dreadfulness and general immorality. There will be a momentary flurry of gossip, which the next scandal will quickly supplant."

She was too damned logical, curse her.

"I have never heard anything so idiotish," he said.

"It is not idiotish," she said. "It is perfectly reasonable."

"We have *made love*, you mad creature," he said. "Several times. Have you forgotten that lovemaking and the arrival of babies are not unrelated matters? Are you proposing to go away—to who knows where—when you might be carrying my child?"

"That is most unlikely," she said. "Use your head, my lord. You are the detective. I was happily wed for twelve years. I have but one child. What does that tell you?"

"Nothing, actually," he said. "I am not Jack Wingate."

She gave a short laugh and returned to the window. The rain continued at the same furious rate. "It had nothing to do with Jack," she said. "I conceived several times and miscarried."

"Oh," he said.

He ought to be relieved, for her sake at least. Childbirth was a risky business, even for the privileged. The Princess Charlotte, heir to the throne, had died in childbed four years ago.

The trouble was, he had never developed the skill of lying to himself. He knew he was too selfish to be relieved. He knew he was disappointed. Worried, too, because he was running out of acceptable excuses.

"You cannot go away," he said. "It is not good for Olivia."

"I have considered this," she said. "It can be good for her if I take her to the right place: one of the German states, where teachers are very strict."

"Bathsheba."

"I see a dark blur," she said. "Someone is coming."

Benedict went to the window. He discerned a single, large blur. He went to the door and opened it before the arrival had time to knock.

Rain dripping from his hat and cascading down his coat, Thomas stood in the narrow entryway. He carried a large, wrapped parcel.

"Which it looks like the rain means to keep on all day and night, my lord," he said. "Which is why I went to the house and laid up supplies. They'll send a proper dinner later, but meanwhile I've brought sandwiches and tea and a flask of something stronger in case of cold, which it is, the temperature dropping considerable since morning."

THOUGH THE MAN was not dressed like a Bow Street officer, Olivia had seen enough thief-takers to recognize the type, even in a downpour. She watched him slither out from the darkness of the stables. Then he stood in the doorway and waited while Gaffy gave his horse into the ostler's care.

Olivia and Lisle were waiting for him under the inn's gallery, out of the rain. As soon as the strange man appeared, though, she grabbed Lisle's arm and dragged him back into the shadows.

"What?" he said. "What?"

She pointed to the stranger. He was speaking earnestly to Gaffy. The peddler frowned, took off his hat, and scratched his head.

Then the thief-taker held up a coin.

"Run," said Olivia. "Just run."

Chapter 16

BENEDICT WATCHED BATHSHEBA MAKE A PRE-
tense of eating the sandwiches and later, a pretense of eating dinner. In between, she sat at the window, watching,
though the rain never abated, and it remained impossible to
see anything.

When she returned to the window after dinner, though,
he decided enough was enough.

"It is night," he said. "Even if the rain stops, you will
see nothing."

"Lanterns," she said. "If Lord Northwick's men find the
children, they'll come to tell us. They'll carry lanterns."

"If they come to tell us, they'll knock at the door," said
Benedict. "Come, sit by the fire in a comfortable chair and
drink your tea. Stop fretting about the children. Stop
thinking about the children. Lord Northwick has scores of
competent persons out combing the countryside as well as
Bristol."

"A search party," she said, still staring into the darkness.
"Exactly what we had tried to avoid."

His uneasiness returned. "What ails you, Mrs. Wingate?"
he said. "Where is the belligerent woman who refused to

let me search alone? Pray do not tell me that disagreeable meeting with your relatives yesterday morning crushed your spirit. I refuse to believe you can be so easily vanquished."

She turned, and to his relief, the blue eyes flashed up at him. "Certainly not," she said. "They were merely cold and distrustful, which is precisely what I expected. Really, Rathbourne—as though such a thing would depress my spirits." She rose. "You seem to have confused me with those fragile creatures who populate your social circle."

"They are not all so very fragile," he said. "You ought to meet my grandmother."

She settled into one of the two thickly cushioned chairs Thomas had placed by the fire.

"I have met Jack's grandmother, and that was enough, thank you," she said. "After my encounters with his family, a merely unfriendly reception is nothing."

She poured tea.

Benedict took his cup and settled into the empty chair by the fire. "I should have guessed," he said. "When they couldn't make Wingate change his mind, they worked on you."

He had not thought of that. The collision with her estranged relatives must have awakened old memories, unhappy ones. No wonder she brooded.

"I was sixteen years old," she said, studying the contents of her cup as though the memories lay within it. "They all had different tactics. The grandmother told me I would never be accepted in Polite Society. Meanwhile, Jack would live to regret his decision. If I was lucky, he'd abandon me. If I was unlucky, he'd stay on, and I would share his misery and bitterness until death did us part. His mother wept and wept. His father tore my conscience to pieces. There were aunts and uncles and great-aunts and lawyers. I was ready a dozen times to give Jack up, only to make them stop tormenting me. But he said his life would not be worth living without me, and I was only sixteen—a girl, Rathbourne, a mere girl—and I did love him so."

What was it like, he wondered, to be loved so?

What sort of man would seek to be loved so, knowing it

could only lead to her enduring more of the misery and abuse she'd borne as a defenseless girl?

"Sixteen," he said, careful to keep his voice light. "How long ago that seems. I was someone else altogether."

"Were you in love?" she said.

"Oh, yes, of course. Who ever is so much in love as at that age? Was that not Romeo's age?"

She smiled. "Tell me about her," she said.

He had not thought about the infatuations of his youth for a very long time. He hadn't allowed himself to do so. He considered it unwise to compare the excitement and idealism of those days to the bored discontent that seemed to permeate his adulthood. One might begin to brood. One might even become so irrational as to long for what was gone forever.

Yet the memory had not vanished. It only waited to be let out. He let it out for her, as he had done so much else.

He told her of a schoolmate's pretty sister, who stole his heart when he was sixteen, and broke it, and took away all his reasons for living . . . until a month or so later, when he met another pretty girl.

As he told the tales, his mind cleared.

Love, in that long-ago time, had been a grand, terrifying, bewildering thing. And so painful. Since he had not let himself dwell upon his youthful experiences, he'd forgotten about the pain. The memories remained, but the feelings were vague, distant.

His schoolboy infatuations now seemed as insubstantial as dreams, though at the time they'd been real enough.

Everything faded, though.

Young love. Youthful dreams.

Grief faded, too, as did the guilt that so often accompanied it.

He had not loved Ada. By the time he wed her, he'd convinced himself that romantic love was the stuff of poetry and drama but not real life. Now he wondered whether he'd stopped believing because, in adulthood, he had failed to find anyone who stirred strong feelings in him.

Still, in his insufficient way he had cared for his wife,

and her death was a shocking blow that left him completely at sea for a long time.

He had been so angry—at her at first, then at himself—as he began to make sense of what had happened between them. Yet in two years' time, even that searing guilt had dwindled.

What he felt for Bathsheba Wingate would fade, too, he told himself. This time with her was a dream, merely a moment of his life. A few strange and thrilling, out-of-the-ordinary days. An aberration. *A brief affair,* she'd called it. A passing fancy. A peccadillo.

He must view it that way, for her sake.

And so he looked and sounded amused as he confessed his handful of youthful infatuations. Then he went on to entertain her with Alistair's much more numerous and exciting romantic catastrophes, and Rupert's mad escapades. In contrast, there was sober Geoffrey who, unlike the others, had made up his mind when he was a boy and never changed it, and wed his cousin, to nobody's surprise.

Benedict was speculating about Darius's recent behavior and his future when a log shattered in a sputter of sparks, startling him out of his reveries. He wondered how long he'd been talking.

"You are too good a listener," he began. Then he paused to look at her. Her elbow rested on the arm of her chair, and her cheek upon her hand. Her eyes were closed. Her breathing was even.

He smiled ruefully. He had planned to put her to sleep. But not this way.

He rose and went to her. Gently he gathered her up in his arms. He carried her to bed and laid her down. He took off her shoes, and drew the bedclothes over her. She scarcely stirred.

She was tired to death, poor girl, he thought. Tired to death with watching and waiting and worrying, about everything and everyone, including him, especially him.

He bent and kissed her forehead. "Don't fret about me, sweet," he murmured. "I'll do well enough. I always have."

* * *

IT WAS THE quiet that must have wakened her, the end of
the steady drumbeat of rain. Or perhaps it was the light. It
was not daylight, that silvery glow. The sky had cleared,
and she lay in a pool of moonlight.

Bathsheba put her hand out, and even as she did so, she
knew he wasn't there. The warmth was missing. She shivered, though not from cold. She had not felt so alone since
those first bleak months after Jack died.

"Drat you, Jack," she whispered. "You had better not be
laughing. A fine joke, you'll think it, that I should make the
same mistake twice."

She heard a sound in the room beyond. She sat up.

Stealthy footsteps.

"Who is that?" she said.

"Roaming bands of soldiers," came a familiar rumble.
"Brigands and cutthroats. Ghouls and goblins."

Rathbourne's tall, dark form filled the doorway. "Or
perhaps it was simply me, galumphing about while fondly
imagining I was stealing noiselessly about the place."

"Were you walking in your sleep?" she said.

"I thought I was walking in my—er—awake," he said.

"You told me not to fret," she said. "Were you fretting,
Rathbourne?"

"I was not pacing, if that is what you are implying," he
said. "I never pace. Caged animals pace. Gentlemen stand
or sit quietly."

"You could not sleep," she said.

"I was trying to work out a plan for dealing with
Peregrine—or his parents, actually," he said.

He folded his arms and leant against the doorjamb. It
was so like his pose at the Egyptian Hall, when she'd first
seen him, that her breath caught, as it had done then.

"I'd forgotten," she said. "The business about the peddler's daughter won't work now, obviously."

"I am considering making a scene," he said. "Turning
the tables on them. Before they can commence their histri-
onics, I shall start striding back and forth, waving my fist
and clutching my forehead by turns."

"You are fond of that boy," she said.

"Well, yes, of course. Why else should I put up with him?"

He ought to have children, she thought. He would make a good father.

She could not give him children. He didn't need an aging mistress with a malfunctioning womb. He needed a young wife who'd fill his nursery.

"If you like, I'll help you devise a scene tomorrow," she said, "while we watch for our wanderers."

"It is tomorrow, actually," he said. "Last time I looked at my pocket watch, it was one o'clock, and that was a while ago."

"Then it is past time you came to bed," she said.

"I see," he said. "Is that what woke you? A desperate longing for me?"

"I should hardly call it a desperate longing," she said. "I should call it a vague sense of something amiss."

"The fire's out and the bed's cold," he said.

"Why, so they are," she said. "That's what it is. Well, you are big and warm. That should solve the problem."

He laughed.

Oh, she would miss that low laughter.

"Rathbourne," she said. "We haven't much time, and you're wasting it."

HE CAME INTO the room, pulling off articles of clothing with every step. In a few minutes, he was naked, miles of hard, muscled male glowing in the moonlight.

In the next minute, he was pulling back the bedclothes, and stripping her with the same ruthless efficiency.

She thought it would be quick and desperate, one last bout of madness.

But when she was naked, he lay on his side next to her and brought her round to face him. He lifted his hands to her head, and drew them down, over her face, then down her throat and down, slowly, over her breasts and waist and belly and lightly between her legs. He moved his long, gentle hands down her legs, then all the long way up again, as though he would memorize her.

Her eyes filled as her own hands went up to tangle in his hair, then to trace the shape of his face—the noble nose, the strong angle of his jaw—and powerful neck and shoulders. Then down she brought her hands, over the hard contours of his torso, so familiar now, and over his taut waist and belly, the narrow hips, and his manhood. She smiled, remembering their drunken night, and he remembered, too, because she saw it in his answering smile. She continued her journey, as far as she could reach down those miles of leg, and up again, her heart aching.

I love you I love you I love you.

He drew her close and kissed her, and it was cool and sweet, then hot and sweet, then dark and wild. She tangled her legs with his and pressed closer, and forgot about tomorrows. She let her hands rove over him again and again, as though she could imprint him somehow, though it was impossible: taste and scent and touch and sound—all so fleeting. This moment. That was all one ever had: this moment.

She took all she could, drank him in and memorized him, in endless, deep kisses and tender caresses, until at last he made a choked sound, and pushed her onto her back.

He entered her in one fierce thrust, and the world shattered. She rose up and wrapped her legs round his waist, her arms round his shoulders, to hold on to him, as tightly as she could for as long as she could. He grasped the back of her head, and kissed her, and she clung, rocking with him, while the heat built and blotted out thought, and while grief, and tomorrow—above all, tomorrow—all vanished.

Only the joy of being joined remained, and they let that happiness sweep them to its pinnacle, and over. Mercifully, it swept them into sleep, in each other's arms, in the silver glow of the moonlight.

NO ONE KNOCKED at the door of the New Lodge until morning. Then it was only Peter DeLucey, accompanied by a servant carrying a basket from the kitchens.

It was early morning, though, forcing Benedict and

Bathsheba to make a hasty toilette. They had no time even for a few private words.

Still, at least DeLucey had not arrived while they were still abed together. Thomas—who had been awake at dawn, as usual—had spotted Northwick's son while the young man was yet a good distance away, and promptly alerted his master.

Not that it was any use trying to protect Bathsheba's reputation, Benedict knew.

After all, Northwick had allotted them his love nest, had he not? Neither he nor anyone else who saw them together would have the smallest doubt that Bathsheba Wingate was Lord Rathbourne's mistress.

Still, Northwick had acted generously and honorably.

When Lord Mandeville found out, Northwick would pay for his generosity and honorable behavior.

That was the trouble with doing what was right. One was sure to suffer for it.

A gentleman does what is right, and accepts the consequences.

Bloody damn rules, Benedict thought.

"I do apologize, my lord," Peter DeLucey said.

Benedict gazed blankly at him for a moment, wondering how much of the conversation he'd missed. "I fail to see why you should apologize," he said. "I'm the one who wasn't paying attention."

"Lord Rathbourne was thinking," said Bathsheba. "That soul-freezing look was not aimed at you, Mr. DeLucey. You merely happened to be in the way. Take something to eat, Rathbourne. One can't concentrate properly on an empty stomach. Thomas, his lordship needs more coffee."

Everyone followed the lady's orders.

She presided as hostess at one end of the small table. The two men sat opposite each other.

"While your mind was elsewhere, Mr. DeLucey was explaining how his men lost the children last night," she said.

He'd been speaking of the peddler, Benedict recalled. DeLucey had been telling them about Gaffy Tipton, whom Lord Northwick's agents had found last night at one of the several Bristol hostelries known as "the Bell."

"He said he knew the children were of good family," Peter went on. "He guessed they were runaways. But he didn't know who it was they'd run away from. For all he knew, he said, the men claiming to work for Lord Northwick were villains."

"In short, Tipton was uncooperative," Benedict said.

"People had to be sent for to vouch for our agent, before the peddler would tell anything."

"Meanwhile, my dear Olivia can spot a constable, debt collector, or thief-taker from a mile away," said Bathsheba. "She would have taken one look at the agent and bolted. It is perfectly understandable."

"By gad, you're taking it well," said DeLucey. "In your place, I should have been wild. As it was, I was longing to throttle the agent. The children were within his reach—and he let them go."

"He didn't *let* them," Benedict said. "As I reminded Mrs. Wingate some days ago, neither my nephew nor her daughter is a trusting child. They are both intelligent. And crafty."

"Father was furious," DeLucey said. "Keeping Grandfather in the dark is not the easiest task in the world. The longer this takes, the more likely he will become suspicious. Once that happens, he'll learn the truth in short order, and then we're in for a prodigious row."

"I'm amazed he hasn't got wind of it yet," said Bathsheba. "Lord Mandeville seemed in no way decrepit to me. His mind is sharp enough and he did not appear at all enfeebled."

"Oh, he's able enough, but over the years he's left more and more of the tedious business side to Father," DeLucey said. "Grandfather would far rather hunt and fish and entertain."

"Then Lord Northwick is well accustomed to organizing and directing his people," Benedict said. This was not always so, he knew. In too many cases, the head of the family insisted on maintaining control of everything to his dying breath. This left the heir with too much time on his hands and no purpose in life but waiting for his father to die. The present king, to Benedict's thinking, amply illustrated all the drawbacks of this method of upbringing.

Lord Hargate's method, on the other hand, was to heap responsibilities upon his eldest, on the principle that the devil made work for idle hands.

"Father has our men combing Bristol from top to bottom, front to back," DeLucey said.

Benedict nodded. "A logical approach. The trouble is, the brats are never where we expect them to be. At what time were they last seen?"

"Gaffy Tipton arrived at the Bell in the early evening," DeLucey said. "He sent the children to stand in the shelter of the gallery while he tended to the horse. This was usually Lord Lisle's task, he said."

"Peregrine?" Benedict said. "My nephew acted as his groom?"

"A quiet, obedient, and useful boy, according to Tipton," DeLucey said.

"Quiet and obedient," Benedict said. "Peregrine. Behold me dumbstruck." He looked at Bathsheba. "Is that Olivia's influence, do you think?"

"Are you joking?" she said.

It came to him without warning, the scene as vivid in his mind as though it had happened but a heartbeat ago: the breathtakingly beautiful face turned up toward his, the blue eyes drowning him, and the note of laughter in her voice when she told him she'd tried to sell Olivia to gypsies.

Was that when it had happened?

Had he been lost long before he realized?

Had all his world begun to change from that day, while he stupidly imagined he was the same?

He was not the same and never would be again.

He doubted Peregrine would be the same, either.

"Tipton said they both made themselves useful," DeLucey said. "He sounded surprised about it, too. Last night, though, he saw to stabling his horse, on account of the rain. He didn't like to risk the children's taking a chill. He sent them to wait under the gallery, out of the wet. That was the last time he saw them."

Benedict considered. "From the heart of Bristol to the gates of Throgmorton is no great journey," he said. "A few hours on foot. They might easily find a ride for some part of the way. Even if they walked, or rode on the slowest wagon, they might easily be at Throgmorton by now."

"You think we should concentrate our efforts here?" DeLucey said.

"I do not like to tell Lord Northwick his business," Benedict said. "On the other hand, he cannot wish to waste his time and the talents of his staff—and the sooner he is rid of us, the better for everybody."

Peter DeLucey started to make the expected polite protest. Benedict cut him off. "Kindly tell your father I wish to speak to him," he said, "as soon as he finds convenient."

Tuesday afternoon

"We can't go through the front gate," Peregrine said. He grasped Olivia's arm and tugged her in the opposite direction, before anyone at Throgmorton's entrance spotted them.

"It's a visiting day," she said. "You heard what Mr. Swain said. Tuesday and Thursday afternoons."

They had spent the night in the shop of Mr. Swain, a pawnbroker, because that was one of the few places where Olivia felt safe.

Peregrine was not sure he had felt safe. Still, it was warm and dry, and he had definitely felt less conspicuous in the dark little shop, through whose door a number of drenched and ragged persons passed, carrying their pitiful stock of goods.

After five days' traveling, he and Olivia looked as dirty and bedraggled as any of Bristol's unfortunates. If they entered a respectable inn or lodging place, they would attract suspicious attention. Of course, they could easily enter a not respectable place. But then they would face worse risks than being caught by constables or detectives.

Mere days ago, Peregrine had wanted to be caught.

That was before.

Now he was glad that he and Olivia had found sanctuary for one more night, even if it was a none-too-clean pawnshop and they had to sleep on the floor.

It was all thanks to Olivia, who apparently knew everything there was to know about pawnbrokers, including the names and addresses of half of those in London and every last one in Dublin. She and Mr. Swain had a fine time exchanging anecdotes and gossip. She had no trouble at all learning all she wanted to know about Throgmorton.

This was fortunate, because the park and grounds covered thousands of acres, and they had no map. Swain, however, had gone to Throgmorton twice for celebrations. He'd sketched a rough plan of the place. Though Swain had never visited the mausoleum, he had glimpsed it, and had heard that it looked like a Roman temple, with two statues guarding the stairs. Peregrine now had a general idea of the mausoleum's location.

"I don't see why we can't simply slip in among the crowd," Olivia said.

"Because there won't be any crowds," Peregrine said. "This isn't like a balloon ascension in Hyde Park, or a race at Newmarket. There won't be great masses of people pouring through the gates. There won't be pickpockets and bookmakers, beggars and prostitutes, mingling with ladies and gentlemen and family groups. Perhaps a handful of people will visit today, and they'll need to look respectable, which we don't. This isn't like Chatsworth, where they let anybody in to wander wherever they like. Even if we did manage to get past the gatekeeper, we'd be watched every minute—and chucked out promptly at the end of visiting time."

While he spoke, Peregrine towed her down a narrow, rutted road. "But the main entrance isn't the only way in," he went on. "After all, one can hardly have the estate workers hauling manure through the main entranceway—the same route the king takes."

"Heaven forfend," Olivia said. "Someone would have to hold His Majesty's nose. Or can he hold his own?"

Peregrine ignored this. "There will be several other gates, much humbler," he said. "But the landscaping will conceal them from view of the main house, so they don't spoil the scenery."

She shot him a look. "I never thought of that. But I've never lived in the country."

"Obviously," he said. "If you had— Oh, never mind. The point is, I'm the expert now. Which means it's your turn to hold your tongue and do as you're told."

He had to give her credit. She kept quiet and let him lead the way, just as though she were a rational person, instead of a lunatic female who actually believed she had a prayer of finding a pirate's treasure chest buried alongside her ancestors.

Peregrine knew they had about as much chance of finding pirate treasure at Throgmorton as they had of finding a unicorn. He could not imagine how they would get near the mausoleum without attracting attention.

But then, he'd never imagined he would have made his way from London to Bristol with nothing more than a handful of coins and his own and his companion's wits to sustain him.

Whatever happened, it was sure to be interesting.

An adventure.

It would be years before he could hope for another one.

SPIRITS SINKING, BATHSHEBA watched the sky cloud over. The wind strengthened, and she drew her cloak more tightly about her.

She stood a short distance from the New Lodge, at the top of the pathway that declined gently in the direction of the mausoleum. This part of the park being thickly planted with trees and tall shrubs, the pathway vanished from view for a time, then reappeared, much wider, climbing the slope toward the ornate structure in which the last few generations of DeLuceys were entombed.

Clouds swirled above the imitation Roman temple, growing thicker and blacker as the wind drove them harder. In her fancy, the clouds were the demonic ghosts of Dreadful DeLuceys, dancing madly over the bones of the good ones.

Even as mere clouds, they boded ill. This was how the sky had looked yesterday before it loosed the torrents that drove them indoors.

Below and to the east of the New Lodge, one caught

glimpses of Throgmorton's large lake, between the trunks and branches of the trees and shrubbery bordering it on this, its western side. On the eastern side lay a series of temples and grottoes, cunningly situated so as to be visible only from certain points along the pathway. At its southern tip, the lake narrowed and spilled into a picturesquely steep cascade that tumbled into a river. In the decreasing intervals of sunlight, the restless waters sparkled. Mainly, though, they were murky, like the sky.

Rathbourne, Lord Northwick, and Peter DeLucey stood talking a few yards away from her. Occasionally they looked up from their discussions, to study the heavens.

Though the aristocratic countenances revealed little emotion, she doubted the conversation was optimistic.

If it rained as it had done yesterday, the children would seek shelter, and they had all too many hiding places to choose among. If it rained as it had done yesterday, searching for them would be far more difficult, nearly impossible.

The afternoon was waning. In a few hours, night would fall.

Another day would be lost.

I'll have another night with him, Bathsheba thought.

She wanted another, and another. She wanted that badly; at the same time she doubted she could bear another day. The passing hours were hard enough.

She'd steeled herself for the break, today.

She was ready to be strong, today.

She was not sure for how much longer, though. She'd already had her nerves wrung to pieces with a series of false alarms. Three times Lord Northwick's search parties had cornered tenants' children by mistake. Once, they'd cautiously surrounded what turned out to be an escaped pig rooting under the shrubbery near a "ruin" built in the last century.

Out of the corner of her eye, she saw Rathbourne step away from the others and start toward her. Northwick and his son set out in the opposite direction.

She quickly returned her gaze to the clouds roiling above the temple.

"Northwick is sending men out to investigate the latest rumors," came Rathbourne's low voice beside her. "One of the local women thinks she saw the children at some point along the eastern boundary wall, not far from the main gate. Another report puts them nearer a gate along the northern boundary. I've told him we'll stay where we are. It makes no sense for us to chase every rumor. At any rate, it is time we had our tea."

"I'm not hungry," she said.

"You're pale and chilled," he said. "You ate scarcely anything at breakfast, and nothing at midday. If you faint dead away when the prodigals finally put in an appearance, people will mistake you for one of those fragile creatures you insist you are not. That would be extremely awkward for me, considering the pains I have taken to assure Northwick that you are a determined woman of strong principles."

"A waste of breath," she said. "He would never believe one of my ilk knew what a principle was."

"He does believe that you are determined to leave Throgmorton as soon as you retrieve your daughter," Rathbourne said. "He has agreed to put a carriage at your disposal."

"A private carriage?" she said. "Have you taken leave of your senses? All you need do is lend me coach fare."

"No, I do not," he said. "You dislike stagecoaches. On account of the jolting and crowding and drunkards and puking and vermin, remember?"

"Then a place on the mail," she said. "Or a post chaise, if you must be extravagant. But I beg you will not send me away in one of my relative's private carriages."

"I am not sending you away," he said. "*You* are sending you away. Because of noble principles. Which I am obliged to respect, curse you."

She turned and looked up into his handsome face, though it hurt her. He wore the same bored expression he'd worn at the Egyptian Hall, but his dark eyes were gentle. Oh, it was affection she saw there, worse for her. If he were truly bored and distant she would not long so much to touch his cheek.

"How do you think I feel?" she said. "I have a handsome, wealthy aristocrat in the palm of my hand, and I must let him go."

"Dream on," he said. "I find you merely tolerable."

"Imagine how I feel," she went on. "I can look back on generations of utterly amoral, conscienceless DeLucey ancestors, any one of whom wouldn't have hesitated to ruin your life and bankrupt you for good measure. Why couldn't I be like the rest of them? But no, I must be the one cursed with scruples."

He smiled. "I shall never forgive you for that, Bathsheba. For that and a great deal else. I believe I shall nurse a . . . grudge . . . to the end of my days."

"Ah, well, at least you won't forget me," she said.

"Forget you? I should as easily forget a bout of whooping cough. I should as easily— Damnation."

He looked up and raindrops splattered his face.

"Come inside," he said. "There is no point—"

"M'lord!" came a shout from not far away. "Sir! This way!"

They both turned toward the sound.

"It's Thomas," Rathbourne said. He ran that way. Bathsheba ran after him.

Chapter 17

WHILE LORD NORTHWICK'S MEN WERE SEARCH-
ing the northeastern section of the estate, Peregrine and
Olivia had been making their way in the opposite direction.

A high wall surrounded Throgmorton's park, as Peregrine had expected. Since Swain the pawnbroker had said
the mausoleum was in the southwestern corner of the park,
this was the way Peregrine led Olivia. Eventually they
came to the stream Swain had mentioned. Thanks to the recent rain, its waters were high and muddy, rushing along a
route it more usually meandered at a leisurely pace.

Peregrine was sure there would be a bridge, and near
it a gate, to accommodate carts and wagons. Not many
yards farther on, the bridge appeared, and the expected
gate, which, though locked, was not guarded.

Climbing over it was no problem.

Once inside the property, they kept to the cart track,
which followed the boundary wall. At first the thickly
wooded landscape hid the rest of the park from view. But
after a few minutes, the track began to climb, and Peregrine spotted the lantern-topped dome of the mausoleum.

"There it is!" Olivia cried.

Birds flew up from the trees, squawking.

"Be quiet," Peregrine said. "I can see. Do you want all the world to know we're here?"

But she was already hurrying up the hillside, along a narrow path that did not seem to be used very much. Peregrine glanced up once at the sky, then followed her. He did not like the looks of the clouds. At this point, though, it made no sense to travel all the long way back to the Bristol Road again because of bad weather.

They could take shelter from the rain at the mausoleum, he thought, under its portico. If they had to spend the night—and that seemed likely—they could do it in one of the numerous other buildings adorning Throgmorton's park. Peregrine doubted they'd all be locked—not that he supposed mere locks could stop Olivia.

He saw her slip, and hurried to catch up with her.

"Do watch where you're going," he said. "Can't you see the ground's still wet? Do you want to break an ankle?"

She didn't seem to be listening. Her eyes were on the mausoleum.

"It's bigger than I pictured," she said. "Fancier, too. They've put a dome on top of the roof, and a rectangular box on top of the dome, and a little ball on top of the rectangular box. And they've stuck all those urns or pots or whatever they are on every roof corner."

The decoration didn't surprise Peregrine. What did surprise him, when they reached the top of the hill, was how secluded the place was. The mausoleums he'd seen had been built for show, and dominated their immediate surroundings. Though this was typically grand, it was very private, with only a small stretch of lawn about it. A dense wall of tall shrubbery and trees almost completely enclosed the space.

"This isn't the fanciest part," Peregrine said. "It's obviously the back of the building. The entrance will be under the portico." He led her round to the front. "Much more elaborate, you see."

It had a wide stone staircase, with balustrades, upon the ends of which stood two stone figures about eight feet tall. From the staircase, a wide pathway wandered down the slope, then seemed to continue up another hill nearby. Everywhere else, the trees blocked his view of the parkland. Peregrine guessed that beyond those trees would be more of the same: the usual rolling landscape. He couldn't be sure, though, since the greenery shut out all but that bit of pathway.

"I'll wager anything that Edmund DeLucey buried his treasure at the foot of one of the statues," Olivia said, calling his attention back to the mausoleum. "But which one?"

"Maybe if we knew who they were meant to represent, we could guess," Peregrine said. "Gods or demigods, probably. Funny, isn't it, how our lot carry out their strict Christian burials under pagan symbols. I know that at least one member of the peerage has a mausoleum in the shape of a pyramid."

Olivia, as one would expect, was not interested in the burial rituals of the British aristocracy. "I suppose we'll have to dig in both places," she said. She looked about her. "I doubt anyone will notice."

Peregrine had to agree with at least the last statement. If Edmund DeLucey had buried anything here, he wouldn't have had to worry much about attracting attention.

Peregrine's family had a park like this, where features of the landscape, interesting structures and such, were artfully hidden along the pathways among trees and shrubbery, so that the visitor arrived upon them unexpectedly, or saw them at a distance only from the ideal vantage point.

Meanwhile, this building's foundation rose about six feet off the ground. Anyone digging at its base would be very hard to see, unless the observer stood in exactly the right spot.

Of course, one must remember that the surrounding trees wouldn't have been so thick and tall a hundred years ago. The hill might have been bare, for all one knew.

Not that Olivia would care what anything was like a century ago. She'd only want to know where they might find spades and shovels. And maybe pickaxes.

As Peregrine stooped to study the ground at the base of the balustrade, he felt the first cold drops of rain.

He straightened. "We'd better get under— What's that noise?"

Olivia turned her head at the same time he did.

A man was running down the pathway on the nearby hill, waving at them and shouting. He was barely a hundred yards away.

Peregrine looked at Olivia. She looked back at him, her blue doll eyes wide.

"No," she said. *"No."*

And *NO!* he wanted to shout.

He wasn't ready to be found.

Not yet. He wasn't done.

He needed only seconds to decide what to do.

His punishment would be horrendous.

He might as well deserve it.

He grabbed her arm and dragged her away from the stairs and toward the nearest opening between the trees. "Run!" he shouted. "Just run!"

THOMAS WAS RUNNING down the path. Benedict started after him in time to see Peregrine grab Olivia and plunge into the woodland to their right: the lake side of the hill. The steepest side.

Benedict could hardly believe his eyes. "Stop!" he roared. "Are you mad?"

The children didn't stop.

He quickly calculated the best angle for intercepting them, and charged into a narrow path nearby. . . . With any luck, he'd catch them before they got far.

He heard the hunting horn's blare.

The signal, summoning the other men from all parts of the estate.

Benedict didn't pause.

"Olivia!" a voice cried.

Bathsheba, calling her daughter.

Benedict didn't look back or waste breath telling her to stay where she was.

He pushed past branches and leapt over roots.

The ground was slick with fallen leaves and pine needles. He ran, wishing she wouldn't run, too, yet knowing she would.

Please, don't fall and break your neck.

As he raced down the slope toward the lake, the pathway narrowed, the forest giving way to shrubbery nearly as tall and much denser.

"Peregrine!" he shouted. "Olivia!"

No response.

Evil children. When he got his hands on them—

"Olivia!" came Bathsheba's voice again from somewhere behind him.

He ran on. The rain beat down now and the curst path twisted and turned, but in the wet it offered surer footing than the children would have among the trees and undergrowth, where wet leaves and pine needles carpeted the sloping ground.

Curse the brats! When I catch them, I'll throttle them.

That was his last coherent thought. His toe caught on a gnarled root, and Benedict pitched forward.

PEREGRINE HEARD THE shouts behind him.

He heard Olivia, too, panting behind him, so close she was.

A part of him wanted to stop, but another part wouldn't, couldn't. He kept on, though he was wet through, and he'd lost the path. It was harder here, because there were fewer trees and more shrubs. The low branches grabbed his clothes and slapped his face. He kept running.

Then he saw it: an opening, at last.

He burst through it—and saw, too late, the short, steep embankment and the swirling water below. He grabbed for a branch, but his feet slid out from under him, and he tumbled headlong down the slope.

"Olivia!" he shouted. "Look out!"

His hands and feet skidded over the slick mud of the embankment, and he plunged into the rushing water.

RUNNING ONLY A few steps behind Peregrine, Olivia heard his cry an instant too late. She was already stumbling after him, arms flailing. As she slid over the edge of the embankment into the water, her hand struck something rough and thick, and she caught hold and held on tightly with both hands.

"Help!" she screamed. Icy water swirled around her, tugging at her, while the rain beat on her head and her hands, which were turning numb. She saw Peregrine thrashing in the water while the current carried him away.

"Lisle!" she cried. "Peregrine!"

His head went under the water.

THOMAS ARRIVED A moment after Benedict fell. The footman hauled him to his feet.

"Mrs. Wingate?" Benedict gasped, brushing muddy leaves from his face. "Where?"

"Caught her dress on a bush," Thomas said. "I begged her to stay there and show the way to the others. Then I run off before she could say no."

That was when they heard Peregrine's shout. Olivia cried out an instant later.

The two men hurried downward, toward the sounds.

Benedict stumbled through the bushes and out onto the path along the embankment.

No Peregrine.

An instant later, the pale head popped up, and Benedict's heart began to beat again.

"Help him!" came a cry from his right.

He turned that way, and saw the girl, clinging to the branch of a fallen tree.

The rotten tree had caught on something. That was why she wasn't yet drifting down the waterway after Peregrine. The boy, meanwhile, was struggling against the current.

"He's tiring, sir," Thomas said.

Another fifty or more yards and he'd be tumbling over the cascade . . . and breaking his neck, if he didn't drown first.

Benedict's gaze shot to the girl. Any minute now, the swollen river could carry away Olivia's tree.

"I can swim it, sir," said Thomas.

"No, keep to the lake path and go to the cascade," Benedict said. He pointed. "Try to stop him going over. I'll come as soon as I can."

Even while he spoke, he was climbing down the slippery embankment and making his way along the water's edge toward Olivia.

Thomas set off at a run toward the cascade.

"Not me!" Olivia screamed. "He's going to drown!"

Benedict stepped down into the water and continued toward her. Though bitter cold and thick with mud and debris, this part of the stream was not as deep as he'd feared. It rose no higher than his waist.

Still, the current was surprisingly strong, forcing him to move more cautiously than he wanted. It seemed to take hours to cover the few yards to the girl.

"Not me!" she screamed. "Not me! I told you!"

"Hush," Benedict said. He prised her stiff fingers from the tree branch, dragged her up into his arms, and staggered back to the embankment. He hoisted her up and set her down on the wet ground.

"Are you hurt?" he said, trying not to gasp.

"N-n-no," she said through chattering teeth. "I t-told you. Get *him*."

She was soaked through. Rivulets of water poured down her face. She was shaking in every limb. And furious.

She was so like her mother.

"Stay," Benedict said. "Stay right here."

"Yes, yes, only *go, please.*"

Benedict went.

BY THE TIME Benedict caught up with his footman, Peregrine had drifted dangerously near the cascade. The water here was over his head. He was trying to swim, but he was too tired—or hurt or both—and the current carried him on toward the cascade, not a dozen yards away.

Thomas was already starting into the water. Benedict went in after him. "M'lord," Thomas protested.

"We need to make a chain," Benedict said.

He didn't have to explain.

Thomas moved deeper into the water. Grabbing his hand, Benedict pushed on toward his nephew. Each step took him deeper, the water rising to his shoulders. The current tried to pull him off his feet, but Thomas kept him steady.

"Peregrine!" Benedict stretched out his arm. The boy grabbed for his hand, missed, tried again.

The second time his fingers caught, and clung to Benedict's.

A small tree branch drifted past them. It spun to the edge of the cascade and over.

Fighting to keep his balance, Benedict pulled Peregrine away from the steep tumble of water and rocks. The water tried to pull them back, but Thomas never budged, though Benedict felt the footman's arm tremble with the effort.

It seemed to take an eternity. In reality, only a few minutes passed before Benedict had pulled his nephew to shallow water. Then he would have carried Peregrine out, but the boy let go as they neared the water's edge, and stumbled out on his own power. He clambered up onto the muddy pathway and collapsed.

Benedict dragged himself out of the water and up to the pathway. "I'd better carry you," he said.

"I'll carry him, sir," said Thomas.

"I can walk," Peregrine gasped. "I only need a minute. To catch my breath."

"A minute, no more," Benedict said. "I left Miss Wingate in a shivering heap upstream. Let us hope she does not take a fatal chill."

Peregrine sat up shakily. His teeth chattered. He set his jaw and rubbed his face. "I'm sorry, sir," he said.

"You will be sorrier than you can imagine," Benedict said. "But later. For now, I must see to your partner in crime."

THEY FOUND OLIVIA waiting where Benedict had left her, and still shivering. Ignoring her incoherent protests, Benedict scooped her up in his arms and started along the pathway. She was completely sodden. Here and there, rotting—and reeking—vegetation clung to her. Peregrine was in much the same condition.

Benedict knew he didn't look or smell any better.

"S-someone sh-should carry *him*," she said, looking over Benedict's shoulder at the boy, stumbling behind them.

"I don't need to be carried," Peregrine said indignantly.

"N-neither do I," she said, teeth chattering, limbs shaking. She turned back to Benedict. "I w-want you t-to p-put m-me d-down." She looked up at him with her mother's great blue eyes. They filled. "I w-want m-my m-mother," she said. Her lips trembled.

"Oh, never mind being pitiful," Peregrine said. "Don't waste your energy getting the waterworks going. Uncle isn't taken in by such tricks. He isn't like everyone else, you know."

Apparently Uncle was, for the little witch had got her hooks onto his heartstrings and might have played him like a fiddle had Peregrine not intervened.

"I don't doubt you want your mother," Benedict said with all the cool indifference he could manufacture. "The question is whether she wants *you*."

THE LAST THING Bathsheba wanted to do was stay and wait.

But a moment after Thomas had left, her skirts tripped her up again, and would have sent her sailing headlong down the hill, if she hadn't managed to regain her balance. She did not want to add to Rathbourne's problems.

And so she waited as patiently as she could, and when the first group of men arrived—Peter DeLucey at the head of them—she pointed the way Rathbourne and Thomas had gone.

Shortly after that contingent vanished into the tall shrubbery, Lord Northwick came running down the hillside.

"That way," she said, gesturing.

As he turned to follow her direction, his foot slid off to one side. He lurched that way, then the other, trying to

regain his balance. Then she watched in horror as he went
down in a tangle of arms and legs, and rolled, over rocks
and broken branches and into a large rhododendron some
twenty yards down the hill.

Bathsheba picked up her skirts and hurried down to him.

He lay very still, on his side.

She knelt in front of him. His hat was gone and there
was a red mark on his face, but he did not appear to be
bleeding.

"My lord." Gently she touched his shoulder.

"Damnation," he said. He opened his eyes. He started to
pull himself up and winced.

"I'll call for help," she said, starting to rise.

"Don't be absurd." He dragged himself up to a sitting
position, obviously in pain. "I haven't broken anything."
He tried to stand, and his face creased into taut lines.

"You'd better stay for a moment," she said. "Let me
make sure nothing is broken. If you have fractured any
ribs, you must be taken back to the house immediately. The
wet will do you no good. I had better call—"

"I'll do," he said. "I doubt I've fractured anything more
vital than my pride. I must have looked a complete clown."

"You are a very bad clown," she said. "I saw it happen,
and I was not even mildly amused."

"In your secret heart, you enjoyed it," he said. "Your
hard-hearted relative brought low."

"I do not enjoy that sort of thing," she said. "You are not
hard-hearted, and we are related only very distantly. How
could I enjoy your discomfort, when you have been so
kind? Let me check your ribs."

"Absolutely not."

A shout interrupted the argument.

Peter DeLucey clambered up the hill. "We've got
them," he said breathlessly. "They are being wrapped up in
blankets. Lord Rathbourne told me to come ahead and set
your mind at rest, Mrs. Wingate. The lake narrows into a
stream at the southern end, and the children seem to have
tumbled into the stream."

"Great Zeus!" said Lord Northwick. "They were not
dragged over the cascade, I hope."

"No, no, Father, they did not get so far. Lord Rathbourne and his servant fished them out. Everyone is wet and cold, but no one is injured, apart from some scrapes and bruises." He paused then, belatedly comprehending the sight before him. "Father, what's happened?"

"I fell," said his lordship. "One of my legs is not cooperating. Kindly help me up. Mrs. Wingate is threatening to check my ribs."

"Fractures can be insidious," she said. "That is how my husband died. You are being unreasonable. You must let me—"

"Peter, help me up," Northwick said. "And you, Mrs. Wingate, will do better to spend your anxieties on your child."

"Mr. DeLucey says she is not hurt," she said. "In any case, children do not break as easily as adults. Young bones are more flexible."

"I assure you, neither of the children is broken," Peter DeLucey said. "They are very wet, though."

"Deuce take it, Peter—your hand!" his father snapped.

Peter gave his hand, and Lord Northwick got up, with a painful effort he couldn't quite conceal.

"There, that is better," said his lordship. "I shall do."

She gave up. Men were so obstinate. "Very well, but you must take great care when you walk," she said. "If you notice a sharp pain—"

"Looking for fractured ribs again, Mrs. Wingate?"

She looked toward the voice, deep and so familiar.

Rathbourne pushed through the greenery. Rain beat on his hatless head and poured down his neck, sending streams of mud downward. He had Olivia in his arms, tucked inside his greatcoat.

"Mama," she said in the most piteous manner.

For once in her life, the brat looked guilty.

Bathsheba decided not to forgive her too quickly.

"Olivia," she said briskly. "You are filthy."

She returned her attention to Rathbourne, who gave her a faint smile of understanding. "Lord Northwick took a dreadful fall," she told him. "He will not admit he is hurt."

"I took a ridiculous one," said Northwick. "But never mind that. Let us get these children to the house."

Though he moved less gracefully than usual, he did not seem to have endured any serious injury.

So she thought, at any rate, until they reached the pathway leading up to the New Lodge. Instead of going up the path he took its branch, which led in the other direction.

"I knew it!" Bathsheba cried. "You have a concussion. I knew you hurt yourself badly."

Northwick turned and looked at her.

"The New Lodge is up the hill," she said. "To the west, not the east."

"I said 'the house,' " he answered. "Meaning Throgmorton House. It is this way, Mrs. Wingate, and it is the way you are to come."

Chapter 18

IGNORING BENEDICT'S AND BATHSHEBA'S protests, Lord Northwick sent his son ahead to prepare the earl and enlighten him regarding certain of their guests' identities.

Then, limping, Lord Northwick led the drenched and shivering party to the ancestral home.

There Lord Mandeville and the ladies stoically watched as the group passed through the hall, leaving muddy footprints and a far from pretty fragrance in their wake.

While the earl would have happily tossed Bathsheba and her offspring out on their ears, he wouldn't dream of offering the same treatment to Lord Rathbourne and his nephew, Benedict knew. It didn't matter how disgusting they looked and smelled.

Lord Mandeville understood his duty, and would do it, though he might gnash his teeth the whole while.

A gentleman considers his duty first and his own comfort last.

Accordingly, the visitors found hot baths quickly readied for them, and freshly made up rooms in the guest wing. Servants swarmed in to attend to them. A physician arrived to examine Olivia and Peregrine—then Northwick, at Bathsheba's insistence. Naturally, his lordship objected. But his wife and mother took Bathsheba's side, and he was obliged to submit, though he did not do so meekly.

In a few hours, all were clean, dry, warm, and fed.

Benedict told himself he had nothing to complain of.

Though he could not make love to Bathsheba this night, he told himself he was not disappointed, because he had not expected to make love to her ever again. Meanwhile, all else had proceeded far more happily than he could have hoped. Olivia did not appear to be ill, and both she and her mama were treated kindly and respectfully.

He told himself they were no longer his responsibility.

He made himself focus on Peregrine, who was.

Bathsheba and her daughter shared a room in another part of the guest wing. Lord Lisle, though only a boy, had been given a large chamber next to Benedict's. Before going to bed, Benedict went to look in on him, to make sure he had not turned feverish.

He found his nephew broad awake, sitting on the rug before the hearth, watching the flames. When Benedict entered, the boy rose hastily, his face red.

"You ought to be asleep," Benedict said. He sat in one of the chairs Peregrine had ignored.

"I'm sorry, sir," Peregrine said. "It was impossible to sleep until I apologized for causing you so much trouble. I couldn't say it properly before, with so many people about. But if I am to tell the whole truth, as I have resolved to do, the truth is, that's all I'm sorry for."

He squared his shoulders and lifted his chin. "If I had it to do over, I should probably do the same thing. I couldn't let Olivia go with Nat Diggerby. He was an idiot and a bully and I didn't trust him. I couldn't let her go alone, either. She would have done, you know, because she didn't care what I said or how I said it. I try to speak to people exactly as you do, but the effect is not the same. No one heeds me. I could scarcely manage her at all—not that I am blaming her, merely explaining the facts as I saw them."

He stood so stiff, it was obvious he was steeling himself.

Against hurt. Rejection.

He was prepared for the usual reaction, in other words.

He had never been a submissive, obedient child. His elders found him annoying at best and infuriating at worst.

Benedict wondered what it was like to be Peregrine. Adults either swatted him out of the way or tried to crush him. What was it like, to grow up being made to feel like an insect?

"Tell me what happened," Benedict said. "From the beginning."

The lad told him, stiffly at first, then, as he realized his uncle was listening, not judging, he relaxed, and grew more animated.

When he was done, Benedict was silent for a long time. He was not trying to keep the boy in suspense. He simply couldn't speak. He knew, too well, what these last few days had been like for Peregrine, and why he had kept on, even today, when he was surrounded and had no hope at all.

But the lad was looking anxious. It was unkind to make him worry.

Benedict spoke past the constriction in his throat. "I shall send an express letter to your parents," he said, "though I suspect they will have taken alarm by now and may already be on their way to London. It is impossible to say what will happen. Matters are . . . complicated."

They were a good deal more than that.

But scenes were for the stage. Grand passions and the heartbreak that went with them were the stuff of melodrama. They had no part in the life of a gentleman.

Benedict refused to brood about the state of his heart. He would endure it, as he'd endured his depressing marriage. None of this affected Peregrine. What did affect him was the scandal about to break.

One could not predict precisely how Atherton and his lady would react. Benedict doubted they'd drop him on account of a scandal. After all, half their friends figured in society gossip.

Still, they might prefer not to have Peregrine spend time with his uncle while the uncle was the darling of the scandal sheets and his caricature appeared in print sellers' windows and umbrellas. Perhaps, after all the excitement died down, Benedict might regain a little of the ground he'd lost. Perhaps he might yet have a say in the boy's future. It was a most uncertain "perhaps."

Benedict rose. "Clear thinking and optimism are difficult when one is fatigued. Go to bed, Lisle, and we'll look at the matter fresh tomorrow."

The taut expression on the young face eased. "Yes, sir," Peregrine said. "Thank you, sir."

"Mind you, I am not at all pleased about the clandestine correspondence," Benedict said as he watched the boy climb into bed. "It is ridiculous at your age. It is absurd at any age. Prying servants are forever finding illicit letters and demanding large sums not to publish them. It is the sort of thing that belongs in a stage farce."

Peregrine winced. "I know that, sir. I knew I ought to resist them, but I simply couldn't."

There was a pause while Benedict beat down emotion and reassembled his sangfroid.

"Other than that, your behavior was ... acceptable," Benedict said.

"Was it, really?" The boy's countenance brightened further. "I have not disappointed you?"

"You are thirteen years old," Benedict said. "One makes allowances. I do, at any rate. What my father will say to you, on the other hand, when we return to London . . ."

Peregrine's eyes widened.

"On second thought, you need not be anxious about Lord Hargate," Benedict said. "He will be too much occupied saying things to me to have breath to spare for you." He patted the boy's shoulder. "Go to sleep, and be glad you are not quite grown up yet."

"LORD FOSBURY HAS never seen his granddaughter?" said Lady Northwick. "How foolish that seems. She is the very image of Jack Wingate."

"But for the eyes," said Lady Mandeville. "She has the DeLucey eyes."

Bathsheba had been greatly surprised when the servant

had come with a message from the ladies, asking if they might visit this morning.

Now they were here, she was not so surprised. They were curious about Olivia.

And Olivia, the little beast, sat, all limpid innocence, while the maid brushed out her hair. The maid would enjoy that, naturally, because Olivia had beautiful hair like her father's. The soft red curls did not tangle into nasty knots, as her mother's did.

"Perhaps it is for the best," Lady Northwick told Bathsheba. "If Fosbury had seen her, he might have taken her away from you."

"But then she would grow up with every advantage," said Lady Mandeville. "A mother ought to consider her child's future above all things."

"I believe I have," Bathsheba said tightly.

"I am sure you have," said Lady Northwick soothingly. "Perhaps, Mama-in-law, you have forgotten that Mrs. Wingate has only the one child. Those of us who have larger broods could perhaps spare one more easily."

"Atherton has given his only son to Rathbourne," said Lady Mandeville. "One makes such sacrifices for the good of the child. Lisle will have a superior upbringing among the Carsingtons."

"I do not believe he has given him up, precisely," said Lady Northwick.

"If he has not, he ought to," said Lady Mandeville. "The Dalmays are famously undisciplined. Atherton would be utterly hopeless had he not spent the better part of his youth with Rathbourne's family."

The elderly countess regarded Bathsheba for a long while, her expression completely inscrutable. Then she said, "It was Lord Hargate's mama who sponsored me in my first Season. When I found myself in the fortunate position of choosing among several acceptable suitors, she recommended Lord Mandeville. I have always considered myself under the greatest obligation to her ladyship."

Lady Northwick gave a little sigh. Then, like the tide drawn to the moon, she left her place beside her mother-in-law and went to Olivia.

"I do not wish to distress Lord Hargate's family or place yours in an awkward position regarding them," Bathsheba said in a low voice to the older lady. "If not for Lord Northwick's fears for Olivia's health, we should have been gone from here yesterday."

"Where do you mean to go?" said Lady Mandeville.

"The Continent." It was harder than Bathsheba would have thought to keep her voice steady.

"Heavens, I can hear your stomach growling, Miss Wingate," said Lady Northwick. "Mama-in-law, we must not keep them from their breakfast."

"Oh, I am in no hurry," Olivia said, so softly and diffidently. "A maid brought me chocolate before. On a silver tray. With a flower. It was beautiful."

"What a sweet child," said Lady Northwick, lightly stroking Olivia's hair.

"No, she is not," Bathsheba said. "Pray do not be taken in."

"Mama!" The blue eyes flashed indignantly.

"We are not staying here, Olivia," Bathsheba said. "You may bat your eyes all you like and pretend to be shy and sweet and innocent, but you are wasting your talents. We are leaving directly."

Lady Northwick stared at Olivia, then at Bathsheba.

"That is a Dreadful DeLucey," Bathsheba said. "Now you will know, if you ever encounter another one. You may stop admiring yourself in the glass, Olivia. It is time for your exit scene."

"It is not yet time," said Lady Mandeville. "You and Olivia will join us for breakfast. I want Mandeville to make her acquaintance."

"IT IS DREADFUL," Bathsheba whispered to Benedict. "I cannot possibly control her at this distance. She ignores every look I send her. Oh, it is too much. She is giving him that wide-eyed gaze, as though he were the sun and the moon and the stars."

Benedict gazed down the length of the table at Olivia, who sat to Lord Mandeville's right, apparently hanging on his every word. "That is how you have looked at me," Benedict murmured. "I thought you meant it."

"Of course I did not mean it," she said. "I only wanted to wrap you about my finger. I find you merely tolerable. Can you make out what she is saying?"

Perhaps because it was more than a family gathering, they breakfasted in state, in the dining room rather than the morning room. Still, Benedict was as surprised as Bathsheba when the countess placed Olivia at Lord Mandeville's right hand and Lady Northwick on his left, and directed Benedict and Bathsheba to sit next to each other at the hostess's end of the table.

Their hostess, however, was conversing with Peregrine at present. He, too, was watching Olivia, though he was making his best effort at polite behavior. For once, Peter DeLucey, seated beside Bathsheba, was not staring in that aggravatingly dazed way at her. He was gazing raptly at Olivia.

Even Lord Northwick showed signs of succumbing.

Now at last Benedict saw what the trouble was, and why Bathsheba feared her daughter would go straight to the devil. Olivia was not merely clever and cunning. She had a strong personal magnetism. The combination was exceedingly dangerous.

But she was not his problem, Benedict told himself.

"All I can discern is that she is taking care to speak softly and shyly," he said. "It is useless to try to read her lips, because she ducks her head, so that the gentlemen must bend their heads very close to hear her."

He dared to bend his head toward Bathsheba. He gazed at her silken skin and remembered its scent. He could not draw near enough to drink it in, as he longed to do. He could only watch the pink wash over her cheekbones. He could only stare at the black curl that had hooked itself over the top of her ear.

"You must not look at me in that besotted manner," she said in an undertone. "You are making a spectacle of yourself, Rathbourne."

"I don't care," he said. "Everyone here knows I am besotted."

She met his gaze, then turned quickly away, and returned to pushing the food about on her plate. "No one knows any such thing," she said. "If you would only maintain your dignity, everyone will assume I was merely a passing fancy."

"I shall be maintaining my dignity for the rest of my life," he said tightly. "I think I am entitled to look foolish this once."

"But of course it is nonsense!" Lord Mandeville said, loud enough to bring the other conversations to a halt. "What fanciful creatures you females are."

Benedict looked that way in time to catch the spark in Olivia's eyes.

"Papa said there was a treasure," she said. "Papa would never lie to me."

"Olivia," Bathsheba said warningly.

"It isn't nonsense." Olivia narrowed her eyes at her host. "You may *not* call my father a liar. He was a *gentleman*."

Peregrine looked at her. "Any moment now," he muttered. "Off she'll go, like a rocket."

"We are all aware that your father was a gentleman, Olivia," Benedict said in his most excessively bored voice. "I should have thought that an educated girl of twelve could discern the difference between a lie and a theory or supposition. If this distinction eludes you, Lord Lisle will be happy to explain it to you after breakfast. For the present, let us turn your attention to the basic rules of proper conduct. Since I have no doubt your father and mother took pains to teach you these rules, I can only suppose that you have suffered a momentary lapse of memory. You may wish to leave the room until you recover it."

The blue eyes flashed at him. He gave her a bored glance and returned to his breakfast.

She looked at her mother, but Bathsheba was looking at him . . . as though he were the sun and the moon and the stars.

Olivia excused herself and marched out of the dining room, chin aloft.

There was a silence.

Footsteps broke it, from the hall beyond. Benedict heard the confident click of boot heels on marble.

The footsteps paused, and Benedict heard a very low rumble, then Olivia's indignant soprano in answer: "Lord Rathbourne sent me out of the room to remember my manners."

More rumbling.

The footsteps recommenced.

The butler entered.

Benedict braced himself.

"Lord Hargate," said Keble, and Benedict's father strode into the room.

AFTER A BREAKFAST that Benedict gave up pretending to eat, Lord Hargate spoke privately with Lord Mandeville in the latter's study.

Two full hours later, Benedict was summoned there.

He found Bathsheba in the hall outside, pacing. She stopped short when she saw him.

His heart stopped short, too, before recommencing unsteadily. "I thought you had gone," he said. "I ordered a carriage. There is no need for you to endure this . . . annoyance."

"I am not a coward," she said. "I am not afraid of your father."

"You *ought* to be," he said. "Most sentient beings are."

"I refuse to run away and leave you to bear all the blame," she said.

"It is not as though I am going to be hanged," he said. "He won't even beat me. He never beat us. His tongue was much more effective. Oh, and his gaze. One look was worth a thousand blows. But I am no longer a boy. I shall emerge from the interview reeling rather than utterly crushed."

"I will not let him make you unhappy," she said.

"I am not a damsel in distress," he said. "I do not need you to slay dragons for me, you addled creature. Now I understand where Olivia gets her mad ideas."

"I want you to go away," she said. "Go for a ride or a walk. Leave this to me."

"Think again," he said. "I can guess what you have in mind. You imagine you can try some of your DeLucey tricks and lures upon him, and wrap him about your finger

and have him eating out of the palm of your hand. You have
no idea what sort of man you are dealing with."

"I don't care what sort of man he is," she said. "You are
not going in there alone."

"Bathsheba."

She knocked once on the study door, opened it, and
swept in, closing the door behind her.

He heard the key turn in the lock.

"Bathsheba," he said. He raised his fist to pound on the
door, then paused.

Scenes belong on the stage.

He turned away and walked quickly down the hall.

LORD HARGATE ROSE when she entered, his expression
polite. It was the same courteously blank look he'd
accorded her at breakfast. He did not so much as lift an
eyebrow at her bursting in on him or locking the door.

She understood where Rathbourne got his inscrutabil-
ity. And his height and bearing.

But Lord Hargate's hair was brown threaded with silver,
not black, and his eyes were a dark amber and as empty of
expression as if they had been made of a mineral.

The earl gestured to a chair.

"I prefer to stand, my lord," she said. "What I have to
say will take little time. I only wished to make it clear that
what has happened is not Lord Rathbourne's doing. I deliberately put myself in your son's way. I did everything
possible to enslave him."

His lordship said nothing. His face told her nothing. A
mask would have had more expression.

"Rathbourne hadn't a prayer," she said. "I left him no
avenue of escape."

"Indeed," said Lord Hargate. "You engineered the children's disappearance, then?"

The question took her aback. She had rehearsed her
speech. She'd had plenty of time. This element had not occurred to her, however. She had been too agitated to think
beyond a few simple points—the obvious ones. She had
only to appear to be what everyone believed she was.

She decided against saying yes. That was too far-fetched, even for a Dreadful DeLucey.

"No, but I used their disappearance to further my plans," she said.

"And these were . . . ?"

"I wanted a wealthy lover."

"A great many men qualify for that position," said his lordship. "Why Benedict?"

"Because he was perfect, which made him a challenge," she said. "The Dreadful DeLuceys prefer to play for high stakes."

"So I have heard," said Lord Hargate. "From what I have observed, you have won. This being the case, I am vastly puzzled at your undoing your work by admitting it to me."

"I should think the answer would be obvious," she said. "I am bored with him. So much perfection is tiresome. I want to go away, but I am afraid he will follow me and make a nuisance of himself."

A loud thump nearby made her start.

Lord Hargate calmly turned to regard the window. A large dark shape filled it. Then the window opened, and Rathbourne climbed through. He closed the window behind him, brushed off a few leaves, and turned to face his father.

"I beg your pardon, sir," he said. "Something seemed to be wrong with the study door. It wouldn't open."

"Mrs. Wingate locked it," said Lord Hargate. "She wished to tell me that she has used you for her own purposes, but now she is bored with your perfection and wishes to go away. She is concerned that you will follow her and make a nuisance of yourself."

"I think Mrs. Wingate must have fallen and hit her head," Rathbourne said. "Not ten minutes ago I was urging her to leave. I even ordered a carriage for her. She will not go. Talk of nuisances."

"I came to your father for money," she said.

Rathbourne looked at her. "Bathsheba," he said.

"I want fifty pounds to go away," she said.

This time Lord Hargate's eyebrows did go up. "Only

fifty?" he said. "It's usually a good deal more than that. Are you sure you didn't mean five hundred?"

"I would mean five hundred if I supposed you carried that much about with you," she said. "The trouble is, I cannot wait for you to get more. Olivia is getting Ideas." About servants and silk gowns and slippers and thick featherbeds and two dozen different dishes laid out merely for breakfast.

"No, Olivia is getting a spade," said Lord Hargate. "Lord Mandeville is taking her and Lisle to the mausoleum to dig for treasure."

"Oh, no." Bathsheba turned to Rathbourne. "What is wrong with him? Could he not see what she is like?"

"She rose to her father's defense when she thought Mandeville had impugned his honor," said Lord Hargate. "Her reaction moved Mandeville deeply. I believe he means to intervene with Fosbury on her behalf."

"No!" she cried. "Rathbourne, you must not let them. The Wingates will take her from me, and she is all I h-have." Her voice broke then, and she did, too. All the anxiety and heartache she'd suppressed welled up and overcame her, and the tears she'd held back for so long spilled down her cheeks.

Rathbourne came to her and put his arms around her. "They will not take her away, and she is not all you have," he said. "You have me."

"D-don't be so th-thick," she said. "I d-don't want you." She pushed him away and hastily wiped her eyes. "I want f-fifty pounds. And my daughter. And then I will go away."

"I regret that is not possible," said Lord Hargate.

"Very well. Twenty pounds."

"Twenty quid?" Rathbourne said. "That is all I am worth to you?"

"Your grandmother insisted that it would be a great deal more," said Lord Hargate. "I am comforted to learn she was wrong in that at least."

"Grandmother knows what's happened?" Rathbourne said. "Oh, but why do I ask? Of course she does."

"Who do you think it was who told me of your mad escapades upon the Bath Road?" said his father. "She had a letter from one of her spies in Colnbrook. Naturally I did not believe any of it. For some reason, your mother did. We had a wager. Perhaps you can imagine my feelings, to discover it was all true. Perhaps you can imagine my feelings, upon learning from that busybody Pardew, of all people, that my eldest son was brawling—on the public highway!—with a lot of drunken clodhoppers in the middle of the night. It is the sort of thing one expects of Rupert, naturally—but not one's eldest son . . . who has always stood as a shining example to his peers as well as his brothers. Of all of them, I had thought that you at least knew where your duty lay, Benedict."

"He knew it until he became besotted with me, and lost all powers of reason," Bathsheba said.

The cool amber gaze returned to her. "Then I agree it would be well if you were on your way, madam. However, Mandeville and I have decided that, to prevent any future unfortunate episodes, it were best for your daughter to discover for herself the truth about Edmund DeLucey's treasure. Mandeville prefers that you do not take her away until she and Lisle have done excavating. I cannot in good conscience pay you any sum until then. The structure is large. I doubt they will finish before tomorrow."

Chapter 19

OLIVIA AND LISLE RETURNED, DIRTY, WEARY, and dispirited, at nightfall. Even a bath with perfumed soap and two maids in attendance did not cheer Olivia. She picked at the meal the liveried servants carried up on a silver tray, complete with a golden chrysanthemum blossom in a silver vase.

She not only climbed into bed without being told a dozen times, but did so two hours earlier than usual, saying she was tired.

"It is very good of you, Mama, not to say 'I told you so,'" she said as Bathsheba tucked her in. "But it is true. You told me so. Lord Lisle told me so, too."

"Adults might be told that such and such a thing cannot exist, or such and such a wish is hopeless, yet they will persist in believing or wishing," Bathsheba said.

"Still, I wish I had thought it through more carefully," Olivia said. "I wish I had not caused you so much trouble. It wasn't what I meant to do. I thought I would find a treasure and make you a fine lady." She smiled ruefully. "And me, too, of course. Well, I shall have to find another way."

"There is another way," said Bathsheba. She told Olivia

about Lord Mandeville's wish to present her to her paternal grandfather, Lord Fosbury. "Lord Mandeville can smooth the way, and you might grow up as a fine lady," she concluded.

"But that is no good if they will not take you as well, Mama."

"Indeed, it is." Bathsheba ruthlessly described the advantages. In detail.

"No, it is not the right idea," Olivia said. "That is never the way I pictured it. I promised Papa I would look after you. My idea didn't work and your idea won't do." She patted Bathsheba's hand. "We'll go away tomorrow, Mama, and seek our fortune elsewhere."

HE ALREADY LOOKED like an idiot. Why not wander out into the garden after the household was abed? Why not linger outside her window?

And then, why not throw pebbles at it?

Scenes are for the stage.

And rules were all very well, to a point.

Benedict stood looking up at the window.

Yes, of course it was ridiculous. He'd see her tomorrow, before she left for good. But others would be by.

He only wanted to see her once and speak to her once while no one else was looking on or listening.

He would not sing melancholy airs. He would not recite poetry.

He would not see her, either, it seemed, for the minutes crept past, and she did not appear.

He had better not try again. He might wake Olivia as well—and she would probably throw the pebbles back at him. And maybe a chair as well.

That was understandable. There had been times when he had wanted to throw things at his father. Children needed discipline. It was their elders' duty to administer it—and be hated for it.

Certainly Benedict had wanted to throw something at his father today. What Lord Hargate had said of Benedict's behavior while Mrs. Wingate was present was nothing to what he'd said later, out of doors, in the garden, where no one could eavesdrop or intervene.

From the highest standing, as one of the aristocracy's most respected members, you have sunk to a mere laughingstock.

That was only the beginning and the mildest part of the speech.

The window opened. A dark head, crowned with a scrap of white nightcap, emerged.

"Bathsheba," he whispered.

She put her index finger to her lip. Then she took it away and pointed within the room.

She did not want to wake Olivia. Neither did he.

"I only wanted to say . . ." he began softly.

She shook her head and held up the finger, signaling him to wait.

He waited.

Minutes slid away.

He was watching the window, and nearly jumped out of his skin when he caught the flash of white to his left. She hurried toward him, grabbed his arm, and drew him away from the house into one of the formal gardens.

He pulled her into his arms and kissed her, deeply and desperately. She answered with the same wild desperation. But then she pulled away.

"I did not come for *that*," she said. "Only to say good-bye. And it is truly good-bye this time. I wish it were not, Rathbourne. I wish so much. But you know that. You ever were able to see through me."

"I knew it," he said. "I knew I was worth more to you than twenty quid."

"Oh, my dear, a great deal more." She laid her hand upon his cheek, in that way she had. "I was awake, trying to write you a letter, because I could not bear to go away without telling you the truth. It does no good, I know, but I have felt so sure that you care for me, too, and I could not bear to leave you coldly or hurt you in any way, even if it were the smallest hurt."

"A small hurt," he said. "That is like saying the guillotine blade nicks a bit. I shall be wretched, and you know it, and worse, we shall be martyrs, which is nauseating. I detest being noble and self-sacrificing. I have done enough of that this day, for I listened to my father and never once gave in to the urge to throttle him."

"Oh, was it very bad?" she said. She drew her hand away, but laid her cheek against his coat, which was better. He could hold her close then, and let his hand stroke down over her hair. "I guessed he would hold back while I was present."

"My brothers have given the gossips' tongues reason to wag from time to time, but they never give anyone cause to ridicule or *pity* them, he told me."

"Oh, no."

"My behavior has sunk to the level of the king and his brothers," Benedict went on. "It is impossible, as you know, to sink lower than this. They are dissipated to the grossest extent, obscenely expensive, and far from intellectually astute. At best they are tolerated. At worst they are hated and despised."

One royal duke's mistress had sold military commissions and promotions. Another of the king's brothers had ten children by his actress mistress, whom he could not support, leaving her to continue her stage career or starve, along with their brood. Yet another royal duke was the most hated officer in the army, and another a violent reactionary. But these and their other doings were trifles compared to the grand melodrama of King George IV's life.

"According to my father, my only hope is the king," Benedict went on. "If he commits another of his outrages, that might draw attention away from me—though we cannot be sure it will be enough to undo the damage. In one act, you see, in a few days, I have undermined all the good work I have done in the last decade and more."

"That is not true," she said, lifting her head to look at him. "No one who knows you can lose respect for you over such a small thing—because you were foolish about a woman, even the most notorious woman in England? He is wrong. I wish I had been there, for I would have told him so. He sadly underestimates you. Only very narrow-minded and stupid people would let one minor episode of your life taint their view of you and all you have done. Admittedly, there are a great many of this sort of people in the world. But you should want nothing to do with them."

The interview with his father had left Benedict chilled. He hadn't realized how much until now, until her words warmed him, driving out guilt and shame.

She had warmed him from the start. He hadn't realized how cold he was until he felt her warmth. He hadn't realized how empty he was until she'd taken hold of his heart and filled it.

He smiled down at her, at her ferocious loyalty.

He remembered Olivia fearlessly defending her dead father's honor at breakfast.

The girl was not altogether a Dreadful DeLucey. Something of her mother and something of her father lived inside her, and only needed to be nourished.

Benedict could have nourished it . . . but he must not think of that. Not now. He'd have the rest of his life to dwell on might-have-beens.

Gad. The rest of his life.

Years. Decades. His family was horribly long-lived.

The Dowager Countess of Hargate was fourscore and five. Her spouse, the previous earl, had lived into his seventies, and many of his siblings were still alive. Mama's family was equally tenacious of life. Her parents were in their eighties.

Benedict might live another *half century*!

Without Bathsheba.

"You're right," he said. "I want nothing to do with them. I want nothing to do with anybody who'd ridicule or pity me because I love you."

She went suddenly still. "You—"

"I love you," he said. "They may all go to blazes. If no one will take the trouble to see what you are really like, if they will drive you out of England, then I shall go with you."

SHE INSISTED HE would not go anywhere with her.

He insisted he would.

The three men who stood but a few feet away, behind
the garden wall, listened while the argument grew fiercer.
Then the debate abruptly stopped, and different sounds indicated that Rathbourne had changed his tactics.

Whether it worked or no was impossible to say. The
voices dropped to murmurs. Then came good-byes.

When at last the lovers had gone their separate ways,
Lord Mandeville said, "You had it right, Hargate. It is like
Jack Wingate all over again, only worse, far worse."

"You are more observant than I, my lord," said Lord
Northwick. "I had not realized matters had gone so far."

"He is my son," said Lord Hargate. "I ought to know
him, even when he is not himself. Certainly I know it is
time to put an end to this madness."

RATHBOURNE HAD PROMISED he would take a full
two weeks to reconsider, and Bathsheba had given her
word that she would keep him apprised of her whereabouts
in the meantime.

She was sure that once she was out of the way and he
had time to think coolly, he would change his mind about
abandoning his life, his family, all he'd achieved and hoped
to achieve, for a woman.

No matter what he did, the title and a great deal of property would be his eventually, unless Fate intervened and
his father outlived him. Still, he would break his parents'
hearts, and his brothers would never forgive him. He could
never hope for a happy homecoming. If he abandoned
his life here for a life with her, he could never hope to regain the position of honor and trust he'd held in the Great
World.

Unlike Jack, Rathbourne would come to regret what
he'd lost, for he'd a great deal more to lose. Unlike Jack,
Rathbourne would come to resent her for what she'd cost
him. He would end up bitterly unhappy and she would feel
like a murderess.

A fortnight would do the trick, she thought. It would
give him time to calm down and his family time to bring
him to his senses.

Meanwhile, there was breakfast to be got through.

Lord Mandeville had commanded their company at breakfast. Otherwise, Bathsheba would have happily breakfasted in her room. Or upon the road.

This time they all crowded about a round table in the morning room, a circumstance not conducive to private conversation.

Thus, when Olivia told Lord Mandeville that she and her mama were going to Egypt, the news reached everyone simultaneously.

"Egypt?" several voices, including Bathsheba's, repeated.

"The idea came to me when I woke this morning," Olivia said. "It occurred to me that if one was looking for treasure, one ought to go where one is likely to find it. A great many people are digging for treasure in Egypt. You told me so yourself, Lord Lisle. You said you were going to Egypt one day and look for treasure."

"*One day,*" he said. "That means the future. I can't go now." He paused, his expression considering. "Unless there was a school they could send me to. At any rate, *you* cannot go to Egypt. That is even more ridiculous than digging for pirate's treasure at Throgmorton."

Olivia's eyes flashed.

"You know nothing about the place," he plowed on. "It is not like England or even the Continent. Women are kept confined. The rule of law as we know it does not exist there. If you tried to travel about Egypt alone, you would be kidnapped instantly and sold into slavery."

"Even with a large party, travel in Egypt can be dangerous," said Lord Hargate. "Certainly, it can be difficult. Still, for those willing to brave the hardships, there are rewards, though not necessarily monetary. Signor Belzoni, for instance, has not profited as greatly as everyone supposes—as Rupert's bride makes a point of reminding me."

Bathsheba noticed that the earl had shadows under his eyes. His face was drawn. He must be weary. He had traveled all the day before yesterday. Last night he must have lain awake worrying about his eldest son. Later, she must find a moment to reassure him—though her compassion might stick in his craw.

"Signor Belzoni brought back such big things," Olivia said. "Giant statues and mummies and such. People can't make up their minds what they're worth. But I shall look for small things: jewels and coins. I know what those sorts of things are worth. I shall also collect papyri. Lord Lisle said there is a great demand for these documents, and Egypt has thousands and thousands of them."

"You have to take them from people who've been dead for a thousand years or more," said Lisle. "The mummies hold the papyri in their hands or have them between their legs. Uncle Rupert said the mummy dust clogs your nose and the smell is disgusting. You have to go into small holes in the ground and crawl about narrow tunnels. It's very hot. And you won't have a lot of servants about to bring you lemonade and sandwiches or to cart away the dirt. It isn't like digging up Lord Mandeville's lawn."

"We are not going to Egypt, Olivia," Bathsheba said. "I recommend you put that idea out of your head."

Olivia's countenance took on a familiar mulish expression as she opened her mouth to answer.

Rathbourne threw her a look.

Though she set her jaw, the contrary expression vanished, and "Yes, Mama," she said, to Bathsheba's astonishment.

"At any rate, I cannot understand why you prate about traveling halfway across the world," said Lord Mandeville. "You have not finished your excavation here."

Bathsheba's heart began to pound. He could have no reason for indulging Olivia except to delay her departure. He must have written to Fosbury, who could have the letter as early as today. He could be here in how many days? One? Two? Or was it simply a matter of hours?

Before her panicked mind could compose a polite refusal, Lisle spoke.

"We've dug a moat round the entire mausoleum," he said. "I don't see how we could have missed the treasure if it was there."

"Lord Lisle has a very orderly system," Olivia said. "I know we covered every inch of the ground."

"Perhaps not," said his lordship. "I have talked it over

with Northwick, and it occurred to us that you mightn't have dug deep enough."

"Recollect that Edmund DeLucey's pirate days were a hundred years ago," said Lord Northwick. "Over time, buildings settle and sink, gardens are redesigned and replanted. The ground about the mausoleum has been built up and filled in several times. One must remember, too, that the gardeners apply layers of lime and fertilizer at regular intervals."

"I should dig deeper if I were you," said Lord Mandeville. "Unless, that is, you have lost heart."

A dismayed Bathsheba saw her daughter's countenance light up. Lisle's expression was only a slightly muted version of Olivia's.

The children looked at each other, and it was clear that neither could wait to get at their spades and pickaxes.

But Olivia surprised her mother yet again.

"Thank you, my lord," the girl said, "but I must leave the treasure hunt to Lord Lisle. Mama and I depart today."

"It isn't my treasure hunt," Lisle said. "It's yours. Edmund DeLucey was *your* great-great-grandfather, not mine. I should feel like a great idiot, digging all by myself while everyone looked on. Besides, what fun would it be to find it if you're not there? This was *your* quest."

"It is more than a treasure hunt," said Lord Hargate. "It is a quest to put old ghosts to rest. Unless the matter is settled for good and all—unless every possible avenue is exhausted—Edmund DeLucey's descendants will continue to believe in the treasure. Then one or another of them will turn up to hunt for it. Then once again they will disrupt both the family and the workings of the estate. How many men have been taken from their regular work to chase after you pair?" he demanded, directing a frigid glare from one to the other. "Have you any notion of the burden you have placed upon the servants, not to mention the inconvenience to the family? The least you can do is complete the job you began and do it thoroughly."

"Yes, my lord," said Lisle.

"Yes, my lord," said Olivia.

And "Yes, my lord," Bathsheba had no choice but to

say, because he was absolutely right. One or another of the Dreadful DeLuceys would take courage from Olivia's daring act and try again.

The matter had to be ended once and for all.

And, as usual, she would simply have to make the best of it.

WHILE THE OTHER men went out with the children, Benedict stayed behind, saying he had letters to write.

He had meant only to write to his mother, to assure her he was well, but his mind wandered to his brothers, each of whom would be affected, though to different degrees, by his decision to go away with Bathsheba.

Then he thought about the report he had promised to write for one of the parliamentary committees, and the letter to a barrister regarding one of his clients, and the letters he needed to write seeking royal clemency in two troubling criminal cases.

He must find successors to head his various philanthropic endeavors, too.

He sat at a writing desk in the library, the pen in his hand, the paper before him still blank.

"Rathbourne, I must speak to you."

He turned at the sound of the familiar voice.

Bathsheba stood for a moment in the open French windows. A breeze from the garden wafted in.

He dropped his pen and rose. "I thought you meant to go with the treasure seekers," he said.

She closed the doors and came inside, and the room brightened several degrees.

"I ought to be there," she said. "There ought to be a witness from Edmund DeLucey's side. But they will find nothing today. Everyone knows that, except the children."

"I know what you are thinking," Benedict said. "I saw the panic in your eyes when Mandeville told them they hadn't dug deep enough."

"You know he will keep contriving excuses to delay our departure," she said. She began to pace the room, her hands tightly folded against her stomach. "Today, they must dig deeper. Tomorrow he will make a case for digging at the New Lodge. You know he is not concerned with laying ghosts to rest, whatever your father says. Mandeville wants to give my daughter to Jack's family. He thinks—everyone thinks it—that I am not a fit mother. He wishes—and who can blame him?—for Olivia to have every material advantage. And perhaps he wishes to make peace between the families before he dies."

"I told you I would not let anyone take Olivia from you," Benedict said. He crossed to her and took her tightly folded hands in his.

"By law a child belongs to her father, and thus to her father's family," she said.

"Fosbury will have to take it to the law, then, and be prepared to spend the next decade or more in expensive legal wrangling."

"You forget," she said tightly. "If you go away with me, you will not be able to afford expensive lawsuits. If you go away with me, you will have no influence over Lord Fosbury and any of his sympathizers. You will no longer have the king's ear."

He knew all this. He knew what he would lose.

But he was intelligent and capable, and he would soon make a new life for himself. A happy life, with a woman he loved and a child to whom he'd already become attached.

"Then I shall have to be clever and cunning instead," he said. "We shall simply have to take Olivia away in the dead of night." He drew Bathsheba into his arms. "Stop fretting. Have a little confidence in me. Try to remember I'm perfect."

She laughed then, and he felt the tension go out of her.

"The trouble is, I am not," she said. "I am not at all sure it is right to deprive her of— What is that noise?"

Birds, he thought at first. The shriek of angry crows.

Bathsheba went to the French doors and opened them. The sound came again.

Not birds.

A scream.

Bathsheba picked up her skirts and ran.

He raced after her.

* * *

"MAMA!"

"Coming!" Bathsheba cried. Rathbourne was ahead of her, his long legs carrying him farther, faster.

"Mama!"

Olivia burst out from a turning and ran toward her mother, arms outstretched. She was filthy, black from head to toe, but she was running, unhurt. A moment later, Lord Lisle appeared, equally dirty. "Sir!" he called. "Uncle!"

Bathsheba slowed and stopped. Rathbourne did, too.

"Mama," Olivia gasped. "We found it!"

Chapter 20

"IT" WAS A SMALL, DIRT-ENCRUSTED BOX ABOUT a foot in length, and perhaps nine inches in height and depth.

One of the outdoor servants who'd assisted in the excavation carried it to the terrace. There, family and guests gathered round to watch as another servant stepped forward to brush off the dirt. But Peregrine took the brush and cleaned the box himself. He worked steadily and as gently as if the thing were made of alabaster, though his hands shook with excitement.

In fact, the box proved to be made of wood and covered in brass-studded leather.

It also proved to be securely locked.

"We'll have to saw it off," Peregrine said. "Or pry it open. It's quite old. The wood is probably rotted. One good kick ought to break it open."

"Wait." Olivia knelt to study the lock. "An ordinary key might work," she said. "Or I could use hairpins. Locks are not usually very complicated."

Benedict edged closer to Bathsheba. "She can pick locks, too?" he whispered.

"Why do you think I wanted to move to a better neighborhood?" Bathsheba said. "She has learnt a great deal too much."

Olivia was trying her hairpins, without much success.

"Try this," said Lord Hargate. He handed the girl his penknife.

She eyed it warily. "I might spoil the blade."

"It can be sharpened."

Benedict met his father's amber gaze.

And blinked.

That could not be a twinkle he saw there.

Lord Hargate never *twinkled*.

The girl fiddled with the penknife, then tried the penknife together with a hairpin.

The lock sprang open.

She took a deep breath, then lifted the lid of the trunk, revealing . . .

Rags. She took out one, and carefully set it down, then another.

"Old clothes," Peregrine said. "Oh, that is so provoking. Why on earth—" He sucked in his breath.

So did everyone else.

Something glittered among the remaining rags.

Still, with the same cautious deliberation, Olivia removed the last of the rotted covering.

Red and yellow and green and blue, silver and gold burst into view. Coins and jewels, chains and medals glittered in the afternoon light.

"Well, well," said Lord Mandeville gruffly. "Did I not tell you not to lose heart?"

Peregrine peered inside the box. "I can't believe it. Is it real?"

Olivia took out a ruby ring and examined it with a practiced eye. She scratched the metal with her fingernail. She bit it. "It's real," she said.

She looked up at her mother, blue eyes shining. "It's real, Mama. The treasure. I knew I would find it. You'll be a grand lady now." Her brilliant blue gaze shifted to Lord Mandeville. "It *is* Mama's, as you said? You must tell her so, or else she will make me give it to you."

"Then let me say it before all these witnesses," said Lord Mandeville. "You, Olivia Wingate, are the descendant of Edmund DeLucey. You and your trusty—er—squire—have taken great risks and endured great hardship. You have even performed mighty labor, digging with your own hands. You have found it. The treasure rightfully belongs to you, to dispose of as you choose."

Benedict looked about him. Lord and Lady Mandeville. Lord and Lady Northwick. Lord Hargate. Peter DeLucey. Bathsheba. The children. Several servants stood near at hand. Others were clustered in the windows of the house, looking down on the scene.

Scenes belong on the stage.

He looked at his father again. Lord Hargate still watched Olivia but now wore an expression Benedict knew all too well.

It was subtle. Lord Hargate was never obvious. But Benedict knew his father well—better than most did—and he clearly discerned it.

This was the same expression his lordship had worn on Alistair's wedding day.

This was the same expression he'd worn when Rupert brought his bride home from Egypt.

Triumph.

Both times, Benedict had fully understood. Against all odds, and to the earl's vast relief, his wayward younger sons had wed perfectly suitable girls of more than suitable wealth.

But this time, for the first time, Benedict was not at all certain what his father was looking so smug about.

WHILE OLIVIA WAS having several inches of dirt scrubbed off, Bathsheba sought out Lord Hargate, to tell him she would not need the twenty pounds after all, and to quiet his mind regarding his eldest son.

The servants directed her to the gothic ruin on the eastern edge of the lake. The ruin had been built in the last century to create a melancholy aspect, conducive to contemplation and poetry.

Though Bathsheba doubted Lord Hargate was the sort of man who had poetic thoughts, she supposed he had plenty to be melancholy about.

She found him frowning up at a crumbling turret. He was not so preoccupied, though, as to fail to hear her approach.

He turned and nodded. "Mrs. Wingate," he said, showing no sign of surprise. But then, he was good at showing no sign of anything. "I collect you've come to tell me that you have freed my son from your toils and we shall soon be shed of you at last."

She paused and blinked. "Yes, actually." She explained about the fortnight's cooling-off period she'd given Rathbourne.

Lord Hargate showed no reaction to this, either.

"Surely, in two weeks' time, you and other family members can make him see his error," she said.

"I think not," he said.

"Of course you can," she said. "He has a strong attachment to his family. And no matter what he says, I know his parliamentary work and his philanthropic schemes give him great satisfaction. He would miss them sorely. He is a good man, Lord Hargate. He is not idle and dissipated as so many of his fellows are. He will do a great deal of good in England. He has a noble career ahead of him. He knows this. He only needs to be reminded—while I am out of the way. I had counted on you to manage this, sir. Everyone says you are one of the most powerful men in England. Surely a fortnight is enough time for you to work your will upon your son?"

"I doubt it," said Lord Hargate. "But here he comes, and we shall see how much power I have."

Bathsheba whipped round. Rathbourne was striding rapidly up the path. He was hatless, and the October wind flung the dark curls this way and that. As he drew nearer she saw that his neckcloth was crooked and one of his coat buttons was not buttoned.

"You did not imagine he would not guess your next move, I hope," said Lord Hargate. "Benedict is an experienced politician. Furthermore, he has always taken an unhealthy interest in criminal behavior."

"Has she come to give me up again, Father?" Rathbourne said. "Bathsheba is always giving me up and saying good-bye. It is her way of expressing affection, you see. That and stealing my purse and clothes."

"I only wanted to set your father's mind at rest," Bathsheba said. "It is obvious he did not sleep a wink last night."

"That is because he was up all night plotting with his fellow conspirators," said Rathbourne.

"Plotting?" she said.

"My dear girl, you come of a long line of liars and cheats," said Rathbourne. "Surely you can recognize a swindle when you see one."

SHE HAD NO idea, obviously.

Her gaze went from Benedict to his father.

As though Lord Hargate's countenance would ever reveal his thoughts, Benedict thought. She might as well look for enlightenment in the ruins behind them. She might as well try to read a brick.

"I know it was all a sham, that scene a little while ago on the terrace," Benedict said, careful to keep his voice level, though he was baffled and angry. "What I could not make up my mind about was *why*. Did you and Mandeville and Northwick go to all that trouble merely to be rid of Bathsheba as quickly as possible? I should think you understood that wasn't necessary. She is determined to set me free, as she sees it."

"I believe my understanding remains in reasonable working order," said his father. He folded his hands behind his back and walked toward the lake and looked out across it.

Bathsheba threw Benedict a puzzled glance. He shrugged. After a moment, they joined his father at the lake's edge.

There was a long silence.

Benedict determinedly waited it out. His father was a master of manipulation. It was no use trying to wrest control from him.

Birds sang. The wind swirled through a pile of leaves, shuffling and scattering them.

Having drawn out the moment for as long as possible, Lord Hargate finally spoke. "You were mistaken, Mrs. Wingate," he said. "I came to Throgmorton carrying a great deal of money as well as several pieces of jewelry my wife and mother contributed. We were prepared to bribe you handsomely to go away forever. I was prepared to do so yesterday, when you came to the study, even though by then I had realized that matters had grown more serious than we had supposed."

"By then you saw that she was not what you had supposed, either," Benedict said.

"There was that," his father admitted. "I have never in my life had so much trouble keeping a straight face as when Mrs. Wingate offered to give you up for twenty pounds. I cannot wait to tell your grandmother." He smiled a little.

But the smile vanished as quickly as it had come, and he went on, "I have always wished I had daughters, Mrs. Wingate, because my sons are an endless source of trouble."

Not I, Benedict wanted to shout, childishly. *Why do you always blame me?*

"You always say that," he said. "It does not strike me as at all reasonable. I have not given you trouble since I was a boy." Then he recalled an incident at Oxford. And another. "Well, not since I came of age, at any rate."

"My sons are an endless source of trouble, of one kind or another, Mrs. Wingate," his obstinate father repeated. "My eldest has been unhappy for a very long time."

Had Lord Hargate said that his eldest son was a traveler from the moon, Benedict would have been less surprised.

Surprise was a completely inadequate word for what he felt. The world had turned upside down.

He blinked. Twice.

His father's deep amber gaze met his. "You used to be filled with devilment," Lord Hargate said. "You used to lead your brothers into every sort of scrape. You used to laugh. I have not heard you laugh in years."

"But of course I laugh," Benedict said. "This is absurd."

"He laughs," Bathsheba said. "I have seen and heard

him do it. A few nights ago, I thought he would do himself an injury."

"You make him laugh," Lord Hargate said to her. "I came here and saw the devil in his eyes. I saw happiness there, too. I know my eldest is no fool. He has never been as susceptible to women as some of his brothers. He is acutely observant. He would recognize an opportunist, I told myself. He would recognize a parasite. Even so, I was uneasy. Even the wisest men can make fatal errors regarding women. But then you came to me with that diverting story about being bored with him and wanting twenty pounds to go away. Then he came in through the window. And then it was quite plain that the pair of you were in love to a perfectly ridiculous degree. I am sorry my wife missed that scene. She would have found it highly gratifying. At any rate, I described it as best my limited powers would allow in the letter I wrote shortly thereafter."

Gratifying.

Benedict hadn't realized how tense he had been until now, when he dared to breathe freely. He hadn't realized how great a weight lay on his shoulders until now, when it finally began to lift.

"Father . . ." he began, his throat tight.

"But leave it to one of my sons to make matters as difficult as possible," his father interrupted. "It was too much to hope you'd choose one of the perfectly suitable girls we have been putting in your way this age."

Bathsheba looked at Benedict. "You never told me they were matchmaking."

"He didn't notice!" said his father before Benedict could answer. "He didn't notice handsome young misses of unexceptional family. He didn't notice beautiful heiresses. We tried bluestockings. We tried country girls. We tried everything. He didn't notice! But Bathsheba Wingate, the most notorious woman in all of England, he noticed."

"We notorious women tend to stand out," she said.

"Perhaps it is his unhealthy interest in the criminal classes," said Lord Hargate. "At any rate, he chose you, and you make him happy. You—of all the women in all the world, the one woman who could never, under any circumstances, be accepted in Society."

"I do not blame you for feeling . . . vexed, Father," Benedict said, "but—"

"It would *never* happen," his father cut in. "It is quite impossible."

"In that case . . ." Benedict began.

"Which makes it a pretty challenge," his father went on. "But if I could get Rupert properly wed, I can do anything. In any case, we have had a piece of luck: Mandeville is eager for our families to become connected."

"He can't mean through me," Bathsheba said. "He would never acknowledge me as a member of his family. He *loathes* me."

"The prospect of becoming connected to the Carsingtons has effected a change of heart," said Lord Hargate. "Perhaps he relishes the idea of thumbing his nose at Lord Fosbury. I cannot be sure. All I know is that he eagerly joined in our conspiracy to make you respectable."

"I told you it was a plot," Benedict said.

Light dawned in her blue eyes. "Olivia's treasure," she said.

"There is nothing like a thumping great fortune to make a girl respectable," Benedict said.

"The treasure," she said. "It isn't Edmund DeLucey's."

"Technically, it is DeLucey treasure, for the most part," said his father. "Mandeville had a number of old coins bearing King George II's likeness, which I bought from him. We knew those too-clever children would instantly recognize modern coins. He and Northwick contributed other items from the family collection, and I put in the jewelry my wife and mother had donated. In all, it does not amount to a great deal. But it looks like treasure, and nearly all the servants saw the chest being opened."

"I should have guessed," Bathsheba said. She closed her eyes. "I can see it now. Sunlight flashing on coins and jewels. A crowd gathered about the children. I did not look up, but I don't doubt the servants were glued to the windows." She opened her eyes. "The servants."

"Servants will talk," Benedict said, "as you pointed out to me some days ago."

"More important, they will embroider and exaggerate," said Lord Hargate. "By the time word reaches London, Edmund DeLucey's treasure chest will be overflowing with rubies, sapphires, emeralds, and diamonds. People will say that Mrs. Wingate is worth twenty or fifty or one hundred thousand pounds. And that, as everyone knows, changes everything."

BENEDICT'S FATHER LEFT soon thereafter, to continue his perambulation round the lake. He would be composing letters to his other relatives, Benedict knew.

"Well," he said once the lump in his throat subsided, "I am very glad I did not throttle him, after all."

"I can hardly believe it," Bathsheba said. "When I woke up this morning I was notorious. Now I am respectable. All it wanted was a fortune—just as Olivia believed. It did not even have to be a real fortune."

He took her hand. "You will have to marry me now," he said. "And we shall have to live in England. No running away to the Continent and living like gypsies. No dismal set of rooms in the shabby part of town. No outrunning the bailiffs. It will be fearfully dull for you."

She scowled at him. "That is the most uninspiring proposal I have ever heard of. And you an experienced politician. You can do better than that, Rathbourne."

He laughed and scooped her up in his arms. "Is that better?"

"It is a slight improvement," she said.

"I am taking you to the New Lodge," he said. "There I shall make passionate love to you, repeatedly, until you say 'Yes, Benedict, I shall marry you.'"

"And if I do not?"

"You will," he said.

She did.

Epilogue

THE LETTER, WRITTEN THREE MONTHS EAR-
lier, reached Peregrine in June 1822.

My Lord,
  *Thank you for your letter, which was vastly interesting,
and for the little Egyptian Man, whom I am happy to report
arrived safely and not all in pieces as you had Feared. It
was most kind of you to think of me. I am truly happy—and
Mama is truly happy, which is most important—and yet I
should have so liked to go to Egypt with you and Uncle Rupert and Aunt Daphne. I still do not understand why Lord
Rathbourne and Mama were so adamant about SEPARAT-
ING US. It is not as though anything Terrible happened on
our Quest to Bristol. We did not commit any Crimes—no
Capital Offenses, at any rate. In fact, we performed a <u>No-
ble Deed</u>, in bringing Mama and your Uncle together.*
  *Still, I am sure you are the one who deserved the Treat,
and you will make better use of it than I. Aunt Daphne was
very clever to think of it—and in the nick of time, too, because I did believe your father and Lord Rathbourne were*

on the brink of EXCHANGING BLOWS. This would have been Exciting. The trouble is, there would have been a good deal of <u>screaming</u> by the Women, and as Mama told me later, it was not good for your Mama to become so Overset in her Condition.

You have got a Brother, by the way. He came five days ago. He is very red and wrinkled and he looks like a Monkey, but Miss Velkel said that is how Babies look when they are New. I think it must be on account of their being squashed in ladies' corsets. I know it is shocking of your parents, at their age, but one must look on the Bright Side. The more other children, the less notice they will take of us. Yes, I include myself, as I suspect Mama is in a Condition now.

But as to Egypt—I pretend, as Aunt Daphne told your parents, that you are merely away at School, except that this time, you have found the perfect school in the perfect place, and they can be sure that this time you will not get chucked out of it. (I know Uncle Rupert was only joking about Throwing You To The Crocodiles.) You shall travel up the Nile and discover Great Wonders in between your lessons with Aunt Daphne.

Meanwhile I take my lessons with Miss Velkel. She is German and very strict. But I have resolved to learn, because I am Lord Rathbourne's stepdaughter, and it is essential that I <u>Learn to Comport Myself In a Manner Befitting My Station.</u> It is not all Dull Propriety, though. Once a week I visit the DOWAGER LADY HARGATE, and we play whist with some of her friends. They know all the best Gossip and they never miss a Trick. I have learnt a great deal from them. At the moment, their main topic is Uncle Darius and WHAT IS TO BE DONE ABOUT HIM. I don't know what needs doing, as I have seen very little of him. I think of him as the Elusive Uncle, for he's never about. But then, he is a Bachelor, and they lead unsettled lives.

I look forward to the day when I become a Bachelor. I should like to live an unsettled life. I have thought about the future a great deal, and have several Ideas.

*But here comes Mama to make me put out the candle.
Best of luck with your studies, and may you discover many
Great Marvels. I shall write again soon.*
    Yours Most Sincerely,
    Olivia Wingate-Carsington

Read on for a special preview of

CAPTIVES OF THE NIGHT
by Loretta Chase

Available in May 2006 from Berkley Sensation!

THE COMTE D'ESMOND WAS THE MOST BEAUTI-
ful man Leila had ever seen. In real life, that is. She'd en-
countered his like in paintings, but even Botticelli would
have wept to behold such a model.

Greetings were exchanged over her head, whose inter-
nal mechanisms had temporarily ceased functioning.

"Madame."

Francis' nudge brought her back to the moment. Leila
numbly offered her hand. "Monsieur."

The count bowed low over her hand. His lips just
brushed her knuckles.

His hair was pale, silken gold, a fraction longer than
fashion decreed.

He also held her hand rather longer than etiquette
decreed—long enough to draw her gaze to his and rivet all
her consciousness there.

His eyes were deep sapphire blue, burningly intense. He
released her hand, but not her gaze. "This is the greatest of
honors, Madame Beaumont. I saw your work in Russia—a
portrait of the Princess Lieven's cousin. I tried to purchase
it, but the owner knew what he had, and would not sell.

'You must go to Paris,' he told me, 'and get one of your own.' And so I have come."

"From Russia?" Leila resisted the urge to press her hand to her pounding heart. Good grief. He'd come all the way from Russia—this man who probably couldn't cross a street in St. Petersburg without having to fight off a hundred desperate painters. Artists would sell their firstborn for a chance to paint this face. "Not merely for a portrait, surely."

His sensuous mouth eased into a lazy smile. "Ah, well, I had some business in Paris. You must not think it is mere vanity which brings me. Yet it is only human nature to wish for permanence. One seeks out the artist as one might seek out the gods, and all to the same purpose: immortality."

"How true," said Francis. "At this very moment, we are all slowly decaying. One moment, the mirror reflects a well-looking man in his prime. In the next, he's a mottled old toad."

Leila was aware of the faint antagonism in her husband's voice, but it was the count who held her attention. She saw something flash in his fiercely blue eyes, and that brief glitter changed not only his face but the atmosphere of the room itself. For one queer instant the face of an angel became its opposite, his soft chuckle the Devil's own laughter.

"And in the next moment," Esmond said, releasing Leila's gaze to turn to Francis, "he's a banquet for worms."

He was still smiling, his eyes genuinely amused, the devilish expression utterly vanished. Yet the tension in the room increased another notch.

"Even portraits can't last forever," she said. "Since few materials are permanently stable, there's bound to be decay."

"There are paintings in Egyptian tombs, thousands of years old," he said. "But it hardly matters. We shall not have the opportunity to discover how many centuries your works endure. For us, it is the present that matters, and I hope, madame, you will find time in this so-fleeting present to accommodate me."

"I'm afraid you'll want some patience," Francis said as

he moved to the table bearing a tray of decanters. "Leila is just completing one commission, and she's engaged for two more."

"I am known for my patience," the count answered. "The tsar declared me the most patient man he'd ever met."

There was a clink of crystal striking crystal and a pause before Francis responded. "You travel in exalted circles, monsieur. An intimate of Tsar Nicholas, are you?"

"We spoke on occasion. That is not intimacy." The potent blue gaze settled again upon Leila. "My definition of intimacy is most precise and particular."

The room's temperature seemed to be climbing rapidly. Leila decided it was time to leave, whether her allotted ten minutes had passed or not. As the count accepted a wineglass from Francis, she rose. "I had better get back to work," she said.

"Certainly, my love," said Francis. "I'm sure the count understands."

"I understand, and yet I must regret the loss." This time Esmond's intent blue gaze swept her from head to toe.

Leila had endured far too many such surveys to mistake the meaning. For the first time, however, she felt that meaning in every muscle of her body. Worse, she felt the pull of attraction, dragging at her will.

But she reacted outwardly in the usual way, her countenance becoming more frigidly polite, her posture more arrogantly defiant. "Unfortunately, Madame Vraisses will regret even more the delay of her portrait," she said. "And she is one of the *least* patient women in the world."

"And you, I suspect, are another." He stepped closer, making her pulse race. He was taller and more powerfully built than she'd thought at first. "You have the eyes of a tigress, madame. Most unusual—and I do not mean the golden color alone. But you are an artist, and so you see more than others can."

"I do believe my wife sees plainly enough that you're flirting with her," said Francis, moving to her side.

"But of course. What other polite homage may a man pay another man's wife? You are not offended, I hope." The count treated Francis to an expression of limpid innocence.

"No one is in the least offended," Leila said briskly. "We may be English, but we have lived in Paris nearly nine years. Still, I am a working woman, monsieur—"

"Esmond," he corrected.

"Monsieur," she said firmly. "And so, I must excuse myself and return to work." She did not offer her hand this time. Instead, she swept him her haughtiest curtsey.

He answered with a graceful bow.

As she headed for the door a tightly smiling Francis hurried to open for her, Esmond's voice came from behind her. "Until next we meet, Madame Beaumont," he said softly.

Something echoed in the back of her mind, making her pause on the threshold. A memory. A voice. But no. If she'd met him before, she would have remembered. Such a man would be impossible to forget.

Continue reading for a special preview of

THE LION'S DAUGHTER
by Loretta Chase

Now available from Berkley Sensation!

FROM A DISTANCE, THE DURRËS HOUSE SEEMED a ramshackle heap of stones piled upon a ledge overlooking the Adriatic. It was smaller than their previous abodes, comprising but two tiny rooms: one to live in, one to store supplies in. To Esme Brentmor, it was a beautiful house. In all her peripatetic life, this was the first time she'd lived upon the sea.

The sea brought them fresh fish nearly all year round. A short distance from the ledge, Esme's garden thrived in surprisingly fertile soil. Even the chickens, in their own irritable way, were happy.

At the moment, Esme was not. She sat cross-legged upon the hard ledge, her eyes on her folded hands as she conversed with her very best friend, Donika, who was leaving the next day for Saranda, to be married.

"I shall never see you again," Esme said gloomily. "Jason says we must go to England soon."

"So Mama told me—but you'll not leave before my wedding, surely?" Donika asked in alarm.

"I fear so. He's made a promise to my English aunt, who is dying."

Donika sighed. "Then nothing can be done. A promise on a deathbed is sacred."

"Is it? *She* held nothing sacred." Esme hurled a stone into the water. "Twenty-four years ago she broke her betrothal vows to him. Why? Because one time he got drunk and made a foolish mistake—as any young man might. He played cards and lost a piece of land—that's all. But *she* told him he was weak and base, and she wouldn't marry him."

"That was not kind. She should have forgiven him one mistake. *I* would."

"She did not. But he's forgiven *her*. Twice this year he's gone to visit her. He tells me it was not her fault, but her parents' doing."

"A girl must obey her parents," said Donika. "She can't choose a husband for herself. Still, I don't think they should have made her break a sacred vow."

"It was worse than that," Esme said angrily. "Not a year after she drove my father away, she wed his brother. She was of a noble family, and wealthy, and you'd think Jason's family would have been appeased. They were quick enough to take *her* in, but my father they made an outcast forever."

"The English are very strange," Donika said thoughtfully.

"They're *unnatural*," Esme returned. "Shall I tell you what my English grandfather wrote when he received the news of my birth? The words are burned in my heart. 'It was not enough,' he said in his hateful letter, 'that you disgraced the Brentmor name with your reckless debauchery. It was not enough to gamble away your aunt's property and break your mother's heart. It was not enough to run away from your errors, instead of remaining, like a man, to make amends. No, you must compound our shame by joining the ranks of Turkish brigands, marrying one of these unspeakable barbarians, and infecting the world with yet another heathen savage.'"

Donika stared at her in horrified disbelief.

"In English, it sounds even worse," Esme grimly assured her. "This is the family my father wishes to take me to."

Donika placed a comforting arm about her friend's thin shoulders. "It's hard, I know," she said, "but you belong to your father's family—at least until you're wed. I'm sure your father will find you a husband in England. I've seen some Englishmen. Taller than the other Franks, and some quite handsome and strong."

"Ah, yes, and I'm sure their kin are just dying to welcome an ugly little barbarian into the family."

"You're *not* ugly. Your hair is thick and healthy, filled with fire." Donika smoothed the wavy dark red locks back from Esme's forehead. "And your eyes are pretty. My mama said so, too. Beautiful, like evergreens, she said. Also, your skin is smooth," she added, lightly touching Esme's cheek.

"I have no breasts," Esme said glumly. "And my legs and arms are like sticks for kindling."

"Mama says it doesn't matter if a girl's skinny, so long as she's strong. She was skinny, too, yet she bore seven healthy children."

"I don't want to bear children to a *foreigner*," Esme snapped. "I don't want to climb into bed with a man who can't speak my language, and raise children who'll never learn it."

"In bed, you won't need to converse with him," Donika said with a giggle.

Esme threw her a reproving look. "I should never have told you what Jason said about how babies are made."

"I'm glad you did. Now I'm not at all frightened. It doesn't sound very difficult—though perhaps embarrassing at first."

"It's also rather painful at first, I think," Esme said, momentarily distracted by the titillating subject. "But I've been shot twice already, and it can't be worse than having a bullet dug out of your flesh."

Donika threw her an admiring glance. "You're not afraid of anything, little warrior. If you can face marauding bandits, you should have no trouble with even your English kin. Still, I'll miss you so much. If only your father had found you a husband here."

Donika tossed a stone into the water. "They say Ismal wants you," she said after a moment. "He isn't old or desperate, but young and very rich."

"And a Moslem. I'd rather be boiled in oil than imprisoned in a harem," Esme said firmly. "Even England, with relatives who hate me, would be better than that." She considered briefly, then added, "I never told you before, but I was afraid once that it would happen."

Donika turned to her.

"When I was fourteen, visiting my grandmother in Gjirokastra," Esme continued, "Ismal and his family were there. He chased me through the garden. I thought it was a game, but—" She paused, flushing.

"But what? But what?"

Though there was no one else about to hear, Esme lowered her voice. "When he caught me, he kissed me—*on the mouth*."

"Truly?"

Esme shook her head from side to side in the Albanian affirmative.

"What was it like?" Donika asked eagerly. "He's so handsome, like a prince. Beautiful golden hair, and eyes like blue jewels—"

"It was *wet*," Esme interrupted. "I didn't like it at all. I knocked him down and wiped my mouth and cursed him soundly." She looked at her friend. "And he just lay there on the ground and laughed."

Donika laughed. "I can't believe this. You knocked down the cousin of Ali Pasha? You could have been executed."

Esme turned her gaze to the sea. Any day now it would carry her far away from all she knew and loved . . . forever.

"My father is no unwanted suitor, no enemy," she said quietly. "I can't fight him. When at last he confessed he was homesick, I felt so ashamed for arguing with him. I'll make the best of it, for his sake."

"It won't be so bad," Donika comforted. "You'll be homesick at first, but once you're wed, with babies of your own, think how happy you'll be. Think how rich and full your life will be."

Her gaze upon the pitiless sea, Esme saw only empti-
ness ahead. But her friend was, miraculously, in love with
the man her family had chosen for her. No more self-pity,
Esme resolved. No more gloom. This was Donika's happy
time, and it was unkind to spoil it.

"So it will," Esme said with a laugh. "And I shall teach
my babies Albanian, in secret."

Also available from
BERKLEY SENSATION

Duchess of Fifth Avenue
by Ruth Ryan Langan
The *New York Times* bestselling author of
"heartwarming, emotionally involving romances"*
brings the Gilded Age to life.

0-425-20889-3

The Penalty Box
by Deirdre Martin
From the *USA Today* bestselling author, a novel
about a hockey heartthrob, a stubborn brainiac,
and a battle of wills that just might end in love.

0-425-20890-7

The Kiss
by Elda Minger
After she finds her fiancé with another woman,
Tess Sommerville packs up and takes a road trip to
Las Vegas, ready to gamble—on love.

0-425-20681-5

Dead Heat
by Jacey Ford
Three beautiful ex-FBI agents have founded a security
firm—and their latest job uncovers a fatal plot against
America's top CEOs.

0-425-20461-8

Library Journal

Available wherever books are sold or at penguin.com